ROYAL BITE

The Immortal Reign Series

Book 3

ARIEL MARIE

Cover by Pretty In Ink Creations

Edited by Emmy Ellis with Studioenp.

Ebook ISBN: 978-1-956602-25-8

Paperback ISBN: 978-1-956602-51-7

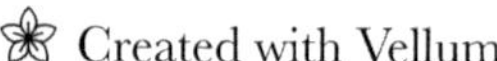

WARNING

Due to the explicit language and graphic sexual scenes, this book is intended for mature (18 years +) readers only. If things of this nature offend you, this book would not be for you. If you like a good action story with hot steamy scenes with lesbian vampires and their human mates, then you have chosen wisely…

Prologue

Downtown Wichita, Kansas, was no place to be once the sun went down. Stormey Jaymes scurried along the sidewalk with terror in her heart. Sounds coming from an alleyway left her fearing for her life.

It was the sound of vampires feeding.

And it didn't appear to be consensual.

Stormy knew better than to leave this late. Her manager at the Jade Inn had called her, asking if she could pick up a shift.

Another employee had gone missing, and they were short on housekeepers.

Even though today had been her only day off

for the week, Stormey had accepted the offer. The pay at the inn wasn't the best, but it was something. Every penny she earned would be put to good use.

The inhuman screams that echoed behind her sent her heart racing. She was practically running at this point.

Two more blocks and she would be at work. It would be safe there. She vowed that the next time they called her in, she would come right away so she wouldn't get caught out late.

On her one day off each week, she spent the entire day volunteering at the orphanage. She had a soft spot in her heart when it came to children who were the forgotten casualties of the war. So many were left without anyone to love them.

Stormey knew what it felt like to lose the two people who had meant the world to her. At the young age of three, she had lost her father in the war and then her mother to cancer. She could barely remember their faces, and to be quiet honest, she wasn't certain the images she held dear were their real faces.

What if the images were something her brain had concocted all of these years? Stormey didn't want to even consider it was a possibility. She blocked that notion from her brain.

She had been so young, and there was no family to take her in, so she'd become a ward of the state. Many of her years as a youth were spent growing up in an orphanage. She may not have had family who were blood related, but she had an extended family who helped her navigate life. She had a claim of about twenty brothers and sisters who had been her rock throughout her younger years.

She just wished she would have been able to keep in communication with most of them, but thanks to the war, she had lost touch with some.

Footsteps thudded behind her. Stormey dared not turn around. She had watched plenty of the older films from before the war that showed what happened when someone did that in those horror movies. It was a favorite pastime she loved to indulge in whenever she could get the chance.

The person behind her quickened their pace. There was a growing number of rogue vampires in their town who didn't follow the vampire laws. They did what they wanted and didn't heed the rules.

Stormey knew all about the vampire laws. She had been infatuated with learning all about this new race of beings from the moment she'd been old enough to understand what a vampire was. When she wasn't volunteering at the orphanage she was reading as much as she could to learn about the vampires.

According to folklore, vampires were the undead who were stronger, faster, and needed to consume blood to live. They were allergic to sunlight and lived long lives.

But Stormey knew she couldn't believe everything she had heard. Vampires weren't the undead.

They were pretty much beings who were alive, just like humans, only with a different thirst.

Only, humans were their food and apparently could be their mates.

And one of them was probably behind her. More footsteps could be heard.

"Oh, look at what we have here," a deep, raspy voice called out from behind, confirming her suspicion.

She tried to move faster but she felt their presence behind her. Stormey's vision blurred. This was not the way she had hoped to die. She had figured she would live a long, full life, find a life partner, and maybe have a kid or two.

Maybe fate had something else planned for her.

She was yanked back and thrown into a brick building by an unseen assailant. Their strength was definitely not human. Stormey was a pleasantly plump woman weighing around two hundred and fifty pounds. She wasn't blessed in the height factor, but the Lord had seen fit to give her ample curves and a plush body. She glanced to her left and saw she was practically steps from the inn.

Damn, she was going to die on her way to work.

"Such a pretty thing like you shouldn't be out at night by yourself," the voice rumbled.

Stormey winced, the foul, warm breath of the vampire greeting her. They trapped her, three of them standing before her. Laughter and growls filled area. More vampires raced by as if in a pack. Her eyes widened at the number of vampires running around on the loose.

What the hell was going on?

Screams pierced the air. These vampires were on the attack and causing a ruckus. These attacks always came in waves. Usually, Stormey would be safe and secure inside when they occurred.

Her heart pounded. She sent up a small prayer to any of the gods who may be listening. A rough hand forced her face toward them. It gripped her chin hard and wrenched her to look at the monster standing in front of her. Stormey assumed he was the leader.

"She smells good," one of his vampire goons groaned. "Let me get a taste of her."

"No, you don't get to go first," the other one snapped.

"I get first bite," the one holding her growled.

Stormey shook at the sight of his fangs descending. They were massive and sharp. They would tear into her flesh and make minced meat of her.

"Maybe I will leave something for you two."

"Let me go," Stormey whispered. Her body trembled out of control.

Apparently, her plea was hilarious to them. The three barked hefty laughs at her expense. There were other vampires dragging a man toward an alleyway. He begged and pleaded with them, but they ignored him.

"Oh, no. You don't get to go anywhere." The leader pressed closer to her.

She turned her face away from him, his tongue connecting to her cheek. She whimpered, nausea overtaking her. She tried to lodge her hands in between them so she could push him away, but it was like shoving a steel wall. He didn't budge.

"Please," she cried out.

"Damn, you taste good," he breathed.

His hands went to her hair and grabbed her low

ponytail, tilting her head back. She struggled, trying to break free, but he was overpowering her. The other two licked their fangs and narrowed their gazes on her, waiting for their turn at her. Stormey grew frantic and jerked her knee up, connecting with his inner thigh. He howled and backhanded her. Pain burst out on her face from the force of his blow. She fell back against the wall and tried to break free but was snatched by her waist.

Stormey screamed.

"Help me!"

"No one will come and help you," the second one growled.

Stormey was slammed back on the wall. The leader glared at her. He gripped her by her throat, crushing her windpipe. She scratched at his hand, trying to free herself so she could breathe. Her lungs burned the second they tried to bring in air.

"What the hell?" The third one paused. His eyes grew wide while a thin line of blood appeared on his neck. An arrow protruded from the side of his neck. He fell to the ground, his body shaking.

"Fuck, it's royal guards." The second one turned and backed away.

"They aren't going to take my meal from me," the leader snapped.

He drew Stormey to her and bent his head with the intent very clear. Stormey cried out, bracing for the pain she knew was coming. This was it. The end of her life was upon her. His body jerked repeatedly, his hold on her neck loosening.

He fell to his knees before her. She stepped back, tripping on her feet and landing on her bottom. The vampire fell toward her. Stormey darted to the side and avoided having him fall on her. She glanced down. Large holes appeared on his back. A dark substance leaked from them, staining his jacket. Her three attackers appeared to be dead.

Stormey glanced up and took in the fighting that ensued around her. She stared, mouth agape, as she watched the royal guards swarm in, fighting the vampires who had been attacking the humans. Their uniforms were dark with purple patches that symbolized the house of Princess Hegna Riskel, the eldest daughter of the vampire king. These highly trained warriors overtook the area and were no match for the lousy vampires who overran her town.

She scrambled to her feet and pressed her back against the wall. She wasn't that far from the inn and knew she would have to take the risk and run. With a prayer on the tip of her lips, she took off toward the tall building on the corner. The sounds of swords and weapons firing filled the air. She didn't look back but kept her eyes on the door.

Stormey arrived and found it locked. She jingled the handle frantically and glanced behind her. The fighting was growing more gruesome, and her heart all but leaped into her throat.

"Open up! It's me!" She banged on the wooden door.

She peered through the window and took in the sight of Melissa rushing toward the door. It flung open with Melissa ushering her in.

"Oh my god. Are you harmed?" Melissa asked. She slammed the door shut and bolted it locked.

The hotel's foyer was empty. Stormey glanced up the stairs. A few faces peered down at her. There were protocols they had to follow when under attack. The hotel would go on lockdown to protect the employees and patrons. She was lucky Melissa had even come and opened the door. To protect everyone, they could have left Stormey outside.

"Thank the fates, no." Stormey raced over to windows, unable to resist looking out. She pushed the drapes aside. The scenery out there was growing worse. Where the hell were all of these vampires coming from?

She had never seen this amount of rogues before in one place.

"Are you crazy? Get away from the windows!" Melissa screeched, but Stormey ignored her.

The windows of the Jade Inn were enforced and could withstand tons of pressure. There was something deep down inside her that had made her go to the window. There was something she had to see. She didn't know why, but her gut was telling her to stay where she was. The royal guards were winning. Bodies of the rogues lay strewn around on the streets and sidewalks.

Stormey's breath caught in her throat as a certain figure caught her eye. It was the princess.

The heir to the vampire throne.

Hegna Riskel.

And she was every bit of the badass warrior they said she was.

The vampire princess was dressed in black fighting leathers, her dark hair scraped back away from her face in intricate plaits. Her expression was cold and hard. Her speed and skills fighting hand-to-hand were breathtaking.

Stormey's face was pressed against the glass while Hegna slid her duel swords out from their sheaths at her sides and engaged with the foolish vampires who thought they could take on the princess. Stormey bit her lip, watching the woman.

She was powerful.

Lethal.

And Stormey was infatuated with the vampire.

"Stormey, get away from the window," Jack, her manager, snapped.

He grabbed her by her arm and dragged her off. Stormey resisted for one slight moment to get one last glimpse of the princess.

CHAPTER ONE

Stormey pulled her coat closed and slid her gloves on. She noticed small holes on the tips of the fingers and frowned. She would have to go and see if she could fix them later. She couldn't afford to purchase new ones, and these she'd had for a few years. Grabbing the shovel, she walked outside the front door of the Jade Inn. Jack had asked for a favor.

She should have known it was something that wasn't in her job description, but what was she going to say?

No?

She snorted.

It was hard to find a good-paying job. Stormey wasn't going to risk him telling her to pack her bags and go. There would be at least ten people lining up to take her job and probably for less money.

So, if he wanted the stairs cleaned off from the snow, then that's what she would do. It wasn't that much, and she did enjoy the biting fresh air. She inhaled sharply and took in her surroundings. It was a beautiful day, and there were even some people ambling down the street.

Stormey blew out her breath and giggled at the sight of it in the air. The crisp winter chill would set in soon. Her coat wasn't the thickest, and she sensed the cold already settling in her bones.

"Let me hurry," she muttered.

The small shovel was balanced against the wall near the door. She grabbed it and got to work. Her shift would be ending soon, and she had plans that included stopping by the orphanage. The winter was hard on the children, so she made sure she put in extra time to help cheer some of them up. Adoptions were down, and the place was getting a little crowded. She worried about some of the older children who would be aging out soon.

She paused and straightened. Her back muscles

protested slightly at the manual work. She made her way to the bottom stair and glanced across the street. A tremor snuck through her at the memory of that night she'd almost lost her life.

But then she had shown up.

The princess.

The rogue vampires had been dealt with.

The people of her city had wondered when the princess was going to do something with the over-population of rogues who were flooding their city. It had become extremely dangerous to be out after the sun went down. There were so many missing person reports filed every day. The news held daily segments showcasing the photos of the humans who had disappeared.

Since the war, humans had become dependent upon the protection of the vampires. The human governments around the world were in shambles. The United States government officials answered to the vampire king and his wardens. There were human police departments, but they had no jurisdiction over the vampires, nor did they have the ability to fight them.

Stormey tore her eyes from the site where she had been cornered and turned back to the inn. The stairs were now free and clear of the few inches of snow that had covered them. She walked back up the stairs and placed the shovel back where it was. She went inside and stomped her feet on the rug.

"Thanks for doing that," Jack called out from behind the check-in counter. His dark mop of hair was uncombed and fell forward into his eyes.

"No problem." Stormey nodded to him and headed past the counter toward the employee lounge where she could hang her coat back up. She had worked at the Jade Inn for a few years now and was thankful for the inn. It allowed her to have a small home of her own, allowed her to feed and dress herself.

Life since the war had been hard. It had certainly taken its toll on the world. Life as humans knew it had changed the moment vampires presented themselves. Humans who were unaware that others existed amongst them were cocky and thought they would be able to eradicate the vampires.

The humans had their asses handed to them.

Vampires were the superior beings. They were masterful hunters and didn't hide the fact that humans were their prey.

Many humans had lost their families to the war. The human governments put a gun in any able-bodied human's hand and sent them off to fight. The draft had been unfair and was forced. Many humans tried to outrun being sent to war. Some were successful in evading their imposed duty while others weren't. The loss of human life had been astounding. The numbers were depressing but were on the rise again. As with any deadly event in history, there was a boom in the number of children born.

Stormey dreamed of a day where she would find that special someone in her life.

She arrived at the lounge and shucked off her coat and hung it up. The air in the hotel was chilly. She doubted Jack would want to turn up the heat in the areas that were designed for employees. She changed her shoes and moved to the closet where her cart was. She was sure Jack had a few rooms that needed to be cleaned from late checkouts.

She got her assignment and saw that she only had one room to clean.

"Room two thirty-seven. Perfect," she muttered. She pushed her cart and headed over to the service elevators. It wouldn't take her long to clean this room. It was a standard, and by the time she was done, it would be time for her to clock out.

She arrived at her destination and knocked on the door.

"Housekeeping," she called out. Even though Jack had listed this room as one that needed cleaning, it didn't mean the people had actually left. Hearing no sounds from the other side of the door, she opened it with her key. Stormey wrinkled her nose at the stale air that greeted her. She turned back to her cart and grabbed some gloves and slid them on.

She entered the room and immediately found the remote. She turned the television on so she could watch the news while she cleaned. She was unable to afford a television of her own, so she got all of her news at work. There were a few shows on that she was guilty of watching when they were on while she worked. Also, she took advantage of being able to watch some of the old movies that were streamed.

She flipped through the channels and didn't see any of the news programs on. She found a movie and set the remote down on the dresser. She hadn't seen this one before. She spun around and got to work.

Even with the TV to keep her company, her mind wandered. She still couldn't get the image of

Hegna Riskel fighting the rogues out of her mind. Stormey would admit she had a little crush on the princess who was the warden who oversaw her area.

There was just something so fascinating about the vampire. She was tall, beautiful, strong, and quite older than Stormey's age of thirty-five. The princess was said to be around two hundred and thirty-six years old.

"She looks good for an old woman." Stormey chuckled. She stripped the bed of its sheets and blankets while trying to not think of what a few of the stains she spotted were. She became lost in her thoughts while working. She hummed to herself, occasionally glancing at the television.

"She's my mate," the man on the screen swore.

Stormey froze in place, her attention now on the television. The movie that was playing just so happened to be an old vampire flick from the twentieth century. The man, a vampire, had dark hair, pale skin, and he fought against another trying to get to a woman. He was frantic and desperate.

How ironic that this movie played. The real vampires of the world were all in search of their mates. It was one of the reasons they had presented themselves. Aside from securing more food for their people, they were in search of their fated mates.

Stormey found it fascinating that the vampires had come up with a way to find them. They had used science and designed a test that would connect them with their intended.

The draft.

This was instilled by the ruling vampires once they came into power on this planet. Humans, when called, were to submit a blood sample. A simple test where the results would determine if the donor had a vampire mate. If the human matched to a vampire, then they would be shipped off to the vampire.

Not all humans wanted this. There were plenty of protests from groups on both sides, human and vampire. These anti-vampire groups felt that humans should not be forced to become a vampire's mate or food. According to them, it was against human rights to make them submit to a vampire.

Then there were the anti-human groups that felt vampires should not take humans as their mates. They were against a mixing of the species. Mating with humans and producing children was an abomination, and the vampire race should remain pure.

Stormey had heard both arguments. There was no way to get away from it. Both sides were fierce in their protests, and one couldn't go anywhere without running into one side voicing their disgust.

Stormey was captivated by the movie on the screen. She knew what she wanted.

She wanted to belong to a vampire.

Her heart quickened just thinking about it.

Who did she dream of belonging to?

None other than Hegna Riskel.

What she wouldn't give to be taken from this life and given to the warrior princess. Stormey desired to be loved, cherished, and protected. She'd heard rumors that all the mates to vampires were satisfied. She didn't know anyone personally, but she'd heard from others who did know someone that vampire mates never wanted to leave their vampires.

Stormey's infatuation may be next-level stalking. She had researched everything she could find about the heir to the throne. The amount of information that as available left Stormey confused on how the world hadn't known about vampires before the war. Stormey knew everything about the vampire that was made public. Her obsession with the princess was like that of a schoolgirl crushing on a famous rockstar.

It wasn't the wealth that was attractive. Stormey wasn't that shallow.

It was Hegna's sense of strength and power. That night where she and her vampires had come in and defeated the rogues was still ingrained in her mind. The way her army followed her commands had been impressive.

The woman was downright sexy. Her dark hair, toned body, and ice-blue eyes. Stormey had viewed multiple pictures of her on the web. She had spent many hours at the library doing her research into vampire history, traditions, and the Riskel family.

Stormey had caught stories of the princess's prowess on the news. There were tales of her lovers and her love of adult entertainment. The heir to the throne was the last of the Riskel daughters to be mated. Her sisters, Velika and Lethia, were mated to their human women via the draft. Hegna was considered one of the most eligible bachelorettes on the continent, if not the world. The princess had been photographed with various unnamed women, and Stormey could never confirm if she was in a relationship with any of them.

She couldn't wait for the day her name was picked so she could go down to the government lab and get her blood drawn.

She wanted someone to claim her.

Stormey knew she would make a damn good

mate to whoever. She had skills that would be helpful. She was a great cook, but vampires didn't consume food. Her cooking skills could be useful for entertaining. She was kind, loyal, and at times a night owl. She could get used to the nocturnal way of life.

She chuckled and shook her head.

"Enough daydreaming," she muttered. She walked to her cart and grabbed clean linen. She turned around and went back in to finish her job. Once she got home, she could daydream about Hegna Riskel until she drifted off to sleep like she had done so many other nights.

STORMEY'S BODY ACHED, but she ignored her complaining muscles. It had been a long day at work, but she wasn't done yet. She was going to stop by the orphanage, Friends of Greta, which was on her way home. Friends of Greta was run by Greta Brothers, a former nun. She was an older woman who'd started the orphanage thirty years ago. After the war, her orphanage had been flooded with children in need.

Volunteers like Stormey helped her to keep it

running as smooth as could be. Greta was getting up there in age and needed all the help she could get to keep up with the rambunctious children.

The war had caused so much devastation. The vampires had swept through their world and destroyed everything. Life as humans knew it was never the same. Humans were no longer at the top of the food chain.

And lately, the world had been in another uproar. It would appear that it wasn't just vampires they had to deal with.

Now there were the lycans.

Stormey shivered at the thought of the wolf shifters. It felt as if she were living in a paranormal movie. Shifters and vampires? Who would come out next?

It would seem that humans had been so arrogant to think they were the only ones inhabiting the planet. Stormey was sure there was so much more out there that they didn't know about.

She hefted her bag onto her shoulder and marched out of the employee lounge. A new wave of energy flooded her with the thought of spending some time with the kiddos. She pushed open the door that led to the hotel's front desk and saw Jack on the telephone.

"Goodnight," she called out and waved.

"Stormey." Jack motioned to the phone. "Phone is for you."

"Me?" She skidded to a halt. Who would be calling her? Whoever it was, the call must be important. Unfortunately, she didn't have a phone of her own and gave her work number for anything important. Her heart seemed to leap into her throat. Her feet were heavy as she walked toward the front desk. "Who is it?"

"I'm not your secretary." Jack blew out a deep breath. "I understand why some of you give out this number, but I'm not in the business of taking messages."

He thrust the phone into her hand. She swallowed hard and lifted it to her ear.

"This is Stormey Jaymes. How can I help you?" Her voice didn't shake, and she was proud of that.

"Yes, Ms. Jaymes, this is Lucy Donovan from the Wichita Draft Office. I need to ask you a few questions to verify your identity." The woman's voice was cold and lifeless.

"Yes, of course." Stormey answered the simple questions. She had to contain her excitement. She had been waiting for this day to come. Deep in her gut, she knew her life was about to change forever.

"Thank you, Ms. Jaymes. You have been identified as a human who will need to report for the draft. Do you understand what this means?"

"Yes, I do." Stormey had to fight to keep a smile from forming.

"Good. You will need to report to the following lab. Do you have a pen and paper to write down the address?"

"Give me one second." She motioned to Jack to give her a pen while she snagged a blank notepad from the counter.

He rolled his eyes and passed her the one in his hand.

"I'm ready." She scribbled down the address and recognized that the place wasn't too far from where she worked. She hadn't even realized the lab was so close.

"You are to report there within the next two hours. If not, you will be in violation of penal code—"

"Don't worry, I'm on my way now," Stormey interjected. She could no longer contain her excitement.

Jack rolled his eyes at her again as she hung up. "You are excited about being called down for that draft?" He folded his arms in front of his chest.

She tossed the pen down on the counter and ripped the piece of paper from the notepad. She stuffed it into her pocket and grinned.

"Have a great night!" She ignored his question, tossed him a wave, and was out the door in a matter of seconds. She didn't want to know his opinion about the draft, nor did she care what he may think of her.

Stormey glanced at the sky and took in that the sun was still out. She had a few hours left of daytime before she needed to seek shelter. She pulled out the piece of paper and stared at the address. She walked down the street in the direction she needed to go. It should take her about thirty minutes if she hustled hard.

Stormey couldn't keep the smile from her face. Her body heated at the thought of being matched with a vampire. She had read studies that revealed the test was one hundred percent accurate on revealing fated mates. They would take a sample of her blood, and by tonight, she would know if there was a vampire out there for her.

Now, she knew not all vampires were registered at the moment. It was a big deal when the vampire princesses were entered into the database. The media and tabloids went crazy. From what Stormey had read, the queen herself had entered her daughters into the draft. The two youngest daughters had been matched right away, and their mating had even led to the birth of the royal family's next generation.

Stormey sighed. Her hand drifted down to her stomach. She yearned to have a family of her own. She had dreamed of the day where she could hold her little bundle of joy. There was no doubt in her mind that she would be a great mother. She may not have been lucky enough to be raised by her own, but Stormey knew what she'd missed out on growing up and vowed that her children would never go without and would always know of love.

She took in the area, having become lost in a daydream. She laughed and sped up. She rounded the corner and glanced down at the piece of paper again.

"Almost there," she murmured.

She nodded to a woman who was walking with a little one in tow. The small boy grinned at her, revealing his two missing front teeth. She chuckled and waved at him. Her ovaries quivered at his cuteness.

Yes.

Her life was going to change.

Stormey paused and looked at the brick storefronts, not seeing one with a sign. She eyed the paper again and searched for the address. She continued down the sidewalk, scanning the area.

"Bingo." Her gaze landed on a building across the street that was unmarked. She jogged across, narrowly being hit by a speeding car. The driver laid on their horn as they flew past her. Stormey hopped up on the curb and gripped her bag handle tight. She stared at the entrance, the butterflies in her stomach fluttering to life.

Even almost getting run over couldn't kill her vibe.

The unmarked building was plain, brick, and didn't give off the appeal that it was a medical facility. Stormey exhaled and moved to the door. She gripped the handle and opened it. She was immediately met with the scent of antiseptic. Inside, she found herself in a waiting area that was filled with people. Chairs were lined up, and there were only a few free.

"Hello." Stormey arrived at the check-in desk.

There was a man sitting behind it, focused on the computer screen, his fingers flying along the keyboard while he worked. His skin was extremely pale, and his dark hair was perfectly combed away from his face. Small fangs peeked out from underneath his top lip. Vampire. Interesting. It was daylight. How was he working here?

She glanced back at the doors and windows and took in the special coverings. "I received a call and was instructed to report here."

"What is your name?" He paused his typing and pulled out a clipboard.

"Stormey Jaymes." She even spelled it out to ensure he had the correct spelling. She wanted to make sure she got credit for showing up. She was used to people misspelling both her first and last names.

"Initial here then fill out this questionnaire." He flipped the page and set the clipboard on the counter in front of her then slid another piece of paper beside it. He placed a pen down for her.

Stormey scribbled her initials then filled out the short form. Her name, address, place of work, family status, height, and weight. She paused. Why did they need to know her clothing sizing? Shaking her head, she quickly finished filling out the form then gave everything back to him.

"Do you have your birth records with you?"

She nodded, reached inside her bag, and removed her wallet. She handed him a copy of her birth certificate and her identification card. He scanned them into the computer, offering the documents back to Stormey. She always kept her records on her just for this moment. She figured she would always be ready for when she was called down for her donation.

"Please stand over there so I can take your picture."

Stormey did as she was instructed.

A few moments later, he motioned to the waiting area. "Have a seat. Here's your number, and they will call that when they are ready for you."

She took the small piece of paper that held her number.

Three hundred and sixty-six.

This would be her lucky number.

Stormey made her way through the sterile waiting area and found a seat in the corner. She rested her bag in her lap and relaxed. With the number of vampires searching for a mate, she was sure there was one out there for her. She understood things between her and the vampire may be awkward at first. She just hoped that over time a loving relationship would develop and grow.

The decor of the waiting room was simple and resembled a doctor's office. Plastic plants, old magazines resting on a few tables scattered around the room. Even light music played through invisible speakers.

Time passed, and Stormey watched the room. She could see fear written on some of the people's faces who were around her. There was a slight tension in the air. No one knew for certain if they would match with a vampire. Numbers were called out, and the person holding the correlating one would stand and follow the orderly to the back.

Stormey shifted in her seat, anxious for hers to be called. No one spoke while they waited. She noticed it didn't take long for the donation. Each person who was called back would be leaving shortly afterwards. Her leg bounced uncontrollably. The woman sitting across from her kept staring at her leg.

Stormey paused the motion. She offered the woman a smile. She scowled at Stormey before turning away from her.

"Three sixty-six."

Stormey's heart stuttered.

It was time for her to give her sample. She stood and walked over to the desk where the same vampire who'd registered her sat. A short woman stood by the desk.

"You called my number. Three sixty-six." Stormey held up the piece of paper.

"Follow me, please." Her dark hair was pulled up in a tight bun. She was dressed in navy-blue scrubs and walked briskly through the halls.

Stormey hefted her bag up on her shoulder and followed. She bit her lip and didn't say a word. The scent of antiseptic filled her nostrils. She was impressed by the sight of the place. This was run by the vampires. The human government didn't have money to run something so elaborate.

"How long have you worked here?" Stormey asked in an attempt to make small talk.

The woman glanced back at her with a raised eyebrow.

"A few years," she responded.

"Do you get a lot of people every day?" Stormey couldn't stop the questions from tumbling from her mouth. She was downright curious. She had waited forever to get here, and now that she was, her curiosity was getting the best of her.

"Yes."

"And do you know how many people are actually matched?"

The woman drew to a halt and faced Stormey. She rested her hand on her hip, and it was then

Stormey saw her fangs peeking from underneath her lip.

A vampire.

Stormey swallowed hard and clutched her bag to her.

"I don't keep up with the humans once they give their samples." She turned and motioned for Stormey to follow her again.

She had increased her pace, and Stormey struggled to keep up. She was beginning to think the woman was irritated by her questions. Did others not ask questions when they came to give their sample?

"Do vampires come here to give their samples, too?" Stormey asked. What would be the chances that she and her future mate gave blood at the same laboratory?

The woman replied with a snort and shook her head. "No, their facilities are different." She stopped outside a closed door. She opened it and motioned for Stormey to enter. It was small and looked like a medical exam room. "Please have a seat. They will be with you soon."

The woman slid a file into the plastic holder on the door. She gave Stormey one last look that was very familiar. One that she'd received plenty of times when people found out she was for humans mating with vampires. The woman shook her head and closed the door.

Stormey removed her coat and hung it up on the hook on the wall. She took the seat and waited.

CHAPTER TWO

Stormey let herself into her tiny home. She shut the door behind her and engaged the locks. She didn't live in the best part of town, but everyone in her neighborhood was like her. Part of the lower working class. The home she rented was just in her price range. It was less than four hundred feet. It was an open floor plan with the living room and kitchen connected. There was a small bathroom in the back, and her bedroom was in the loft.

It wasn't much, but it had been her home for the last few years. It was decorated sparsely with only the necessities. She had an oversized chair and a table in the living room as her only furniture.

She was proud of her house. As a child who'd bounced around between orphanages to foster homes, she had been so excited to find a place of her own. She had moved countless times. There were some families who'd taken her in. Some had been good while others were questionable. She had tried to be a well-behaved kid in hopes someone would want to keep her and adopt her, but it always ended with her being sent back to an orphanage.

Many of the families who'd fostered her did it for the money. The government paid them to look after children. They didn't really want her but wanted the benefits of having a foster kid.

That was what drove her to find someone to love her.

She wanted to belong. She wanted to share all of the love she harbored inside her. When she was sixteen years old, a woman by the name of Lori Silver had agreed to house her. Finally, she had found a foster mom who cared for her. Those last two years in the foster system were the best of Stormey's life. They had lived in a small town in Alabama.

Stormey still communicated with Lori whenever

she got a chance. They exchanged letters to keep each other updated. Lori was getting up in age, but she was still caring for older foster children. Whenever Stormey had extra money, she sent it to Lori. The woman never thought of herself. Stormey insisted that the few dollars she sent be spent on her. Lori was stubborn, and Stormey was sure her foster mother spent that money on her children.

She took her coat off and dropped it onto her chair along with her bag. She rushed to the ladder that led to her small bedroom.

She stripped off her work clothes and threw on her best outfit. If tonight was going to be the night she met her mate, then she wanted to look her best. She chose a pair of black leggings and a soft cream sweater she had found at the secondhand store. It was thick and long, stopping just below her plump bottom. She frantically gathered her belongings together and tossed them into her bag. Clothes, shoes, some personal trinkets, and the letters from Lori.

She wanted to make sure that if—no, when—her name was drawn, she would already have her belongings together. She didn't own much. Once she left, she was sure her home would be rented out by the next morning. Her landlord would not miss her at all. The only thing that mattered was keeping someone in the house so he could get paid. Not that he fixed anything. There was plenty that needed attention in her home. She didn't want to complain and risk getting thrown out. So she patched up what she could.

"This is sad," she murmured, staring at her bag on her bed. She hadn't realized that all of her personal belongings fit in one duffle. Not that it mattered. After she paid the few bills she had, she donated as much as she could to the orphanage. Those kids needed it more than she did.

Stormey carried the bag downstairs and sat it on the floor near her chair. She scanned the rest of the house to see if there was anything else she wanted to take. She didn't keep anything of value downstairs. If someone broke into her home, she didn't want to make it easy for them to take from her.

She moved over into the kitchen. Her stomach grumbled, alerting her that she hadn't eaten since earlier that day. She opened the fridge and found there wasn't much in there. She frowned, unable to remember the last time she had gone to the market.

"Today will be a day to splurge." She slammed the door shut and went over to her bag.

She peeked inside her wallet to make sure she would have enough to cover dinner. She tossed her coat back on and decided she would go to the local diner near her home. They served good, hot food, and she had enough time to grab something to eat and could watch the draft on their television.

With it being wintertime, the sun didn't stay out as long. Ever since the princess and her small army had come to town, attacks on humans had decreased drastically. There were even guards and human police who patrolled areas, making it safer for humans to be out at night.

Martha's was a cozy little diner that was located a few blocks from Stormey's neighborhood. Stormey locked up her home and left. She slid the straps of her bag across her chest to be able to hold on to it. She picked up her pace and stayed aware of her surroundings.

It wouldn't do her any good to donate her blood, be matched, but be found dead in an alleyway.

Stormey blew out a deep breath and increased her speed. She made it in record time. She entered the restaurant and was immediately hit with the aroma of good, home-cooked food. The decor was that of the late twentieth century. It may be a little outdated, but it was clean.

"Hello there. Just one?" a short lady with olive skin and jet-black hair greeted her. The woman's smile was infectious. Her tag held the name Cecilia.

"Yes, please." Stormey returned her smile.

"Would you like a booth or table?" Cecilia grabbed a menu and waved for her to follow.

"A booth would be perfect." Stormey glanced around and took in the other patrons. There were a few couples, a family, and some singles spread around. "Can I be near the television? I just want to catch the news."

"Of course." Cecilia walked over to a booth and set the menu down.

Stormey removed her coat and slid into the booth. She settled her belongings on the seat next to her before picking up the menu.

"Can I get you something to drink?"

"Water would be fine." Stormey began going over the short menu. She wanted to save some of her money. Luckily enough, water was free.

"Want a lemon for it?" Cecilia asked.

"Sure, thanks."

Stormey turned her attention back to the menu once Cecilia disappeared from her table. Everything sounded good, but she needed to stay within her budget. When Cecilia returned, she had her decision made and placed her order.

Her anxiety was rising. She peered down at her watch and saw that it was time for the news. She glanced back over to the television, and the opening credits were rolling. Stormey wiped her hands on her leggings and reached for her water. She pushed her lemon in it, picked out a few sugar packets from the table, and put them in. She chuckled as she took her spoon and mixed it together. She sipped then settled back and turned her attention to the television.

The anchors were discussing the latest string of robberies and investigations. None of this appealed to Stormey, but she knew they had a job to do to inform the public of the latest happenings in their city and across the nation.

One of the stories caught her attention.

"Another lycan sighting has been reported," the male anchor announced.

Stormey inhaled sharply. She leaned forward to listen better. She was terrified at the thought of encountering one of these wolf shifters. Nothing she had heard was good about them. Between rogue vampires and lycans, she didn't know which would be worse.

"Tom Jones has more on this story. Tom?"

The picture cut to older bald gentleman standing outside. He and the camera crew appeared to be in one of the public parks.

"Thanks, Michael." The camera swung around and focused on Tom. "We are here where multiple people have stepped forward claiming to have seen lycans. Now we all know from mythical tales that lycans are beings who can shift into a beast. A ferocious wolf who is larger than their natural counterparts and is extremely dangerous."

"Can these lycans be identified from regular wolves?" Michael asked.

"Oh, most definitely. These shifters are three to four times the size of a regular wolf and will attack at will. Allegedly, their bite is infectious and can pass on the virus that will turn a human into one of them."

Gasps went around the diner. Stormey's eyes grew wide at the announcement. She took another sip of her free lemon water and couldn't take her eyes off the screen.

"Has this been confirmed?" Michael asked.

This same question was on the tip of Stormey's

tongue. She knew vampires could turn humans, but it wasn't off of one single bite.

Word on the street was the human would have to be on the brink of death, bleeding out, and then would have to drink from the vampire. She had heard multiple stories that the drinking of vampire blood was only the beginning of the process. She had read conspiracy theories that said the human would need a full blood transfusion of vampire blood, or the vampires had a venom in their bite that they called forth that would initiate the change. There were so many stories floating around that Stormey didn't know what to believe. She didn't know anyone who had been changed into a vampire.

"We are waiting to hear confirmation from the Centers of Disease Outbreaks and the Vampire Caucus. As soon as we have word, we'll share. Back to you, Michael."

"Here you go, dear." Cecilia returned with Stormey's food. She placed a plate with honey butter chicken, biscuits, and a side of broccoli.

Stormey couldn't help the splurge. This was her celebratory meal for finally being called down to the government lab. She had a good feeling deep down inside. This would be the last night she would have to worry about money and food.

She was going to be drafted.

She just hoped her vampire wasn't too old and would be welcoming to her. Maybe they could start out as friends and it could grow into something more. Stormey was optimistic that everything was going to work out.

"Thank you." Stormey's stomach grumbled. The food looked amazing, and she was happy that she had decided to come out to eat. Whatever she would have scraped together at home wouldn't be anything like this.

"Let me know if I can get you anything else." Cecilia rushed over to another table.

Stormey dug into to her food. The taste exploded onto her tongue. It was delicious and everything she had hoped it would be. She turned her attention back to the news. She was growing impatient. Why didn't they do the draft at the beginning of the show to get it over with? She couldn't be the only person interested in seeing if they matched with a vampire.

"Good evening, America. Here are your nightly draft picks." A beautiful brunette came into view on the television. The news broadcast was interrupted by the draft.

Stormey dropped her fork down and crossed her fingers. She sent up a prayer that she would hear her name called. Her heart raced while her leg bounced.

Would she hear her name?

A man's name and photo came onto the screen. It had to be his photo from his registration at the lab. Another photo was shown, and a name was read. This time it was a young woman. They continued revealing photos and names.

Stormey Jaymes.

Her photo appeared on the screen.

Stormey bit back her excited scream. She felt eyes turn to her. She blinked a few times in disbelief. The odds of being drafted was one in a million.

Her name had been called. She held back a smile as she took in the sympathetic looks of the patrons in the diner. She didn't want to appear like a weirdo and grin at them. Instead, she nodded and gave them a tight smile. She pushed her plate away just as Cecilia returned to her table. Suddenly, she was no longer hungry.

"Here's your check, hun. Pay when you're

ready." Cecelia gave her a look of pity as she sat the small piece of paper on the table.

"I'm ready now." Stormey gave a dry laugh.

Cecilia just didn't know how ready Stormey was, and she wasn't talking about paying for her meal. This was something she had been waiting for. She stood and walked to the front and paid her tab.

"STORMEY JAYMES?"

Two large men were waiting for her at her home. A dark-colored SUV was parked on the road in front of her house. She swallowed hard at the size of them. They were pushing six and a half feet tall, muscular, and she pitied anyone who tried to fight them or run.

She slowed down and paused close to them.

This was it.

She hadn't thought they would arrive that fast. But then again, they were probably alerted before the draft was announced. She imagined there were many humans who didn't want to be drafted and sent away to a vampire. She had heard of people who had run and been captured. Occasionally there was a news story of a human who was evading the draft and there was a manhunt for them. These two would get no fight out of her.

"Yes, that is me." She cleared her throat and tightened her grip on her bag.

"You are to come with us. We are your escort," the one with long dark hair said.

"Am I allowed to get my things?" she asked. Stormey walked toward her home and prayed she would be able to take her things with her.

"Of course." The blond one kept his hair cut close to his head.

They parted to allow her to go inside. Blondie followed her in. His massive size made the place feel like a small closet. He took up basically all of the living room.

"Pack one bag with anything of value to you."

"I'm actually already packed," she admitted sheepishly.

His eyebrows rose, but he didn't say a word. Stormey took one last look at the house. She wouldn't miss anything here.

She turned back around to Blondie. "I'm ready."

Stormey followed him out. She closed and locked the door behind her. The dark-haired escort held the SUV's back door open for her. Blondie took her bag from her and walked to the back of the vehicle. She got in the truck and settled back in the plush leather seat.

She took a final glance at the house that had been her haven for the past few years. Her vision blurred slightly, but she blinked back the tears. She wouldn't be sad, no, this was a joyous occasion. She felt it deep in her bones that her life was truly just beginning.

Her two escorts entered the SUV. They soon sped away from the life she knew. Once she was settled, she would send word to the orphanage of her being drafted. She hated that she hadn't had a chance to say goodbye to the children and Ms. Greta.

"Are you able to tell me where we are going?" she asked.

There was a snort from the front seat. She couldn't tell which one of the guards it was.

"We are not to give you any information," Blondie said.

"Not even the state or the city?" She gasped. Well, that was unfair. They had been traveling for a short while now, and it was going to kill her to not know where she was going.

"We can at least tell her the town," Dark Hair

muttered. He was driving the SUV. He guided them onto the nearly empty highway.

Stormey leaned forward so she could see Blondie.

"Who am I going to tell if you give me a tiny bit of information?" she stated. If they could just give her a little, it would calm her nerves. She rubbed her palms on her thighs.

"Fine." Blondie sighed. He ran a hand along his face.

She couldn't tell if they were vampires or human. It was widely known that humans were employed by vampires. With the size of these two, they had to be vampires.

"Our destination is Black Hollows, Oklahoma."

"Black Hollows…oh." Stormey's eyes widened. Black Hollows was the home of Princess Hegna Riskel. Her heart pounded at the thought of being so close to her crush. She settled back in shock. "Thank you for sharing."

"Don't ask any more questions. The only reason I'm telling you that is you are making this job easy." Blondie grunted.

"Well, I'm glad," she said. She folded her hands together on her lap. "Most people think I'm crazy for accepting vampires and wanting to be drafted."

The vehicle was silent. She hadn't expected a response at all from the two of them. She turned and watched the scenery pass by. Darkness surrounded them, and it was slightly comforting. She stared at the sky, wondering if her mate had been notified of her impending arrival. Was that person happy? Were they frantically getting their home ready for her?

"You're not crazy," Dark Hair replied gently.

Her head whipped around in shock.

He met her gaze in the review mirror. "Vampires are not all bad. My wife is a vampire."

Stormey's breath escaped from her. She didn't want to get in trouble by asking any more questions. She was definitely intrigued that this big man was the mate of a vampire. She yearned to ask if he was part of the draft.

"I can see the question on your face, and the answer is yes. I was drafted. My wife is my entire world." He turned his attention back to the road ahead.

Stormey smiled, her heart full of hope. She leaned toward the window and dreamed of her meeting with her mate.

It wasn't long before they arrived at a small airport. She was escorted onto a private jet plane.

The ride wasn't long. Once they were on the ground, she was whisked away into another SUV.

Oklahoma was a state she had never visited before. Most of her life she had lived in the south. She had moved to Kansas to find employment. It was hard to find jobs in Alabama that didn't involve her selling her body. It wasn't uncommon for humans to move around the country to look for safe places to live and to secure work.

Stormey held back a yawn. She had been up for most of the day, and it was starting to take a toll on her body, but she refused to fall asleep. She sat up straight, taking in the area. It was hard to see with it being so dark outside. This was her new town, and she vowed to explore and get to know it. She wasn't sure her vampire would be rich, and it didn't matter. If the person was a vampire and had been around for a few centuries, she hoped they weren't poor. That wouldn't make sense at all. She bit back a chuckle at the thought.

Stormey was no stranger to hard work, and she wouldn't mind getting a job. No matter if they were rich, she would need something to do with her time. Hopefully, when it was time to talk children, she could work part-time or quit all together. She was determined to be a fully accessible mother and would love to stay at home with her children.

The SUV turned down a long winding road. She took in a large body of water that was noticeable through the thicket of trees. Curiosity got the best of her.

"Are we almost there?" she asked.

"Yeah. We should be there in a few minutes," Blondie answered.

Stormey jerked forward and reached into her bag. She pulled out her brush and ran it through her thick, dark hair. She wanted to ensure she looked her best for her mate. She finished and applied a coat of lip gloss. That was the extent of her makeup. It was a luxury she couldn't afford.

Stormey tossed everything back in her bag and glanced up. She froze in place at the building coming into view.

A castle.

A freaking castle.

The air in her lungs was snatched out of her. She couldn't breathe. There was only one castle that she knew of in Black Hollows and who lived here. Stormey shook her head. The fates couldn't be this good to her. This had to be a joke, or maybe her mate worked at this castle and they were just bringing her here to meet them.

Dark Hair hit the brakes, bringing them to a stop in front of the stone stairs that led to the entrance.

She gulped.

"Who is my mate?" she asked. Her voice was hoarse and cracked at the end. She gripped her bag tight. This had to be a dream.

Yes, she must have fallen asleep in the truck. She reached over and pinched herself. The pain burst out from underneath the skin on her wrist where she had nipped.

She was awake.

Blondie got out of the car and opened her door. He held his hand out for her. She stared at it for a moment before sliding hers into his larger one. He assisted her from the SUV and shut the door.

"Miss Jaymes, you have been matched to Princess Hegna Riskel." He bowed his head to her.

She snatched her hand back from him and stared at the castle.

"You are lying," she whispered. Her pulse thundered in her ears. She stepped back, falling against the SUV. Were they playing a cruel trick on her?

Did someone know how much of a crush she had on the princess?

"A draft match is nothing lie about. We take this very seriously. It is true. You have been matched with none other than the heir to the throne." Blondie stood firm, staring at her.

She swallowed hard. She had lost count of how many times she had fantasized about being mated to the vampire princess. Never in her wildest dreams would she have thought she would be matched to her.

"Come." Dark Hair strode around the truck and motioned for her to follow him.

It took her a few attempts before her legs were able to move on their own. She walked behind him while Blondie ambled along beside her.

The castle was a large and imposing structure made of stone. It was giving off fairy-tale vibes, and Stormey couldn't wait to see what it looked like during the day. It was sure to be a magnificent building. She had only seen pictures of it in the news or the papers.

The doors opened, and a gentleman dressed in a suit stood waiting for them. He had to be the butler of the residence. All places like this had one. She wondered if he was a human or vampire.

"We have Miss Jaymes for the princess," Dark Hair announced.

They arrived at the top of the stairs and stood on the landing. The elderly man's eyes swiveled toward Stormey. He did a quick perusal of her, but she was unable to read his expression.

"The princess is not here. She is away on business, but we will get Miss Jaymes settled," the butler said.

Dark Hair handed him Stormey's bag.

"Miss Jaymes, Edward will take care of you from here," Blondie said.

He and Dark Hair stepped down a few stairs. She turned to them and offered them a warm smile.

"Thank you for escorting me here," Stormey said.

They both gave her a nod.

"Will I see you again?" she asked. "I don't even know your names."

"I am Elwin, and this is Caleb," Dark Hair replied.

"Thank you, Elwin and Caleb. I will remember your kindness." She gave them a tiny wave and entered the castle.

CHAPTER THREE

"Your Grace. Are you sure we should be here?" Corbin exclaimed. He strolled along next to her.

Hegna Riskel sensed the worried gaze of her trusted advisor. Corbin had been by her side for well over a century. His advice was always sound, but tonight, Hegna wanted to make bad decisions.

She was the oldest daughter of the vampire king and queen. It was she who had been deemed the heir to the throne. She was always supposed to play by the rules, do what was expected of her. In truth, she had no problems doing what was expected of her, but there were certain aspects of her life where she wanted to maintain control.

And deciding when to mate and who to mate was one of them. A scowl formed as she thought of her mother's treachery.

How dare she enter Hegna into that wretched draft without consulting her. This was not the right time for her to be matched with a mate. There were more important factors she had to worry about. Such as this bitch of an alpha wolf who'd decided to wage war against the vampire nation.

That was top priority.

Not falling in love.

She wouldn't give in to the mating bond. She wouldn't be a slave to the notion that one other person was her sole purpose in life. As a future queen, she had to think of every vampire in the nation. Only she determined her fate. When that time came, Hegna preferred to have some sort of say-so.

But that had been taken from her the day her mother, the queen, had entered her daughters into the draft.

One day in the future, Hegna would sit on the throne as queen, ruling the vampire nation. Once her people were at peace then it would be appropriate to find a mate. Not when they were seconds away from a war again with the lycans. She bit back a snarl at the thought of the lycan alpha causing waves in their lives.

"I can go anywhere I damn well please," Hegna growled.

Her personal guards walked in front of her and Corbin. They paused at the shut doors of the unlabeled property. Cesar, her most loyal guard, banged on the door.

They were at an establishment where Hegna enjoyed blowing off steam and to feed. Madam Rice, one of the most well-known madams across the nation, owned discreet feeding clubs that allowed vampires to not only sample the goods but fuck them if one desired. A vampire could have their choice.

Food or sex.

Or both.

Most times Hegna preferred both.

The humans who were donors were well compensated for their time and blood. Madam Rice had establishments all across the country. There was even one in Hegna's town that she frequented.

"I didn't say you couldn't come here. As your advisor, I am highly suggesting we go back to your sister's home so you and your family can have a much-needed royal family meeting to strategize against the lycans." Corbin turned to her and met her ferocious gaze head-on. He was one of few people who did not cower from her. Due to their friendship, he had become desensitized to her fierce nature.

Their friendship dated back to when she had just turned one hundred and had been a member of her father's army. Corbin's coven had come under attack, and it was Hegna who had dragged him out of a burning building. He had felt he was in debt to her for saving his life. He had refused to leave her side, first serving as her assistant, then working his way to her advisor. Over the years, they had grown as close as siblings.

She eyed her friend. He was tall, lean, with an odd shade of greenish-blue eyes. She made him train to ensure he would be able to protect himself. As the advisor of the future queen, he would always have a target on his back. His hair was silver, falling just below his shoulders. His fangs peeked through from underneath his top lip.

"And as my friend, what would you suggest we do?" Hegna smirked and moved closer to him.

His eyes flicked to the building. Lust and desire

appeared briefly in them. Her friend was easy to read. Thankfully, he was not a warrior. His expressions would give away any and all of his battle strategies.

She snorted. "You can't hide your thoughts from me, my friend. You desire to get your dick wet, and you shall while we are here."

Hegna clapped Corbin on the back and grinned.

A small window opened on the door.

"Who goes there?" a sniveling voice asked from behind the door.

"The Princess Hegna Riskel, first born daughter of King Niall and Queen Mira Riskel, heir to the throne, warden of the central—"

"If that door doesn't open in three seconds, I will enter by force and slaughter every living being inside," Hegna barked, interrupting Cezar. She didn't have time for formal introductions. She was in the mood for a curvy female with a sweet cunt and delicious blood. Just thinking of soft, supple thighs had her fangs descending.

Her guards shifted next to her. It would only take one order and her warriors would carry out her wishes without questions. Patience was not one of her virtues. She strolled to the front of her security detail. She brandished her fangs at the doorman.

"Does that answer your question?" Hegna snapped. Her hand rested on her daggers that were sheathed on her waist. Tonight, she had changed up her outfit. Normally, she would be in her fighting leathers, but instead of leather pants, she wore her leather kilt with a matching sleeveless tunic. Her knee-high black boots added four inches to her already six-foot frame.

It was her casual warrior look.

"Yes, of course, Your Grace. My apologies," the voice exclaimed.

The sounds of the locks being undone filled the air.

Hegna ignored Corbin's muttering about her being rude and impatient. The mistress of this establishment had been alerted that she would be attending. This was the type of welcoming reception they offered their future queen?

"No manners," Hegna grumbled. Madam Rice would hear her complaint. It was wintertime, and they were currently in Washington state. As a vampire, she didn't feel the cold as much. Her legs were bare, and maybe she should have worn pants, but knowing where she was going, she wanted to have easy access.

"They both were acting correctly," Corbin said. He came to stand next to her. "It is customary for you to be announced formally, and that vampire was doing his job. You would question if they just let anyone in without screening them."

Hegna scowled, refusing to acknowledge that Corbin was right. They entered the establishment. It had not been updated and was reminiscent of a time when vampires were underground. The entrance was dreary. Stone walls on each side of the dark hallway were crumbling slightly. Fire burned in sconces that lined the walls, giving off a little light. Not that she or her vampires needed it. Her vision was impeccable in the dark.

Hegna passed the doorman who gave a low bow, his gray hair hiding his face. She continued on through the short hallway and entered the waiting grated elevator. Corbin stood next to her while her four guards filed in around them. Cezar pulled the grate down and guided the elevator down to the lower level.

"There's no way I can change your mind?" Corbin leaned over and asked.

"Not for all the blood in the world." She

smirked. Her men deserved to relax and enjoy carnal pleasure. Tensions had been running high ever since the lycans had revealed their numbers were on the rise. "Tonight, men, everything is on me."

She was met with celebrating cheers and laughter.

"Your Grace, it is much appreciated," Cezar said.

"No need to thank me. Keep serving me well." Hegna glanced around the small car and gave each man a nod of respect.

Cezar, Kendrick, Rodin, and Joran were loyal to her. They'd fought alongside her for years. They were her detail that she had chosen to travel with her. She had left Bijou, her second-in-command, and her captain of her army, Nezera, in charge. Those women would keep everything running smoothly in her absence.

Hegna was one lucky vampire to have such a team surrounding her, and she appreciated each and every one of them. A future queen would need to be surrounded by those she could trust. If ever one of them were to betray her, it would gut her, but it wouldn't keep her from killing them.

They arrived with a ding of the bell, deep

underground where they were met with sensual music.

Hegna exited the elevator behind Cezar and Kendrick. She ran her tongue along her fangs, the desire for blood growing inside her. The hall was short, but the club was visible around the stone columns.

Everything about the establishment was pleasing to the eyes. This one was decorated almost the same as the club back in Black Hollows. Sheer black curtains hung from the ceiling. There were plenty of chaises, long chairs for anyone to use them as they pleased. Naked bodies were everywhere. Women being taken up against a wall, men being bent over with their lovers behind them, all crying out their ecstasy. The air was filled with the delicious aroma of sex and blood.

Human servants walked around with transparent clothes that alluded to what was underneath them.

Men and women were enjoying the carnal pleasures that were offered.

Open feedings were occurring. Hegna's own arousal heightened. This was exactly where she needed to be. Not in some stuffy room strategizing about a lycan alpha. Tonight was her night to release. She'd worry about war in the morning.

"Your Grace." A small woman in a silk black robe, pale skin, and large blue eyes appeared in front of their group. Her dark hair was pulled up into a high bun, showcasing her neck.

Cezar and Kendrick parted to allow Hegna to walk to the front to greet the woman.

"My name is Opal. I am Madam Rice's assistant, and I must apologize for the delay of your entrance."

"It's quite all right, Opal. Please share with Madam Rice that it shouldn't happen again," Hegna growled.

"I agree. With the string of lycan attacks, we've had to up our security and screening to protect our patrons." Opal bowed her head before glancing back up to meet Hegna's gaze.

"I will discuss this with my sister and ensure there is enough protection in this area for your fine establishment," Hegna said.

Her gaze drifted away to a female vampire being serviced by two human males. Her cries were growing louder as each male was pounding into her simultaneously.

"We would offer many thanks. If you come this

way, Your Grace, I have a special area reserved for you. Would your entire party be staying together?" Opal asked, eyeing the five men with Hegna.

"My men are free to go where they please. Send the bill to my house," Hegna instructed. She turned and nodded to her men. She would not need protection. Hegna was a deadly vampire and didn't need coddling.

Her guards returned the nod, separating and leaving her side. Hegna raised an eyebrow at Corbin.

"I'll be at your side, as always." He smirked. He shrugged and moved to her side.

Hegna bit back a chuckle. She knew he would be changing his mind and probably leaving her side once he saw someone who captured his attention.

"Please, follow me," Opal said. She spun around on her heel and led them through the club.

The building was windowless, protecting vampires from the sun. There were tastefully erotic paintings hanging on the walls. Madam Rice ensured that all of her facilities were top notch. There was even a bar on one side that provided alcohol and blood, for those vampires who may not want live donors. Madam Rice even offered lodging at her establishment for those who may need a place to stay to wait for the sun to go down, or for those who chose to have privacy with their donors.

Hegna walked with her head held high. Some vampires who weren't completely busy with their humans gave her appropriate nods of greeting. Opal guided them to an area at the back of the club that allowed them to have an open view of everything. There were large columns with drapes that could be pulled closed should they desire to keep their party private.

There was a comfortable half-circular bench with plush pillows for them to sit. A low, round table was perched in front of the sofa. Directly behind the seating was a massive bed topped with a comfortable-looking mattress and tons of pillows.

"Is this to your liking?" Opal asked.

Corbin went over and took a seat on the couch while Hegna stood near a pillar. She leaned against it and eyed the club. She quickly made all of the exits, the warrior in her calculating how fast she and her men could be out if something were to occur. Satisfied with what she saw, she gave a nod before turning to Opal.

"It is exceptional," she replied.

Opal brightened at the compliment.

Hegna took her seat, crossing her legs. She

leaned back, sensing her hunger growing. "My favorite blood type is—"

"O negative," Opal interjected with a smile on her lips. She folded her hands in front of her. "Your Grace, I have the perfect young lady for you. She's twenty-two years old and has never had a vampire drink from her. She should be a good choice for you." She appeared certain of her choice.

"A virgin?" Hegna raised an eyebrow.

"Only to the bite of a vampire."

"Very well. She sounds lovely, but I want two." Hegna leaned forward, resting her elbow on her knee.

"That shall not be a problem." Opal turned to Corbin, her gaze curious. "And, sire, what shall you require? Male or female? A certain blood type?"

"You appear to know the princess so well. I want you to surprise me." Corbin smirked.

"As you wish, sire." Opal leaned forward in a deep bow. Wisps of her hair broke free from her bun and fluttered into her face. She straightened and left their area.

"You want to be surprised?" Hegna arched an eyebrow at her friend and settled back against the pillows.

"Yes, you know I don't have a preference to

male or female." He grinned, showcasing his fangs. "As long as their blood is thick and sweet, that's all that really matters. Besides, both come with holes to fuck."

Hegna barked a laugh. This was her friend, Corbin, not her advisor. His sense of humor matched hers on every level.

"But women have an additional hole the males don't have."

"That is true." He chuckled.

They both turned back to the view, taking in the scenes before them. Sex and feedings went hand in hand for vampires. The intimate nature of feedings could lead to sex, or vice versa.

Hegna took in the carnal scenes playing out before her and licked a fang with her tongue.

"Your Grace. May I present Kala and Velvet." Opal stood in the entrance.

There were two females standing behind her. Opal certainly did know her well. The first one was petite, long, flaming-red hair, a slender nose, wide eyes, and pouty lips. Her body was draped with sheer white material that did little to hide her dusky nipples. The other female was tall, long legs, short black hair, large, full breasts. Her sheer material was black, like the others.

"Are they to your liking?

Hegna growled low in her throat.

Yes, this would make up for the snafu at the entrance.

"Yes, Opal. You shall be rewarded handsomely," Hegna replied.

The smaller one in white appeared nervous. The white symbolized her being untouched by a vampire's fangs.

"And, sire, I have two young gentlemen for you. Warren and Max." Opal motioned to two tall, lean men who wore black sheer material wrapped around their waists. Their long, thick cocks were semi-hard as they eyed Corbin.

Her friend's expression was that of a predator on the hunt. Sharp and full of hunger.

"Will they do, or would you—"

"Leave us," Corbin growled. He stood and removed his jacket, not taking his eyes off his human donors.

Opal gave a nod, a pleased look on her face. She stepped through the humans and disappeared.

Hegna agreed. Presenting these humans in front of them was like teasing an animal with its meal.

Hegna was ravenous, not having had a decent

meal in a day or two since traveling to her sister's home.

"Come." Hegna waved the two women over to her. Corbin's humans were already at his side. Hegna eyed the smaller one. "You are Kala?"

"Yes, ma'am," Kala replied with the hint of a Southern accent. She ambled over to stand in front of Hegna.

Velvet stood next to her. The taller woman's gaze was locked on Hegna's bare legs.

"You sit here by me." Hegna patted the seat next to her.

Kala immediately complied, kneeling on the cushion beside her. The scent of the humans was overwhelming Hegna. She could hear the pounding of their blood. Kala's eyes were wide as she stared at Hegna.

She didn't want to instill terror in the girl. The last thing she wanted was her blood laden with the acidic taste of fear. Velvet was a woman Hegna could tell was used to servicing vampires. She slid her coverings off, leaving her naked. She stood tall and proud, meeting Hegna's gaze. Hegna uncrossed her legs and widened them. She lifted one leg and rested her foot on the seat.

Her pussy was completely open and exposed to

Velvet. Hegna crooked a finger. Velvet sauntered over to her, leaning down over Hegna, offering her lips. Hegna crushed her mouth to hers in a harsh and demanding kiss. Even though these two women were to please and feed her, she would ensure they enjoyed their time with her. A side effect of being fed from a vampire was intense orgasms.

That was why many humans flocked at the chance to be live donors in settings such as these. Aside from it paying an above-average wage, they all got a euphoric sense from the bite of a vampire. Some humans were even known to become addicted to vampires' bites, just as they would to the synthetic drugs that were sold.

Hegna pulled back, cupping Velvet's chin.

"On your knees, human. I want these lips and tongue on my pussy," Hegna commanded. She removed the belt that housed her daggers and set it down on the table.

"Yes, Your Grace." Velvet kneeled before her.

Hegna eyed her large breasts and made herself a promise to taste them. Velvet's gentle hands rested on her thighs and pushed them apart even more. She leaned her head down and slid her wide tongue along the slit of Hegna's pussy. Hegna groaned, now understanding why her name was Velvet. That tongue of hers was wide, smooth, and very talented.

Hegna reached up with her hand closest to Kala and slid it up to the base of her neck, freeing her from the white material. She turned her attention to Kala, taking in her satiny, young body. Her breasts were small but perky. Her dusky areolas appeared soft and sweet.

Hegna groaned from Velvet's assault. She had captured Hegna's clit and was suckling it, slow and steady.

A deeper moan, that of a male, cut through the air. Hegna couldn't keep from peeking in on her friend. Corbin was relaxed with his pants around his ankles while the human male, named Max, was on his knees swallowing Corbin's cock. Corbin was locking lips with the one named Warren, and from the looks of things, they were getting hot and heavy. It pleased her that her buddy was enjoying himself.

Hegna turned back to Kala, tearing the material away. She wanted to see all of her. She guided the younger woman to her, capturing her lips in a kiss. She slid her hand down to cup her tantalizing breast. Her mound was pillowy and supple. Hegna guided her other hand down and threaded her fingers in Velvet's hair, holding her in place. Hegna was very talented at being a multitasker. She thrust her hips, fucking Velvet's masterful mouth.

Kala returned her kiss, shy at first before becoming bolder. Hegna tore her mouth away and dropped kisses along her chin and down to her throat. She moved her hand down Kala's torso and dove in between her legs. The girl was drenched. Hegna's moans were breathless. She dipped her finger into Kala's hot core to be rewarded with her sweet cream.

Kala's hands were busy, undoing the top of Hegna's tunic. There was a button at the base of her neck that freed her breasts. Kala folded it down, exposing Hegna's. Her small hand gripped and molded to Hegna's mound, eliciting a growl from her.

Kala's hips rocked against her hand as she stroked her clit. Her moan was music to Hegna's ears. Now that she had this shy little bird, writhing, her blood would be flowing fast and would be just so sweet.

Hegna nuzzled Kala's neck. The girl tilted it back, presenting the full length. Hegna licked her soft skin. She opened her mouth wide and sank her fangs deep into the column of her throat. Kala stiffened for a moment, a gasp escaping her lips. Her breaths turned to pants, and her hips bucked harder against Hegna's hand.

Hegna pulled her thick, delicious blood in, drinking it down. Just as she'd known, the girl was sweet. O negative, just as she was promised. Hegna drank greedily from the girl. The coppery, nutritious substance gave her everything she needed. Madam Rice ensured all of her humans were on kenaf weed, an herb that would help replenish their blood stores.

Kala pinched Hegna's nipples as she reached her climax. The girl screamed out her joy, her muscles growing taut. Her blood continued to flow freely. Hegna drank a little more than she should since she was close to reaching her climax. She tightened her hold on Velvet's hair. The woman pushed two fingers inside Hegna, twisting them around. She pumped them hard while humming.

It sent Hegna crashing into an orgasm. She tore her mouth from Kala, exhaling through her first release. It wasn't life-shattering, but it was hard enough to steal her breath away and take the edge off the lust building inside her. She had all night if she chose, to get her pleasure from these two, more if she wanted to. It would only take one request to bring more women to satisfy her.

Velvet took another swipe of her tongue before sitting up. A pleased look was on her face, and she held out her wrist to Hegna without a word. Her lips were shiny with the proof of Hegna's release. Hegna snatched her arm and pulled her forward.

Velvet giggled, falling against Hegna. Her breaths were coming fast, and she waited for the bite. Kala fell back onto the couch, still riding the high of Hegna drinking from her. Hegna glanced at the young girl and took in her chest rising and falling rapidly. She continued to writhe on the couch, her moans and gasps filling the air. This was how most humans were after their first bite. It was an aphrodisiac for them. Soon, Kala would be coming back to her for more.

"She'll be fine," Velvet murmured, her gaze flicking back to Hegna. Her slick lips curved up into a smile.

Grunts and groans were coming from Corbin and his humans. Max was on Corbin's lap, riding Corbin's cock while her friend drank from the other human male. Hegna was glad that she was able to talk her advisor into coming with her to the club. He needed a night off to enjoy their way of life.

What was the purpose of being a vampire if one could not indulge in all the things that were meant for them? She brought the woman's wrist to her lips. She bathed the site she'd chosen with her tongue.

Velvet leaned forward and captured Hegna's nipple with her lips.

Hegna rewarded her by sinking her fangs into her wrist. Her warm blood flooded Hegna's mouth. From the first taste, Hegna could tell she was slightly older than Kala.

Velvet lifted her head, her eyes closed. The same euphoric feeling was overtaking her that Kala had experienced.

"Yes," Velvet hissed.

Her free hand slipped between her own thighs. She played with her pussy, and Hegna pulled more of her delicious blood from her. Velvet's arm jerked feverishly as she fucked herself. Hegna watched her, unable to tear her gaze from her. Velvet's throaty cry joined those who were also reaching their climaxes nearby.

Hegna eased back from her, eyeing her wrist. There was a bruise forming. Hegna licked the pinpoint holes, using her saliva to heal them. Velvet fell forward, her head resting on Hegna's stomach. Hegna ran her fingers through the dark hair, pushing it back from the woman's face. Velvet smiled, lifting her head. She returned to her suckling of Hegna's breasts. Kala, now awakening from her euphoric state, sat up. She smiled shyly at Hegna and moved back next to her.

"Let me see your neck," Hegna murmured. She wasn't so cruel as some would make her out to be.

Kala tilted her neck, revealing blood still seeping from her wounds. Hegna brought her close and licked her bruising skin, sealing the holes over.

"Oh, my. I've never experienced anything like that before," Kala whispered. The human was addicted.

Hegna brushed her hair from her face. "I'm sure you will now enjoy your work immensely."

"God, yes." She wrapped her arms around Hegna's neck and drew her forward.

Hegna grinned, knowing tonight was going be very interesting. They shared hard, short kisses, before Hegna turned to Velvet, tugging her in for a few as well.

"Get on the bed," Hegna growled.

It was time to take their party to the large bed behind them. Kala and Velvet grinned, both scurrying from their positions over to the bed. Hegna stood and faced the big monstrosity. She hadn't even realized Corbin had already moved his males over there. Her friend was pounding his cock into Warren from behind while grinning the whole damn time.

And he hadn't wanted to come.

"Your Grace."

Hegna spun around, glaring at the royal guard standing at the entrance. He was dressed in official royal uniform, a gold patch on his chest.

Hegna swore.

It was one of her mother's guards. She doubted her father would send someone searching for her. She reached down and yanked her tunic up over her breasts.

"What the hell do you want?" she snapped.

"Your mother requests your presence." He stood firm with his message.

Hegna narrowed her gaze on him. She couldn't kill him. The sounds of Corbin finishing made her actually jealous. He wasn't being summoned.

She was.

"I'll be there at dusk." She turned her back to him. She walked toward the bed, her gaze locked on Kala and Velvet already starting without her. Their lips were locked in a deep, passionate kiss with Velvet's hand buried between Kala's thighs. She peered at the guard.

"She said immediately." He swallowed, still meeting her hard gaze.

She would have to give him credit for his bravery. She had killed many men for less than what he was doing now.

"According to the queen, if you don't return with me now, she will come down here herself."

Hegna growled and reached up, buttoning her tunic. She stretched for her belt off the table and put it back on. She brushed her twin daggers with her fingertips. She glanced over at Corbin who lay watching her with both of his males lying in his arms. She turned and faced the club, catching hints of her men enjoying themselves.

"Corbin, I'm going to meet with my mother. You men continue your fun. I'll see you later." She didn't wait for a reply and strode toward the guard without looking back.

CHAPTER FOUR

"A brothel? That's where you were?" Queen Mira growled.

Hegna's mother was a fierce woman who was a force to be reckoned with. She glared at Hegna, resting her hands on her waist. The queen dressed in a long flowing gown that would look outdated on some but was the queen's signature. The woman was five hundred and eighty years old and didn't appear a day over fifty. Her long blonde hair was pulled away from face and hanging down her back. She embodied the look of a queen. All of her daughters resembled her, only Hegna had inherited her dark hair from her father.

"You were to come here immediately upon arriving to Ensfield, not go to the local seedy whorehouse."

Hegna stepped from the shower and wrapped her towel around her. She ambled over to the sink and reached for her brush. She should have known that her mother would come searching for her. When she'd returned to Velika's castle, she had come to her room with the intent to shower first before searching for her mother. She'd made the mistake of lying across the bed after she'd removed her shoes and had fallen asleep. Her belly was full of delicious blood from her two donors, and her body was slightly satisfied. Sleep had quickly claimed her.

She sighed.

What she wouldn't give for a life-altering orgasm with any of her lovers. Not that she didn't enjoy any climax she could reach, it just wasn't one that she would write home about.

Hegna didn't want to argue with her mother. Hegna may be two hundred and thirty-five years old, a hardened warrior, and a warden of her own territory, but she respected her mother and would take the tongue-lashing she knew would come. There were some things her mother and her would never see eye to eye on, and visiting a place like Madam Rice's was one of them. According to her mother, a future queen shouldn't be seen in establishments like that.

"Hello to you, too, Mother. I needed to feed," she replied calmly. She brushed her dark locks to detangle them. She sensed her mother's presence near her. She kept her gaze forward, not wanting to meet her mother's gaze. Her brush snagged on a few tangles. She paused and carefully worked the knot, before continuing on. "And it's not a brothel. It's a clean facility for pleasure feeding—"

"A brothel," her mother snapped. She leaned back on the counter and stared at Hegna until she could no longer avoid meeting her gaze. A deep scowl was embedded in her refined features. "Was sex involved?"

"Yes."

"Did you pay for the services of said club?"

"Yes." Hegna's teeth ground together. She knew where her mother was going with this line of questioning.

"Then it's a brothel. A whorehouse." Mira threw up her hands, clearly exasperated with

Hegna. "I don't know why you constantly want to frequent a place like that. If you needed to feed, your sister has plenty of human donors waiting."

"Mother. I'm not a child. A royal going to Madam Rice's facility helps improve the economy. Others will frequent the club that is safe for humans. They are paid well, they are taken care of and under the watchful of talented physicians. Vampires feel safe going there and can feed without looking over their shoulders. Everyone gets what they want. Not everyone has a line of human donors waiting to be called."

Hegna slammed her brush down on the counter. She rested her hands on the marble and stared into the sink. She had never raised her voice to her mother before and immediately regretted it.

"And so what if sex is involved. Everyone is there of their own free will. Would you want to take something away from the community that is one thing that brings vampires and humans together? Is that what you would have me do? Shut down the madam? That, I promise you, will not look well for the royal family."

They were in a stare-off. Hegna had heard stories that she was just as stubborn as her mother.

The queen was a fierce vampire who always put the good of vampires before herself.

"I see there is nothing I can do at the moment to change your mind." The queen sighed. She rested her hand on Hegna's.

Hegna, no matter how mad she was at her for entering her into the draft, couldn't stay mad at her when she was in her presence. She covered her mother's hand with hers and met her glance. "No, you won't."

"As a mother and queen, one thing I have learned is to carefully choose my battles. If you think that establishments like the madam's helps vampires, then I will leave that to you as long as it is spun in a positive light."

"I will. I must speak with Velika about patrols in that area. I was alerted that lycans had been spotted there. We need to ensure that human and vampires alike will remain safe when enjoying each other's company." Hegna straightened to her full height, towering over her mother.

"Speaking of lycans, we are meeting tonight to discuss these wretched animals." Mira walked by Hegna's side as they left the bathroom and headed into the attached bedroom.

A servant was in the room laying out clothes for

Hegna across the bed. She turned and gave a deep bow to Hegna and Mira.

"Will you be needing assistance getting dressed, Your Grace?" the servant girl asked.

"I'll be fine dressing myself," Hegna grumbled.

The girl gave a nod and scurried from the room. Hegna took a seat on the edge of the bed.

"You should be kinder, dear," Mira said. She went over to the window.

Dusk had finally settled. The window coverings must have lifted when Hegna was in the shower. She threw on her clothes in a rush. She wouldn't have time for anything else.

"I was kind. Making her stay to help me get dressed would have been torture for her." Hegna smirked. Her mother was probably hanging around to ensure she didn't disappear again. She slid on her fighting leathers. There was no telling what would be needed from her. She was under the same roof as her two sisters. Maybe they could go lycan hunting together. It had been a while since the three Riskel siblings had fought side by side.

"Have you heard anything regarding the draft?" Mira asked.

Hegna froze in place. Her breath caught in her throat. She slid her tunic down over her head and glared at her. Was that the true nature of demanding her presence back at Velika's castle?

"No. Have you?" Hegna didn't want to even think of that wretched draft. Mated life may be suitable for her sisters, but it wasn't for her. She continued getting dressed while eyeing her mother wearily.

"Of course not. If I had, I would have been retrieving you from that brothel—club—myself." The queen sniffed.

Hegna paused and stared at her. The woman was honorable and wouldn't lie about such a thing.

And she was right.

If she knew Hegna had been matched, it would have taken the queen herself to drag Hegna from the club.

Hegna tugged her boots on and zipped them up. She adorned her body with her knives and daggers under Mira's watchful gaze. She returned to her bathroom and pulled her hair back into a loose ponytail. Once she was satisfied with herself, she strolled back into the bedroom.

"I'm ready now. Are you going to escort me to the meeting?"

"You are just like your father," Mira snapped. She marched toward the door, muttering.

"Muttering isn't queen-like." Hegna snickered.

Mira hated when she and her sisters spoke under their breath. She'd reprimand them for doing it in her presence. To witness her mother do it, she couldn't help but point it out.

"Shut it, Hegna Riskel." She threw open the door and glared at Hegna over her shoulder.

Hegna flashed her fangs and followed her out the door.

"AZURA IS TAKING RISKS NOW. She's becoming more dangerous," Velika hissed. She slammed her fist down on the table.

Hegna Riskel eyed her youngest sister. Velika was more like her than Lethia. She was headstrong, stubborn, and spontaneous. Her blonde hair was held back in intricate braids. Her brow deepened with a scowl.

"Any more than she has been?" Hegna murmured.

She settled in her high-backed chair while her family was spread out around the table. They were all meeting to discuss the impending war with the lycans. Apparently, her family had been waiting for her arrival to hold this meeting and solidify a cast-iron plan against the lycan alpha. They were locked away in Velika's war strategy room.

Corbin sat her to her left. He looked refreshed and had a spark in his eyes that had been missing as of late. She hadn't been able to speak with him before the meeting began, but she could see he was well rested and the night at the madam's did him well.

Both Velika's and Lethia's advisors joined them. The room was heavily guarded, as was Velika's property. They couldn't be too careful when the entire royal family were together. Security was thick not only around the castle, but the town of Ensfield itself.

They would be going to war. Azura Michaels, the new alpha of the lycans, was a ticking time bomb. She was determined to take over everything the vampires had fought for.

Vampires who were once living in hiding as much as the other non-human races were. The vampire rulers around the world decided that they no longer wanted their people to live underground. They no longer wanted to hide who they were and what they were. It was time to present themselves.

The past few centuries before the war, it was

discovered that the amount of vampires born was on the decline. Vampires were only able to procreate with their fated mates. And that was an issue because vampires were having a harder time finding the one person fate had designed for them.

This had been a vital issue that had to be addressed.

Vampire leadership around the world agreed that they had to do something or in the coming centuries, they ran the risk of going extinct.

The vampire kings united and faced the humans. They offered a peaceful opportunity to them, but they were met with a hostile resistance. Humans had been ignorant in assuming they were the only ones inhabiting the earth and thought they were the stronger race.

Thus, the war.

And the humans lost.

Now they lived in a world that was governed by the seven vampire kings. The Riskel family ruled the North American continent.

It was discovered by the royal scientist that humans were compatible and would be another option vampires could seek out for matings. A test was developed that would require a simple blood sample that could match a vampire with their mate.

With this new test, a database was created. After the war, the king put it into law that humans would have to submit their blood sample. The human government, or what was left of it, backed this law. They didn't want to risk the wrath of the vampire kings.

That was how the draft had been founded. It had a one hundred percent success rate, and the vampires who had participated were extremely pleased with their matches. With this proof of success, more vampires donated their own samples in order to be matched with their mates.

The queen, Mira Riskel, had even taken it upon herself to enter her daughters into the draft. She determined that it would be a good look for the royal family to participate. She wanted to show that her family was not above the draft. The moment the public had got word of Velika and Quinn's mating, everything had gone crazy. More vampires stepped forward to donate their blood in search of their mate.

Then Lethia was matched with her mate, Alima. Their union gained even more popularity, and again there was a rush of vampires signing up. Due to the rush, the number of drafts had to increase to meet the demand.

Now all eyes were on Hegna.

Hegna snorted. She didn't want a mate. Velika had once been like her, but she'd fallen for her human and was in love. They had even gone through the process of impregnation and now had a son. Hegna's heart softened at the thought of her nephew. Prince Blayze was the first royal dhampir and had everyone wrapped around his little finger.

One day, she too would have children. That she knew without question.

Just not now.

"That is why we need to squash this lycan now," the king growled.

Her father, a great warrior, had fought for centuries for their people. Hegna had always idolized him. When she had been at a young age, he had put a sword in her hand and trained her. She, the future queen, would need to be a deadly warrior, a cunning diplomat, and have a large heart for her people. All of the traits that her father embodied and had instilled in her.

But he didn't just focus on only her, being the heir. All of the Riskel daughters had trained hard their entire lives. They had higher expectations to meet than any other warrior because of their last name. Each one of them had earned the title of warden.

"We don't know much about this alpha. I have just returned from the summit of kings," Niall continued. All eyes in the room were on the king. He scowled, the look the same as Hegna had seen on her own face and her sisters'. "There have been lycans spotted throughout the world. Azura at least spoke the truth. Their numbers are growing, and we need to take action. Killing their alpha will be the first step. It will weaken them. Lycans will need a leader to follow."

"Well, if they are spotted all over the world, that would mean there is more than one alpha, correct?" Lethia asked. Dressed like their mother in a dramatic gown, she glanced around the room.

The middle sister may fancy wearing expensive clothing, but it didn't mean she was unarmed. Hegna wouldn't be surprised if she didn't have at least four blades hidden somewhere on her body.

It had been Lethia who had fought the lycan alpha and was wounded. Hegna's gums burned as her fangs threatened to descend. There was a bounty on the alpha's head, but she had outsmarted every bounty hunter out there so far. The queen had issued a very hefty bounty on the alpha—dead or alive.

Only it was Hegna who wanted to be the one to end the alpha's life for what she had done to Lethia. No one messed with her sisters. It was only a matter of time until the alpha made a mistake.

And Hegna would be there to take her head off.

"That is what the other kings are now looking in to. We agreed to meet again virtually once they all have more information. I shared with them everything that I know, but it wasn't much," Niall said.

"Your Graces, may I ask, what all do we know?" Lethia's advisor, Aubrey Lafayette, asked. She held her electronic tablet in her hands. The vampire was a whiz when it came to electronics. Lethia had shared that her advisor had a way of finding information on that little contraption of hers. "She's highly intelligent if she's been able to remain under our radar and grow her numbers, she's pissed at the Riskel family, and she's been negotiating with some humans. Anything I miss?"

"Do we know her motive?" Corbin asked.

Hegna's advisor frowned. It was apparent the wheels in his brain were turning. Hegna knew what that look meant. He was quickly piecing things together. He was one who had to understand all of the parts of a problem. He'd always shared with her that the best way to defeat an enemy was to have a clear understanding of them.

"Why go directly after vampires?" he said. "Why not just come out to the world?"

"Besides the fact that vampires have been eradicating their kind since their rebellion?" Lethia rested back in her chair. Her eyes were dazed slightly as if she were reliving some memory. "There is some history that we don't truly know of between her and our family. She purposely chose to go after our family."

The holographic device in the middle of the table roared to life.

"Incoming call," the box announced.

Everyone froze in place, not saying a word. The air grew thicker with tension. Hegna glanced over at her youngest sister and arched an eyebrow.

"Isn't this line secured?" she asked.

"Of course it is," Velika hissed.

"Well, answer it," Lethia suggested. She shrugged one shoulder. "We are all safe here, and what if it is one of our contacts trying to report something?"

"I agree," Niall said. He sat forward, his gaze narrowed on the box. "Answer it. I'm curious as well as to who would be so bold to call your secured line that shouldn't be available to anyone but those who need it."

Velika reached forward and tapped the box's button. The image that came forth was not one that Hegna would have expected.

Azura Michaels.

"Well, well, well. The royal vampire family, the Riskels." Azura grinned, flashing fangs. She sat in a chair and crossed her legs, appearing as if she were invited to this meeting. "I'm sure there is no need for introductions on my behalf."

"How did you get this number?" Velika snapped.

"Don't worry about that." Azura chuckled. Her gaze scanned the room and landed on the king. "King Niall, just the vampire I wanted to speak with. You are certainly hard to get a hold of."

"You can find me anytime," the king said. He pushed back from his chair and stood. Her father was a seasoned, deadly warrior. Being king did not mean that he stayed off the battlefield. He was still physically fit, muscular, and was an expert swordsman. His hand gripped the hilt of his sword that sat in the sheath on his waist. "Why don't you come meet me in person."

"I'm so tempted, considering what you did to my family. Your head would make a great accessory on my wall." Azura growled.

Hegna, Lethia, and Velika stood immediately. A threat to their father elicited a violent response. No one threatened their parents or any member of their family and lived to tell about it.

"Watch your tongue, wolf," Hegna bit out. She and her sisters flanked her father, with her standing in front of him. She rested a hand on her hilt of her dagger. "I'm going to take great pride in cutting it from your mouth."

"The three princesses protecting their murdering father," Azura barked. She stood from her chair, planting her hands on her waist. The woman didn't look as if she had been injured at all on the day she'd fought Lethia. The alpha had been shot multiple times with argentite-filled bullets that should have been deadly to her. "The vampire king who murdered lycans and their babies. That is who you are protecting? A king who ordered the killing of children."

Hegna held back her shock, keeping her face clear of any emotions. Her father had ordered the deaths of children?

"Those days we were at war," Mira said from

where she stood. The queen, who was no stranger to war and fighting, glared at the alpha. Their mother had been a warrior for her father and could still wield any weapon as well as her daughters.

"War, you say? War would insinuate two parties battling each other. What happened was a massacre that started with your king beheading my grandfather in front of his entire pack, then having his wife's and son's throats slit. Boys aged eight and thirteen. Then their three-year-old daughter was tossed into the river to drown. That is how you define war?" Azura paced back and forth.

Things were starting to fall in place. Everyone knew of the story of King Niall fighting the lycan alpha, Ariston. The clash of the vampire and lycan kings. Niall had led his vampires into battle against the lycans. Azura surely had it mixed up with some fable that was told to blame vampires for her ancestor's death. It was a tale that had been told to Hegna and her sisters as bedtime stories. It was a grand tale of how vampires had defeated lycans.

"Anything I did was in the name of my people," Niall said. "Your kind—"

"Wanted to live," Azura screamed. Her breaths were rapid, her crazed eyes locked on them. "Just as you have done, we wanted to live in peace. Free from the tyranny of the vampire reign. But no, if you couldn't keep lycans as slaves, then you hunted us down and murdered us. But no more. No longer will you hunt my people down. We are stronger and will not cower from a fight. Everything you have done to us, we will return the favor tenfold to honor all of our dead. And your family will watch as we destroy what you have built, then I will kill you, King Niall. Slit your throat as you did my grandfather."

Azura's figure disappeared, the call terminated.

"If your name is not Riskel, leave us," the king roared.

Hegna stared at her father, seeing him in a new light. Had what Azura said been true? She'd never questioned her father's orders before. She was a warrior for him, fought in battles and wars, but never had she carried out something as heinous as the murder of babes.

Their advisors and few guards immediately exited the room without question. The door shut behind the last person, leaving her along with her family.

"The past is the past," Velika said. She folded her arms in front of her chest. "But that lycan doesn't get to make threats. We will go after her father. My sisters and I will destroy her."

The king didn't say a word but walked over to his wife. He gripped his sword and shook his head at her.

"You know I would have never ordered the killing of children," he said.

Mira stared at him with wide eyes. Her fierce expression hardened. "I know, Niall. What Velika said is true. The past is the past. There is nothing we can do to change it."

"If you didn't order that, then who would have carried out something like it under your name?" Hegna demanded. If her father was innocent of the murder of children, then who would have been so bold to do so? She would gladly avenge her father's name. She felt slight movement from her sisters and knew without question they were thinking along the same lines as she was.

"That person has already tasted the end of my sword and is no longer breathing," her father said.

Hegna was sure there was s story behind this, and she was dying to hear it.

"But here we are, still cleaning up his mess," her mother hissed. Mira's sharp gaze moved to her daughters. She stalked to them and stopped in front of Hegna. "This is a prime example of knowing who you keep close to you. Be it a queen or a warden, you need to ensure the people who you trust will always be loyal to you."

"Enhance security. I don't want to take any chances that Azura will come after Blayze," Niall ordered. The fierce warrior king was back. He stood tall while he took them in. There was nothing that her father wouldn't do for them, and the sentiment was mutual. Riskels fought together and protected one another. "It is too dangerous for us to remain together. Azura knew we were all here. Leave, go back to your territories. Prepare your men. We will be going to war."

Velika growled and backed away, spinning on her heels, and headed to the door. Hegna was sure her mate and child were at the forefront of her mind. Their father was right. Blayze, a young babe of six months old, was their future. He needed to be protected. The door burst open with one of Velika's staff entering.

"Your Grace. I apologize for this intrusion," she gasped, out of breath.

"It's quite all right, Jaden. What is it?" Velika rested her hands on the young woman's shoulders.

"There's an urgent message for your sister,

Princess Hegna." Jaden turned to Hegna. She gave a short bow and walked over to Hegna. She held out the envelope in her hand.

"What is this?" Hegna asked. She took it and flipped it over, noting the seal of her house. She broke it and pulled out a slip of thin parchment paper.

Princess Hegna Riskel, firstborn daughter of King Niall and Queen Mira Riskel, heir to the throne, commander of mid America, has been matched with her fated mate. The female human has been delivered to the commander's castle in Black Hollows and is awaiting the princess's arrival.

A growl vibrated deep from within Hegna. She crumpled the paper in her fist and let out a roar.

CHAPTER FIVE

It had been a few days since Stormey's arrival. She sat in the chair and allowed her newly appointed vampire attendant, Cici, to do her hair. This was something Stormey had to get used to. She had not been comfortable having someone waiting on her hand and foot, but she was informed it was expected of her. She hadn't wanted to insult Cici by refusing her services.

It would seem that she was the first human Cici had ever served. She was hired specifically to assist Stormey. She was a young vampire woman with pale skin, and large brown eyes that were odd for a vampire. She was tall and lean with deep auburn hair. She'd immediately greeted Stormey with a wide grin which had made Stormey feel comfortable around her.

"I love how thick your hair is. It is so easy to braid," Cici murmured. Her fingers were like magic.

Stormey felt relaxed and calm as Cici ran a comb through her long hair. It was something Stormey took great pride in. Not having many friends to experience life with, she enjoyed taking care of her hair. She was proud that her thick hair was down her back. She had been growing it out for the past few years and only used natural substances in it. She couldn't afford the haircare products that were sold in stores.

"Thanks," Stormey murmured. As much as she wanted to enjoy this, she couldn't help be worried about the first meeting between her and the princess. Hegna Riskel was known to be a hardened woman who was deadly in combat. She was a fierce vampire who protected her people.

"Almost done," Cici said.

Her gentle tugs were enough to almost send Stormey back to sleep. A yawn escaped her. She glanced over at her bed and secretly wished she could crawl back in it.

"Are you still tired, mistress? I'm sure it's hard to acclimate to the nocturnal life."

"Just a little, but I should be okay. I'm anxious to learn more about the castle."

Cici had started giving her tours around the building. She'd introduced her to many of the employees, human and vampire. Her favorite so far was the chef, Val. Stormey had thought she'd had good food before, but she was wrong on so many levels. Val's food was an experience. She looked forward to seeing what he had cooked for her today.

And Cici was correct. Stormey was having a hard time getting used to the nocturnal life. She was sure in a few days she would be fine. She wanted to make sure she would be a nocturnal being once Hegna returned. Worry filled Stormey at the thought of meeting Hegna. She had read as much as she could about the matings of humans to vampires. In the castle was a jaw-dropping library with an endless amount of books and even a computer with the internet.

Stormey had been like a child in the candy store the moment she had sat in front of the computer. Before she had come to live in Black Hollows, she had to travel about five miles by public bus to get to the only city library that had survived the war. Now she had not only many books at her disposal but access to the internet a few floors under where she slept.

"All done," Cici announced.

Stormey jumped up from the chair and walked over to the floor-length mirror that rested on her bedroom wall. Three days in Black Hollows, and she was already in love with her private living quarters. It was much larger than the tiny home she had lived in. A king bed with a plush mattress and fluffy pillows that had her getting the best sleep she'd had in a long while. She had awoken on her second day and found her closet filled with clothes sized perfectly for her. Stormey felt like a modern-day princess.

The bathroom and all the amenities it came with held everything Stormey had ever dreamed of. A large soaking tub, a shower that was encased in glass with multiple showerheads, a vanity that held makeup and more products that she would ever use. She'd taken advantage of the shower this morning and the bath the night before. Stormey was so used to conserving her resources such as water so her bill wouldn't be high. Here, she wouldn't need to worry about that. Her shower today was a long twenty-minute one.

"You certainly are talented," Stormey breathed.

Cici had placed intricate braids and created a crown around her head. Her neck was free, and she really liked having her hair off her neck. She stared at her reflection, barely recognizing herself. The castle could be a little drafty, so she had chosen a thick red sweater that had a V-neck, jeans, and a pair of nice leather boots.

"I'm glad you like it." Cici beamed from behind her. "Come, mistress. We'll stop at the kitchen first so you may break your fast."

Stormey didn't need to be told twice. She spun around and followed Cici to the door. They were met with a guard standing outside her room. This was another thing she had to get used to. Stormey had never felt more protected.

"Good morning—evening, Desmond." She smiled at her guard.

He was an extremely large vampire. She had to crane her neck back to meet his gaze. He, like most other of the vampire guards, appeared lethal, stoic, but respectful to her.

"Evening, Miss Jaymes." He gave a slight bow of his head to her. Desmond was dressed in his royal guard uniform; the patch with the Riskel family crest was purple.

Stormey knew from her research that each warden had their own banner colors. Purple for Hegna, Lethia blue, and Velika red with the king's colors of gold.

"Mistress, we will let you lead to see if you remember how to get to the kitchen," Cici said.

"I'll be able to get there." Stormey laughed. She paused and glanced at the room across from hers. She was told that it was Hegna's personal living quarters. Her smile slowly faded. The princess had been gone on official royal business. "Do you know when the princess will be here?"

"The last word I received was that the princess would be returning soon," Desmond replied.

Stormey was not going to question any further. She turned and headed toward the wide staircase. The castle was a few hundred years old and was full of history. She breathed in deeply as they took the stairs. They would have to go down two floors to reach the dining room and kitchen. The walls were stone, with long windows that were currently blanked out by the steel coverings that kept the sun out. The handrail was a thick mahogany wood, smooth to the touch.

Once on the first level, Stormey headed into the direction of the dining room. The hallways were lengthy, and she took a few turns and successfully arrived at the dining room. She pushed on the tall double doors and entered. It was a grand room with high ceilings with two chandeliers made of pure crystals and gold. The table was long and could easily seat twenty people. It was decorated for a ritzy party. Flowers, candles, and ancient china dinnerware. The walls held sconces with fires burning. Again, the windows were concealed with the steel. Soon they would be rising once the sunrays were no longer a danger to the vampires. Stormey stared at the table but didn't want to take her meal here. It would be lonely and cold.

"Excellent." Cici clapped and came to stand next to Stormey.

"I want to eat in the kitchen at the island," Stormey announced.

"The kitchen? But we had the table made up so beautiful for you." Cici's face fell. She walked over to the table. "Is it not to your liking? I can have the servant fix it—"

"No, it's gorgeous. It's just that I would feel lonely being in here all by myself," Stormey tried to explain. She'd prefer to watch the bustle of the kitchen. She had learned that even though the vampires didn't require food to live, the kitchen fed all of the humans who worked at the castle. They served meals where the humans could come and grab food. Their dining hall was located in another part of the castle that she had yet to see.

"Okay, well, if you are certain. Come." Cici waved her on to follow her.

Stormey smiled, feeling slightly excited. They exited through the swinging door on the opposite side of the room that led to kitchen. They had to walk through a short hall before they entered the room where all of the salivating scents were coming from.

"Val, I have a guest for you."

Val, a big, burly Italian chef, was piling something into the stove. He shut the door and spun around.

"Ah, Miss Jaymes. Good evening," he greeted her with a warm smile. His words were slightly accented with a hint of his homeland. His dark hair was pushed back away from his face, and his skin was a dark-olive complexion that was highlighted by his white chef's jacket. He waved a finger at her. "I have something special for you this evening."

"I can't wait. I hope you don't mind if I take my

meal here at the island." She moved over to the chairs and hopped up onto one.

"Not at all, as long as you don't mind the bustle of the kitchen."

The kitchen was a professional chef's dream. It was big enough to be able to feed the hundreds of humans the castle employed. The staff could easily cater large dinner parties with ease.

"Yes, I don't mind watching. I'd love to see what all you cook and be able to speak with some of the castle's employees." Stormey turned to Cici and Desmond. She was interested in getting to know the human staff. If she were to be a lady of the castle as the mate to Hegna, she wanted to begin by getting to know everyone and allowing them to know her. She wanted to be open. She was no stranger to tense relations between humans and vampires. Black Hollows was no different than Wichita, she was sure.

"I'd have to clear that with my superior," Desmond said.

"Clear what with your superior?" a new voice asked.

Stormey swiveled her head around to the newcomer. No introductions were needed. Stormey knew who the woman was immediately.

Bijou Goldis, Hegna's second-in-command. She was in charge of the warden's armies and was a legendary warrior in the vampire community. When Stormey had researched Hegna, Bijou's name constantly came up.

Stormey slid to her feet, not knowing if she was to bow or what. So she did what was a human greeting. Held her hand out to the general.

"General Bijou Goldis. It's a pleasure to meet you. I'm Stormey Jaymes," she said. She offered a wide smile.

Bijou's eyebrows arched in surprise. The woman was dressed in fighting leathers, her body adorned with knives. Her dark hair was pulled back in a low ponytail. She was the epitome of a badass warrior. No way would Stormey want to be on her bad side.

"Well, it would appear introductions truly aren't needed." Bijou's lips cracked a slight smile. She took Stormey's hand in a brief, strong shake before pulling away. "My lady, please forgive me for not seeking you out before and welcoming you to Black Hollows castle."

"Oh, I'm sure my arrival was as unexpected as my departure from home was." Stormey took her seat but turned it around so she could continue her conversation. She understood the nature of the matching rules. Humans were swept away from their homes immediately and literally dropped into the laps of their vampires to keep them from having time to run away.

"It would appear our future princess has done much research on vampires," Cici announced. "She knows much about our kind."

"Is that so?" Bijou appeared impressed. She came to stand by Stormey, jerking her head to Val. "I'll take a goblet, please. I'll dine with Miss Jaymes."

"Coming right up," Val said.

"You are not troubled by being matched with a vampire?" Bijou asked.

The woman apparently was very direct, but Stormey didn't mind. There were those humans who were like Stormey in wanting to match with a vampire. Not many, but they still existed. Her dark gaze studied Stormey.

Trying to not fidget underneath her gaze, Stormey reached for the wine glass Val had set out for her. She didn't know when a dinner place setting had arrived on the counter where she sat. She took a sip of the red wine and held back a groan. Val was well worth whatever Hegna paid him in salary.

"Actually, no. I've always had a curious nature.

It led to me love researching and reading. I wanted to know who this new race was that we were living beside and try to understand them."

"And do you? Understand vampires?"

"Not at all. Just like humans, vampires are complex," Stormey admitted.

"Ain't that the truth," Bijou murmured.

Cici and Desmond moved away from her, but Stormey called out to them.

"Why don't you take your meal with us? There's plenty of room." She motioned to the two other empty chairs at the island.

Desmond's gaze flicked to Bijou's.

"Your future princess would like to have a meal with you. Take a seat," Bijou said.

They took their seats. A young female dropped off Bijou's goblet. The copper scent that floated through the air alluded that it was blood for the vampire.

"Ayah, Cici and Desmond will be dining with us."

"Yes, General." She smiled and scurried away.

"And for Miss Jaymes, as promised." Val returned and set a platter in front of Stormey with a silver top hiding what was underneath.

"Oh, my. The presentation is wonderful."

Stormey laughed. She was curious as to what was underneath. She excitedly lifted the top and gasped, her eyes widening at the dish. There were thick noodles, a red sauce with some kind of black shells. It was garnished with fresh basil leaves. "It smells so good. What is it?"

"It is mussel fettuccine with a Napoli sauce." Val straightened to his full height. He took the top from her and set it aside.

"I've never eaten mussels before." She tore her gaze away from the beautiful plate. This was fancier than anything she'd ever been served.

"Then you are in for a treat." He laughed. He held up a block of cheese and a grater. "Parmesan, my lady?"

"Please," she gushed.

She watched him shave the cheese on top of her food. The aromas had her stomach announcing it was starving. He stopped once she waved her hand. She was a little skeptical on the mussels, but she was willing to try them.

"Here goes nothing."

She lifted the first shell and ensured she had a little sauce with it. She slid the meat into her mouth and chewed. The flavors burst out on her tongue. Her eyes widened in surprise.

"Oh, my goodness," she groaned. She reached for her fork and dove into the noodles and sauce. She brought it to her mouth and closed her eyes, truly enjoying the food.

"I almost want to try it." Cici giggled.

Ayah, the kitchen assistant, brought over her and Desmond's goblets. She stared down at her cup before eyeing Stormey's plate. "It looks much better than what we have here."

Stormey chuckled. She prayed she never would have to give up food. She knew that vampires could turn humans and hoped she wouldn't have to be turned in order to live as Hegna's mate.

"Have you ever had food?" Stormey asked the vampires seated with her.

They all shook their heads.

"Aw, I'm sorry."

"Food can be a love language for humans," Val said.

"It can be," Stormey agreed. She loved cooking, and if she couldn't feed Hegna, then she'd have to find another way to show her appreciation for her. It was weird that they hadn't even met yet and she was already thinking of ways she could please her vampire mate. "Val, you will have to let me cook. I make a mean fried chicken and macaroni and cheese."

"Of course. Anytime you want to come down here to cook, you are welcome. There is plenty of space." Val grinned.

"Thanks. I really appreciate it." Stormey beamed.

He gave her a slight bow then went and joined the staff who were bustling around cooking and baking. She finished her food while asking little questions of the vampires. She wanted to get to know them and was surprised about the things she had learned. Outside of working for the princess, they all had normal-sounding lives that if they weren't vampires, she would assume they were human.

Bijou was single, loved being out in nature, and loved drawing in her spare time. It helped her unwind from the stress of being a general in an army. Cici was dating a young vampire and loved horse riding. Desmond was mated to his destined mate. He and his mate loved traveling and journaling about all of the cities they'd seen. He even compared cities from the different time periods which she found really interesting.

"Would you mind if I read your journals? That

is a fascinating take on it. I would have loved to visit Paris in the eighteen hundreds, in the nineteen hundreds, and now just to compare."

"But of course, my lady." Desmond had relaxed slightly and even offered her a genuine smile.

"The answer to the question earlier is yes. If Miss Jaymes would like to meet the human employees, she can. This is her home, and she has full rein to go where she would like." Bijou stood from her seat.

"Thank you, General," Stormey said. It pleased her to hear that she would not be treated like a guest or an object owned by Hegna. There were so many rumors going around amongst the humans on how the vampires treat their human mates, and Stormey wasn't seeing any proof since she'd come to Black Hollows castle.

"No need to thank me. And please, call me Bijou."

* * *

"TELL ME, Cici. Do you enjoy working here?" Stormey asked.

They had begun the next tour of the castle. It would take Stormey a while before she was comfortable moving around herself. Certain areas such as the kitchen and dining room were somewhere she would definitely need to know where to go if she wanted to eat. There was an offer for her to eat in her room, but she'd turned that down.

"I do. Before I was promoted to your servant, I worked in the castle's concierge department." Cici strolled along beside Stormey.

They were on the second level of the castle, and Cici had been pointing out artwork and priceless items. Stormey enjoyed these walks around the building. There were so many beautiful rooms throughout the place that she was making a list of her favorites so she could go back to them.

"Really?" Stormey was surprised. A concierge department?

"Yes, we cater to any and all of the guests. We assist with events that are held here on the property when the princess entertains."

"And this was a promotion? Attending to me?" Stormey asked. She jumped at the sound of the window coverings moving. It was a whirring sound that echoed throughout the castle. She hadn't realized the night had passed by so quickly.

Daylight was coming.

"Oh, yes. It's a great honor to be chosen to care

for the mate of our princess. One day the two of you will rule. My family is very excited for me and have been bragging to everyone they know that I am your servant."

"Well, it is I who am thankful that you are assigned to me. I appreciate how kind you are and open to sharing things with me when I have questions."

They stopped outside a closed room. The doors were massively tall and looked to be made of heavy wood. It was so dark, it appeared black. The Riskel family crest was carved into each door. The artwork engraved along the doorframe in gold captured her attention. Stormey stepped forward and ran her hand along the grooves, entranced by its beauty.

"What room is this?"

"This, my lady, is the princess's office."

Stormey stepped back, curious as to what was behind the doors. She wasn't going to ask if they could go in there. She was pretty sure the answer would be no.

"What is she like?" Stormey asked.

"She's a fair employer. We all are loyal to her. She's a good warden and will make a great queen. Vampires follow her because she is passionate about our kind," Cici said.

That wasn't much to go on, but again, Cici may not know the princess personally to be able to actually answer the question. There was something about her. Cici appeared nervous, her fingers fiddling with each other. She had a hard time meeting Stormey's gaze.

"What are you not telling me?" Stormey stiffened.

"I'm sure you have heard that the queen entered her three daughters into the draft without their knowing or consent," Cici began.

Something passed in her eyes that Stormey couldn't read. "Hegna has probably been the most vocal of the three about the queen submitting her to the draft."

Stormey took a step back. She hadn't thought that her vampire would be one that wouldn't want a mate. She had been so excited that she had been matched that she hadn't taken the time to think how Hegna would take this.

"So what you are saying—"

"I think you are a very nice woman and I think you will be a good fit for our princess, but there is a chance that she won't want you."

The words echoed in Stormey's head.

She won't want you.

Well, Stormey was used to not being wanted. She would do what she had to do to win over the princess. She had studied the royal family and knew everything that was made public. She would find a way to get the princess to like her. She may not ever love her but at least she would like her.

Complete the mating bond.

Harsh footsteps echoed down the hallway. Someone was coming up their stairs. She moved over next to Cici. Desmond had remained silent and a few feet behind them to give them space. He moved to stand beside her, his hand resting on the sword that was sheathed on his waist. Stormey stood to the side, needing to see who it was.

But deep down, she knew who it was.

The princess.

Stormey's breath hitched in her throat. Two massive guards arrived on the landing first. Then behind them was the princess dressed in all leather, walking alongside a male who was tall and lean with long silver hair. Another two guards filed up the stairs behind her.

Stormey's heart pounded. The guards drew closer, and it wasn't until they had stopped in front of them that she took notice of Cici and Desmond bowing. She was unsure what she was supposed to do. Did she bow? Curtsey? She never got the chance to make a decision.

Hegna's icy-blue gaze landed on her. The vampire warrior stalked to her. Desmond moved aside as she came to stop in front of Stormey. Her gaze slowly drifted down Stormey's body, taking her in. Stormey stood tall and refused to cower from the vampire. This was her mate, and she would show that she wasn't afraid of her. Hegna's eyes returned to meet Stormey's.

"So you are the human."

CHAPTER SIX

Hegna hadn't thought she would meet the human outside her office. She had recently returned home and wanted to talk with her team before seeing the human. According to the law, she couldn't have the female returned. She had spent an hour speaking with the matching officials. No matter how much she'd yelled or threatened to stake them, they wouldn't make an exception. What good was it to be the heir to the vampire throne if she couldn't throw her weight around regarding this matter?

"My name is Stormey, not the human," the woman said.

Hegna bit back a smirk. This Stormey had spunk. Hegna could appreciate it, but too bad they weren't going to get to know one other. She had to decide what to do with the female since she couldn't send her away.

"Well, Stormey, it would seem you and I need to have a discussion, but now is not the time. I will send for you when I am available." Hegna tried to not stare too deeply in the human's deep bedroom eyes. Her gaze dropped down to Stormey's plump lips, and she found herself imagining tasting them.

Hegna cut that train of thought. She didn't want to admit it, but she found Stormey to be beautiful. The woman's smooth brown skin practically glowed. Her voluptuous frame had Hegna's hands itching to touch her. Stormey's womanly curves were perfectly highlighted by her low-cut sweater, and jeans that looked as if the woman was poured into them.

Hegna bit back a curse and scowled.

"You're sending me away?" Stormey asked.

The expression on Stormey's face had Hegna's hand balling into a fist. She had only been in her presence a few minutes and she was already being affected. Hegna needed to put some space between them.

"How I wish I could, but I can't," Hegna snapped. She turned her attention to the young female who must have been assigned to her mate—human. "See to it that she is kept entertained. I have important business to attend to."

"She can hear you perfectly fine," Stormey spat. She spun on her heel and marched away.

Hegna stared off after her, watching the sway of her hips. That one certainly had a fire to her that needed to be controlled.

"Will do, Your Grace." The young vampire bowed her head before racing after her charge.

The guard, Desmond, gave Hegna a nod and followed the two of them. Hegna spun around to enter her office to find her guards gone and Corbin standing in the doorway.

He pinched the bridge of his nose and let out an audible sigh.

"What?" Hegna brushed past him and entered her office. She strolled over to her desk and sat in her plush leather chair. Her office was where she handled all of her warden business and held her meetings with human and vampire officials.

Her territory was the largest of her sisters. It expanded into Canada, covered the entire midwest United States and went down into Mexico. By the piles of papers adorning her desk, there were matters that needed to be addressed but would need to wait.

"You could have handled that better," Corbin said. He sauntered into her office and took a seat in one of the chairs that faced her desk. He placed his leather attaché bag down on the floor near his feet. He was dressed in a gray button-down shirt, with the top button casually left open, dark slacks, and black boots. He had left his silver hair down, flowing past his shoulders. He narrowed his gaze on her, steeping his fingers.

"I think I handled it well." Hegna snorted. She rustled the papers before her, looking to see if anything needed to be addressed immediately. She really didn't want to have this conversation with her friend. His expression was easy to read. His advice would be something she wouldn't want to hear.

Mate with the human.

Now if only Bijou and Nezera were to arrive. She needed to discuss what was learned at Velika's with her general and captain. Defending her territory against the crazed alpha was important. She and her family would be meeting again soon, but it would be via hologram call. With the lycan's threats, it would be safer if they didn't convene together.

"Not sure what your definition of well is, but that was far from it."

"I'll worry about her later. I have more pressing matters at hand than to worry about a human who is said to be a match to me," she snapped.

The door opened with Bijou and Nezera entering. Hegna stood from her seat, glad to have them present so the topic could be changed. The matter of the human could wait.

"General. Captain."

"We came as soon as we could," Bijou announced.

The women strode forward. Hegna motioned to the round table for them to sit there. Corbin joined them. He eyed her, and she knew that wasn't the last of their conversation.

"Congratulations on your matching," Bijou began.

Hegna whipped her head in her direction. Not her, too. She sighed and closed her eyes, rubbing her temples. A slight ache was forming behind her eyes.

"Your mate will make a great princess and future queen."

"And how do you know this?" Hegna ignored the congratulations. This was not a joyous occasion for her. Only a slight issue that she would figure out how to deal with.

"I've spent some time with her. She's a very caring human who wants to make this mating work. She already has ideas that I think you should hear," Bijou responded.

Hegna stared at her second-in-command. Had the woman been hit on the head one too many times? Bijou had fought at Hegna's side for centuries and was as dedicated to their kind as Hegna was. Didn't she understand why now was not the time for Hegna to mate?

"A lab test doesn't mean that we are compatible. No one will tell me who is the right person for me. Only I get to choose that, and I alone will determine how my future will go," Hegna ground out. She leaned forward, eyeing all three of them. These were the women and man who she trusted without a doubt. She would lay down her life for any of them and she knew they reciprocated the same feeling.

"What did I miss?" Nezera asked. There was befuddled look in her eyes.

Hegna sniffed. So only Bijou was dazzled by the human.

"Nothing for you to worry yourself about. I called this meeting because Azura interrupted the meeting of my family," Hegna said.

The air grew tense.

"She attacked?" Nezera asked. Her captain was a deadly vampire who had worked her way up the ranks of the army and earned her title of captain. Her insight into strategic battle-planning was top notch, and the woman was a great warrior.

"No, but I wish she would have so that we would not be having this discussion because she would have tasted the silver of my daggers," Hegna snapped.

The image of the lycan brought a snarl from her. She updated her team on what she had learned. They remained quiet, allowing her to finish uninterrupted.

"It goes without saying that you do not leave this castle without a personal escort at all times," Bijou said.

"I can take care of myself," Hegna assured.

"Be that as it may, humor us all. We are not going to take chances that Azura somehow finds a way to get her hands on you. The future queen is to be protected at all times." Bijou narrowed her eyes on Hegna.

"Don't forget who you are speaking to," Hegna warned.

"My princess, my future queen, and my friend," Bijou growled.

Hegna closed her eyes and rubbed her temples again. She and Bijou were two stubborn vampires. There would be no winning with the general.

"Fine. One guard at all times. We can't waste resources with our guards and warriors coddling me." Hegna was willing to compromise. What kind of warden would she be if she didn't listen to her council?

Bijou stared at her at first as if she was going to argue but must have thought better of it. She gave a nod and relaxed slightly.

"Aubrey forwarded me information on the locations of all known packs across the country." Corbin pulled out a tablet from his attaché bag and turned it on. He sent the file to the hologram device sitting in the middle of the table. A map of the North American continent appeared before them in the air.

Hegna growled at the amount of packs marked on the image. There were plenty in her territory, and she didn't appreciate it at all. These filthy wolves needed to be stopped.

"How has this happened and we've not known?" Nezera murmured.

"I want increased patrols in every city and town. We are going to include the human government. Reach out to the mayors and governors and send a message," Hegna began.

She glanced at Corbin who gave a nod. He had cultivated a relationship with the human leaders, and she felt comfortable allowing him to handle them. He had a way with words and a way with humans that she had never perfected as he had.

"We can use the lower-class warriors to assist with patrols," Nezera suggested.

"Good. We need a solid plan of how we are going to protect our people and hunt down this bitch."

Hegna refused to end this meeting until they had a stringent plan in place.

HEGNA STOOD behind her desk and picked up one of the papers that had *urgent* written across the front of it. She glanced up and took note that Bijou was still in her office. Their meeting had concluded, with them having a definite plan in place. Hegna was not going to wait for the alpha or any of the lycans who followed her to act first.

It would be her who would make the first move.

Any lycan who followed Azura Michaels would be killed. Nezera and Bijou would put together teams of warriors who would begin hunting the wolves down. There were one too many lycan attacks documented, and they would pay for it dearly.

"Is there something else we need to discuss?" Hegna asked. She held the paper while she waited to hear what her second had to say.

"About the human," Bijou began.

Hegna rolled her eyes. Of course, the conversation was going to be about the woman.

"What about her?" Hegna snapped. She didn't want to keep thinking of the brown-skinned beauty. The paper crinkled in her hand. She didn't want to think she was beautiful. Her gums burned as her fangs pushed against them, wanting to descend.

Wanting to sink into the soft flesh of Stormey.

Hegna tried to push all of those thoughts away.

"Get to know her. I know that the draft and the matching is not something you want, but you can't ignore her."

"Why can't I?"

Bijou stared at her, and it was as if she were seeing through Hegna. The woman knew how Hegna thought, and it made her uncomfortable. Aside from Corbin, Bijou knew her the best.

"Do you really want to pass up on an opportunity to mate with the woman that fate has chosen for you?" Bijou asked.

"Fate? It was a fucking test done at a lab. Has it been proven that fate had any part of the decision of who matches with who?" Hegna tossed the paper down the desk and rested her palms on it.

"Don't start with that argument. You've seen the research and know the numbers. Matings from the draft are one hundred percent successful. It is working. Children are being born from it, vampires are flocking to sign up to it in masses."

"Yeah, but how do I know that the human who was sent here is mine?" Hegna didn't want to admit she could feel tiny wisps of something strange inside her that she suspected was the mating bond.

"You mean your mate? Or better yet, Stormey. That is her name."

"You've certainly taking a liking to her. How much time have you spent with her?"

"Oh, please. I've had one meal with her and learned a lot from her. You could have been saddled with a human who didn't want to be here and made your life a living hell." Bijou folded her arms in front of her chest.

"That actually might have worked better," Hegna muttered. A human who was a flight risk would have been perfect. They could have run away, and Hegna could have 'looked for her' and then been 'unsuccessful.' She smirked at the thought. Maybe what she needed to do was make the woman uncomfortable to the point where she wanted to leave. Hegna would be willing to purchase *Stormey* her own home and give her a living allowance. She didn't care where the girl would want to go as long as it was far from her.

Yes, that was what she would do. She'd make the woman not want to be around her any longer.

"I don't like that look on your face." Bijou sighed.

"I don't know what you are talking about."

Hegna sniffed. She straightened to her full height and wiped her face of all emotions.

"In your absence, Edward took care of things. He assigned Cici to attend to your mate, had clothing purchased for her, gave her the room across from yours. You may want to follow what your sisters did for their mates."

"And that is what?"

"Education about our kind so she can learn about our society and way of life, and self-defense classes. From what I heard, Lethia worked with her mate on her own."

Hegna didn't want to risk the bond forming even more. Education? Sure, it would help for the human to learn about vampire society norms. Self-defense would be a must. She may not want the human, but she'd be damned if a lycan attacked and harmed her.

The human.

She wasn't going to start claiming her now.

"Fine. I'll have Corbin set up her education and have Nezera find someone to train her." Hegna gave a nod at her decisions. It was the least she could do. She'd have to thank her butler, Edward, for managing well in her absence.

"Sure. I'll pass the message on to Corbin and Nezera, and don't forget, eventually the coven will demand an official meeting with Stormey. The announcement was sent out everywhere about your match." Bijou spun around on her heels and marched to the door. She paused, glancing over her shoulder. "But I'm sure you know that and have a plan for that."

She left the office and shut the door behind her. Hegna blew out a deep breath. When did her friend become so observant of the goings-on of the castle, and when the hell did she start bossing Hegna around? But she couldn't be mad at her. Bijou was right. The coven was going to want to meet Stormey. A celebration would be planned. They would have to make a public appearance.

Fuck.

Maybe she couldn't send Stormey away. Maybe she could have a wing of the castle remodeled for her. She could have her own area far away from Hegna.

Yes, that may work.

She glanced down at the paper she had been holding and saw it was a request from the human mayor of Black Hollows. There was an appeal for a donation for a charity ball for orphaned children.

She'd take care of it later and have money sent.

She had a soft spot in her heart for orphaned children.

The ache in her head was growing slightly. She stretched and decided to call down to the kitchen for some blood. She'd had a long night, and the sun had risen. It was time for her to get some sleep. She'd deal with all of this craziness in the evening.

CHAPTER SEVEN

Stormey entered her room and shut the door. A change of the guard had occurred, and it would seem that her other one, Jasper, would be posted outside her room. She blew out a deep breath and took in her bedroom. She leaned back against the door and tugged her boots off and wiggled her sock-covered toes.

She strolled across and went into the closet and tossed her boots. She smiled softly, taking in her wardrobe. She had imagined that her mate had put all of this into motion while she had been away on business. Her smile slowly faded. She sat on the comfortable plush chaise and stared at the ceiling.

Stormey felt like such a fool. She'd been living in a fantasy, thinking that her vampire mate would return home, sweep her off her feet, and complete the mating bond between them. She had even imagined they would fall deeply in love from the moment their eyes met and live together happily ever after.

No, the situation was far from a happy ever after.

Her vampire mate didn't want her.

Stormey could even see the princess had rejected the notion of having a relationship with her.

After marching away from the princess, Cici had taken her on the rest of the tour, but Stormey's mind wasn't there. She had even got the chance to go outside on the grounds, but she couldn't get Hegna out of her head.

The vampire was even more gorgeous in person. Stormey's fantasies of her did little justice to the real woman. Her icy-blue eyes were mesmerizing, and her body draped in her fighting leathers highlighted her toned, muscular physic.

Stormey's breath paused in her chest as a memory came to her.

Hegna's eyes had been filled with lust when she had perused Stormey's body with her gaze. Just the memory of it had Stormey's body heating.

The vampire may have said one thing with her mouth, but her eyes had revealed something she didn't want anyone around them to know.

She desired Stormey.

That gave Stormey a foot in the door. Hegna may not want her now, but they could begin somewhere. A physical relationship wouldn't be a bad start. Thinking of burying her face between the vampire's thighs had her core clenching.

What would she taste like?

Was she a boisterous lover?

Did she like to dominate and take control?

"Oh God, I hope so." Stormey would love it if Hegna took control of her and gave her endless amounts of pleasure and orgasms. She had read that the vampire princess loved frequenting feeding clubs. Stormey had never visited that type of place before but had heard whispers of what went on there.

A shiver slid along her spine.

She sat up and swung her legs around, resting

her feet on the floor. She eyed the area of the closet where her lingerie was. There were some risqué items hanging. She pushed up and strode over. A plan was forming in her mind.

She would seduce her vampire.

Stormey wasn't above using her body to get what she wanted, and that was for her vampire to at least like her.

Love could come later.

Stormey's hand landed on a black lace dress. She grinned and held it up. She spun around and knew this plan of hers could work. What hot-blooded woman—vampire—could resist a sexy, curvy woman who was barely dressed?

Stormey raced out of the closet and placed the delicate dress down on her bed. She walked over into her bathroom and stripped her clothes off. She threw her shower cap on and jumped in the shower. She grew giddy at the thought of what Hegna's face would look like when she saw her.

She quickly washed her body, scrubbing the day away. Tomorrow, Cici had promised to take her to the dining hall where the humans ate their meals. She smiled, excited about meeting them.

Once she was done, she cut the water off and snagged her towel that was waiting on the hook outside the shower. She dried off as best as she could before wrapping the plush towel around her. She left and went over to the vanity where her lotions and perfumes had been placed. After moisturizing her body, combing out her braids until her hair hung down her in soft waves, she even applied simple makeup. She wasn't a professional at it, but she tried her best, and she looked damned good.

Satisfied, she went back into her bedroom and stood before her bed. She stared down at the beautiful lace dress. She had never worn anything like this before. She fingered it, tracing the stitching.

"You can do this, girl. Claim your vampire," she whispered to herself. The dress had a low neckline, and with her overly large breasts, her cleavage was going to be on display. She had boobs for days and wasn't ashamed of them at all. When she was younger, kids would tease her, but she now knew those girls were just jealous that she had blossomed before they had. She slid the dress on and had to adjust it. "What is going on?"

She walked over to the mirror and chuckled. She had to reposition her breasts and straighten out the dress. It fit her well. She gasped as she took herself in. Her boobs looked amazing. With the sheerness of the material, her areolas were on display. Her nipples beaded into taut buds, pressed against the soft material. She bit back a moan at the feeling. Her figure appeared hourglass as her waist tapered slightly then her hips had a grand flare.

Stormey stepped back and didn't recognize herself at all.

Who was this woman staring back at her?

She turned around and giggled. Her backside was basically left out. There was a corset backing that she had tied as best as she could. A 'V' opening at the bottom of the dress exposed her ass.

Her face warmed at the thought of why someone would need easy access to their bottom. She pressed her hands to her cheeks and laughed.

It wasn't like she was a virgin. She'd had sex before and had even enjoyed it, but it had been a long while since she had liked someone enough to gift them an invite into her bed.

"Showtime," she announced. She took one last look at herself and tilted her chin up. She was smoking hot. Hegna was not going to be able to resist her.

She went back into her closet and found a robe. Jasper was standing outside her door, and it would not be appropriate for him to see her as she was. She was sure he would know why she was going over to Hegna's room, but she was sure he'd keep his mouth shut.

Stormey went over to her door and cracked it open. Sure enough, Jasper, in his royal guard attire, stood posted.

"Is there something you need, my lady?" he asked, glancing to her. He was a black vampire with deep-brown skin. His hair was kept cut short to his head, and he, like the other guards, was massive and tall.

"Has the princess returned to her quarters?" she asked.

"No, my lady. She has not."

"And you can let me in her room, right?" she asked. Stormey's gaze flickered over to the doors that faced her room. She bit her lip and drew up the courage. It would be now or never.

"Um, my lady?" He raised an eyebrow at her.

"Has anyone told you that I'm not allowed in her room?" She stepped out of hers and shut the door behind her. She marched over to the wide double doors. They, too, were decorated with the Riskel family crest like her office doors. Stormey spun around and waited for a reply.

"No, my lady. There are no orders regarding you going into the princess's private quarters." He walked over to her, pulling a set of keys from his pocket. He slipped the appropriate key inside the lock and turned it. He pushed open the door. "The servants have already prepared her room for her arrival."

"Thank you, Jasper." Stormey grinned, sliding past him. She spun around and giggled. "Don't tell her I'm in here. I want to surprise her."

"Of course, my lady." He gave a bow and headed back over to her room and took up his post.

She closed the door and leaned back against it. Her breath escaped her as she took in Hegna's quarters. She was currently in the sitting room that had oversized couches that faced each other. The room had an old-world feel to it. She felt as if she'd been thrown back into the eighteenth or nineteenth century. Her room was slightly modernized, but this looked as if Hegna preferred an earlier time period.

Stormey eased off the door, eyeing the large fireplace that had a roaring fire burning bright. She continued her journey, finding the next room to be a cozy dining area. She wasn't sure why a vampire who couldn't eat food would need such a place. It was as tastefully decorated as the sitting room. On the round table sat a rectangular vintage silver platter with a beautiful brass goblet that was embossed with a lush floral design. Stormey stepped closer to the table and picked up a distinctive metallic smell.

Blood.

She backed away. Jasper had shared that the servants had prepared Hegna's room for her return. They'd left her a goblet of blood to drink. Stormey's hand came to rest on the side of her neck.

Once they were mated, would Hegna only drink from her? Or would she still need to be supplemented by blood banks or live donors? This was something she would have to ask. That hadn't been in any of her readings.

There were a set of french doors that opened into a vast bedroom that was much larger than hers. A monstrous fireplace sat on the left side of the entrance. The fire burning bright in it warmed the air.

Warm colors decorated the room. Massive drapes lined the windows, softening the sight of the metal shades. Stormey's gaze landed on the bed that was at the center of the wall opposite her. She walked across to admire the handiwork of the wood. Four posts rose high. Deep sangria drapes were organized around the bed. She imagined they allowed Hegna to enclose herself and whoever shared the bed—

Stormey didn't want to think of Hegna with any other female. Her hands balled into fists at the thought. She suddenly had the urge to want to commit violence against the faceless women.

She glanced around and tried to figure out where it would be best for her to wait for Hegna. She eyed the rug in front of the fireplace. It would be perfect. The hearth would keep her warm. She slid the robe from her shoulders and padded over to a chair in the corner. She tossed it on the chair and made her way to the rug. It was located a few feet from the fireplace. She knelt and waited.

* * *

HEGNA GAVE a nod to the guard, Jasper, who stood outside the human's room. She inhaled sharply, unsure why they had put her in that room. But then Edward wouldn't have known how Hegna truly felt about mating.

"Good morning, Your Grace." Jasper bowed his head and thumped his chest over his heart in fealty to her.

"Everything is well?" she asked. Her gaze

flicked to the door again. The ache behind her eyes pulsated slightly.

"Yes, Your Grace." He straightened and met her gaze.

"Good. Well, see you in the evening." She spun away and let herself in her room. It was odd that the door was unlocked. She had gone away, and usually her door would be locked. But seeing the fire blazing in the fireplace, she remembered the servants would have come to prepare her room. Jasper was manning the hall and would have alerted her if something was out of the ordinary.

She winced slightly from the headache and leaned back against one of the couches and removed her boots and socks, dropping them onto the floor. The servants would take care of them later. She walked into the dining area and took notice of her waiting goblet. The delicious aroma of the sanguineous drink waiting for her would be what she needed. The pain in her head was probably a result of an extended time between feedings.

Hegna lifted the goblet and brought it to her lips. She took her first healthy gulp and immediately glanced down into the cup. The taste was slightly off. It wasn't terrible, but something was different.

She sniffed it and didn't pick up on any poisons or chemicals. The scent appeared to be fine.

Then why was she sort of put off by it?

Maybe it was because it wasn't her favorite type. She shrugged and took a small sip. She needed some sort of nourishment before she went to bed. It had been a long night, and she just wanted to unwind. She undid the belt that held her daggers and placed it on the table. She moved down to her ankles and took off the two smaller knives that were strapped to them. She dropped them down beside the other weapons and hefted up her goblet.

She strolled into her room and immediately drew to a halt. With a grimace, she drank more blood, draining the cup almost dry. Hegna paused, the hairs on the back of her neck rising. Someone was in her room who shouldn't be there. She slowly turned her gaze to the fireplace in her sleeping quarters and paused.

Never would she have imagined she'd come home to something that beautiful and tempting.

The human knelt on the rug, dressed in something that hid none of her body. Hegna's grip tightened on the goblet. It bent slightly from her hold. Her eyes greedily took in the brown-skinned female who watched her with wide brown eyes. Her dark hair, no longer in braids, flowed around her shoulders. Her voluptuous body was encased in a lace dress that put her full breasts on display.

Hegna wanted to see her closer. Her fingers itched to tear it off of her so she could have her in all of her glory.

"What are you doing here?" Hegna rasped. Her throat constricted slightly. She swallowed hard, trying to wet her suddenly dry esophagus. Why else would words barely be able to come out of her mouth? She couldn't look away from her human if she tried.

"I think we got off on the wrong foot." Stormey's hands slid along her bare thighs, garnering Hegna's attention.

Hegna had the strong urge to part those thick thighs so she could find the delicious cunt that would be waiting for her. She inhaled sharply, detecting the sweet aroma of her human's arousal.

"Is that so?" She arched an eyebrow and slowly brought her gaze up to meet the human's. The goblet fell from her hand, ignored. Was the woman part witch? Did they not screen her enough to detect the heart of a witch? It could be the only reason why Hegna was feeling like she was under this woman's spell.

She blinked, finding herself standing in front of the human. She had somehow managed to walk over to her. The aroma of her arousal was thicker. Hegna's gums burned and stretched as her fangs forced their way through and descended.

"Yes, we did." Stormey's lips curled up into a sensual smile. She held her hand out to Hegna. "Hello, Your Grace. My name is Stormey Jaymes."

Hegna eyed the small brown hand extended to her. She took it and immediately felt a jolt of energy race up her arm. She gasped, holding on to Stormey's hand. She hadn't wanted think of her by her name, but she couldn't help it any longer.

"Hello, Stormey. My name is Hegna Riskel." Hegna didn't recognize her voice. She slid her tongue along her sharp fangs. Her gaze was drawn to Stormey's neck and locked in on the sight of her pulse pounding away. Hegna could hear the rush of the delicious blood she knew was waiting for her. "Why are you on your knees, Stormey?"

"I wanted to please you," Stormey replied softly.

Hegna's gaze snapped to Stormey's face. Her expression was open and honest. The yearning burning in Stormey's eyes almost brought Hegna to her knees. She reached out with her other hand and cupped Stormey's chin.

"I've waited for the day to belong to someone. Have someone who would want me. I know that I may not be what you want in a mate, but I promise I will try my hardest to be that woman for you."

Had no one wanted this woman?

Had she been abandoned?

Had someone hurt her? Hegna's grip tightened slightly at the thought. Whoever had laid a finger on her would die on her order.

"And me? Am I the person you would want to belong to? A vampire?"

"Yes. I've dreamed of this day. I have been interested in vampires since I can remember. You have been someone I fantasized about meeting for years. About six months ago, you may not remember, but you sort of saved my life."

Hegna inhaled sharply. She had saved Stormey's life? If that was the case, she would have remembered. Stormey was not a woman to be forgotten.

"You must be mistaken." Hegna couldn't stop touching Stormey. She slid her hand along her jawline and up to her hair. Her dark strands were soft to touch. Her fingers easily glided through them.

Stormey leaned into her touch. "It was in Wichita. There was a rogue vampire attack—"

"There was a human woman who had been cornered and trapped. It was Nezera's bow that struck the rogues down…"

"Allowing me to run free to the hotel I worked at."

Hegna remembered that night. The rogues had been a pain in her side. She was already having to deal with the increased lycan complaints, then the rogues decided to come out in force. It was one trip that she and her captain had taken. It had been just the fight she had been looking for. She briefly remembered a curvy female racing across the street and into a building. She had hoped the rogues hadn't attempted to turn her. Humans sometimes did not survive the change.

Hegna didn't want to admit it, but there was a chance that fate was working. What were the odds that she had gone to Wichita to fight? That trip honestly hadn't called for the warden to go and personally handle something her warriors could have done.

But something had drawn her to the city.

"And here you are," Hegna breathed. She took in the woman with all of her sensual curves kneeling before her, and her chest rumbled with a growl. Lust and desire for her filled Hegna. She wanted her.

"Here I am."

"And you want to please me?" Hegna murmured.

Stormey nodded, her eyes darkening. Hegna flashed her fangs, and if she didn't know any better, the scent of Stormey's arousal intensified. She took Stormey by her chin and turned her face away, assessing both sides of her neck.

"Have you ever been bitten before?"

Another growl rippled from her at the thought of someone sinking their fangs into her woman's neck. She didn't see any evidence that Stormey's skin had been pierced. Vampires had the ability to control their donors and put them in a trance. They could even erase the memory of the act.

"No. I've never been bitten before," Stormey replied. Her breathing was growing faster, her breasts rising and falling.

Hegna licked her lips. She wanted to remove the damn dress so she could have access to them.

She reached for her tunic and pulled it over her

head. This was a dangerous game she was playing. In the back of her mind, a voice screamed to send the human away. She had promised herself that she would not find herself like Lethia and Velika, mated.

But then something else was telling her to taste what was hers.

What harm would it do to taste her?

It had been a few days since she'd taken a lover.

Hegna's body was heating up, and the ache behind her eyes was lessening. But no amount of pain was going to keep her from Stormey's lush body. Small hands landed on the edge of Hegna's pants. Stormey had raised herself on her knees and began undoing the buttons of her pants.

Hegna's pussy grew slick with need. There was something about this woman before her on her knees that had her ready to explode. Hegna tugged off her bra, leaving her upper half bare. Her nipples were pebbled into little buds. The air kissed her nipples, and they grew even harder.

Stormey guided her pants down and helped her out of them. Hegna kicked them off to the side while trying to control her breathing. Stormey paused and took her in. Hegna fought to keep from puffing her chest out and posing. She knew what she looked like. One did not become a warrior for the king and not be in the best physical shape they could be in. She was naturally toned, but with her training, her muscles were more defined, and she had little fat on her.

Stormey reached for her tiny panties and slid them down her legs, tossing them aside. There, she was finally naked in front of Stormey. Her human's gaze roamed her body, pausing at her breasts which weren't large, but they definitely could feel a woman's hands. She continued on and stopped at her mons.

Hegna could no longer hold back. She shot her hand out and gripped Stormey's thick hair, threading her fingers through it. She arched Stormey's head back so she could meet her gaze.

"Stand," Hegna demanded. Curiosity had Hegna wanting see the entire outfit before she peeled it off.

Stormey did as she was told. Hegna appreciated that she didn't argue but complied.

Hegna slowly took in how the dress stopped mid-thigh. The lace was transparent enough to showcase Stormey's areola and nipples. Hegna continued her assessment, her gaze trailing down Stormey's torso and landing at her mons, hidden by her soft belly and thighs. Hegna clenched her fists and walked around to Stormey's back. Her eyes drifted down to the corset-like closure in the back. An opening that gave easy access to Stormey's ass was perfect. Whoever designed this needed to be thanked personally. Hegna stepped forward, her fingers going to the leather ties. She slowly undid them, loosening the dress and widening the V-shaped opening. More of Stormey's rounded ass was revealed to her.

"Bend over," Hegna rasped.

Her gaze was locked on Stormey as again she did as she was told. The new position put her core on display. Her plump labia were slick with her honey already trailing from her.

Hegna reached out and ran a finger along the slit, eliciting a moan from Stormey. She dipped her fingers into the slit and ran it along the length of it. She removed her fingers, finding them coated with Stormey's nectar.

She brought them to her lips and licked the creamy substance off. Stormey's unique taste exploded on her tongue. Hegna's breaths came faster. She needed more.

"This needs to come off, now," Hegna snapped.

Stormey straightened to her full height and

reached for the edge of the dress, but Hegna was too impatient. She tore it from Stormey's body. Stormey whimpered as Hegna tugged the shredded material from her and tossed it over her shoulder.

Hegna closed the gap between them, wrapping her arms around Stormey from behind. She frowned at the feeling of her soft curves in her embrace. She couldn't help but feel as if this was right. This was what she had been missing all this time.

"You're so soft," Hegna murmured. Her hands came up to cup Stormey's breasts. The mounds were much larger than Hegna's hands.

Stormey leaned back against her with a sigh.

"Is that a problem?" Stormey's question appeared hesitant.

Hegna pinched Stormey's perky nipples and growled.

"Fuck, no. I love a female who is womanly and curvy." She nuzzled Stormey's neck, inhaling her scent.

Stormey arched her head away, allowing Hegna to have more access of the column of her neck. Hegna took advantage of the move and slid her tongue along her supple skin. The faint rushing of her blood reached Hegna's ears.

"These breasts, your thighs, your ass, are all delectable, and I shall taste them."

"Yes," Stormey hissed. She turned her face to meet Hegna's gaze. "Please."

Hegna took her chin and crushed her mouth to hers. The kiss was hard, and fast. Stormey's lips parted, allowing the invasion of Hegna's tongue. Stormey met it shyly at first, then grew bolder. Hegna spun her around in her arms, breaking the kiss. She pressed another to Stormey's lips before she guided her back down on her knees.

"On all fours," Hegna demanded.

She watched Stormey move into position, and her chest rumbled from the growl that wanted to come out. Light from the fire flickered, highlighting Stormey's brown skin. Hegna followed her down on the rug behind her. She licked her lips at the sight Stormey presented.

She placed a hand on the center of Stormey's back and pressed her head down onto the rug. Stormey was open for her. Hegna ran her fingers along Stormey's labia, spreading them open. The slick pinkness of her opening was revealed. Her clit was swollen and protruding from her slit.

Hegna pushed two fingers inside Stormey. Her channel was tight and wet. She withdrew them, thrusting them back inside. She lowered herself to where her face was level with Stormey's ass. Hegna slid her tongue along her puckered rim. She withdrew her fingers so she could spread Stormey's cheeks farther apart. She took her time trailing kisses over her cheeks. The meat of her ass was firm but yet soft to touch. She nipped and kissed her way back to Stormey's pussy.

Her tongue slithered to her delicious core. Her tongue dove into her slick opening. Her honey was sweet and thick. She withdrew it then continued on up to her swollen bud. She captured it with her lips, teasing Stormey's clit. She suckled it into her mouth, playing with it.

Stormey's muffled groans were growing louder.

Hegna continued feasting on her human's addictive cunt. She drank in her slickness as it eased from her opening. Hegna pushed her two fingers inside Stormey again while her tongue made its way back to her rim.

Stormey's body writhed underneath her. She rocked her hips back, welcoming Hegna's mouth and fingers.

Hegna lifted her face and fucked Stormey hard with her fingers. She watched as her pale fingers disappeared into Stormey's warm heat. She paused, pushing them as far into Stormey as they would go. She reached out and grasped Stormey's hair and brought her head up. She withdrew her fingers and brought them around to Stormey's mouth. She opened her lips and suckled Hegna's fingers, cleaning them off.

"Such a good girl. Now turn over so I can have my fill of you."

CHAPTER EIGHT

Stormey rolled over and spread her legs wide. Her core repeatedly clenched, demanding that Hegna push those fingers back inside her. She shook from the anticipation of what was to come. Hegna had been teasing her with her tongue and her fingers. She had brought her close to orgasm only to back her away from the edge of ecstasy. Stormey wasn't above begging for her release.

Hegna crawled over her, resting her hands on each side of her head. Her large, icy-blue eyes bored into her, sending a shiver down her spine. Stormey couldn't resist resting her hands on

Hegna's waist. Her breasts hung down, brushing against Stormey's. She inhaled sharply, loving the feeling of their breasts touching. She wanted to feel the entire weight of Hegna on her. She brought her down completely on top of her. Stormey sighed. Hegna's muscular frame felt so good on her.

Hegna lowered her head, her mouth claiming Stormey's. The kiss was slow and erotic. It left Stormey's breathing ragged and harsh. There was almost a desperate passion behind it that she had never experienced before. She stroked Hegna's tongue with hers in a sensual manner. Her tongue brushed Hegna's sharp fangs, and a shiver raced through her imagining them sinking into her neck.

Stormey arched her back in pleasure. A growl came from Hegna who tore her mouth from Stormey's and pressed kisses on every exposed part of Stormey. Hegna cupped Stormey's breasts in her hands. Stormey groaned. The vampire's calloused hands sliding along her nipples elicited a groan from her. The rough part of her hands teased her taut nipples. Hegna molded her mounds, trying to palm them, but her hands were not large enough.

Hegna dipped her head down and captured one nipple with her lips. She tugged on it, soothing it with her tongue. Her other hand mimicked the action, but pinching and pulling on her nipple. Stormey threw her head back, unashamed at the sounds of the moans and gasps spilling from her lips.

Hegna suckled from her as if she were a starving babe, sliding her tongue along her sternum and arriving at the other breast. She bathed Stormey's areola with the flat pad of her tongue, sucking the nipple into her mouth. Stormey didn't know where to put her hands. She lifted them above her head, her breasts pushing forward.

Hegna released her and trekked down Stormey's body, stopping to place kisses along her soft belly. Her tongue swirled around her deep belly button then continued on. A growl echoed in the air once Hegna arrived between her thighs. She pushed them apart and paused, staring at Stormey's center.

Worry had filled Stormey earlier that maybe Hegna wouldn't be attracted to someone of her size. She hadn't had many issues in the past with her prior lovers. There were plenty of people who loved someone her size. But she had never been with a vampire before, and to think that she was matched with Hegna who had no say, she'd had a brief moment of doubt.

But fate didn't make mistakes.

At least not that she had read.

Then Hegna had answered her, practically making her knees weak.

Fuck, no. I love a female who is womanly and curvy.

Hegna's fingers skirted along her slick labia, spreading them apart. Stormey was soaked for her. Her slickness ran down the crack of her ass.

"You are so fucking wet." Hegna inhaled sharply. She dipped down, her tongue circling Stormey's clit.

Stormey cried out, her sensitive nub being licked and suckled. Hegna concentrated on her clit, swirling her tongue around it. Her legs trembled. She was so close again and she wanted to come, but she didn't want to release too soon.

Hegna continued to feast on her. The woman was an expert at eating pussy, and Stormy was thankful fate had matched her to the vampire. Her skin grew sensitive, goosebumps forming on her arms. She cried out again from the intense pressure on her clit. Hegna had latched on to it and sucked it deep into her mouth. Stormey couldn't help but entwine her fingers in Hegna's hair. Her hips rocked bath and forth, and she rode Hegna's tongue. Heat swirled in her belly at the intense need to climax burning inside her. Hegna's tongue released her clit and slid through her drenched folds.

"Hegna," Stormey moaned.

She was rewarded with two fingers sinking inside her. A hand gripped her breast. Hegna continued to suck her clit while fucking her with her fingers. Stormey panted, grinding her hips down against her face.

The hand on her breast ran across her, focusing on her nipple. Hegna pinched her hard. A sharp pain exploded that had Stormey crying out. She trembled, chanting Hegna's name, her hips recklessly jerking on their own.

Stormey glanced down and caught sight of Hegna feasting on her, and she could no longer hold back. Her legs drew up, she fisted Hegna's hair, and screamed.

Her climax slammed into her, sending her tumbling through the waves of pleasure that washed over her. Hegna didn't let up on her clit. The woman fastened her mouth on it, suckling even harder. Stormey writhed and cried, tears spilling down her cheeks. She flopped back onto the floor, barely able to move.

Hegna released her clit and withdrew her fingers. Her tongue languidly licked every inch of her, cleaning the release that she felt resting on her pussy and inner thighs. Hegna pressed her hands on the back of Stormey's thighs to keep her legs up in the air and her pussy displayed for her. The vampire moaned as she continued to lick Stormey clean.

Stormey slowly came down from the high of her climax. She blinked her eyes open and stared at the ceiling. She had never come that hard before.

Ever.

She was still out of breath and was fighting to catch it. Sweat beaded along her forehead. Her skin was slightly damp from the fine sheen of perspiration that encompassed her. The heat from the fireplace was now a bit too much. She'd at first thought it was chilly in the room, but it would seem that all she needed was Hegna and her talented tongue to warm her up.

Hegna raised her head and dropped her hold on Stormey's thighs. Her legs fell to the floor, resting on the rug. Stormey could barely control her limbs. Any energy she had was sucked straight out of her.

The vampire's deep chuckle was low and sent a thrill through Stormey. She blinked and leveled her gaze on Hegna, watching her move up to Stormey's head.

"You said you wanted to please me, did you not?" Hegna flashed her fangs.

"Yes," Stormey whispered.

She eyed the sexy vampire, and a new wave of desire pooled in her stomach. She went to push up on her elbows, but Hegna shook her head, resting a hand on her sternum and holding her down.

"You are perfect where you are," Hegna murmured.

She lifted her leg and straddled Stormey's face. She reached down and brushed Stormey's hair from her face. Stormey's heart raced as she took in the perfect pink pussy hovering inches from her mouth. She licked her lips, ready to get her first taste of Hegna.

This was something she had dreamed of and fantasized about. Her fantasies of eating Hegna's pussy always led to her fingering herself to completion when she would lie in her small bed back in her tiny home.

Now, she had the real thing literally in her face.

Stormey reached up and brought Hegna's pussy down to her. She covered it with her mouth while gripping her ass. She gave it a deep, long lick, taking her first taste. Stormey moaned, her mouth filled with the delicious taste of her mate. Her pussy was sweet and juicy like a peach, her favorite fruit.

Stormey dragged her tongue through her folds, up until she reached her clit. She pulled it into her mouth, her hands resting on Hegna's thighs. She gripped them tight, and Hegna moaned. The vampire rocked her hips slowly. Stormey licked her. She lapped up all of her delicious juices that eased from her slit. Stormey tightened her hold on Hegna, sending her tongue deeper, pressing against Hegna's opening.

"Fuck," Hegna growled. She reached down, raking her fingers through Stormey's hair. "Your mouth feels so good on me."

Stormey beamed at the compliment. When she had admitted to Hegna that she wanted to please her, this was what she'd had in mind. She wanted to devour the vampire's cunt and drink her all in. She wanted the vampire to know that without a doubt they were meant to be together.

The vampire, she was quickly learning, was extremely stubborn.

But Stormey was determined to break through her walls.

And at the moment, Hegna was riding her face

with her gaze locked with Stormey's. A deep connection exchanged between them. Stormey continued to suck on Hegna's clitoris. She rolled it with her tongue, applying pressure to it.

Hegna's gasp was like music to her ears.

"Keep doing that," Hegna whispered.

Her back arched, providing a wonderful view of her perky breasts for Stormey from her position. At the moment, she wouldn't want to be anywhere else.

If she died right this second, she would die a happy woman.

Going out while her woman was riding her face was the ultimate death. No doubt about it. Warriors would want to die in battle. Stormey would want to die while eating her woman's pussy.

Hegna's hips rocked faster. The grip on Stormey's hair tightened, but she couldn't care less. She shook her head and hummed, tugging on Hegna's swollen nub.

"Yes. Yes. Yes," Hegna chanted. She squeezed and fondled her own breast with her free hand. Her eyes had yet to break the connection with Stormey. Her body trembled on top of Stormey, and it was a miracle that she was able to stay erect.

Stormey grew bold and sank her teeth onto her clit.

Hegna's cry pierced the air as she reached her climax. Her thighs clamped down on Stormey's face. Her head fell back, and she groaned. Her hips paused with her resting fully on Stormey's face. Hegna's body trembled violently, her pants loud and harsh. She fell forward, her hands resting on the floor.

Hegna immediately rolled over, breaking the connection with Stormey. She lay on the rug with her eyes closed, her chest rising and falling rapidly. Stormey knew what she was going through. The orgasm had been a hard one and the pleasure overwhelming. She moved and slid up beside her. She smiled when Hegna flopped onto her back with her arms splayed wide. Stormey snuggled beside her, resting her head on shoulder. She closed the gap between them and threw her arm over Hegna's stomach. Her vampire's eyes remained closed.

Completely happy, Stormey closed her eyes and allowed sleep to take her.

HEGNA OPENED her eyes and inhaled. Her legs were pushed open, and someone was gently licking her pussy. She smiled softly and reached down, entwining her fingers in the thick hair of the person who would be rewarded for waking her this way.

She frowned for a moment at the thought of who would be drawing a moan from her. Gentle fingers thrust in and out of her slick core. She blinked hard and looked around, recognizing her bed. The drapes were drawn, putting her and her lover in a cozy little world of their own.

Another moan slipped from her.

Her hips rocked forward, desperate for more.

She blinked again, and it all came back to her.

Stormey.

The human had been waiting for her in her room, basically naked and eager to please her. Hegna had not had the will to resist her. The mating bond was real, and it was sinking its claws into her.

She would send her away.

After she reached her orgasm.

Once they had woken up by the fireplace, Hegna had brought Stormey back to her bed. She had taken the woman at least two more times. She'd even brought in a dildo that they had used on each other. She reached her hand underneath her pillow and found it.

This had not been her plan.

But the sex was out of this world. Hegna couldn't deny that. She had never felt completely satisfied after reaching an orgasm with prior lovers. With Stormey, the pieces fell into place. Only with her fated mate would she have the type of sex that she had been seeking.

"You're finally awake." Stormey's husky chuckle reached her ears. She lifted her head and withdrew her two fingers from Hegna.

Hegna's sharp vision allowed her to watch Stormey bring her hand to her lips. She stuck her fingers in her mouth, sucking the cream from them.

Hegna growled and sat up.

"I am. Come here." Hegna snagged Stormey by her hand and brought her to her. She entwined their legs in a position that put their cunts together. Hegna's hands rested on Stormey's ample bottom.

"You feel so good." Stormey sighed. She thrust her pelvis forward, dragging her pussy slowly over Hegna's.

"As do you," Hegna admitted. She was an ass. She should end this now and send the human away.

Not continue fucking her, taking pleasure, but she couldn't stop.

They rocked against each other, setting a steady pace and rhythm. Their bodies writhed. Their breasts were crushed between them.

Hegna cupped Stormey's chin and claimed her lips. Stormey melted into her, opening her mouth and welcoming Hegna's tongue. Their pace quickened, the moans and gasps filled the air. The sound of their wetness was heard. Just hearing it and feeling how drenched their pussies were fed the fire in Hegna.

Mate.

She gripped Stormey tighter to her, fucking her mouth with her tongue. She slid her hand around to the back of Stormey's neck and held her in place. She tore her mouth from Stormey and laved her tongue along her jawline and down to her neck. The rushing sound of her blood captivated Hegna. Her gums burned and stretched, her fangs breaking free.

Bite her.

Their bodies, coated in sweat, slid along each other with ease.

Stormey arched her head away from Hegna, presenting her neck to her. Hegna's gaze locked on the perfect spot for her mark. She grazed her fangs over Stormey's supple skin, her blood calling her.

Hegna's body was strung tight, close to orgasm.

"Make me yours," Stormey begged.

Something in Hegna snapped. She suddenly came to her senses. She had been close to sinking her fangs into Stormey's neck, biting her, marking her. Completing the bond.

And that wasn't what she wanted.

No.

She pushed Stormey down on the bed, following her. She gripped the human by the neck, squeezing as she continued gyrating her center on Stormey.

"That's what you want, isn't it?" she growled.

"Yes," Stormey's voice was strained.

Hegna tightened her grip on her. A moan was ripped from her. She was on the edge of her release. She threw her head back, giving in to the pleasure of her human's pussy gliding along hers. Their clits rubbed together, and they pumped harder.

Hegna threw back her head and gave in to the pleasure that washed through her. She released the human's neck and held on to Stormey's leg. She brought Stormey's thigh to her chest and continued writhing on her. Stormey's hoarse cries joined Hegna's.

Hegna's thighs were slick from the juices that poured from her and Stormey. She inhaled sharply. Her body shuddered from the sensations coursing through her. She finally drew to a halt, resting her pussy on Stormey's.

Hegna's breaths were coming in pants. She inhaled sharply, trying to get a hold of her breaths.

She pushed off Stormey and moved back against the pillows. She stared at the human who lay sprawled on the massive mattress.

Of course, the human almost had her. Hegna ran a hand along her face, feeling more like herself. The mating bond was slowly enveloping her, but she refused to fall into its grasp. *She* decided when she would mate and to whom.

"What did I say?" Stormey's strained voice broke through the silence. She sat up, confusion in her eyes. The winding of the window coverings kicked in, providing a distraction. Hegna was unsure what time it was. With it being wintertime, the sun rose much later, allowing them to have longer nights.

Hegna slid to the edge of the bed and pulled back the drape.

"I refuse to fall for this." She motioned between her and Stormey. She stood from the bed and turned, taking in Stormey. She bit back growl. A pleased sensation rose in her chest. Stormey looked well-fucked. Her hair was a mess, and her eyes were slightly dazed.

"What do you mean?" Stormey asked. "Am I missing something? We had one hell of a night—"

"That will not happen again," Hegna snapped. She inhaled and immediately regretted it. The scent of Stormey's slickness between her thighs filled Hegna's nostrils. She had to put some distance between them. She balled up her fists to keep from reaching for Stormey.

Azura Michaels.

That was who she needed to concentrate on. She would kill this wolf alpha. The lycans were top priority. She had to protect the vampires and the humans who lived in her territory. The future of their kind and eradicating the lycans were the center of her attention.

Falling in love and sealing a mating bond was not what she wanted.

Her life was going just fine without the stress of having a mate.

"What do you mean? I'm your mate."

Stormey's eyes were wide. Fat tears balanced on the edges of her eyelids, but Hegna hardened her heart. Stormey crawled to the edge of the bed. Hegna backed up.

"Was it me asking for your bite? We don't have to do it now. We can get to know each other. Spend time together."

"No." Hegna shook her head, ignoring Stormey's gasp. She knew what she had to do. She would have the human relocated to one of the other wings in the castle, putting as much room between them as possible. "Get your clothes and go."

"But, Hegna—"

"I said, go!" she roared.

Stormey scrambled from the bed and rushed over to rug in front of the fireplace and gathered her belongings. Hegna spun around and went into the bathroom. A crack appeared in her hardened heart at the sound of Stormey's sniffling. Hegna walked over to the double sinks and rested her hands on the counter. She stared at herself, and she, too, had the look of someone who had been royally fucked.

Her nipples were sore, as was her clit from Stormey's attention. She closed her eyes and tried to block out their night. She would resist the urge to rush after Stormey and bring her back.

Hegna had an agenda, and it didn't include a mate. She would ensure Stormey was well taken care of, but she would not be completing a bond.

A single bite wouldn't have sealed them together, but Hegna wasn't sure how she would react once her fangs were in Stormey's neck.

Her ears picked up the faint sound of her quarter's door opening and closing.

The ache behind her eyes reappeared. Hegna cursed and pushed off the counter and headed over to her shower. She would need more blood soon. As soon as she was done bathing, she'd call down to the kitchen.

She flipped the water on, waiting for it to heat up.

The image of Stormey's large tears in her eyes had her stomach clenching.

She drew up to her full height, refusing to fall for the tears. Hegna walked into the shower, allowing the hot water to soak her skin.

Yes, she had an agenda, and she would follow it.

CHAPTER NINE

"I think this is enough for today," Cici said. She stood next to Stormey who was wiping down one of the tables in the dining hall for the castle's employees.

Stormey looked over at her and offered her a small smile.

"What are you talking about?" She straightened to her full height and put her cloth in the little bucket with hot soapy water in it. Stormey had thrown herself into everything she could become involved in. Since the night she'd been sent away from Hegna's room, she had wanted to keep herself busy.

A pain spread in Stormey's chest at the memory of the cold rejection of her vampire. She had thrown her robe on and left the lingerie on the floor. She wouldn't need it. The walk back to her room had been awkward. She'd held her head high, not saying a word to Jasper, and went into her room. Once inside, she'd fallen onto her bed with sobs racking her body.

And to make matters worse, Hegna had her relocated to another wing in the castle.

Stormey was sure there was talk around the castle. She had made sure she had introduced herself to everyone. If she was to be the other lady of the house, then she wanted to be involved. There was no point in sulking in her room.

The day they'd moved her belongings was the day she decided to have Cici take her to the dining hall. She'd sat for half a day, greeting and speaking with the humans. Everyone was welcoming and kind. She even helped in the kitchen, making dishes that she loved cooking. Val even allowed her meals to be served. The assistants in the kitchen took her recipes, adjusted them for the amount of people who had to be fed, then served them. They were all a hit.

"You shouldn't be in here cleaning." Cici glanced around nervously as if checking to see if anyone was watching them.

"There is nothing wrong with me helping around this place. I just want to be useful." She shrugged. She took her bucket and went over to another table. The workers deserved a clean place to take their meals, and she actually enjoyed the quiet time to herself while she worked. The next lunch rush would be in a few hours.

"But you will be a princess," Cici reminded her.

"Seriously?" Stormey arched an eyebrow at her. She snorted and went back to wiping down the table.

Cici couldn't believe that, still. Hegna had no intentions of doing anything with Stormey. Hegna had approved her vampire society lessons which she enjoyed. Stormey had also started working with a warrior for self-defense education. Zeke was fast becoming a friend to her. He was patient with her. She may have been unfit when they'd first started, but he was quickly whipping her into shape.

"I can't tell. I'm just a human without a purpose here."

"That is not true," Cici gasped. She rested a hand on Stormey's, pausing it in mid-wipe. Her wide eyes softened. "I've received permission for us to leave and go shopping."

"But I don't need anything." Stormey pulled her hand away and tossed the cloth back into the bucket. She literally had anything a woman could want. She was informed that she had a monthly allowance to spend however she wanted. She was still shocked at how much Hegna was giving her. Was she feeling guilty about how she'd treated her? Stormey had not seen the vampire since that night.

She'd picked up on rumors swirling around the castle. She was quickly learning if she wanted to find out anything, just spend time with the workers. They talked amongst each other, and word spread fast. Apparently, this lycan alpha had made threats to Hegna's father and was desperate to overthrow the vampire's rules. War was on the horizon, and Stormey didn't know how she felt about it.

She had been a young babe when the human and vampire war occurred. Over thirty years later, and humans were still recovering. Their world had been destroyed to the point they'd needed to start over. It was taking a long time, and she hoped that someday in the future, their world would prosper, and all beings could live in harmony and peace.

"Sure you do. Everyone needs few trinkets and knickknacks." Cici laughed. "Come on. You haven't left the grounds since you arrived."

"Um, okay. I guess it would be good for me to get out in the town."

"Exactly. Many members of the coven live in the town, and an outing is just what we need. They will want to see the mate of their princess." Cici tugged on her hand and led her out of the hall.

"If you think it's important and a good idea," Stormey said. She trailed Cici through the halls and up the stairs to her new domain. The quarters she had been given were just as nice as the old ones.

"I do, and so does Corbin," Cici said. She guided Stormey inside her bedroom and pushed her toward the bathroom.

Stormey spun around and followed Cici into her closet.

"Wait, you're saying that Hegna's personal advisor thinks it would be best for me to go out in public to be seen? As the mate of Hegna?" Stormey was confused. Hegna didn't want her as a mate. Why did she need to pretend in public?

"Well, you are the mate of the princess."

"I am so confused." Stormey leaned against the doorjamb and tried to figure out what was going on. "So she doesn't want me but has to keep me. I'll still be her mate, but yet not be her mate."

Stormey pinched the bridge of her nose. She was learning that vampires, hers in particular, were truly more complex than humans.

"That sounds about right." Cici held a dress up and hung it on a hook near the door. She rushed around the fancy closet, collecting accessories and shoes to go along with the dress.

"And I can't go out in jeans and a t-shirt to shop?" Stormey eyed the outfit Cici was putting together.

"On no, my lady." Cici looked appalled as if she were asked to never consume blood again. She gathered everything in her arms and scurried out of the closet. She arranged it all on the bed. "We must have you looking your best. Now, go shower, or do you need assistance with bathing?"

"You know I prefer to wash myself," Stormey mumbled. She went into the bathroom and took a short shower.

Cici assisted her with her hair, makeup, and

getting dressed. The spice-colored dress she chose was made of a thick material. The bodice was form-fitting, and the skirt flared out and stopped at her knees. Her tall boots were brown leather with three-inch heels. Cici completed the ensemble with a wide leather belt around her waist.

"You look beautiful, my lady." Cici stepped back and admired her handiwork. "One last thing." She hurried into the closet and returned with a soft cream hooded cloak.

Stormey's hands drifted along the royal crest that was embroidered in deep purple on the left breast. It was a beautiful cloak, and she spun around in it, watching the bottom part flare out around her.

Once Cici was satisfied with her appearance, they left her quarters and walked to the front door.

"Miss Jaymes, your ride is ready for your trip into town." Edward strode toward them. He had yet to crack a smile for Stormey. He had overseen her move to the new wing. With all of the items she now owned, it had taken an hour to get her moved. The six servants who were assigned to help her relocate didn't waste any time.

"Hello, Edward. Thank you." Stormey gave him a nod. She was slightly nervous about leaving the castle. Cici was right. Since she'd arrived, she hadn't left.

He held open the door for her and bowed when she ambled past him.

Three large SUVs were parked out front. Stormey widened her eyes. Guards were standing outside with a few others. Desmond stood by the middle car. Upon seeing her, he opened the back door for her.

"All of this for me to go shopping?" Stormey laughed. She figured one guard would be sufficient. She stopped by the truck and glanced at the other guards who were waiting around.

"Unfortunately, yes," a voice said behind her.

She spun around and found herself faced with Corbin, Hegna's personal advisor. She peeked around him and didn't see any sight of her vampire mate.

"As the mate of the warden of the largest territory and the heir to the throne, you are to be protected at all times."

He offered a smile, and Stormey relaxed. She'd only spoken with him once before. On her tour of the stables, he'd been there brushing down a beautiful chestnut colt.

"And you are offering your protection?" She

arched an eyebrow at him. Her lips curled up in a teasing manner.

"Oh, I'm not a fighter," he scoffed.

Corbin was a handsome man, and his silver hair highlighted his features. She was sure he had people, vampires or human, falling at his feet. He grasped her hand and assisted her into the waiting vehicle. He took the seat next to her. Cici filed in behind them in the third row before Desmond shut the door.

"Hegna has seen to it that I can protect myself."

"Did she train you?" Stormey asked softly. No matter that her heart had been stomped on by the vampire, she still wanted to know about her.

Desmond got into the passenger side while another guard slid into the driver's seat.

"We're ready to leave," Desmond announced, holding his hand up to his ear. A few seconds later, their caravan took off.

"Hegna, train me?" He snorted and shook his head. "One time, and it was a disaster. I was sore for a week, and that was the only time I allowed her to try to teach me. She can be quite hard on us non-warriors, and I refused her as a teacher. Instead, she assigned one of her warriors to teach me."

Stormey felt somewhat better hearing the story.

So far, everything was going well with Zeke. Tomorrow was her next lesson. In the morning, she would work with him, and then after a shower and lunch, she'd meet with Miss Lavana for her other lessons. Both she looked forward to. Her teachers were wonderful, and she was learning so much.

"So, I hear it was you who recommended I get out so people can see me?" Stormey asked. She turned and looked out the window, watching the scenery fly by. The castle was located in a remote part of the town. Nature was beautiful in the state of Oklahoma. Snow covered everything. She was glad Cici had brought out her cloak. It was warm and comfortable. "Why?"

"Not only am I the personal advisor for Hegna, I am her friend. The initial meeting with Hegna was not a normal, chance meeting. She had saved my life, and I vowed to always be loyal to her. When she became a warden and commander of an army, she demanded I be her personal advisor."

"Why did she demand this of you?" Stormey turned away from the window and faced Corbin. He was giving her so many details about her mate that she would not be able to read anywhere nor have her mate share with her. She was like a sponge, soaking up all the little tidbits that she could.

"Because she knew that I am completely loyal to her. I would never steer her wrong. I would always speak my mind and the truth to her."

He paused, a strange look passing in his eyes that she couldn't read.

He ran a hand along his jawline. "I also told her that she was wrong in pushing you away. She needs to stop being so damn stubborn and claim her mate. For some strange reason, she thinks she doesn't deserve happiness and that she has to put her people before her."

Stormey's breath froze in her lungs. She blinked back tears that blurred her vision.

"I think you got it all wrong. She doesn't want me." Saying the words tore open a new wound in her chest. She glanced down at her hands, wondering if Hegna had shared this with him. "Did she really say that?"

"Not in so many words, but my dear friend never knows what is best for her. That's why she has me as an advisor." He smirked. He reached out and tapped her on her knee. "Don't worry, my lady. Hegna knows she will have to deal with you at some point. She just needs time to realize that she can't control everything. In the meanwhile, I'm going ensure that everything continues to move on as it should. While she's out fighting those nasty lycans, I'll help you learn how to run your home. The coven is going to want to see you, and eventually we will have the best damn soirée to introduce you two as a couple and the future of vampires."

Stormey wiped the lone tear that slid down her cheek. She already felt slightly better listening to Corbin. It would seem she had an ally in him. He knew Hegna the best and if he thought she needed more time to acclimate to the notion that there were some things she couldn't control, then Stormey would give her time. She was determined to be the best princess she could be. She was not only going to lead the vampires, but she wanted to include humans as well and bridge the gap between their two races.

"Thank you," she whispered.

"No need to thank me." He waved a hand at her.

Their conversation continued, and she learned a lot about the coven and what to expect from them. She wasn't surprised to know that council members for the territory would be wanting to meet her, and that some may not support human and vampire mating. Stormey was realizing that she was going to have to develop thicker skin. She enjoyed their chat and was sad that it came to an end. They had arrived at the shopping center.

"You will love the market, my lady," Cici gushed. She stepped out of the vehicle behind Stormey.

"And don't be shy about spending my friend's money," Corbin said.

They headed toward a building that was an old Catholic church that had been renovated. It was breathtakingly beautiful with its vintage look, a stone construction with gargoyle statues placed along the roof. Spotlights highlighted the two towers that soared up toward the skyline, one with a bell housed in it. It was around ten o'clock at night, and the street was bustling with people as if it were mid-afternoon.

"Oh?" Stormey arched her eyebrow at him.

The security guards spread around them, and she felt like true royalty. She had never felt as safe as she did right now in public. Peering over one's shoulder while scurrying down a public road after the sun went down was what she was used to.

They walked up the stone stairway and entered the church, pausing in the entryway. Her breath escaped her at the scene before her. The building was much larger on the inside than it had appeared outside. The pews had been removed, and the open concept of the parish allowed rows of vendors to hawk their wares. The original altar remained, with rows of burning candles. Stormey wondered if anyone used the altar for prayers. The beauty of the stained-glass windows was breathtaking, while fire burned bight in the sconces anchored to the walls.

The marketplace was busy with plenty of consumers milling around. Aromas filled the air that had her inhaling deeply. Her first public appearance.

She could do this.

"Hegna is far richer than one could probably comprehend." He laughed. "Now, come. Everyone will be watching you. Act like your normal self."

"I don't know what is normal. I haven't shopped for myself in eons," Stormey said.

She removed her hood and blew out a deep breath. A few of the guards had entered before them and began spreading out, disappearing into the crowd.

"Shall we?" Corbin held out his arm to her.

She offered him a tight smile and took it. Cici walked behind them, and they strolled around. Eyes were on her as he said they would be. She didn't want to appear quiet and timid. Wouldn't they want the mate of their princess to be strong, kind, and with a big heart? At least that was what she would expect.

She held her head high and met each curious gaze with a smile.

"Atta girl," Corbin murmured. He brought her up to the first booth.

An older woman with salt-and-pepper hair, bright-green eyes, and a wide smile greeted them. Her eyes were outlined in dark kohl, and her black blouse was a wraparound with the tie resting underneath her breasts. Her skirt was made of the same material, flowing around her feet. Her gaze dropped to the crest on Stormey's cloak for a brief moment.

"My lord, how do you do?" She turned her focus to Corbin.

On her table was gorgeous handcrafted jewelry on display. Stormey released Corbin's arm, stepping closer so she could see better. Silver, copper, bronze, and even some small gold trinkets. Bracelets, rings, necklaces, and pendants. The woman before her was certainly talented.

"I'm doing well, Clementina. May I present

Miss Stormey Jaymes, mate of our warden, Princess Hegna." He motioned to Stormey with a nod.

The woman's eyes widened and flicked back to Stormey.

"My lady." The woman dropped down in a deep curtsey. She straightened up to her full height, her lips curved up into a smile.

"It's nice to meet you." Stormey returned her smile. She focused on the items on the table. She picked up a bracelet that caught her eye. It was brilliantly made. Bronze bangles attached to each other. There were small designs on them with words she couldn't decipher. "Did you make all of this?"

"I did. That is a pair." She lifted the identical bracelet and held it out to Stormey for her to try them on.

Stormey slid them onto both of her wrists, immediately feeling a warmth to them.

"They are lovely," Stormey whispered. She traced the tiny words with her fingers. "What does the wording mean?"

"It's a simple spell to help balance one's chakra and make one feel more beautiful." Clementina smiled.

Stormey's eyes widened. Was the woman before her a witch? She glanced at Corbin, who must have read her mind and gave her a slight nod as if to answer her unasked question.

Stormey didn't believe in chakra or spells, but she loved the bracelets. She had never purchased herself something so stunning before.

"We'll take them," Corbin announced.

He carefully watched her. She turned away from his gaze and looked at the table again. She caught sight of a ring that held a pretty stone on it that reminded her of Hegna's eyes. She picked it up and immediately felt drawn to it.

"Yes, of course." Clementina beamed and reached for a leather packing for the bracelets.

Stormey slid them off and handed them to her. She bit her lip and stared at the ring.

"We'll take this, too." She thrust the ring at the woman.

Clementina practically danced in place as she took it from Stormey.

Stormey realized she hadn't even asked the price. She turned to Corbin who had taken care of paying for her jewelry. "Um, we didn't ask a price—"

"You don't need to." He patted her on her shoulder with a wide grin. "You have money now,

Stormey. Whatever you want in life, it can be yours."

Clementina handed her a linen bag with a handle that held her purchase. Stormey smiled and thanked her. Corbin guided her along the aisles, allowing her to stop at any vendor she wanted. Quickly, word was getting around about who she was. Many vendors vied for her attention. She wanted to purchase from them all, but it was hard for her to just turn off that part of her brain that remembered what it was like to struggle and penny-pinch.

The wonderful aroma of fresh-baked goods reached her. She eyed the area and saw a young woman and a few children behind the table. She smiled at the one who appeared to be about four or five. She was dressed in jean overalls with a pink, long-sleeved shirt underneath it. Her brown cheeks were chubby, and her hair was braided with colorful beads on the end.

They were human children, and it was their table that had cookies, cakes, and muffins. Stormey wondered how the woman and the children were out at night by themselves. Nighttime was always dangerous for humans.

Stormey had been shocked to see that humans

and vampires could be in one place without fear. There was an atmosphere of support and fun. She'd truly enjoyed the time she had spent here. She'd met humans, vampires, and a few witches. Cici had been right. She did like it. Here, everyone appeared to get along.

"I have to go there," she murmured. She slipped from Corbin's side and strolled over to them. She arrived at the table, and the aroma was overwhelming. Her mouth watered at all of the treats on display. "Hello there."

"Hi." The little one grinned and waved at her. "We're raising money."

"Oh, is that so?" Stormey returned her smile.

The young woman finished her transaction with an older gentleman before her. She turned to Stormey and offered a smile.

"Yes, she's right. We are selling baked goods as a fundraiser. What you see here is what we have left." The woman beamed. Her gaze roamed Stormey, and she swallowed hard. "So is it true? You are the princess's mate. A human?"

"Yes, I'm human. My name is Stormey." She held her hand out to the woman who took it in a brief shake then motioned to Cici who arrived at her side. "And this is Cici."

"Brandi," the young woman said. She gestured to the children next to her. The other two were older than the little one. They looked around ten or twelve. "This is Ricky, Lauren, and the little tyke right there is Maisie."

"Hello, everyone." Stormey leaned her hands on the table and had already made up her mind that she was going to buy out the rest of their table. She would take the baked goods and put them in the dining hall for the employees. They would love them.

"Aren't you all just so adorable." Cici smiled while waving to the kids. She glanced at the table and groaned. "Everything smells so heavenly."

"What are you raising money for?" Stormey asked casually.

"All the proceeds are going to the children at the Fountain of Hope Orphanage," Brandi answered. She threw her arm around Ricky and smiled. "We want to renovate their playground and give them a better place to run out all of their energy."

Stormey stared at the children. They were orphans. Her heart pounded. She hadn't known there was an orphanage in Black Hollows. Why had she not even checked? She felt guilty that she hadn't.

"I'll take everything," Stormey blurted out.

"What?" Brandi's eyes grew round. The kids laughed and giggled their excitement. "Are you serious?"

"Yes, I'll take everything you've got." Stormey grinned.

"Oh, my. We appreciate it. Come on, kids. Let's bag everything up for this nice lady," Brandi said.

The kids kicked in and immediately began cleaning off the table and packaging everything in the boxes behind them. Brandi came from around the table and wrapped her arms around Stormey.

Immediately, Desmond was at her side, pushing Brandi away. Stormey hadn't even realized he was near.

"Remove your hands from Miss Jaymes," Desmond growled, placing a hand on the sword at his side.

Everyone within earshot of the table paused and glanced in their direction. Brandi stepped back, fear on her face.

"It's quite all right, Desmond," Stormey said. She rested a hand on his forearm. His muscles relaxed, and he glanced at her. "She was just thanking me for buying out her entire table."

"What's going on?" Corbin arrived, looking at all of them.

"Nothing. Everything's fine. I promise." Stormey didn't like that they were the center of attention. She had been since she'd arrived, but she didn't want anyone thinking Brandi was causing issues. She turned back to Brandi and took her hands in hers. "I have a soft spot in my heart for orphans."

"Really?" Maisie asked. She crawled under the table and joined them. She plainly ignored the big vampire guard and turned her back on him. She stared up at Stormey with wide eyes. "Did you not have a mommy and daddy, too?"

Stormey's heart lurched. This little girl tugged on her heartstrings. She bent down to where she was eye level with her.

"No, I didn't have any family, and I spent most of my childhood in an orphanage that I'm sure is similar yours."

"Wow," the two older kids breathed.

"What happened to your mommy and daddy?" Maisie asked.

A lump formed in Stormey's throat. She smiled and took Maisie's hand in hers.

"Well, my daddy was sent off to war and never

came back home, and my mom, she got really sick and died," Stormey shared.

"And you're a princess now?" Maisie asked.

The innocence in her eyes just made Stormey want to wrap her up in her arms and take her home with her. Stormey laughed at her question.

"Not officially, but soon, I will be." She held up her hand, and the little one gave her a high five.

"I'm going to be a princess when I grow up, too!" she shouted, jumping up in place.

"Come on, Maisie. We have to let Stormey go about her day. I'm sure she has more shopping to do," Brandi said.

"But—"

"No buts. It's already late, and I promised Miss Emily that I would have you home at a decent time." Brandi held out her hand to Maisie.

"How are you getting home?" Stormey stood to her full height. She would hate for something to happen to them with it being so late.

"We have a van. The guards here walk us to it to ensure we are safe, then I drive straight to the orphanage."

It sounded like she had done this plenty of times, but Stormey wanted to ensure they were all right. She'd hate to think of something happening to them on their way back.

"I want a guard to ensure they make it home okay." Stormey turned to Desmond. She didn't ask, nor did she hesitate. This was something that she wanted and she'd fight anyone who dared oppose her.

"Yes, ma'am." Desmond nodded. He presented his back, speaking into the small device on him.

"You don't have to do that," Brandi gushed.

"Yes. Just humor me. It will allow me to sleep better knowing that you and the kids arrived home safely," Stormey said.

The kids had packaged everything up and had it on the table waiting for her.

"Okay." Brandi's smile stretched from ear to ear.

"Their escort will be here in ten minutes." Desmond turned back around and announced. "And someone will be here shortly to take these boxes and load them up in the trucks."

"Thanks." She faced Brandi and the kids. "I want to come visit and see how I can help."

"We'd like that." Brandi gathered the kids and fussed at them to put on their coats.

Stormey backed off with a smile and waved.

She spun away, happy that she had come to the marketplace. She was determined to go visit the orphanage and see what she could help with.

As Corbin had said, she had money now. She could do what she wanted with it.

CHAPTER TEN

"Has there been any word yet?" Hegna asked.

She and Bijou strolled through the training facility. During the middle of the winter, their workouts were held inside a special building that had been constructed for them. It housed multiple weight rooms, sparring rooms, Olympic-sized pools, areas for them to do agility training, and more. It had been worth every penny. When it was built, she had taken an idea from her sister and had underground tunnels built that connected it to the castle.

Their warriors trained hard faithfully and were some of the most lethal men and women on the planet. Hegna was proud of the members of her army. Her men and women were spread out throughout her territory.

Currently, Nezera and a team were off scouting an area that had documented lycan activity just over the border into Canada. Another team would soon be dispatched. Hegna had been working nonstop since that day. She tried to not think of the night she had sent Stormey away.

She inhaled and tried to harden her heart even more. She didn't know what she had thought was going to happen after she'd sent her away. She had thought Stormey would be screaming and throwing a temper tantrum, but she'd done none of that and just left. Even when she was ordered to move to the other wing, she had not complained.

Hegna received daily reports on her human. She was kept up to date on her education sessions, her self-defense, and even her activities in the kitchen. Hegna did not know how she felt about Stormey working in the kitchen. She would soon be a princess and did not have to work.

"Nezera reported in, and so far, a few random lycans were spotted. She promised to reach out again when she has more information. They are tracking them now," Bijou said.

Hegna's gaze swept the room, and there was no sign of Stormey. She was to be at her self-defense class with the warrior Nezera had chosen. Hegna wanted to ensure Stormey would be able to protect herself should she find herself in a position that would call for it. With the announcement of their matching, it had put a target on her back.

She and her sisters had been hunting down Azura hard. Velika's tech team was having a difficult time tracing that incoming call. It bounced around on several satellites before the trail went cold. Sightings of the alpha around the continent had led to dead ends. It was like she had disappeared into the wind.

Even the bounty hunters were coming up empty-handed. The queen was not pleased and had upped the amount on the lycan's head.

Hegna was growing frustrated. The lycan had the nerve to come forward and threatened her father then disappear. She was a coward, no true alpha.

"It has been a long time since we've spilled blood on the battlefield," Hegna began. The promise of battling the lycans had lit a fire under her warriors. They hungered to take down the mangy beasts in the name of their king.

"Yes, it has. Peace is only the result of war," Bijou said.

"But have we truly known peace since the last war?" Hegna questioned.

For over thirty years since the ending of the war between humans and vampires, she hadn't felt completely at peace. They'd had to deal with insurrections from humans, rogue vampires causing an uproar in their communities, and now the lycans. Would they ever get to a peaceful time where they could live without the threat of enemies?

They walked down the hall to the next rooms. It was good to show her face while her warriors trained. There were many days where she joined them. Correcting maneuvers, working with the young warriors who were new recruits, and even training with the most experienced of her men and women. Hegna believed in creating an air of camaraderie amongst her army. She had an upcoming trip scheduled to travel to other cities and towns where groups were posted, providing protection for her territory.

Hegna inhaled, sensing the ache in her head was reappearing. It had been coming and going for the last couple of weeks. She gritted her teeth and tolerated the pain. She didn't know what was plaguing her and causing this pain. She tried to increase her blood consumption, and when she did, then her stomach ached.

"Is today her self-defense lesson?" Hegna asked casually.

They arrived at the next area of the building. This room was filled with sparring mats. Weapons adorned the walls where one could train and practice with them. There were several of her more experienced warriors wrestling on the floor. She and Bijou circulated the room.

"Yes, it is," Bijou answered stiffly.

Hegna didn't look over at her. She didn't want to see the disappointment in her general's eyes. It would appear that Stormey was slowing winning everyone over to her. Everyone gushed about her and liked her. Even the butler, Edward, had good things to say about her.

Apparently, Stormey was falling into the role of mistress of the castle. Deep inside, Hegna was impressed. Stormey could have stayed to herself, but she was proving to be a person with a big heart.

"There she is with Zeke." Bijou pointed to the corner where the last mat in the rows were situated.

Hegna's heart all but leaped into her throat as she watched her human. Stormey was dressed in black leggings, a matching sports bra, and was barefoot. She had a long staff in her hands, and the way she held it had Hegna wondering if she'd ever used the weapon before.

Stormey was graceful as she swung the stick at Zeke who expertly dodged it. He swept his own staff, connecting with Stormey's. Hegna's hands balled into fists, and she pushed down the urge to race over there and protect her.

Stormey grunted, her brows narrowed in concentration, and she advanced on Zeke, swinging the stick. She spun around, giving herself more momentum, landing a blow to Zeke's stomach. He fell back a few paces, tripping over the mat and hitting the floor.

"Oh, my goodness. Are you okay?" Stormey cried out. She threw down her stick and rushed to Zeke.

Hegna narrowed her eyes on the two. Stormey's lips curved up into a smile. Her eyes softened, and she listened to Zeke.

"Good job, my lady," Zeke said. He scoffed and pushed Stormey's outstretched hand away. He stood and bent, picking up his staff. "You can knock me down, but I refuse to allow you to help me up."

"Seriously? Why, because I'm a girl?" She

snorted. She grinned up at him, playfully pushing him away. "Don't tell me your ego is so large that I can't help you up."

Hegna could no longer hold back. She didn't like the playful banter. This should be a serious training. Someone could get past their defenses and take her human. They needed to make sure Stormey could protect herself until help could arrive to her side.

Hegna growled low and made her way over to them. Bijou's soft curse was faintly heard beside her. Hegna ignored the bows and fist bumps to the chests made by her warriors. Her focus was on Stormey who was bestowing her beautiful smile on a man.

"Let's do it again—" Zeke's words died off when he saw Hegna and Bijou approaching. He turned to them, his smile disappearing. He was a mid-level warrior who was climbing the ranks of her army.

She studied his face and would consider him to be a handsome vampire. Bright-blue eyes, short brown hair that ended in curls, tall, and muscular. Hegna's nails bit into the palm of her hand. Zeke stood to attention, his arms at his sides. He then bowed his head and thumped his fist over his heart.

"Your Grace. General."

"At ease, warrior," Bijou announced. "Walk with me, Zeke."

Bijou and Zeke walked away, leaving Hegna alone with Stormey. This wasn't a place for them to have a personal conversation. There were at least twenty warriors in the room, all vampires and all with heightened hearing.

Hegna stared at Stormey. This was the first time she had been this close to her since that night.

"Do you need something from me?" Stormey asked. She rested the staff on the floor and gripped it close to her.

Hegna swallowed hard, truly unsure why she had come over here.

"No." Hegna cleared her throat. Her eyes greedily took in Stormey's curvy frame. A fine sheen of sweat rested on Stormey's brow, neck, and her arms. Hegna had the sudden, intense urge to drag her tongue over the small trails of sweat that ran down Stormey's body. She blinked, and instead, jerked her chin toward the staff. "You seem really comfortable with that."

"Well, I had plenty of practice back in Wichita." Stormey rolled her eyes. She brought it up and rested it on her shoulders with her hands holding on to it. The move pushed Stormey's breasts out.

Hegna had a hard time keeping her eyes from the mounds she had worshipped before. Her eyes locked in on a trail of sweat sliding down from her neck and disappearing into her cleavage.

"What does that mean? You were a fighter?" Hegna had finally read all of the paperwork that had been sent to her regarding her mate, and there was no mention of fighting experience. That wasn't something they would have left out.

"Not officially. I was a housekeeper and used a broom a lot. That broom came in handy when men would try things with me."

"You were attacked before that night?" Hegna growled. She may take a trip back to Wichita and deal out lessons. Human males just had no manners. If one of them had harmed Stormey, then she would gladly go back to Wichita and teach him a lesson, by ripping his arm off.

"I was never hurt, thanks to my handy-dandy broom." Stormey chuckled. She glanced away, biting her lip.

Hegna distinctively remembered how sweet those lips tasted.

"Why were you laughing and smiling at Zeke?"

Hegna couldn't help but ask. Something that she assumed was jealousy was rearing its ugly head inside her. She had never been jealous before and didn't know how to deal with it.

"What? Why do you care who I laugh and smile at?" Fire blazed in Stormey's eyes. She narrowed them on Hegna and swung the staff down to stand it beside her.

Hegna stiffened. There were very few people who questioned any of her motives, but they certainly didn't do it when her men were around. Hegna glanced over her shoulder and caught Zeke's eye.

"Give me your staff," she ordered.

He jogged over and passed it to her. She slid her hand along it. This weapon wasn't one she preferred. It had been a while since she had used one. Not that it mattered. She was a lethal vampire, and anything could become a deadly weapon in her hand.

If her human wanted to test her in front of other men, then she'd punish her for doing so.

"You were lucky in striking Zeke," Hegna began. She twirled the long stick with one hand before holding it up in front of her. She loosened her knees and flashed her fangs. "Try that on me."

The room grew silent. Hegna didn't have to turn around to see that all eyes were on them. She was sure her taunt was heard by every man and woman in the room. Hegna watched as the wheels turned in Stormey's head. It didn't take long for her to reach her decision.

Stormey gripped her weapon with both hands, fury burning bright in her eyes. She drove forward, swinging her staff at Hegna who raised hers and blocked the attack. Hegna brought hers back and aimed it for Stormey. Her mate jumped back and sidestepped, barely missing the taste of Hegna's staff.

"Footwork needs to be improved," Hegna snapped. She was speaking to both Stormey and Zeke. If the human ever had to defend herself, she needed to be quicker on her feet. She would never be able to outrun a vampire or a lycan, but it would help if she didn't trip over her feet.

Hegna moved forward swiftly, twirling her staff around in her hands, sending it again in a downward motion at Stormey. A satisfied grunt left her when Stormey brought her stick up, blocking Hegna.

Stormey cried out from the force of Hegna's staff meeting hers.

"Why are you going so hard?" Stormey gasped. She was panting, sweat pouring down her face. She quickly found herself on the defensive, backing away from Hegna's advances.

They danced around the mat, all the warriors surrounding them now to watch.

"I'm supposed to be learning."

"And you don't think this is a lesson?" Hegna said. Her human just didn't understand that in the midst of war, no one would give any of them a break.

Stormey gave a short growl of her own, forcing her way forward, sending a combo of hits at Hegna.

"Good." Hegna twisted her stick around and knocked Stormey's out of her hand.

It flew over into the spectators. A hand reached up and snagged it in the air then dropped it on the floor. Everyone knew during a spar, no one was to interfere. Stormey's eyes widened. Her gaze flicked to the area where her staff had gone.

Stormey was going to make a run for it.

Hegna easily read her expression.

Stormey raced toward it, but Hegna used her vampire speed to rush forward, catching her by surprise. She tossed her staff down and wrapped one arm around Stormey, clutching her tight.

"Don't give up. Fight me."

Stormey swung her elbow back to Hegna, almost catching her in the face. Stormey clawed at her arm, then stomped on the inside of Hegna's ankle. Pain exploded in her leg, and her grip loosened slightly. Stormey had wiggled free of Hegna's hold, but she didn't make it far. Hegna leaped forward and tackled Stormey. They fell down on the mat with Hegna rolling on top of her. She pinned Stormey's wrists down to the mat.

"Just admit that you hate me," Stormey spat. Her chest was rising and falling rapidly. Tears flowed from her eyes. She struggled to buck Hegna off, but she was no match for her strength. "And I don't know what I did to make you hate me so much."

Hegna paused, staring down into her big brown eyes. She blinked and glanced down at Stormey's plump lips that were slightly parted. Her skin flushed, drenched in sweat, was soft and so supple.

Hegna's blood was pumping from the excitement of sparring with her human. Having Stormey underneath her again brought back the intense need to claim her.

"Leave us," Hegna ordered.

She didn't recognize the huskiness in her voice, but she didn't have to repeat herself. The shuffling of feet echoed through the room as everyone filed out. Once the sound of the door shutting rang out, Hegna spoke.

"You think I hate you?" She tightened her grip on Stormey's wrist. The human couldn't be further from the truth. She released one of her wrists and wiped a tear that fell from her eyes. Just because she didn't want to complete the mating bond did not mean she disliked the human. "If you were a person I hated, you would feel the wrath of my hatred."

That was for certain.

"Then why are you doing this? You send me away then have me relocated across the castle. Do you know how that made me feel? That there are whispers going around the castle, people are trying to figure out why you wouldn't want me—"

"Who is this whispering about you?" Hegna demanded. She would cut the tongues out of the mouths of whoever gossiped about her human. Not one vampire or human who worked for her should be spreading lies or rumors. Taking their tongue would ensure those rumors would die out.

"That's not the problem." Stormey hiccupped. She turned her face away from Hegna and closed her eyes. More tears fell from her lids.

Hegna hated the sight of them marring her human's beautiful skin. She grew panicked, not knowing how to stop her from crying.

"The problem is you."

"Me?" Hegna gasped. Disbelief filled her. How could she be the problem? She'd moved Stormey away from her to keep down the temptation of going to her room. She had ensured Stormey had everything she would need and want. "What have I done?"

"You pushed me away and didn't even try. You're such a control freak that you have it in your head that only you can decide what is best for you. Apparently, I am not good enough for you, and fate doesn't know what she is doing. You don't see that everyone around you wants you to be happy. You deserve everything that you are denying me."

Hegna swallowed, not knowing how to respond. Her hand slipped down to Stormey's chin, and she brought her face around so she could meet her gaze. Hegna hated to admit that she had been fighting a losing battle since the moment she'd sent

Stormey away. Memories of their night had been haunting her.

Did she want to complete the mating bond?

No.

Did she want this woman underneath her?

Fuck, yeah.

"I don't hate you," Hegna started. She'd never lied about anything in her life. She only hoped that Stormey saw the honesty in her eyes.

A shudder shook Stormey's body. Hegna slid her hand down her neck and moved to the edge of Stormey's sports bra. Her breaths had slowed to an even pace. The feel of them against Hegna was too much of a distraction.

"Then what is this between us? I can't stop thinking about you. I'll do whatever I need to do to prove to you that we are meant to be," Stormey whispered.

Hegna's fingers snagged the bra and lifted it, exposing Stormey's breasts. She had dreamed of these large mounds. She lowered her head and captured one of Stormey's perky nipples. The small bud was soft and pliable. She rolled it with her tongue, sucking it deep inside her mouth.

Stormey arched her back, a moan leaving her lips.

Hegna molded the other with her hand. Stormey's skin was a bit salty from her workout with Zeke. Hegna didn't want to think of the warrior and the twinge of jealousy that arose in her belly. She teased the bud with her fangs, eliciting a moan from Stormey.

Needing to taste more of her, Hegna moved farther down her body, dragging her tongue along the way. The hint of musk and salt filled her nostrils. Her hands skated along Stormey's curves and stopped at the elastic band of her leggings. Her fingers hooked the material and tugged them down Stormey's legs, baring her soft flesh.

A growl rumbled inside Hegna's chest. She pushed Stormey's legs apart, revealing her pretty brown labia. Desperation filled her. She spread those fat lips open, exposing Stormey's pink core. Hegna leaned down and covered her pussy with her mouth. Stormey gasped, her hips thrusting toward Hegna's mouth. The sweet, tangy taste of Stormey exploded on her tongue.

Hegna gripped Stormey's thighs tight as she devoured the human. Her taste was one that Hegna could no longer resist. She dragged her tongue though Stormey's cunt, lapping up the honey that escaped from her channel. Hegna drank it all in.

She latched on to Stormey's swollen clit, suckling it with abandon and fury.

Stormey's cries filled the air, fueling Hegna's desire to hear her fall apart. Her human's fingers entwined in her hair and held on. The pain that exploded from her scalp was ignored. More of Stormey's juices flowed her mouth as she continued to tease and consume her. Stormey's hips thrust back and forth in a rhythm, and she took her pleasure.

Hegna glanced up at Stormey and found her head thrown back in ecstasy. Her chest rose and fell rapidly, and she writhed on the floor mat.

"Oh God," Stormey cried out.

Her fingers tightened in Hegna's hair, her hips quickened. Hegna could feel her human was teetering on the edge of her release. Hegna focused on the little swollen bundle of nerves in her mouth. She increased the pressure and tugged on it.

Stormey's muscles grew taut under her hands. She thrust her pelvis forward, tremors racking her body. She reached her climax. Her cries echoed around the room. Hegna pushed her fingers into Stormey's channel. Her walls were tight and pulsating. Hegna fucked Stormey, taking her climax even higher. She twisted her fingers around, pumping them faster while her human bucked and shuddered.

"I can't take any more," Stormey whimpered.

"You can," Hegna growled.

She wanted to push her even harder. She latched back on to Stormey's clit and continued to thrust her fingers harder. It didn't take long for Stormey to reach her second release. Hegna's mouth was flooded with her cream.

Stormey fell back against the mat, her muscles relaxed. Only the sound of her breathing filled the air. Hegna took her time licking her cunt until it was completely clean of her juices. She loved the taste of her little human and didn't want to leave her cunt.

Hegna took one last long lick of Stormey before rising onto her knees. Stormey lay on the mat, her face flushed, her breasts unbound and free. Her legs were still open, revealing her delicious cunt, and it was a sight that she never wanted to forget.

Thinking how Zeke had looked at Stormey brought a possessive rage inside her chest. No matter the fact that she hadn't put her mark on Stormey, she was still hers. The match said so, and every vampire had better respect it.

Stormey was hers.

Hegna bit back a curse at the thought. She reached out a hand and cupped Stormey's cunt. Stormey jerked slightly, her eyes flying open.

"This is mine," Hegna rasped. The words tumbled from her mouth before they even registered in her brain.

"It's yours," Stormey whispered without hesitation.

Hegna couldn't take her eyes off Stormey's beautiful body. Her fangs pushed forward, bursting through her gums. The overwhelming need to bite and drink from Stormey was growing. She could do it. She needed the blood. It had become harder to drink her processed blood. She knew what it meant, but she didn't want to admit it.

Her body was trying to communicate with her. Hegna had heard what had happened to her sister, Lethia, when she hadn't drunk from her mate. Her sister had grown weak. Not drinking from her mate had attributed to her getting wounded by the alpha and had slow healing.

But Hegna was stronger than her sister.

She was the heir to throne and could resist the need to feed from Stormey. The thought of it had Hegna's heart screaming at her. Hegna winced, the pain in her head reminding her of what she had always promised her. The conflict inside her was leaving her confused.

What would be so bad about mating with Stormey? She was matched to her. She was trying her best around the castle and had everyone eating out of the palm of her hand.

Hegna's ears picked up the distinct sound of hard footsteps coming down the hallway outside the sparring room.

Hegna stood and held a hand out to Stormey who took it. She brought her up and close. Stormey leaned her naked body against Hegna. Her eyes were wide, and her lips parted.

"I'm willing to wait for you," Stormey murmured.

Hegna's hand rested on Stormey's waist while her other lifted and cupped her cheek. She lowered her head and covered Stormey's lips with hers. Hegna growled. Stormey's lips were soft and parted immediately for her. She thrust her tongue inside her human's mouth, stroking her tongue and coaxing her into a slow duel. She tilted her head, deepening the kiss. Stormey moaned, pressing her bare breasts to Hegna's chest.

Hegna's hand couldn't sit idle while her human's womanly body was in her grasp. She slid her hand lower, to Stormey's ass, cupping it to hold her close. Hegna turned them to where her back was to the door and whoever opened it wouldn't get a glimpse of Stormey's nakedness. Seconds later, it opened.

"Your Grace," a familiar voice spoke.

Hegna raised her head, staring down into Stormey's eyes. Her female was out of breath, her exhalations now slight pants after their kiss. Hegna growled, not wanting to risk someone seeing Stormey.

"What is it, General?" Hegna growled. The use of her friend's title warned Bijou she wasn't in the best of moods. She wanted to drag Stormey into her bedroom and lock them away altogether while another part of her wanted to run far away from her.

"You're needed. There are a few calls that are important," Bijou announced. "I tried to take them for you since I knew you were busy, but it is you they are demanding to speak with."

Hegna wanted to say something to Stormey, but she didn't know the first thing she should say to her.

"Go. It's okay," Stormey whispered. Her face lit up from the smile that spread across her face. She reached up and ran a thumb along Hegna's bottom lip. "It sounds important. I'm sure we are due a conversation soon."

Hegna jerked her head in a nod. Stormey was right. They would need to sit down and have a true conversation. She couldn't keep running from her.

Hegna glanced over her shoulder and met Bijou's eyes. She nodded to the door, signaling she wanted her to shut it. Hegna didn't want to chance her second-in-command seeing her human's body. Once Bijou shut the door, Hegna back away, memorizing Stormey standing there with her sports bra bunched up underneath her chin, leaving her completely naked from the breasts down. She spun around and headed for the door. If she stood there any longer, she would have Stormey flat on her back again.

CHAPTER ELEVEN

Stormey watched Hegna stride out of the sparring room and close the door behind her. Stormey's body still trembled. She felt weak as if all of her energy had been zapped out of her. She bent and grabbed her panties and leggings. She slid them on and fixed her bra, covering herself.

What was that?

She stared at the mat where Hegna had just given her two of the most powerful orgasms she had ever had. Her clit still tingled, and her pussy had a warm sensation pulsing through it. She giggled, knowing that meant Hegna had thoroughly pleased her. She found her boots and slid them back on her feet. She'd go back to the castle and shower before heading down to the kitchen. It was the day that she had chosen to prepare a meal. The human employees loved when it was her day to cook. Not that they didn't like Val's food, but they loved hers because it reminded them of home and of something their mothers or grandmothers made.

Stormey slipped her coat on and headed toward the door. She laughed, noticing that her walk was different. Pushing open the door, she jumped, a squeak escaping her.

"Zeke, what are you doing here?" she asked. She held a hand to her chest, her heart racing from the surprise.

He avoided her gaze at first and gulped.

"My apologies, my lady. I didn't mean to frighten you." He straightened to his full height and offered her a small smile. Something was off about him.

"Was there something you wanted?" she asked curiously.

"I wanted to make sure that you were all right. With you being alone with the princess, I just remained close by should you have needed something."

"Oh," she said. She frowned slightly. "Why would I need help with something?"

"Well, you know." He sheepishly stared down at his feet. He swallowed hard several times before looking back up at her. "There has been talk that the princess doesn't like you. Or, um, doesn't want you."

Stormey was unsure how to respond. She studied him and realized what he truly meant. Had Hegna been about to harm her, he would have stepped in to save her.

Her heart softened for a moment. For she knew that he was no match for the princess. No matter how much he had trained so far, he would never be able to beat Hegna.

Even Stormey knew that.

"I think that is very honorable of you, but as you can see, I'm well," she replied gently.

"Yeah, I heard." Again, his eyes cast down at their feet.

Stormey's cheeks warmed at his response. She was sure anyone within ten miles had probably heard what was going on in the sparring room. There shouldn't be any feelings of embarrassment on her part. She was the mate of the princess. Whether the princess wanted to admit it or not, it was the truth.

And as the princess had reminded her before she'd left, Stormey's pussy belonged to her.

Stormey's heart skipped a beat at the memory. It was a step in the right direction. She just had to be patient, and after seeing the turmoil in Hegna's eyes, it gave Stormey something to hold on to.

"Was there something else you wanted?" she asked.

Movement down the hallway caught her attention. Desmond was making his way to her.

"May I escort you back to the castle?" Zeke offered. He flashed her another smile, this one showcasing his fangs.

"That won't be necessary, warrior," Desmond said, arriving at their side. Her guard stood a few inches taller than Zeke. He shot him a glare that caused Zeke's smile to disappear. "I'm sure you are needed elsewhere."

"Yes, sir." Zeke stepped back slightly. He glanced back at Stormey and bowed his head to her. "Until our next lesson, my lady."

"I'll see you later." Stormey replied. She didn't know what had passed between the two of them, but it was something.

Zeke hesitated slightly before he walked away. Desmond turned to her and bowed.

"My lady. Are you ready to return to the castle?" he asked.

"Yes, I need to shower before I go to the kitchen. I'd hate to show up looking the way I do." She motioned to herself. She was sweaty and could scent herself. Her workout had been intense. Before they'd sparred, Zeke had her going through some strength training.

Desmond motioned to the hall that led them toward the front of the building. They strolled along in silence. Stormey's brain was racing. There were so many thoughts and questions filling her mind. She didn't know what had just happened between her and Hegna. There was an internal struggle going on inside the princess. Stormey could see that in the moment Hegna had stared at her before she'd left the room. The darkening in her eyes, the gentle touch, the kiss, and the hope inside her blossomed.

Was Hegna coming round to the notion that they were mates?

"Can I ask you a question, Desmond?" Stormey zipped her coat up as they came upon the main entrance of the facility. She flipped her hood on and slid her hands into her pockets.

Desmond pushed open the door and stepped out first. The guard scanned the area, motioning for her to follow him.

"Yes, mistress." He grunted.

Their conversations were usually at a minimum. She knew the employees, human and vampire, gossiped. When she was around, some conversations were hushed, and quick gazes flicked to her before glancing away quickly when they saw she'd caught them staring.

"Do people talk about me behind my back? Or why Hegna hasn't claimed me?" she asked. She refused to look at him. It was embarrassing enough to ask her guard, but she was sure he heard things moving along through the castle.

"My lady…" He hesitated.

"Please. Be honest." She peered over at him. It was something she needed to know. Zeke admitting that people were talking had her worried. Did they laugh at her? Did they pity her? Stormey tried so hard to not fall into a pity party when she thought about how Hegna had pushed her away, but then she'd showed up today and rocked her world.

He sighed, and for a moment, she didn't think he would answer her.

"There is a concern on why the princess has not completed the mating bond with you. We were all confused about why she moved you to your new quarters."

"I see." A powerful gust of wind blew, and she stumbled slightly.

Desmond caught her and helped her right herself. They were walking along a path that led to the castle. Even though it was cold outside, she didn't mind the walk. With the way her body had overheated in the sparring room, she welcomed the drop in temperature. The sky was clear with only scattered stars spreading across the dark canvas. The half-moon was visible and shared its light with them.

There wasn't much illumination outside to highlight the walkway. It reminded her that she was going to talk with Edward about having more lamps installed along the many paths that led away from the main house. The vampires may be able to see perfectly in the dark, but the humans couldn't.

"I don't want the princess cutting out my tongue for sharing gossip—"

"You don't have to worry," she rushed to assure

him. She had asked for herself, not that she would ever tell Hegna of what she'd learned. He was right. Stormey wouldn't put it past Hegna to cut out someone's tongue if she thought they were spreading lies.

"No one would ever speak ill of you, my lady," Desmond added. He glanced down at her, a small smile on his lips. "You are loved by all who meet you."

Stormey relaxed, slightly relieved. Then if everyone was wondering why Hegna was resistant to mating with her, hopefully that concern would be gone. With what had happened in the sparring room, Stormey had a feeling deep in her stomach things were going to be changing.

Another strong gust of wind blew by. They picked up their pace, soon making it to the castle. Stormey smiled and acknowledged everyone they passed. They headed up to the third level of the tower her quarters were in. They arrived at her door. She spun toward him.

"Thank you, Desmond," she said.

"For what, my lady?" His eyebrows rose in shock.

"For everything. For protecting me, listening to me when I'm rambling about things, and for be honest with me. I appreciate it." She was sure he hadn't heard that much since this was his job. He had dedicated his life to the crown, serving Hegna, and now protecting her. It was expected of him, but she wanted to ensure he knew how she felt about him.

"It is my honor, my lady." He gave her a deep bow and thumped his fist over his heart.

She'd seen other warriors do the same to Hegna. She placed her hand over her heart and smiled, disappearing into her quarters. She shut the door behind her and leaned back against the wood. The scent of cleaning solutions filled the air, alerting her that the housekeepers had been in her room.

Stormey headed toward her bathroom. She'd shower quickly then go down to the kitchen. She entered the bathroom and passed the mirrors over the sinks. She paused and took in her smile.

Mid-afternoon fighting and sex must have been what she needed. Now she understood vampires a little better. Her adrenaline had already been high, and then to be taken higher on the waves of an orgasm, she was still riding the wave.

Would Hegna come to her again? Would she send for Stormey?

Stormey had meant what she had said. She would do whatever she had to do in order to win Hegna over.

* * *

STORMEY KNEADED the dough and folded it over. Tonight, she wanted to make something savory and filling for everyone and she had a hankering for breakfast. Sausage, biscuits, and gravy were on the menu. It was easy to make, and it helped that the castle's kitchen had a well-stocked pantry.

"Everyone is loving the meal, my lady." Ayah breezed back in the kitchen. She smiled and came to stand next to Stormey.

"Really?" It pleased her to know that people enjoyed what she cooked.

"Breakfast is a hit." Ayah laughed. She wiped her brow with the back of her hand. "I'll go start working on the new batch of sausage gravy for the next wave." She spun around and headed over to the fridge.

Stormey reached over for her biscuit cutter so she could throw these biscuits in the oven.

"You're going to put me out of a job." Val

laughed. He stood on the other side of the counter where she was working.

"Oh, I doubt it. My cooking isn't as gourmet as yours. Mine is home cooking." She giggled. She enjoyed spending time in the kitchen. It had allowed her to feel needed and connect with all of the human employees. It was important for her to show that she cared, and it helped with relations between humans and vampires.

At least once she mated with Hegna.

"I'm not sure if anyone told you, but there will be a dinner with the local human leaders and the princess," Val started.

Stormey tried to hide her surprise. Not that she was kept in the loop on all workings of the castle. If she was going to be running the castle as the mate of the princess, she needed to know these things and be included.

Stormey didn't know if she should speak with Corbin or Hegna herself.

"Okay." She began cutting the biscuits and placing them on the awaiting pan. She didn't want Val to feel guilty that he'd spilled the beans on something that she may not have been included in on purpose.

"And I was wondering if you wanted to help

with the planning of the meals. Something that would be welcoming."

"What's the occasion?" she asked. She had a few ideas and wasn't sure if this was a standard meeting or if they were coming to discuss a problem.

"Well, from what I understand, to meet you, the mate of the princess, and to discuss the lycan issue." Val pulled a small notebook from his pocket on his jacket and set it down on the counter.

"Oh, so an important meal. We should probably do something fancy." She paused and looked over at him. She wasn't sure what they had in their deep freezer stores.

"What are you thinking?"

"I'm thinking you wouldn't want something too fancy that was like a brag. Most humans can barely get by." At least all of the people she knew. She didn't know what how well-off the mayor was or any other local leaders.

"I see your point. Maybe we should do seafood. Something that can be caught fresh in the lakes." He scribbled notes down on the paper.

"That would be perfect. There are plenty of fisherman who we can pay. It's a good way to put money into small businesses," she said.

"I like the way you think. There are a few local guys I'm sure I can call on." Val winked at her and walked away.

She glanced down at the biscuits and sighed. She had so many ideas that she wanted to implement and she was going to have to start doing things her way.

CHAPTER TWELVE

"When are the meetings going to end?" Hegna sat back in her leather chair and glowered at her advisor.

Corbin smirked and glanced down at his tablet resting on his lap. Bijou sat in the other chair next to him.

After leaving Stormey yesterday, she had been called away for meetings that all could have waited. By the time she had wrapped them up, the sun had risen. She had thought to go to Stormey but figured she would be resting. What she would have said to the human, she had no clue.

A sharp pain sliced its way through her stomach. She inhaled, attempting to push it down. The twinges were getting more frequent and the intensity worsening. She opened her eyes and found Corbin and Bijou staring at her.

Nothing apparently got past them.

"When was the last time you had a proper feeding?" Corbin asked.

He folded his hands, resting them on the tablet. His face was devoid of any emotions, and she knew this wasn't her advisor speaking to her, but her friend. Concern was evident in Bijou's eyes. Hegna cursed internally, not wanting to have this discussion with either of them.

"I had some before I came here," Hegna admitted. She held his gaze, tapping a nail on her desk.

"You are looking a little pale there, if I do say so," Corbin replied.

"I didn't ask you how I looked," she snapped. Her gaze flicked to Bijou, daring her general to speak about how she appeared.

"He's right. I can see you are having pain," Bijou said.

Hegna glared at her other friend. So they were going to team up against her. She should have known.

"I assure you both that I am fine," Hegna growled. She held back a wince from the ache spreading behind her eyes. This wretched headache was not leaving her. It came and went. She hadn't lied. The blood she drank was slightly repulsive. She tried to drink the entire goblet, but she was unable to face it all.

Even thinking about her feeding this morning had her stomach quivering. She swallowed hard to will the sourness to leave her. There was no way in the seven hells she'd vomit in front of these two.

"You know what happened to your sister," Bijou said, exasperation lining her voice.

"And I am a stronger vampire than my sister." Hegna sniffed. She didn't know why either of them were concerned. She had been able to complete all duties just fine.

"And more stubborn. Why can't you just admit it," Bijou agonized. She closed her eyes and rubbed them with her fingers. The general seemed as if she hadn't slept well.

"There is nothing for me to admit. Maybe I have a stomach bug." Hegna shrugged.

Corbin snorted and rolled his eyes. "Just forget it, Bijou. She's not going to admit what everyone already knows." The smug look on his face had

Hegna wanting to reach over and slap him in the head.

"And what might that be?" she asked through clenched teeth. She already knew what he was going to say but wanted to see if he was bold enough to speak the words.

"That Stormey is your true fated mate and you just don't want to admit that the test was correct," Corbin calmly announced.

Hegna flew back from her desk and rose to her feet. She glared at him, her breaths coming rapidly.

He was right.

She didn't want to admit the test was correct, but she'd be damned if she would admit *he* was right also.

"You don't understand," she gasped. She rested her clenched fists on her desk. The pain rippling through her abdomen was robbing her of air. Hegna had never experienced anything like this before. She'd been stabbed, shot, hung, and beaten in the past. None of that pain compared to this. It was as if something internally was trying to claw its way out.

"You need blood," Corbin growled. Her friend stood and stalked over to her. He folded back his sleeve and presented his wrist to her.

She eyed his pale wrist and felt, again, the wave of nausea that came. She closed her eyes and shook her head. She focused on her breathing.

Inhale. Exhale. If she were alone, she would attempt a deep meditation. That would help clear her of all thoughts and urges. For now, this exercise would have to do. As the warden, she had little time to devote to her own well-being when so much was at stake for her people.

"I swore I would never drink from you," she whispered. The pain was receding, and her breathing was improving. She straightened to her full height and met his gaze.

"As long as you don't try to fuck me, you can drink from me." His lips curled up into a grin in the corner.

She rolled her eyes and pushed him away.

"You are an idiot," Hegna muttered. She motioned for him to return to his seat. Her knees had grown weak, and she refused to show either of them. She locked them together, hoping she could stand until he sat again. "I have everything under control."

"I highly doubt it. The moment you pass out, I will be calling for the healer," Bijou warned.

The fierce look in her eyes was familiar to

Hegna. It was the same look she gave the enemy before she struck them down. Her general would do as she'd threatened.

"It won't be necessary." Hegna took her seat again, satisfied she was able to smoothly sit without falling into the chair.

Bijou's phone rang. She pulled out the device and hit the button.

"Captain, you're on speakerphone. The princess is here, along with Corbin," Bijou announced.

This was a phone call Hegna had been waiting for. Nezera was to check in last evening, but something had come up. Hegna leaned forward, her attention on the device.

"Thank you, General. Can everyone hear me? We are currently underground," Nezera said.

"We can hear you," Hegna assured her. She needed to know what the captain had discovered so they could correlate findings with the other scouting teams. The Canadian town they were hunting in would be the perfect place for lycans to set up dens. The area was remote and low population. "What do you have to report?"

"We have confirmed the location of the lycan den," Nezera said.

Hegna's gaze narrowed. This was just the information they needed.

"They have taken over the small town of Sanlow, and we haven't seen any trace of humans."

"Are you saying what I think you are saying?" Corbin asked, glancing around the room.

Hegna recognized the human town. It was one of the few towns where vampires were absent. They protected themselves, and Hegna's warriors had only stepped in a few times in the past when rogues had made their way there.

"Everyone in the town has been turned. Men, women, children, young and old."

Her words were met with incredulous silence. This couldn't be the only town of lycans. Azura had admitted their numbers were great. So not only had they been kidnapping humans who were trying to escape their matched mates, they were taking entire towns and turning them. This information needed to be shared with her family.

"Are you sure?" Bijou murmured.

"I'm positive. We have secured an informant, and he's confirmed it."

"And he's trustworthy?" Hegna inquired.

They would need to look into this matter expeditiously. How the hell had the lycans commanded an entire town and they hadn't been alerted to the matter?

"He shared with us that during the town's invasion, they attempted to turn his wife and seven-year-old son, and both died during the process. So do I believe him? Hell, yeah." Nezera snarled.

Hegna couldn't even begin to understand what the lycan had been through. She knew that if anyone laid a hand on Stormey, she would rip their head off and tear them limb from limb. She wouldn't stop there. She would go after their family, friends, and all who were close to them.

"For sharing this information, what does he want in return?" Hegna asked. She felt the gazes of Corbin and Bijou on her. The king had an agenda for the lycans, and it was Hegna's responsibility along with her sisters to carry it out.

"He wants his life to be spared. He says there are others who have similar stories and did not ask for this. From what he told us, the roundup of humans and their turning was quite violent and vicious. He's pleading for their lives," Nezera said.

Hegna stared at the phone. Was it fair to punish those who were innocent and turned against their will? Having an informant who was a lycan, be it forced or not, could be vital to bringing down Azura and her mangy mutts.

"For now, he will be spared. Dive deeper and see what you can find out," Hegna said.

"Yes, Your Grace." The line went dead.

"The entire fucking town?" Bijou stood from her seat and paced the floor. She was in full general mode. The anger radiating from her was palpable.

"When was the last time we had contact with them?" Hegna asked.

"I will find out, Your Grace," Bijou snarled.

"We have to alert your sisters and parents. How many other towns have ben commandeered and we are in the dark?" Corbin asked.

"We need to find out. Send word to every vampire post to check on all neighboring towns and cities. We need to ensure this hasn't happened to more," Hegna ordered.

Corbin scribbled notes on his tablet.

"Send word to my sisters, too."

"Will do. You have another call—"

"It can wait." Hegna pushed back from her desk and stood. This time her legs held all of their strength.

"This can't wait. It's either take this call or he's bound to show up," Corbin said.

Hegna rolled her eyes and blew out a deep breath. The hologram box on her desk alerted them of the incoming call.

Corbin glanced down at his tablet. "He's on time."

"Who the hell is it?" Hegna growled. She didn't have time for this. She needed to formulate a plan, and maybe even travel to Sanlow herself. For a pack to take over an entire town, the alpha had to be there.

"It is Lord Vilson." Corbin eyed her.

She closed her eyes and flopped back down in her chair. Corbin was right. If she didn't take this call, then the coven's council member would show his face here at the castle.

"Make it quick," she grumbled.

He reached across the desk and hit the button on the box. Bijou took her seat as well.

"Your Grace. Thank you for your virtual audience today." Lord Vilson's figure appeared in the room. He stood, dressed in dark clothing with a cloak resting on his shoulders. His long black hair flowed around them. His piercing blue eyes were locked on her. He had been the lead council member of their coven for centuries. There were plenty of times when Hegna and he had butted heads. The elder vampire still insisted on using his official title of Lord from centuries before.

"I'm a very busy woman, Lennix. How can I help you this evening?" she asked. Lennix Vilson always assumed he was of the utmost importance and everything needed to stop when he spoke.

"The entire town has been in an uproar about your future mate," he began. He paced back and forth, his hands dramatically flailing in the air. "The coven is demanding the mating be as soon as possible."

"The coven wouldn't dare demand anything from me." Hegna kept her voice quiet, but her patience was running low. This call could have waited for another day. "What I do with my personal life is my business, not yours—"

"Don't forget your duty is to the coven and to the entire vampire nation as the heir to the throne. You must complete the mating bond with the human as soon as possible. The entire coven is demanding to meet the woman whose beauty and caring nature rumors have spread throughout the town and the territory."

Hegna arched an eyebrow. Stormey had been the talk of the territory? Hegna glanced over at

Corbin's smug face. She itched to land a punch and split the lips that curved up in a smirk.

"Thank you for reminding me of duties that I know more than you do," Hegna snapped. She was done with this conversation. Her annoyance level was through the roof. She had more pressing things than to be reminded of something she'd been told since she was born. "Right now, the lives of vampires are at stake. I'm sure when you are hosting your parties and entertaining members of the coven, that you don't discuss the lycan threat that overshadows us. That is what is important, not who I mate with."

"I have come up with a solution." He paused and turned to her, completely ignoring her barb at his infamous parties he liked to throw. "We will have a small dinner party at the castle where you can introduce us to your mate. We'll worry about an official introduction of the future princess once you have sealed the bond. I will send word to Edward, and we'll work out the date."

"That will be fine," Corbin said, interjecting before she could respond. Her friend must have taken a look at her face and saw the fury that rolled through it.

Lennix bowed, and the call disconnected.

"Where in the seven hells does he gets the balls to try to tell me what to do?" Hegna said.

She glanced between Corbin and Bijou. Corbin had the nerve to grin at her while Bijou shrugged.

"Just remember he's thinking of the good of the coven—"

"He's thinking of himself," Hegna grumbled. She pushed back from the desk, and this time she was officially done with calls. No more. She didn't care who it was, she was not taking another wretched call. "No more calls—"

The hologram alerted her of another one. Hegna growled and reached for it, intent on tossing it out of the window.

"It's your mother." Corbin chuckled.

Hegna glanced at the window and saw it wasn't open. The steel coverings were raised, allowing the moon's rays to come in through the glass. Hegna may be the heir to the throne, but she wouldn't dare not answer her mother's call.

"Hello, Mother." Hegna hit the button.

Her mother's figure appeared. Corbin and Bijou stood and bowed to the queen. Hegna stood from her seat and reciprocated the motion. Her mother was dressed in a royal golden dress that flowed around her body. A purple belt was resting on her waist. Her blonde hair was drawn back away from her face. She was the epitome of a queen, and Hegna could never pull off a look as regal as her beautiful mother.

But Stormey could, a voice in the back of her head mentioned. Her human was beautiful and had a kind soul. An image of Stormey sitting on the throne beside her came to mind. She'd be stunning as queen consort. While Hegna would be dressed in her fighting leathers, her mate would be in the fanciest of dresses, with the most precious jewels adorning her, while they led the nation together.

"Hegna. Corbin. General." Mira nodded to them, turning her attention to Hegna. She walked over to her, assessing Hegna. Her gaze paused on Hegna's face. "When was the last time you fed?"

Corbin snorted.

"I doubt you are calling to check in on the last time I consumed a meal." Hegna held her mother's stare.

The queen sighed and shook her head. "You and your sisters are all the same. You have a mate, seal the bond with her."

"Mother—"

"I don't want to hear it. Lethia refused to bite her mate and drink from her, and look what happened to her when she fought that wretched alpha," the queen snapped.

"I am stronger than my sister—"

"But no smarter," Mira cut her off. Her hologram figure moved away and walked over to a window.

As the future queen, Hegna had been trained since birth on how to rule.

"Again, Mother. To what do I owe the pleasure of your call?" Hegna bit back a growl and rested her hands on her waist.

"In two days' time, we will need to meet via hologram. Your sisters and your father and me. We need to share information that will help in the fight against the lycans."

"I have information that I will give. Something I just found out today, but we will be getting more details."

"Good." Mira turned back to her. She went back over to Hegna and stopped in front of her. "I will be making a trip to Black Hollows soon to meet my future daughter-in-law." The queen spun on her heels and took a few steps away. The call disconnected with her mother's figure disappearing into thin air.

Hegna stood rooted in her spot, shocked.

"Am I not the heir to throne?" she wondered aloud. She glanced over at Bijou and Corbin and threw her hands up in the air. "Apparently, everyone can tell me what to do and what is best for me."

"I'm not going to argue about the queen. She basically can tell all of us what to do." Bijou chuckled.

Hegna ran a hand along her face and moved over to her desk. She leaned back against it, resting her bottom on it.

No one truly knew what it took to be warden or commander of an army but her sisters. The responsibility weighed heavy on all of their shoulders. Hegna was thankful she had people she trusted.

"I'll start reaching out to the guard posts," Bijou volunteered.

"Thank you, General." Hegna paused at the sound of a knock at the door.

Corbin and Bijou shrugged at her questioning look. She wasn't expecting anyone to step by while she met with her personal small council.

"Come in," Hegna called out.

The door opened, and immediately she was hit with the familiar scent of the one person she couldn't stop thinking about.

Stormey stood in the doorway with her attendant behind her. She took in the room and hesitated. Her large brown eyes connected with Hegna. A twinge of her abdominal pain reappeared as if to remind Hegna of what she needed. She cleared her throat and waved for Stormey to enter.

"Stormey. Did you need something?" Hegna asked. Her gaze greedily took in her human who was dressed in thick leggings, high boots, and a blue sweater dress that hugged all of her curves. A floral perfume filled the air, but Hegna was able to scent Stormey's natural aroma. She inhaled deeply, and immediately, her core clenched.

She needed the human.

"I don't mean to interrupt. I can wait. It was nothing," Stormey gushed, her gaze flicking between Corbin and Bijou.

"Well, you are here now. What is it?" Hegna asked, preferring this distraction as opposed to another useless meeting. She folded her arms in front of her chest to keep from reaching for Stormey.

Stormey slowly strolled into the office, her hips offering a gentle sway. Her hair was left down with the front tied back. Stormey stopped a few feet from Hegna who bit back a growl, wanting her closer.

"I would like to go visit the Fountain of Hope. I

was told this trip wasn't authorized," Stormey announced. She stood to her full height and met Hegna's gaze. "I met a few people from there when we went to the marketplace, and I promised them that I would come."

"Fountain of Hope?" Hegna frowned. The name rang a bell, but she couldn't put her finger on it.

"Yes, it's the local orphanage. Volunteering at orphanages was a passion of mine before I came to Black Hollows. I spent time in a few growing up, and it's very dear to my heart," Stormey said.

Hegna turned and rifled through the papers on her desk and pulled out the one with the name Fountain of Hope on it. She had received a letter requesting donations a few weeks ago. She raised it and scanned the letter. They were going to hold an event in the spring to help raise funds, but they needed help getting started.

Maybe she would take an interest in something Stormey liked.

"When would you like to go?" Hegna looked up from the paper.

Stormey bit her lip, her fingers entwined together. "Soon. It's five-thirty, and it would be nice to go now so that it won't be too late for them. They are human and aren't nocturnal like we are," Stormey said.

Like we are.

Hegna liked how Stormey included herself. Hegna dropped the paper on her desk and moved to stand in front of her. She rested her hands on her shoulders.

"You can go now, and I'll come with you," Hegna said.

Stormey's eyes widened at the announcement. "What? Are you certain? You appear busy. I can take my guard with me, and we—"

"I'll go with you, and we'll take a team of vampires with us for protection." Not that Hegna was worried, she could protect her human, but she didn't want to take any chances.

Her mate was precious.

Hegna swallowed hard. She stared down into Stormey's eyes, and a twinge tweaked in her chest. Her heart skipped a beat from the feeling of warmth radiating from Stormey's shoulders. The memory of her mate's taste on her tongue and the sound of her cries came rushing back to her.

"Okay," Stormey whispered. She took a step toward Hegna, closing the gap between them.

"If visiting orphans is something that is a

passion for you, then maybe I should become involved as well," Hegna replied. She ignored the gasps from the room. This was a big step for her, and from the look of excitement and happiness spreading across Stormey's face, it let her know it was the right decision to make.

Hegna realized that maybe she had been difficult.

She had always been a firm believer she controlled her destiny, but maybe this once, fate or that damn test, was right.

Stormey was hers.

Hegna made a vow she would make up for her harshness toward her mate. When she ascended the throne and Stormey was there by her side, she would be ruling over not only vampires, but humans as well. Stormey would be the highest-ranking human on the continent.

"That would be nice." Stormey leaned up on her toes and placed a chaste kiss on Hegna's lips. "I hope you like kids."

CHAPTER THIRTEEN

Stormey sat beside Hegna with butterflies fluttering around in her stomach. She hadn't expected Hegna to come with her. She had been shocked when she had asked for someone to take her to the Fountain of Hope and was told that due to increased security, the princess had to approve her outing.

So Stormey had stalked her way to Hegna's office and had planned on demanding she be able to go to the orphanage, but the second she'd opened the door, her bravery had faded.

Hegna was dressed in her dark fighting leathers with only a few blades on her. The sight of her had left Stormey tongue-tied. Her dark hair had been pulled back. Her sharp blue eyes had watched Stormey as if she were prey.

Stormey had been beyond shocked when Hegna had not only approved her outing but decided she would come along, too.

If visiting orphans is something that is a passion for you, then maybe I should become involved as well.

Was this a sign she was coming around to the notion they belonged together? Stormey could only hope. She glanced over at Hegna who was silent in her seat. She stared out at the scenery as it passed. Stormey wondered what she was thinking. Had she put off something important so she may come with her?

Their caravan made its way through the town. Stormey had only expected she would need two guards to escort her to the orphanage, but Hegna was insistent that they needed a full team of guards to accompany them. Stormey felt like royalty with as many people it took to secure her and Hegna's trip to the orphanage. They were in the back of an armored sedan which, according to Desmond, was impenetrable by bullets. Two large SUVs, with one in front and the other behind their car.

She smiled softly. Deep in her heart, she felt

Hegna was trying in her own way. If she wasn't, then why was she there?

Stormey reached out her hand and took Hegna's in hers. Hegna's head flew around, her surprised gaze meeting Stormey's. She entwined their fingers together and slid across the backseat and closed the small gap between them.

"Thank you," Stormey said softly. Hegna joining her meant a lot to her. This was something she could share with the vampire princess and maybe, just maybe, Hegna would share something personal with her. Stormey was willing to take things slowly if it meant she got her vampire.

"For what?" Hegna blinked.

"For coming with me. This means a lot," she said. She glanced down at their hands, and her heart skipped a beat. Those hands could not only give her the best pleasure she had ever experienced in her life, but yet were deadly.

Stormey wasn't sure why, but the thought of Hegna defending her and taking someone down in her honor sent a thrill through her. She had never been a person who liked violence, but it was comforting knowing the person she was to spend all eternity with was a lethal vampire.

"Why would going to visit children with no

home mean so much to you?" Hegna arched an eyebrow at her.

It didn't escape Stormey she hadn't pulled her hand away. She tucked that away as a win.

"I'm sure you know I was raised in an orphanage. My parents were taken from me at such a young age, and with the war going on, there wasn't anyone who could take me in, so I was sent to an orphanage. I know how it feels to not feel wanted or loved. Sometimes all a child needs is a smile or a hug to brighten their day," Stormey said. She leaned her head on Hegna's shoulder.

Her entire childhood hadn't been horrible, and she did have fond memories of some of the volunteers throughout the years. A small twinge of sadness went through her that she hadn't been able to say goodbye to the children back in Wichita. Good volunteers were always hard to find. In the world they lived in now, not many had much to give. Stormey certainly hadn't, but her time was more valuable than any money she could have given the orphanage.

"Tell me, Stormey. When you left the orphanage, what happened then?" Hegna asked.

Stormey sighed, her thoughts circling to Lori. She made herself a note to send word of her move to her former foster mother. Stormey began telling Hegna how Lori had taken her in. Lori didn't have much and was lonely after her husband died, so she went through the process of taking in foster children. It gave her a purpose in life.

"She sounds like a good woman," Hegna murmured. She reached up and brushed Stormey's hair away from her face. The tips of her fingers lingered on Stormey's cheek.

"She is. Even though I don't live in Alabama any longer, I still send her letters to update her on my whereabouts and to let her know I'm okay." Stormey felt the words tumble from her lips. She was growing entranced by Hegna. Her vampire's fangs were noticeable from underneath her top lip. Stormey's breath caught in her throat at the sight of the sharp teeth. Her body was already reacting to their closeness. She squeezed her legs shut and tried to will her body to calm down.

"We must thank her," Hegna said softly. She lowered her head slightly.

Stormey closed the gap, impatiently pressing her lips to Hegna's. Their lips molded together in a gentle kiss. Hegna's tongue slipped through Stormey's. She opened her mouth wider, welcoming Hegna's invasion. Their tongues stroked each other in a slow, sensual duel. Stormey turned toward Hegna, sliding her arms around her vampire.

Stormey groaned, hating they were in the backseat of a car and had on too many clothes. Hegna released Stormey, her hand cupping Stormey's cheek. Her lips curled up slightly in a small smile.

"I can scent your arousal." Hegna's voice was husky and tantalizing.

Stormey leaned into her hand, almost dissolving into a puddle on the seat. She loved the sound of Hegna's voice when it deepened.

"I promise you later I will take care of you."

"Promise?" Stormey asked.

Hegna nodded and released Stormey. She tucked her into her side and peered out of the window. It was then Stormey realized their vehicle was slowing down. Snow had covered the town, but it looked as if the streets were clear. She stared out her window and didn't see many people out which wasn't a surprise to her since it was after dark. It was early evening, and wintertime meant longer nights and shorter days.

"It would appear we are here."

"IT IS QUITE an honor for us to have you visit," Miss Emily Washington, the head of the orphanage, greeted them. She held out her hand to Hegna and Stormey. Her grip was firm, and her smile was wide. She stepped back away from them and motioned to the building. "This is Fountain of Hope."

Stormey glanced around and took in the decor. It was out of date and was an older mansion that appeared to have been built back in the twentieth century. There was a staircase that led to the second floor. The entryway was once grand, with a chandelier hanging from the ceiling. The paint and the wood had seen better days. It was clean but showed off the wear and tear from over the years.

"This does remind me of a few orphanages I was in," Stormey murmured. She spun around and sighed as memories came forth. She met the gaze of Hegna before turning back to Emily.

"You were raised in an orphanage?" Emily asked, curiosity in her eyes.

"I was. I was taken in at the age of sixteen by a woman who fostered me until I aged out." Stormey glanced up and took in curious faces of children huddling down along the railings at the top of the stairs.

"May I ask what triggered this visit?" Emily asked. She fiddled with her hands in front of her. She switched her attention to Hegna. "I would have to admit when I received the call, I was shocked that you would be visiting our home."

"As Stormey mentioned, she was once an orphan, and children who are like her hold a special place in her heart," Hegna began. She continued on, but Stormey tuned her out. A certain set of brown eyes, big chubby cheeks, and braids with colored beads on the ends caught her eye.

Maisie.

Stormey waved at her, and she must have taken it as a cue to come on down the stairs.

"Princess!" Maisie called out. She ran to the top of the stairs and made her way down them. She was dressed in a purple, long-sleeved t-shirt and sweatpants. Her feet were bare, but they flew down the stairs.

Stormey grinned and opened up her arms. The tyke made it to the bottom and took off, slamming into Stormey. She laughed and wrapped the little one up in a hug.

"You came like you said you would!" Maisie giggled.

"I did." Stormey laughed. She pulled back to

get a look at Maisie. She was such a cutie, and Stormey's heart melted at the sight of her. "Have you been a good girl?"

"No," Maisie said with a straight face, sending Stormey into a fit of laughter. There were a few snickers and snorts from her guards. She glanced up to see Desmond smiling before he turned away.

Hegna stared at Maisie with a raised eyebrow.

"Maisie, you are supposed to be upstairs," Emily gushed.

She reached for Maisie, but she buried herself into the side of Stormey's winter cloak.

"Oh, it's quite all right. Maisie and I met at the marketplace when she was selling the baked goods," Stormey said. She took Maisie's hand and loved how the small one felt. She had always yearned for a child, and Maisie had her biological clock blaring.

"Oh, you're the one who bought out the table? Maisie has been speaking of you nonstop." Emily laughed.

"Yes, and I must say everyone enjoyed the snacks," Stormey said. The baked goods were a hit, and when everyone found out they were from the orphanage, it made it even better.

Maisie leaned against Stormey, peeking around her leg at Hegna. Stormey giggled at the wide-eyed gaze of the youngster. Hegna glanced down at her. She offered the tyke a smile. Her face completely relaxed as she winked at Maisie. Stormey's heart skipped a beat.

"Aren't you a vampire?" Maisie blurted out.

Chuckles went around at her innocent question.

"I am," Hegna replied.

"Then where are your fangs?" the little one asked. This young girl was bold and brave.

Stormey laughed and squeezed her hand. Maisie reminded Stormey of herself at that age.

"Now, Maisie, let's not be rude," Emily sputtered.

"It's fine." Hegna raised her hand. She walked over to Maisie and bent down on one knee, bringing her somewhat eye level with the child. "Do you promise to not be scared if I show them to you?"

"I never get scared," Maisie scoffed.

Emily rolled her eyes, shaking her head. The headmistress of the orphanage certainly had her hands full with this one.

"Then you are a very brave young girl," Hegna replied. Something passed fleetingly on her face. She then grinned, showing off her fangs.

Maisie's quick intake of breath was the only

sound in the room. She moved forward to get a better view.

"Cool," Maisie breathed. "Do you bite people?"

"Maisie!" Emily cried out.

Hegna laughed and stood. Maisie glanced around at the adults, then grinned.

"I'm sure Princess Hegna will answer your curiosity another day," Stormey said.

Maisie laughed and leaned against her, hugging her legs.

"Come. I can give you a tour." Emily waved for them to follow.

Maisie held on to Stormey's hand while they walked through the aging mansion. Some of the children followed at a distance. Stormey was sure word had got around that the princess was visiting them. Humans were aware of the vampire royal family who ruled above the human government. There were about twenty-five kids currently living in the mansion along with a few employees who were like Brandi and traded their services for food and housing.

Emily soon ushered them down a hall and into the living room that had a welcoming feel to it. The furniture was mismatched, but it had all of the trappings of home. This room also needed a good updating, as did the entire building. Hegna and Stormey took a seat on the large couch with Maisie sitting between them. She offered a smile to Hegna and had yet to release Stormey's hand.

Desmond and the guards had spread out with Cezar, Hegna's personal guard, entering the room and standing by the door. Hegna had the other guards remain outside to ensure there was no threat before they had entered the home. It left Stormey wondering if something had happened that she was unaware of.

Stormey turned back to Emily. She continued discussing the history of the orphanage and how she had started it twenty-five years ago. There had been so many children on the streets of Black Hollows and surrounding towns. She and a few others worked tirelessly to get the children off the streets. It was extremely dangerous at night for the youth, and they were unable to protect themselves against rogue vampires and vile humans as well.

This was a subject Stormey was all too familiar with. She was thankful she had never been a kid who had to rely on her survival skills on the streets. Many of the cities and towns she'd lived in, rogue vampires were on the rise, and many teens disappeared.

"Brandi said you were raising money to give the children a better playground," Stormey interrupted.

"Ah, yes. That is one of the many projects we are looking for funding for. These children deserve to have a safe area to play and burn off some energy." Emily leaned back in her chair. The dark circles beneath her eyes revealed she gave every bit she could to the orphanage.

"There was a letter sent to my office," Hegna began.

Stormey was taken aback. Hegna had received mailings from the orphanage?

"It appeared to be a general one seeking funding. What exactly do you need, Miss Washington?"

"Look at this place. Honestly, I would love to have this place renovated, a game room with plenty of activities for the kids when it's too cold to go outside, a library with newer books than ones that are close to fifty years old, the list goes on and on." Emily sighed. She tucked her gray curls behind her ear and shook her head. "I'm sure it would cost in the millions to get this place in tip-top shape. We are just lucky the old building is holding on."

"Can I turn on the television, Miss Emily?" Maisie asked. She had been such a good girl, quiet while the adults were chatting.

"Yes, my dear. Just keep it down," Emily said.

Maisie flew off the couch and raced over to the television. She dropped down on the floor before it and switched it on. She flicked through the channels until she found something on.

Stormey turned and found Hegna watching her with an unreadable expression. This time, it was Hegna who reached out and took Stormey's hand. She gave it a squeeze and returned back to Emily.

"Miss Washington, I want to help," Hegna stated.

Stormey's breath caught in her throat. She stared at her vampire as if she had grown a second head.

"You do?" Stormey and Emily echoed at the same time.

Hegna squeezed her hand again. "I do. The history of our people has been a rocky one, and I admire your passion for wanting to protect the children who were victims of the war, be it directly or indirectly. Everything you have done is considered honorable in my mind, and I want to pay for the complete restoration of this building and ensure you and the children have everything you will need."

The room went completely silent except the low

rumblings of the television. Stormey squeezed Hegna's hand as hard as she could. Tears welled in her eyes. Emily's face was marred with tears as well.

"Your Grace, that is the best news I have heard in decades," Emily cried out. She stood abruptly from her chair.

Stormey and Hegna followed suit.

"Can I hug you?"

"Um, yes," Hegna said, but her words were cut off from Emily already pulling her into a hug.

The older woman's body shook with sobs.

Hegna glanced over at Stormey in alarm. Stormey was sure Hegna wasn't used to being hugged by strangers. Stormey wiped her cheeks and smiled, giving her a nod.

"I'm so shocked and thankful." Emily drew away with a laugh. She came over and hugged Stormey, too.

Stormey returned the tight embrace before releasing the woman.

"Someone will be in touch to get the process started," Hegna said. She tugged Stormey to her side and took her hand again. She glanced down at Stormey with a small smile on her lips. "Stormey, I'm sure, will want to work closely with you on the project."

"My intention when coming here was to find out how I can volunteer and to see what else I could help with," Stormey admitted with a laugh. She leaned against Hegna and was confident the walls Hegna had constructed now had a large crack in them. She was breaking down.

"Miss Emily, this mean lady is on all of the channels," Maisie cried out.

Hegna stiffened beside her. She released Stormey's hand and strode over to the television.

"Excuse me, little Maisie. Go over there with Miss Emily, please," Hegna said. All traces of the light-hearted vampire princess were gone. Now stood the warrior, staring at the television.

Maisie didn't hesitate and did as she'd said.

"What is going on?" Stormey asked. She moved beside Hegna who fiddled with the television to increase the volume. Stormey stared at the woman on the screen who looked vaguely familiar. "Is that—"

"The lycan alpha," Hegna growled.

"People of the North American continent. It is I, Azura Michaels." The lycan alpha stared menacingly into the camera. Her amber eyes glowed, and large fangs were noticeable from under her top lip. She appeared frantic and crazed with her hair wild.

"If you don't know who I am, let me introduce myself. I am the alpha of the lycan nation, or you may be more familiar with the term, wolf shifters. And no, this is not a joke. We do exist."

"Cezar, is this real?" Hegna snapped.

"We are verifying it now," Cezar responded.

Stormey's eyes were glued to the television. She couldn't believe what she was seeing. She knew Hegna and her family were about to go to war with these beasts, but seeing the enemy's face made it all too real for Stormey.

She was terrified at the thought of Hegna going off to fight in a war. Was this how her mother had felt when her father had been drafted to fight? Stormey and Hegna's relationship was only in the budding stage. She didn't want to risk losing her vampire when they had only just found each other.

"I'm sure you are wondering where we have been hiding. But first I'm going to share a history lesson of my race," Azura continued. She sat up tall in the chair she was seated in. The background was blurry as if they were using some form a technology to hide what was behind her. "Hundreds of years ago, my people were peaceful but lived as slaves to your masters, the vampires. These vampires who rule your world are not to be trusted.

We had to fight for our freedom and the right to exist."

"Cesar," Hegna growled.

Her blue eyes flashed with a burning rage that sent a shiver of apprehension through Stormey.

"Princess. We've confirmed this broadcast is live. They're overriding the satellites, and we can't pinpoint where they are." Cesar held a hand up to his ear, listening to whoever was speaking to him through his mini communicator.

"Our fight for freedom led to the vampires declaring war on all lycans. They began annihilating our people with a vengeance. They came close to wiping an entire race from the face of this earth. But no more. My people will rise, and that will be because of you. We will defeat the vampires, and then all humankind will become lycans."

Stormey froze with a sick feeling appearing in her stomach. The television went dark before it switched to a cartoon show.

"Princess." Maisie broke free from Emily and ran to her.

Stormey wrapped an arm around her while the girl buried her face against Stormey's leg.

"Don't worry, little one," Stormey said. Her eyes met Hegna's as she rubbed Maisie's back. "Princess

Hegna won't let that bad woman anywhere near any of you."

"Promise?" Maisie lifted her face and stared at Hegna.

The princess came to kneel in front of Maisie and placed a fist over her heart. "I give you my word as your warden, and as heir to the throne, no one will touch you," she swore.

Maisie studied Hegna, jerking her tiny head into a nod.

Hegna stood and met Stormey's eyes before moving over to the doorway. "It's time to go."

"But wait, we can't leave them unguarded," Stormey said. She glanced down at Maisie's wide eyes, and her heart lurched. She couldn't fathom something happening to them. There was no security here at the orphanage. The children would be sitting ducks. Who would protect them?

"We'll utilize our human team and ensure they are protected. Cezar, tonight, have a couple warriors stay until daylight." Hegna turned back to her, seeking her approval.

Stormey smiled, relieved that the women and children at the orphanage would have some form of protection.

"Thank you."

CHAPTER FOURTEEN

"Your Grace," Cezar called out her name.

Hegna took Stormey's hand and assisted her into the back of the sedan. She turned to him once he arrived at her side.

"Lukas and Spencer will remain behind and guard the orphanage tonight," Cezar said.

"And the human militia?" Hegna asked.

She had commandeered a deal with the local reserve military force. The humans created their own defense services that would defend the territories they created. These men and women who served in the militia were for the protection of their fellow man and had decided to work with Hegna and her armies when needed. In return, Hegna ensured their men and women had the latest technologies when it came to weapons.

"I spoke with their leader who also saw the lycan's broadcast. They will send someone soon and will keep watch over the children and females who live here."

Hegna nodded, satisfied. She hadn't liked the look of fear in Stormey's eyes at the thought of leaving everyone who called the orphanage home unprotected. If the lycans descended on the older mansion, no one would survive.

"Very good," she said.

Cezar slammed his fist to his chest and bowed. She slid into the vehicle beside Stormey and shut the door. Stormey turned to her, a soft smile on her lips. She slipped across the seat and pressed herself to Hegna. She dropped a kiss to Hegna's lips before easing back.

"What is that for?" Hegna asked.

"For everything you've offered to do to help the orphanage and the kindness you showed Maisie," Stormey said. She took Hegna's hand in hers. "Corbin told me I could do what I want with the allowance I'm given."

"You can," Hegna murmured.

Cezar and Desmond entered the vehicle. Soon, they were pulling off and headed back to the castle.

"I wanted to make sure you could do whatever you wanted, or purchase whatever you may need that we haven't already provided."

"That is sweet of you." Stormey chuckled, squeezing Hegna's hand. "You do have a heart under here, don't you?" She reached up and tapped on Hegna's chest above her heart.

"Of course I do. I am many things, but I am not cruel. Those children are probably orphans because of the war, be it directly or indirectly, and I can't stand by and watch them suffer. They are innocent," Hegna said. It was true. She was many things, but cruel toward the innocent was not her. As the warden of her territory, it was her responsibility to see that all were taken care of and protected. "And you are correct. They need protection. Azura needs to be dealt with, and we will ensure that she will not harm anyone."

Hegna hadn't shared with Stormey what she had learned about the Canadian town. Stormey was such a caring person that Hegna was sure she'd be distraught to hear what had happened to the human town.

"You are going to go after her, aren't you?" Stormey asked.

Hegna turned to her mate and hesitated. Was this what she was supposed to do? Share information with her human? She made a note to speak with Velika and Lethia. Did they share duties or plans with their humans?

"I am," Hegna said. This was something she would admit. Stormey would not have to worry about anything. Hegna was a strong vampire, and even though she hadn't fed as she should, she could still take down the alpha.

At the thought of feeding, Hegna's eyes dropped down to Stormey's neck. She inhaled, taking in the sweet smell of Stormey. The pounding of her pulse reached Hegna's ears. Stormey's winter cloak covered her skin, but she could still sense the rushing of her blood as it flowed through her body.

"Can I ask you something?" Stormey asked.

Hegna snapped her attention to Stormey's eyes. Something in her tone set off an alarm in the back of her mind.

"Sure." Hegna cleared her throat and fought the descent of her fangs. She blinked and focused on her mate.

That word sent a rush of desire through her.

She fought to concentrate on Stormey as she turned to Hegna.

"As the lady of the castle, will I be—"

Stormey's words were cut off. Something slammed into the side of the vehicle, sending it spinning. Hegna wrapped an arm around Stormey, holding on to her. Hegna braced herself, waiting for it to hit something. Cezar, who was driving, cursed and brought the car to a halt. Stormey rested back against her seat with wide eyes and panting.

"Are you okay?" Hegna asked.

Stormey jerked her head in a nod, sliding out of Hegna's hold.

"What the hell was that?" Hegna growled. She released Stormey's hand and leaned forward to look out the front windshield. Whatever crashed into them had to be massive.

"Fuck. Lycans." Desmond pointed to the two enormous beasts encircling the royal guard SUV that was in front of them.

Hegna stared at the animals. They were much larger than the ones they had fought centuries before. Were these lycans who'd been turned? Tonight, it wouldn't matter.

Hegna scanned the area, finding them in the middle of downtown Black Hollow. The area was eerily empty. Not a single streetlight was working, casting them in darkness. Only the headlights of the vehicles provided illumination. The hair on the back of her neck rose.

This was a trap.

Somehow, they had been followed. Hegna growled, anger rising inside her. How had they been tailed and not picked up on the presence of the beasts?

From the shadows of buildings crept more of the mangy beasts. Some crawled on all fours while others walked on their hind legs. She didn't have as many weapons on her as she normally would since they had been visiting children, but she still had enough to defend her and her mate.

Hegna bared her fangs, ready for the fight. Her men were already exiting the other SUVs and engaging in battle with the beasts.

"Stay in here." Hegna swung back to Stormey. She reached for her dagger she kept on her waist. The silver blade would prove to be deadly for the lycans.

"What? You're leaving me?" Stormey gasped.

A lycan was thrown against their sedan. The weight of the animal rocked their car. Cezar exited the driver's door and shut it. He quickly used his short sword and sliced the lycan's neck. Blood sprayed on the windows. Stormey turned away from the sight, shutting her eyes for a brief moment.

"This car is basically impenetrable. They will not be able to get to you," Hegna promised. She reached out and cupped Stormey's chin, staring into her eyes. Her heart pounded rapidly. Something inside her demanded she protect this woman. "Desmond, you are to stay in the car with my mate. Nothing is to happen to her."

"Yes, Your Grace," Desmond replied immediately.

"Be careful," Stormey whispered.

"Always," Hegna said. She released Stormey and opened her door. She slammed it shut, hearing the locking mechanism slide into place. Hegna didn't have to tell the warrior that if things didn't go their way he was to drive off and get Stormey to safety.

For now, they would handle these wolves.

She slid her dagger from its sheath and brandished it. A lycan caught sight of her and rushed toward her on his hind legs. She dodged the claws he swiped at her. She swung around, slicing his abdomen with her blade. He made the mistake of leaving his vital areas open. He howled, thrusting his claws at her again. This time she swiftly sank her blade into his stomach and twisted it. She sliced it down, ripping his insides out. He fell to the ground, bleeding out.

She spun around just in time to be hit by a heavy weight. Growling filled her ears, and she crashed down on the concrete with a vicious lycan snapping his jaws in her face. She held on to the handle of her blade and brought her arm up while holding him back with her other hand. He was a strong wolf, but she was stronger.

She brought the blade down into the neck of the lycan. Blood spurted out as she drove it in multiple times. She cried out, shoving him off her to where they rolled with her landing on top. He slashed his claws at her, raking them down her arm.

"Son of bitch!" she spat.

She wedged the blade in again, and this time she pulled it across his entire neck. His body slumped on the street, no longer moving. She pushed up and stumbled off. Her arm burned where his claws had caught her. She stripped off her long coat and tossed it away.

She swiveled around, scanning the area. Her men were dealing deadly blows to the lycans.

Hegna growled at the sight. This was entirely too close to home. One lycan who stood almost seven feet tall turned his sights on her. He watched the fight from the edge of a building and swung his humongous fangs toward her.

Who the hell was this? It certainly wasn't the alpha. Was it one of her right-hand men? An enforcer? There was something about him that was different than the others.

She pulled another blade that was small from the sheath at her ankle.

"Come on, you fucking lycan," she snarled.

Hegna relaxed her legs and bent down in a defensive stance. She dared him to fight her. It didn't matter that he was much bigger than her. He sprang off the building, threw back his head, and howled. It echoed through the air, traveling far. He stalked toward her.

Hegna stood her ground and kept her focus on him. She didn't look at the car, not wanting to alert the lycans that a human was secured in it. The armored vehicle could withstand a lot, but she didn't want to test it against the claws of a multiple lycans. A growl echoed behind her. She shifted her position and saw that there was another lycan approaching her from behind. This one wasn't as big and was down on all fours.

Two large beasts, this was just a walk in the park for her.

She waited for them to make their move. It didn't take long. The newcomer rushed her, but Hegna was ready. She swung around, slicing the lycan's body. It slid on the ground, away from her. It got back up to its feet and circled her with the larger one.

"You both will die tonight," Hegna warned.

The larger one snorted, holding her gaze. The smaller one attacked again and slammed into Hegna. She dropped her blade and encircled her arms around its neck. She brought it close to her and squeezed, then jerked hard, snapping the animal's neck.

Hegna let out a cry from pain exploding in her shoulder muscles. The massive lycan had snuck behind her while she'd been dealing with the other one. He'd sacrificed the weaker animal. His fangs dug deep into the meat of her muscle. The scent of her blood filled the air as it rushed out of her. She snarled and tried to not jerk away from him for it would tear her even more. She picked up her blade and drove it backwards.

He roared, releasing her. She fell forward on her knees. Her vision was blurry with her spinning. She shook her head and stood to her feet. She stumbled, holding her blade tight. A howl pierced through the air off in the distance. The lycans, who were still fighting, paused, turning around and running off.

Who the fuck was calling them back?

The large one who'd bitten her made his way to the alley where he had come from. He lingered and swung round to her. He flashed his fangs, disappearing into the alley. The dead beast remained on the street.

Hegna ignored the blood running down her arm. She stalked toward the center of the road and raised her dagger in the air.

"For the crown!" Hegna shouted.

Her warriors echoed her cry. Hegna faced the car and walked toward it. She blinked, two cars swimming before her. She squinted and tried to focus on ambulating.

"Your Grace!" Cezar called out.

He came to stand in front of her, blocking her pathway to the car. Suddenly, there were two of him. She blinked again, and then there was one.

"You are injured," he said.

"I'll be fine. I need to check on Stormey."

Hegna moved to walk past him, but he blocked her with his body. “Move out of my way, warrior.”

“We need to get you to the healer immediately. You are losing too much blood, Your Grace.” His gaze dropped to her shoulder.

The pain was pulsating. She gritted her teeth and tried to will her mind to ignore it.

“I’ll be fine,” she snapped. She tried to raise her arm, but the damn limb wouldn’t cooperate. Her world tilted over, and warm arms wrapped around her waist.

“I got you,” Cezar murmured.

He shouted out orders to the men and walked toward the car. He was practically dragging her. She refused to be carried, and he didn’t even ask. Cezar knew her well. A future queen and commander of an army would walk.

“Here we are.”

She turned back and looked out at the street. She eyed the unmoving lycans, curious as to why they weren’t switching back to their human forms.

“I want these bodies taken and studied. Any who are still alive, throw them in the dungeons,” she ordered.

“Yes, Your Grace. Let’s get you to the healer.” He opened the door and helped her into the car.

Hegna grunted, releasing her blade to fall onto the floor of the car.

"Oh my god!" Stormey cried out. She moved to Hegna's side, tears sliding down her face. She tore off her cloak and brought it to Hegna, pressing onto her wound. "I saw that wolf bite you. I thought you were going to be killed."

"It would take more than a bite to kill me." Hegna groaned. The pain from her shoulder zipped down her entire arm to her fingers.

Stormey's sobs filled the air while she held her makeshift bandage. Cezar slid into the driver's seat and threw the vehicle into drive.

Hegna rested her head back on the seat while listening to Desmond calling ahead to the castle, alerting them that they would need the healer urgently. She gritted her teeth and tried to breathe. She already knew what she needed to heal completely.

Blood.

The swooshing sound of Stormey's flowing through her arteries filled Hegna's ears. She turned her head away, trying to find something else to focus on. The scenery flew by as Cezar drove like a bat out of hell.

"Are you okay? Talk to me." Stormey hiccupped. "I don't think you should go to sleep."

"I'm fine," Hegna grunted out through her clenched teeth. She closed her eyes and tried to block out the sound of Stormey's racing pulse.

"Is there something you need?" Stormy asked.

"Don't ask me that," Hegna breathed. She kept her face away from Stormey. She tried to think of anything but sinking her fangs into Stormey's neck and taking what she truly needed to heal.

* * *

"YOUR HEALING SHOULD BE FARTHER along than this," Ellanora grumbled.

Hegna grimaced at the tugging and pulling of her skin while the experienced healer sutured the wound on her shoulder.

"You need blood."

"I'll be fine." Hegna groaned. She turned her head away, not wanting to see the older vampire's judging eyes. Hegna had met the healer when she was young and foolish back in her seventies. She had a lot of respect for Ellanora and her talent. The vampire healer had sewn up Hegna more times than she could count.

Once they had arrived at the castle, Ellanora had met them at the back doors. They'd taken Hegna down to the infirmary. A couple of her warriors who had fought beside her were getting treated for minor injuries. Hegna had been brought over to a private area that was closed off by glass. Hegna could see the entire section which was bustling with activity. Stormey sat across the room near the doors. She had refused to leave and go get cleaned up. Hegna's blood coated her clothing, her skin, and even a few spots on her face. Their eyes met, and Hegna held her gaze for a moment.

It was easy to see she wanted to come be by Hegna's side, but Hegna didn't want her near her, seeing how weakened she was.

"I heard through the whispers that you are not drinking from your mate, nor have you bonded to her yet," Ellanora said, apparently catching Hegna staring at Stormey.

Another pierce of the needle greeted Hegna.

Ellanora continued, ignoring the fact that Hegna had turned away from her. "Blood would have had you completely healed by now, and there would probably be a slight scar until your body could continue to work on itself."

"I don't need a lesson right now," Hegna snapped. "And people shouldn't be gossiping."

"Don't go getting an attitude with me. Why didn't you take from your mate? I'm sure she would have allowed you to." Ellanora cut the nylon and tied a knot in it. She set her instruments down on the table beside them. "Have you been able to feed?"

"A little. I've been too busy trying to protect our people," Hegna stated. She tore her gaze away from Stormey and stared at the ceiling. She tried to adjust herself on the uncomfortable infirmary bed.

Ellanora sighed and stepped away from Hegna and busied herself with the items on the table. She paused and glanced over at her.

"I can administer a small blood transfusion that should stimulate the healing process, but, Your Grace, you will need to feed." Ellanora rested a hand on Hegna's. She eased the other arm over, assessing the claw marks.

"Set up the infusion." Hegna jerked her head in a nod. If she bit and drank from Stormey right now, she didn't trust that she would be able to stop. Her mate's blood would be too sweet for her to resist, and she sensed her body was in survival mode. Her fangs had yet to rescind up into her gums.

"Very well, Your Grace." Disappointment filled Ellanora's voice.

Hegna ignored it. She knew what was best for her. She would have to get blood into her, and the transfusion would help take the edge off her. It wasn't the same as consuming the blood from a bite. What she needed was a warm body to draw from. She glanced back over at Stormey and refused to drink from her at the moment.

Not now.

"Do you want her in here with you?" Ellanora followed Hegna's gaze. She moved around the small room gathering supplies.

An assistant peeked their head in at the beckoning of Ellanora. She lowered her voice and discussed the plan. The assistant bowed to Hegna before leaving the room.

"No. I want her to leave and go get cleaned up and rest," Hegna said.

"Then you better tell her yourself. It's already been suggested to her, but she refused to move until she can speak with you." Ellanora leaned against the entrance of Hegna's room.

"Bring her to me," Hegna said.

Stormey was so damn stubborn, but Hegna had to admit it felt good to have someone worry about her. She hadn't had that before. Others worried about her because of her position as the warden, or because she was the princess or even because of her being the future queen of the vampires. But no one truly worried about Hegna, the vampire, the woman.

"Very well." Ellanora bowed her head and stepped outside the room and motioned to Stormey.

She stood and navigated her way through the bustle of the infirmary. Hegna couldn't take her eyes off her. She stopped next to Ellanora, who murmured to her, "She's a little ornery. Beware."

"I can hear you, Ellanora. That is no way to speak about your princess." Hegna smirked. She adjusted the sheet that was over her naked chest. Ellanora had her remove her tunic so she could assess the wounds. Now that Stormey was nearby, Hegna's nipples beaded up into buds.

"I'm sure she is speaking the truth," Stormey said.

She hesitated by the entryway then went over to stand next to Hegna. Her wide eyes took in the wound which Hegna was sure was a mess. From the ache and pain in her shoulder muscles, she was sure it wasn't pleasant to look at.

"How are you feeling?"

"Like a lycan chewed on my shoulder," she murmured.

"I thought vampires were self-healing." Stormey's soft hand slid along Hegna's and entwined their fingers together.

"I'll be fine by tomorrow," Hegna said. Once she got a little blood in her, she'd seek out a human donor. One who would be able to give her what she needed. Her stomach rolled at the thought of feeding from someone who wasn't Stormey, but it was necessary. She refused to risk harming her. "I want you to go and get cleaned up."

"But I want to—"

"I'll be fine," Hegna cut her off. She squeezed Stormey's fingers. "I promise. Go shower, get something to eat, and rest."

Stormey eyed her suspiciously as if she didn't trust Hegna. Her gaze went back to Hegna's shoulder, then moved over to her arm with the claw marks. Her human didn't want to leave her side. She didn't have to say it. It was evident on her face. Hegna sensed an unfamiliar sensation in her chest she had never experienced before.

"We'll talk later," Hegna said.

"Okay." Stormey leaned down and pressed her

lips to Hegna's in a soft kiss. Her brown eyes filled slightly with tears. She blinked them back and rose. "Do what the healer says and don't try to be a big brave vampire."

It would seem her mate knew her well.

Stormey backed away from the bed and paused at the door. She smiled at Hegna then walked through the infirmary toward the exit.

Was this love or another type of emotion that came along with the bond?

Hegna followed Stormey's figure until she disappeared through the door. Ellanora and her assistant returned to the room.

Her mate had ordered her to follow all directions from the healer. She certainly was. Afterward, Hegna would go seek out a donor and force herself to feed.

CHAPTER FIFTEEN

Stormey knew she had been sent away. There was something Hegna didn't want her to see. She felt slightly hurt by it, but she sensed Hegna was truly trying. Their relationship was moving in the right direction.

She felt it down in her bones.

That moment when Hegna had been placed into the car, basically bleeding to death, had almost had Stormey losing her mind. She had watched Hegna from the moment she'd stepped out of the car. There was no question the woman was a badass. She and her warriors didn't back down from the big monsters.

Hegna had fought with one large dagger and a small one. Stormey's heart had seemed to lodge itself into her throat as she'd watched Hegna fight. The woman was fearless and lethal. The instant that huge lycan had sidled behind her and bitten her, Stormey had screamed. She'd had the urge to bolt from the car and warn Hegna, but she had common sense. That would have caused a distraction that could have proved fatal.

Stormey held her towel around herself and walked into her bedroom.

"Mistress, I have brought you something to eat," Cici announced. The vampire was arranging her food on the table for her.

"You are so sweet." Stormey inhaled the delicious aroma that filled the air. She stopped by the table and appreciated Cici's thoughtfulness. She didn't want to eat where others could see her. If she ate in the dining hall, she was sure to be bombarded with questions about the battle that had gone on downtown. She didn't want to answer questions about the princess. Word had made it around the castle that their princess was in the infirmary. "Let me throw some clothes on."

"I took the liberty of putting some comfortable things on the bed for you." Cici smiled softly.

Stormey picked up her worry by the sound of her voice, her facial expression, and the way she stood.

"She's going to be okay. The princess is very stubborn," Stormey said. She picked up a dinner roll and took a bite out of it. The buttery bread was mouthwatering good. She moaned and dropped it back down in the basket.

"Thank you, mistress. The princess is our hope for the future." Cici stood back from the table, fiddling with her hands. She looked pale, even for a vampire.

It was then Stormey understood how much these vampires loved their princess. Even the warriors who fought for her did so with such abandon. They were willing to lay down their lives for Hegna. Stormey wished she could say the same for mankind. Humans didn't have such loyalty to their leaders. History proved how often humans fought each other.

"Well, according to the princess, it would take more than a lycan bite to take her out," Stormey said.

Cici smiled faintly, her shoulders dropping.

"That sounds like our princess," Cici murmured.

Stormey spun around and moved over to the bed. As promised, Cici had laid out thick leggings, an oversized sweatshirt, and warm socks. She quickly got dressed and headed back over to the dining table. Val had outdone himself, but Stormey wasn't going to be able to eat everything he had sent up. She made her plate and began eating.

"When I'm done, I want to go visit the princess," Stormey announced. She took a sip of the wine Val had paired with her meal. She hadn't really drunk wine before coming to Black Hollows, but Val had her try this one, and she had fallen in love with it. "Do you think we can cancel my lesson tonight with Miss Lavana?"

"Yes, mistress." Cici nodded and tidied up the bedroom. She glanced back over at Stormey, looking as if she wanted to ask a question.

"Did you need something?" Stormey asked.

"You saw the battle with the lycans?" Cici asked. She made her way back to the table and took a seat in the chair across from her.

Stormey paused, not wanting to relive the memories, but it was hard to try to push them away.

The sight of the lycan clamping down on Hegna's shoulder would probably give her nightmares.

"I did. Hegna and the warriors are very brave. I didn't know what to expect. I was so scared for them," Stormey admitted. Even though Hegna continued to push her away, she was drawn to her. It didn't help that Stormey had fantasized about the vampire before they'd been matched. She had in her head what she thought Hegna would be like, and she had been completely off. There was no warm welcome, no immediate feelings of love and mating. The lust and animal attraction were certainly there.

She couldn't help but feel something for Hegna. Stormey figured she may be one of the few humans who felt the bond between the two of them. Maybe it was because she had opened her heart and mind to the idea of fate. But Hegna was proving to be much different than how she presented herself. The way she'd been with Maisie had Stormey falling for the princess. She may try to appear tough and lethal, but she had a heart. Who knew the hardened heir to the vampire throne had a thing for children?

Stormey wasn't going to give up on Hegna. She was going to make her want her. There was no doubt the sexual tension between them was through the roof. The looks Hegna gave her always held heat, passion, and possessiveness.

But Stormey wanted more, and she was going to demand it.

She wasn't going to be pushed away any longer.

She had done what Hegna had wanted her to do. Shower, eat, and she would rest next to Hegna. She was tired of sleeping alone, knowing the vampire she belonged to was in an entirely different wing in the castle.

Stormey was going to put her foot down and make Hegna claim her.

"They are, and I'm so thankful. Everyone is talking about the lycan's broadcast." Cici visibly shuddered.

Since Stormey had arrived at the castle, she had grown close to Cici. She considered her a friend and was thankful for meeting her. Cici took such good care of her and was patient explaining things to her. She'd helped Stormey get to know the staff and ensured she knew how to get around this monstrous castle.

"It was scary when we revealed ourselves. We had hoped we didn't have to go to war. We wanted to live amongst humans as we had done before, only not hiding that we were different."

Stormey paused, staring at her. She hadn't really considered how the war impacted vampires who wanted to just live their lives. What would it have been like to hide who she was?

"What did you do before the war?" Stormey asked. It felt funny asking this question.

Cici looked as if they were the same age, but she was quite older. Vampires lived long lives and still appeared so young. Apparently, they aged much slower than humans did. Cici was a pure vampire. She'd shared that her parents were fated mates and she was the product of their union.

Through her lessons, Stormey had learned more about vampires then she had doing her own research. She had known that as the mate of the vampire princess she was going to rule at Hegna's side, yet she hadn't really understood what it all meant. Vampires would come to her and Hegna with issues and problems that they would solve. It was hard to believe vampires would be accepting of her sitting on the throne beside Hegna.

Of course, there were those vampires who were against humans and vampires mating, so they would have to deal with that. She was interested in reaching out to the women who Hegna's sisters were mated with. They were human like her, and she would love to hear advice from them. From what she'd heard, they had been successful in maintaining their territories with their mates. But Stormey would prove to be different. Her mate would one day sit on the throne and rule vampires. Would those who protested humans come out of the woodwork the day it was time for her to sit as queen consort with her mate?

Would it cause a divide amongst vampires?

There was so much to worry about. Thankfully, she had Miss Lavana to help ensure she understood vampire society. Miss Lavana was educating Stormey about the coven's politics and how they loved to host parties and social networking events. Miss Lavana had a hard time meeting her gaze when asked about what went on at the parties. Stormey's curiosity was now officially piqued. According to Miss Lavana, there would be a party in honor of her and Hegna's mating once it occurred. These soirees were also a way for vampires to mingle and would be fun.

"Before the war, I was here, but before I came to work for the princess, I worked as a housekeeper and a nanny for a wealthy vampire family. I was there for about forty years. Before that, I had gone back to school so I could become a nanny because I thought children would be my calling. But my most interesting job was working in a glove factory back in the nineteen thirties." Cici giggled.

"A glove factory?" Stormey smiled.

It was interesting to hear Cici share some of her most fond memories of the past. The vampire acted as if the nineteen thirties were just yesterday. It was a hundred years ago. She thought it was amazing how the vampires were able to live long lives and move through time experiencing different periods. Once Hegna claimed her and sealed the mating bond, then Stormey would be able to live alongside Hegna through the future. She couldn't wait to see what the future held for them.

The part she didn't look forward to was watching people she knew begin to pass away from old age while she remained youthful and aged slowly.

"Yeah. I was able to work the third shift. The owners had started having the factory run twenty-four hours a day, six days a week. A lot of us vampire women blended in and went to work late at night," Cici said.

Stormey pushed her plate away and wiped her mouth with her napkin. Now that her belly was full, she wanted to go speak with Hegna and make sure she was okay. Stormey had been suspicious when Hegna had wanted her to leave. She had been sewn up, but they were waiting for something.

Hegna needed blood. She had been pale and had lost enough of hers. Most of it appeared to be on Stormey's clothing and skin by the time they'd made it to the castle.

If she needed blood, Stormey wanted Hegna to take hers.

"I'm ready to go see the princess," Stormey announced. She pushed back from the table with determination filling her. She was going to force the princess to drink from her. If they were to be mated, Hegna was going to start drinking from her and her body only.

"WHAT DO you mean the princess has left the castle?" Stormey said. Shock filled her at the thought the vampire she had watched get sewn up hours ago, was no longer in the building. Stormey had gone back down to the infirmary and hadn't found her there. According to Ellanora, she had left to go to her room. She had sought out Hegna at her personal quarters, and there was no one there. No guard outside the room.

Stormey had made her way downstairs and sought out Edward. The old butler had become an ally to Stormey since she'd arrived. She'd found him in the main hall near the front entrance. He had stepped out of the receiving room when she'd caught up with him. The hall was grand and wide. The floors were a darker stone while the walls were light in color. There were tables with flower arrangements, vintage art from prior centuries displayed, while sconces provided light.

"The princess took a few warriors and she left the castle," Edward clarified. He was an older man, with gray-streaked black hair and a few scattered wrinkles on his face. He was dressed formally in a black-and-gray suit.

She'd learned he was a turned vampire who had been attacked by a rogue vampire back in the late nineteenth century. He had been a butler before and continued his profession afterward, being hired by Hegna to run her castle.

"But where would she go?" Stormey grew exasperated. Her stubborn vampire should be resting and recuperating from almost dying. She had lost so much blood and had been so pale when she'd been in the infirmary.

"I believe she and the warriors went to Madam Rice's club," he announced.

Stormey glanced over at Cici. She didn't know who Madam Rice was, but from the sound of the club, she assumed she knew what it was for. She swallowed hard, feeling slightly sick to her stomach. She'd thought they had made a little progress in their delicate relationship.

"Is that a…um…" For some reason, she couldn't get the words out.

"A feeding club," Cici finished off. A light dusty-rose coloring appeared on her face.

Stormey's eyes widened at the realization of what normally came along with vampires' feedings. She stared down at her hands. The few times she'd been with Hegna, the vampire hadn't bitten her.

"Oh," Stormey murmured. She blew out a deep breath and knew she wasn't going to take this lying down. She refused to allow her mate to just ignore her, push her off to the side when they were meant to be together. She stood to her full height and met Edward's curious gaze. "Where is this club?"

Footsteps sounded behind her, but she ignored them. She was set on finding out where this place was so she herself could go to it. Knowing Hegna was in a place like that felt as if she was being disloyal to Stormey. Mates were to be only with each other. Why couldn't her stubborn vampire heed what their bodies knew? Stormey felt that Hegna's body wanted her.

"Ah, Edward. There you are," Corbin's voice appeared behind her.

Relief filled Edward's face. He tipped his head to the princess's advisor.

"Lord Apostu." Edward gave a nod to Corbin who came to stand at Stormey's side.

"Miss Jaymes." Corbin smiled at her. His long silver hair was braided away from his face while the rest was left flowing down his back.

"Lord Apostu, you are friends with the princess, are you not?" Stormey sniffed. She rested her hands on her waist and stared at him.

His eyebrows rose sharply at her use of his formal title. She had thought he was on her side, but she should have known his loyalty would be to Hegna. He had said he'd thought Hegna was being a fool and he wanted to help her. But how was he helping her if he allowed Hegna to go to this club?

"You know I am." His smiled disappeared as he eyed her.

She studied him and was surprised he wasn't with Hegna. She'd heard the whispers about him and his personal activities.

"And if I recall, you said Hegna needed to stop being so damn stubborn and claim her mate. Did you not?" She stared at him and tried to will her racing heart down. Her hands curled up into fists. She wanted to hit something to expel this anger that boiled inside her.

"I did say that." He looked uncomfortable and glanced over at Edward who avoided his gaze. "Stormey—"

"If that is the case," she interjected; she was far from done with him, "then why is my mate at Madam Rice's?"

"Hegna does what she wants to do, and no one can get that woman to change her mind," he snapped. "I may be her friend and her advisor, but that's just what I do, offer my advice, and if the princess wants to ignore my advice, then she will do just that."

"Take me there," Stormey demanded. She moved closer to him, tilting her head back so she could meet his eyes. "She will not ignore me anymore. If she needs blood, then she will take it from me."

She felt all of their eyes on her as silence fell around her. Would they listen to her? She would be princess once she and Hegna sealed the bond, but at the moment, she was just a human. She inspected Corbin. War raged in his eyes.

"You don't know what goes on in those types of places," Corbin said. He ran a shaking hand along his face.

"If I am to be sitting at Hegna's side, then I need to see and know everything," she stressed. She rested a hand on his arm, hoping the war inside him was siding with her. "I need to help her. She needs my blood, and if there is something else she wants there, then I will give her that, too."

His eyes flashed to hers. He barked a harsh chuckle and shook his head.

"The only humans who are allowed there are the ones who are working," he said.

"Then call the madam and inform her that her queen is ordering her to allow my daughter's mate to have full rein of her facility," a sharp voice ordered from behind Stormey.

She spun around, her mouth dropping open at the sight of the newcomer.

Queen Mira Riskel stood with a fierce expression.

Stormey didn't have to question or guess who this was. She'd seen the queen enough in the media over the years and in photographs.

Edward, Cici, and Corbin all dropped down to their knees in respect for the queen. Stormey glanced at them and joined them, lowering her eyes to the floor. How had the queen snuck up on them without any of them hearing her?

The queen's heels echoed on the floor and stopped before Stormey.

"Rise, Miss Jaymes," Mira commanded.

Stormey raised her gaze and stood. The queen was a mirror image of Hegna, only her hair was blonde. She wore a deep-royal-blue dress with a black cloak wrapped around her shoulders. There was no doubt this woman was royalty. The air around her screamed that she was a queen.

The queen flicked her hand, allowing the others to stand as well. She assessed Stormey for a moment with a blank expression.

"Your Grace. It's a pleasure to meet you," Stormey said. Her heart raced while under the queen's perusal. Would the queen be upset that Hegna hadn't claimed her? Would she blame Stormey for Hegna's continued rejection?

"It's a pleasure to meet the one who is going to

put my stubborn daughter in her place." The lips of the queen lifted at the corner slightly. She focused on Corbin and arched an eyebrow. "Do I need to repeat myself?"

"No, Your Grace. I will call ahead and notify them of your command," Corbin said.

"And you will accompany Miss James and then ensure my daughter returns back home." She moved to stand in front of Corbin.

His eyes widened a little, but he didn't move away from his queen.

Mira's voice lowered to a threatening manner that sent shivers down Stormey's spine. "If she does not come home, then you will answer to me."

"Yes, of course, Your Grace." Corbin paled slightly.

"I would like to speak with Miss Jaymes alone for a moment," the queen announced.

Stormey smiled softly at Cici who scurried past her. Corbin and Edward followed her down the hall. Once they turned the corner, the queen faced Stormey.

"My daughter needs someone who is direct and just as bullheaded as she is." Mira folded her hands behind her back and slowly ambled around Stormey.

This woman was more intense than Hegna. Stormey could see where her mate got it from. The queen stopped in front of her and smiled. Her face relaxed completely, and Stormey saw more of Hegna in her.

She rested a hand on Stormey's shoulder. "And from the sound of it, you are clearly her mate."

"Everyone sees it but her." Stormey sighed. She stood to her full height and met the queen's eyes. "But I'm done with her pushing me away. I'm her mate, and she's going to respect me as that."

"Then you go to the club. I don't like those places, but Hegna is convinced they are necessary for our people." Mira grimaced and rolled her eyes in an un-queen-like fashion. "But you are right, my dear. As a future princess and future queen consort to my daughter, you need to be fully submerged in our world."

"I'm ready, Your Grace."

"I hope you are." The queen smirked. She gave a squeeze to Stormey's shoulder before releasing her. "When I met my husband, he was stubborn as well, but it didn't take much to change his mind after I bested him in a sword fight in front of his men."

Stormey's eyebrows shot up. She'd heard the

queen had been a warrior in her own father's army. Stormey would love to be able to meet Hegna on the sparring mat as her equal. The first time, Hegna had bested her. Determination filled her. Stormey knew without the queen saying, what she needed to do.

CHAPTER SIXTEEN

"Are you certain, Your Grace?" The young hostess's eyes widened in shock at Hegna's request.

It was an uncommon request from Hegna who frequented the Black Hollows branch of Madam Rice.

Hegna leaned back in her chair and turned back to the small stage before her. A near-naked human female danced around a pole in front of her. The dancer flipped her light-brown hair off her shoulder and bent down, presenting her ass. Hegna smirked and nodded to the hostess.

"You heard me correctly. I will take a glass of

blood. No human donors tonight," she said. She licked her lips and switched her attention back to the woman who gyrated and danced to the rhythm of the music blaring through the club. If this had been six months ago, Hegna would already have had this stripper on her knees with her face buried in Hegna's cunt.

But things had changed.

Hegna didn't want to let on, but the thought of taking blood from a live donor was flipping her stomach. She'd had such an urge to go to Stormey's room and demand she allow her to feed from her, but Hegna had hesitated. The blood transfusion was helpful, but it made the hunger she felt increase.

Hegna was ravenous, and any person she'd sink her fangs into was at risk of being drained dry. There was no amount of kenaf weed the humans could take that would help them make the amount of blood she desired. Instead of a live donor, she would opt for the processed blood from donors. It was still from a human, but it eliminated the intimacy of a bite.

"Yes, Your Grace." The girl dipped down in a quick curtsey and rushed off.

Hegna glanced around and took in the club.

The area she was in allowed for private shows from dancers who would be available for not only entertainment, but for donation and more. There was a small wall that blocked anything that would go on in the semi-private area, but it still allowed Hegna to view the establishment. The warrior in her always wanted to see everything and the exits.

Hegna had left the castle with a few of her men who were scattered around the club. There were ample amounts of vampires taking advantage of all that Madam Rice had to offer. Members of her coven were seen along with vampires she didn't recognize. Security was tight in places like this. Ever since the club in Velika's town had notified them of lycans prowling around, they had increased protection so vampires could continue to enjoy themselves and humans would have a safe place to work.

Hegna settled back against the comfortable chaise while watching the woman who had now removed all of her clothes. She swung up high on the pole with grace and strength. She slid down and twirled around it until her back was to it. She leaned back, doing a sensual dance, running her hands along the swell of her breasts then down her torso.

The hostess returned. “Here you are, Your Grace.”

She set a bronze goblet on the small table next to Hegna. The scent of the copper fluid drifted through the air toward Hegna. She reached into the pocket of her leather pants and brought out a gold coin to tip the hostess.

The young woman’s lips widened as she reached for the coin. “Thank you.”

She disappeared, leaving Hegna to her private show. She took the goblet and brought out another coin and tossed it onto the floor for the stripper. She sipped the blood and held back a grimace. It wasn’t bad blood; it was as if her taste buds were off. The dancer slid down to her knees and crawled over and picked up the coin. She threw a wink at Hegna and rolled over onto her back. She spread her legs wide and pleasured herself with her fingers.

Hegna watched, sipping her blood. It was weird. She felt nothing while watching this woman take her pleasure into her own hands.

“You can go,” Hegna said.

It was cruel to stop a person from reaching their release, but at the moment, Hegna didn’t want to watch. The only pussy she wanted to see belonged to a beautiful brown-skinned woman who haunted her every thought. She tipped her cup to the woman to try to soften the blow. The dancer stood and smiled, taking her gold coin with her, spinning around and exiting the stage.

Hegna sensed someone standing off to her side. She glanced over and arched an eyebrow.

"Madam Rice," Hegna murmured.

It had been a while since she had seen the madam in person. The woman was very busy with her clubs all over the continent. The madam stood tall, with her dark hair pulled away from her pale face. Ruby-red lips and flawless makeup had the woman looking beautiful. She wore a black dress that was mostly sheer with darkening areas around her breasts and her nether region. She was curvy and was once a prostitute who had an eye for business.

A woman starting a successful business centuries ago was almost unheard of. But the madam was determined and had the backing of certain vampires in her corner. This kept the opposers of a woman owning brothels or feeding houses away. The madam and the Riskel family had history. It had been the king's younger sister who had leant her support to the madam.

"What do I owe the pleasure of your visit?"

Hegna took another sip of blood. She kept her face void of emotions, not wanting the madam to sense something was wrong with her. The rolling of her stomach was revealing her body was slowly going to reject blood in general if it wasn't from her mate. The pain that accompanied it was tolerable.

"I heard you were visiting and I thought I would come over." The madam shrugged a shoulder. She took a seat on the chaise next to Hegna. "I also heard you are refusing my donors. Is there something wrong with them?"

Hegna held back her smirk. She figured there had to be a reason the madam had come to speak with her. Hegna looked out at the club and took in humans walking around in white or black sheer material draped over their naked bodies. She caught sight of Cezar sitting in a chair across the room feeding on a female while another one knelt before him sucking his cock. Her gaze whipped across to another area of the club where her other guard, Joran, was feeding off a male.

The room was filled with sexual tension with many taking advantage of the pleasures the madam offered. A vampire woman was being escorted by two human males to the lower level where the private rooms were located.

"There is nothing wrong with your donors. Tonight, I just wanted something different," Hegna replied. Movement from the side of her eye caught Hegna's attention. One of the attendants of the club was spraying the pole and wiping it down.

"Something different, eh?" The madam's lips curved up deviously. She tapped Hegna on her knee. "I have just the person for you."

"Bethany," Hegna called the madam by her first name. She shook her head and held up a hand. She didn't want to insult her by refusing another donor. Coming here was to keep her from going to Stormey. She needed to avoid her until her thirst was under control. "I am just here for entertainment."

"And entertainment you shall have. This donor is new to my employment. She's a virgin to vampire bites, thirty-five years old, and is extremely beautiful. I'm not asking for much. Just help her get comfortable dancing for our kind." A special glint appeared in her eyes. She grinned and stood from her seat. She moved out of Hegna's sight. "If anything else comes of this, I just ask you don't bleed her dry. I can tell that blood in your goblet isn't sitting too well with you."

Hegna bit back a curse and slammed the goblet

on the table. She blew out a deep breath and figured she'd allow the new girl to dance and do whatever, but she wasn't crossing any lines by drinking from her. She'd leave her untouched for another vampire to break her in and tip her well.

It didn't take long for the new girl's show to begin. The lighting that focused on the small stage lowered while slow music played. Hegna's gums burned as her fangs fought to descend. She didn't know why they were demanding to come out. It had taken hours for them to rescind. They burst forth, sliding in place. The hairs on the back of her neck rose, standing at attention. A tremor flittered along her spine.

What was going on?

A curvy figure draped in sheer white material stepped out from behind the black curtain. The woman's back was to Hegna, allowing her gaze to roam her hourglass frame. Her ass was plump and round. Hegna immediately sat forward. She knew this body.

It couldn't be.

The woman turned around, revealing what Hegna's body had sensed before she'd even laid her eyes on her.

Stormey.

Her brown curves were on display; the sheer drapes did nothing to hide her body. Her full breasts with her dark areolas and budded nipples were exposed, her loose white coverings falling from her. She held Hegna's eyes and danced. Hegna was mesmerized by Stormey's movements. She swung her hips around in a circle motion while her hands glided up to her breasts. She cupped them, massaging the mounds while her body sensually swayed along to the beat of the song.

Hegna's mouth watered at the sight of her human dancing without fear. It just showed how strong and fierce she was. Some humans had a hard time entering the world of vampires, and diving straight into a feeding club would be challenging. Her mate came toward her. She gripped the pole and slowly walked around it. She rested back against it, pushing the rest of the material off her, leaving her naked.

A pulse throbbed in Hegna's core. Stormey was arousing her to where it was almost painful. Her pussy grew slick with need. She sat forward even more, her breaths growing rapid.

Stormey spun around and bent down, holding on to her ankles, presenting her ass and core to Hegna. A growl ripped from her at the sight of her mate's delicious center. Stormey brought herself up and then dropped into a squat and used her hands to sweep her hair out of the way. She bounced, the meat of her bottom shaking, teasing Hegna. She looked over her shoulder at Hegna, a smirk on her lips.

She knew what she was doing to Hegna.

"Come here, Stormey," Hegna growled.

She stood and walked to the edge of the stage. Hegna ignored everything else around them. The club faded away as her attention was only on Stormey. Her mate fell to her knees and rolled over to face Hegna. She remained on her knees and crawled to Hegna. The sight of her had Hegna strung tight. Her long hair hung around her shoulders. Her ass swayed in a gentle motion as she came toward Hegna.

Stormey arrived in front of her and fell onto her back, resting on her elbows. She spread her legs wide, showing off the pussy Hegna had been dreaming about. Hegna's hand dropped down to Stormey's center. Her finger ghosted along Stormey's slick labia. Her mate was aroused. Hegna's finger slipped inside Stormey, finding her channel warm, slick, and tight.

"What are you doing here?" Hegna asked. She

pulled her finger out, then eased it in again. She didn't want to think how all of this was arranged. She just knew the person she wanted was here in the club. She'd always enjoyed the clubs, but that was before Stormey had come into her life.

"To give you what you need." Stormey exhaled. Her tongue snuck out and slid along her bottom lip.

Hegna's eyes greedily took in her human's body and paused at the sight of her finger going in and out of Stormey. She introduced a second one, eliciting a moan from Stormey.

"And what is that?" Hegna's voice was strangled. Her throat tightened at the thought that Stormey wanted to be with her. No matter what she'd put the woman through, she was persistent in pursuing Hegna. She rested her other hand on the stage and leaned down, pressing her lips to Stormey's.

Hegna pushed her tongue between Stormey's opened lips and was immediately greeted by her tongue. Their tongues stroked each other and dueled along in a sensual dance. Her fingers continued plummeting inside Stormey. She captured her human's moans with her mouth.

Hegna tore her mouth from Stormey's and

twisted her hand around to where she could rub Stormey's clit with her thumb.

"Tell me, Stormey. What do I need?" She slowly withdrew her fingers from Stormey's warm cunt and put them into her mouth. She groaned at the familiar taste of her mate on her tongue.

"Me. My heart, my body, and my blood is yours," she whispered.

But Hegna heard every word. She cupped her face and studied her. This woman was determined to have her.

"You'll let me have you here?" Hegna lifted an eyebrow, challenging her.

Stormey smiled and brought her legs around to the edge of the stage. Hegna stepped back as she stood. Stormey held a devious look in her eyes.

"I don't know if you know this or not," Stormey began.

She reached for the front of Hegna's pants and undid the button. She drew down the zipper, all the while maintaining eye contact with Hegna. She tugged the pants down Hegna's legs. Hegna kicked them and her boots off.

"But I've been learning about vampire society."

STORMEY HADN'T FELT any amount of embarrassment or shame when she'd danced for Hegna. There had been more eyes on her than Hegna's, but the only person she cared about was Hegna. Her vampire had been unable to take her eyes from Stormey. The flames that burned in Hegna's eyes had fueled Stormey on.

She'd felt empowered, sexy and beautiful. The club had practically paused when she had stepped out onto the stage. She'd held Hegna's gaze and moved her body to the song. It had pleased her to know Hegna had not fed from any women in the club and had only requested the processed blood. Stormey had watched from behind the curtain and seen how she'd sent the stripper away.

Madam Rice had been surprised but kind when Stormey had arrived. She hadn't questioned the motive for Stormey wanting to perform for Hegna. Corbin and a few guards had accompanied her as the queen had ordered.

Stormey blinked, sending her hands along Hegna's muscular thighs. She knelt before her and had to admit being in public with Hegna was heightening her arousal. Who knew she had a sex-in-public kink?

"Will you take everything that I will give you

tonight?" Stormey asked. She placed her hands underneath Hegna's knees and pulled her to the edge to allow her bottom to rest slightly off the couch. She parted them, revealing Hegna's center to her. She licked her lips, wanting to taste all of her vampire.

"You don't know what you are asking of me," Hegna bit out through her fangs. Her icy-blue eyes were locked on Stormey.

A shiver slipped through Stormey. It was Hegna who didn't understand how much Stormey wanted for her to take everything from her. Hegna widened her legs and rested one foot on the couch. She was now open completely for Stormey.

"I do." Stormey leaned down and took one long lick of Hegna's center. Her tongue dove between her labia. The taste of Hegna exploded on her tongue. She covered Hegna's pussy with her mouth and drank in all that was Hegna.

Her vampire's body arched off the couch. Her hand shot out and entangled with Stormey's thick hair. Stormey held back her smile and feasted on her mate. She focused on Hegna's swollen clit and suckled it.

Hegna trembled underneath her, pulling on Stormey's hair. She ignored the pain, focused on bringing Hegna tremendous amounts of pleasure. The orgasms Hegna had given her drove her to want to do the same for her.

"Fuck, Stormey," Hegna cried out.

Stormey released her clit and sank two fingers deep inside her. She slowly thrust them in and out, teasing Hegna's clit with her tongue. Stormey glanced up and caught sight of Hegna's head thrown back against the couch. Pleasure was etched on her face with each thrust of Stormey's fingers.

Hegna's eyes flew open. She struggled slightly with removing her tunic. She pulled it over her head and tossed it on the floor next to her clothes. Stormey's heart leaped; she took in the sight of Hegna's firm breasts. Her dusky nipples were taut little buds that rose and fell with each breath Hegna took.

Stormey skated her free hand along Hegna's torso and arrived at Hegna's bare breast. She fondled it, pulling at her nipples, sending her fingers into her pussy hard and deep. Hegna's muscles tightened, her legs rising in the air. Stormey latched on to her clit and suckled it again, simultaneously stimulating her breasts and fucking her with her fingers.

"Come here," Hegna ordered.

She reached down and tugged Stormey by her arms. She lifted Stormey as if she weighed nothing and brought her on top of her. Stormey's body landed on of Hegna who turned them round on the couch to where Stormey remained above her. She positioned their legs to bring their slick pussies to touch.

Stormey rested her hands on the couch behind Hegna's head and thrust her center against Hegna's.

"Hegna," she cried out.

She shuddered from the intense pleasure that radiated through her body. The sensation of Hegna's clit rubbing on hers had her trembling. Hegna's hands rested on her thigh and ass while thrusting against Stormey.

"Yes, *miere*. Take your pleasure, too," Hegna growled.

Her lips clamped down on one of Stormey's nipples, sending an electric current through her. Stormey didn't know what the word *miere* meant. It was the first time she'd heard it and she made a note to ask about it later.

Their bodies moved in sync with each other. Stormey closed her eyes, riding on the pleasure coursing through her. Hegna lifted off her breast and positioned them closer where there was nothing that could fit between them. Hegna buried her face in the crook of Stormey's neck and shoulder. Her tongue snuck out and trailed along Stormey's neck.

Stormey was teetering on the edge of her release.

She was so close.

Her thighs were slick with the proof of her and Hegna's desire. She threw her head back, rocking her hips, seeking out her peak when a sharp pain exploded on her neck. She cried out, tumbling into her orgasm. The amount of sheer pleasure from her release erased the pain at her neck. She cried out, wrapping her arm around Hegna as she drank. The pull of Hegna drinking from her went down to her core. Her clit pulsated, filling with a hot heat that spread through her body. Hegna continued to writhe against her, intensifying it.

Another strong orgasm ripped its way through her. She bit her lip to keep from screaming. Her body moved on its own, seeking out more pleasure. Her hips gyrated, her back arched, her breasts sliding against Hegna. She was lost in her own pleasure-filled euphoria. She now understood the thrill of a bite from a vampire and how some humans became addicted to it.

Stormey felt as if she were floating amongst the clouds. She was high on adrenaline that coursed through her. She moaned, pure joy at the fact Hegna was drinking from her. She finally descended from her high. Their hips slowed to a halt. Their breasts were crushed between them.

Stormey slowly caressed Hegna's back. Her body felt flushed and sensitive from the tops of her head down to her toes. She sighed, leaning into Hegna, wanting her to take what she needed.

This was her purpose.

She didn't need anything else but this woman whose fangs were buried in her throat.

Hegna withdrew her fangs. Stormey shivered at the move. She licked the area which was just as erotic as if Hegna were licking her between her legs. Once she was satisfied with what she saw on Stormey's neck, Hegna lifted her eyes to her.

The sounds and music of the club were ignored as they stared at each other. Stormey only wanted to be with Hegna and understood life with a vampire was much different than a human. She'd only been inside the club for minutes and had seen open feedings and fucking. Vampires were sensual beings, and she wanted to meet all of Hegna's needs.

Stormey didn't care where they were as long as they were together.

"You are a very determined human, *miere*," Hegna murmured. She brushed Stormey's hair away from her face. Her fangs were peeking from underneath her lip. There was a small amount of blood in the corner of her mouth that ran down toward her chin.

Stormey reached up and wiped it away with her fingers. She leaned down and pressed a kiss to Hegna's lips, tasting a hint of her blood.

"For someone I want, I will be."

"And you don't care that we are here?" Hegna arched an eyebrow.

Stormey looked around, seeing a few eyes were on them, but the majority of the vampires and humans were deep in their own pleasures. She turned back to Hegna with a smile.

"I don't know." She shrugged. She pressed another kiss to Hegna's lips and rocked her hips. "I kind of like it."

"Is that so?" Hegna nipped her bottom lip with her fangs.

"Yes. So people can see that it is me who will serve all of your needs." Stormey laughed as Hegna pushed her down onto the chaise with her back resting on the cushions.

Hegna smiled, bracing over Stormey.

"You are my vampire, and if anyone will feed you and fuck you, it will be me."

CHAPTER SEVENTEEN

"You are daydreaming again," Miss Lavana announced. She sat back in her chair and eyed Stormey.

They were in the large library where they met for all of her lessons. Leather-bound books filled the rows of shelves. There was so much rich history in this room that Stormey loved coming here to learn. Even on the off hours, she snuck down here and pored through the books. Some were written in other languages she couldn't read, but there were plenty she could.

Stormey glanced at Miss Lavana and felt guilty.

She was right and hadn't been paying attention to her. Stormey bit her lip and stared down at her notes and chuckled.

"I'm sorry, Miss Lavana," she said sheepishly.

"You have the look of someone in love," Miss Lavana murmured.

The older vampire had been a wonderful teacher for Stormey. Miss Lavana had stressed that with her new position, it was important for her to learn the history of their kind, if she were to help lead them. Stormey agreed. She was a firm believer one must know where they'd come from in order to know where they would need to go. Mistakes in the future could be avoided if one had a clear understanding of history.

Stormey loved researched, but right now, her mind was occupied with the memories of the night she'd spent with Hegna in the feeding club. She should have been embarrassed or ashamed that she'd had sex with her mate and allowed her to feed from her in front of others.

But she didn't feel any of that. She had heard the whispers that people were questioning why the princess hadn't claimed her.

One thing she'd learned about vampire society was there was lots of gossip. She was sure word would get around about her and Hegna in Madam Rice's establishment. Which was what Stormey wanted. She wasn't ashamed to want people to know that it would her providing for Hegna.

Since she had returned to the castle, Hegna had been ankle-deep in dealing with the lycans. More attacks had been occurring not only in their territory, but all across the country. The lycan alpha was making good on her promise. The same day they'd walked through the doors of the castle, Hegna had been pulled from her, and hours later, Stormey had been notified the princess and a small army had left for battle.

Stormey's heart had been in her throat this entire time. She hadn't even got a chance to see Hegna before she'd left.

"We can finish another day. You are making good progress," Miss Lavana said. Her eyes crinkled in the corners with her smile. She had shared with Stormey that she was almost five hundred years old but didn't look a day over fifty. The vampire worked as a historian for the coven and had been a wealth of information for Stormey.

"I appreciate it." Stormey laughed. She reached up and rested her hand on her neck. The two pinpoints from Hegna's fangs were scabbed over.

Her core clenched when she ran the tips of her fingers over them. She found herself missing her vampire. They'd had one hell of a night with each other, and then duty had called. She glanced up and caught Miss Lavana's eyes on where her hand touched. Her face warmed as she stood from the table. "I do have one question for you."

"Yes, my lady. What would that be?"

"Has there ever been a history of a human sitting on the throne beside the king or queen?" she asked.

Miss Lavana's eyes softened, and she shook her head.

"No, my lady. There hasn't."

"Oh." Stormey inhaled sharply. "And do you think when the day comes, I'll be accepted?"

"There are those who are against humans for anything other than food, but I can honestly say the majority will wait and see who you are and what you are about." Miss Lavana gathered her belongings and inserted them into her bag. At that moment, her eyes revealed her age with the wisdom that shone through them. "They will want to see how you lead, bring our worlds together, compassion, innovation, and more. We are a people used to action, and that's when you would be judged."

"Thank you, Miss Lavana." Stormey smiled. The woman had given her a little hope for the future. She could be all of those things. As a woman who'd started from nothing, she wanted to be that leader for those who had no one to turn to. Vampire or human. "Will the day after tomorrow still work for you?"

"Yes, that will fine, my lady." The older woman bowed her head and left the library, leaving Stormey alone.

She sighed and glanced down at the books on the table. She lifted them and moved around, putting them back where they belonged. She paused while standing in front of the window that overlooked the snow-covered gardens below. She couldn't wait to see what they looked like once the spring thaw came. It was too cold for her to spend much time out there. The bitter winds were fierce this year.

"Mistress," Cici called from the door.

Stormey spun around and headed toward her.

"Yes, Cici. Did you need something?"

"No, mistress. Edward asked for me to come and retrieve you. There is a visitor in the parlor room waiting for you. A Miss Emily Washington from the orphanage is here to see you."

"Oh, okay." Stormey made her way out of the library and followed Cici to Emily. Stormey was excited to see her. They were going to be working together to remodel the orphanage. Stormey had such wonderful ideas that she couldn't wait to work with Emily during the process. She was interested in getting to know the children as well. This would open so many doors for her with her future plans. First, she would start here in Black Hollow, then move forward with reaching out to other orphanages and then shelters for the homeless. There were so many people who were forgotten that she vowed to remember them all.

Stormey opened the double glass-paned doors and entered the room. It was cozy with a couple of sofas, big floor-to-ceiling windows, the coverings open to allow the moonlight to enter. The decor was light, airy, and welcoming.

"Emily." Stormey strode across the room.

Emily smiled and stood from the sofa she was sitting on.

"Princess!" a small voice shouted.

Stormey grinned at the sight of Maisie rushing across the room. She hadn't seen the little tyke when she'd first entered. Maisie's hair was no longer in the braids with the beads on the ends. It was now arranged in two large ponytails with bows in them. Her small figure slammed against Stormey's.

"Maisie, how are you?" Stormey cupped her round cheek, her heart swelling as she looked upon the child.

"I'm good. I've missed you." Maisie grinned.

"I missed you, too. What are you two doing here?" Stormey took Maisie by the hand and went over to where Emily stood.

They shared a quick hug and took their seats on opposite couches. Maisie settled next to Stormey, not letting her hand go.

"Would you like me to have drinks and snacks brought down?" Cici asked.

"Please," Stormey replied.

Cici gave her a nod and stepped out of the room, closing the doors behind her.

Stormey turned back to Emily with a smile. She hadn't really had visitors stop by the castle for her. She sat taller, knowing this would soon change the more she got involved with their community and territory. "It's a pleasure to see you. What can I do for you?"

"Well, since we are going to be working together on the renovations of the orphanage, I wanted to run some things by you. I've already been in contact with the architect that Princess Hegna sent to me."

"Fantastic," Stormey gushed.

Emily pulled out some building blueprints. Stormey was happy that Emily didn't mind her involvement. A servant brought them their snacks and drinks. They consumed the tasty treats while studying the plans. Stormey knew how these children felt, and if they could provide a fun and safe space for them, it would mean all the difference. They pored over the designs, and Stormey offered her recommendations. She was thrilled Hegna was covering all of the costs for the orphanage.

She brought up something to Emily that she wanted to develop more. Her next project would be to get involved with helping these children find good forever homes. There were children becoming homeless daily, and that was an issue she wanted to focus on. No child should be on the streets. It was extremely dangerous to be homeless, especially for children. Not only did they have sick humans who would take advantage of them, but rogue vampires and now lycans.

"I think it is such a blessing that you were brought to Black Hollow." Emily wiped a lone tear that trailed down her face.

Stormey smiled and reached across, taking her hand in hers. "Believe me, I've always wanted to do something of this magnitude but didn't have the means or the resources. Now that has all changed." She glanced over at the sleeping child next to her. Maisie had dozed off at some point after eating her fill of the sweets that were delivered. She trailed a finger along the little one's cheeks.

"She really is attached to you," Emily murmured.

Stormey's heart picked up slightly as she watched the sleeping child.

"You're all she talks about," Emily said.

"She's such a sweet girl. What happened to her parents?" Stormey asked. Maisie was such a wonderful child, and it pained her that she was without a family. She was lucky to be in Emily's care. Not all orphanages were as wonderful and caring as the Fountain of Hope. She lifted her hand as Maisie rolled over onto her stomach, a small snore escaping her.

"Well, her mother was a single mom. Her father sounded like he was never in the picture." Emily reached out and poured hot water in her teacup. She finished doctoring her tea and raised it along with the saucer and took a sip. She glanced over at

Maisie, her eyes softening when her gaze landed on her. "From what I know, she had lived with her mother and grandmother. There was a home invasion where both her mother and grandmother were killed. Maisie was found hiding in the crawlspace underneath the house."

Stormey's heart ached for the little one. She had already been through so much at a young age and she was still able to put a smile on her face. They all could learn so much from these children.

"And there's been no interest in anyone adopting her?" Stormey asked.

Emily shook her head and set her cup and saucer down on the small table. "Unfortunately, adoption has been at an all-time low lately. Not many families can afford to adopt. The fees are outrageously high, and most can't afford them."

"Fees instilled by who?"

"Why, the human government, of course. They are foul and money-hungry. They don't care if any of these children find homes. They want to make money off anything they can," Emily said.

Stormey glanced down at Maisie and would bring this up to Hegna. Something had to be done about this.

* * *

STORMEY SWUNG HER STAFF AROUND, feeling more comfortable with it. She cried out as it struck Zeke's. The force of the two sticks hitting each other sent a strong vibration coursing up her arms. Her workouts with the vampire had been very helpful in boosting her confidence, and she'd even noticed she had shed some weight.

"Good." Zeke stepped back from her. He grinned at her and stepped closer. He motioned for her to lift the stick. "When you swing the stick toward an enemy like that, make sure you grip it with both hands."

He dropped his staff on the mat and helped position her hands. He moved behind her and guided her through a motion. He adjusted her elbow and brought it up higher. She bit her lip and ignored the sense of wanting to put more room between them. She stiffened slightly, and he must have picked up on it and backed away from her.

"Swing again and let me see," he said. He grabbed his stick from the floor and took a few paces back.

She went through the move and noticed a difference when she swung her staff. Using this weapon came easy to her. She wasn't sure she would be able to stab anyone with a knife, but Zeke wanted her to learn both.

"That does feel a little better," she murmured. She paused and stood to her full height.

They were practicing in the sparring room as they did each session. Today, there were only a few other pairs utilizing the room.

"Come. Let's take a break." He motioned over to the wall where a few bottles of water sat.

She blew out a deep breath and walked with him. She tossed her staff on the mat, anxious to have a swig of water. They had been working out for a couple of hours. Her body was not as sore as it used to be when she'd first started working out.

Stormey plopped down on the floor and reached for the ice-cold bottle of water. She twisted off the top and took a long pull from the bottle. She leaned her head back on the wall and closed her eyes. She felt sweaty, and her leggings were sticking to her. She made a mental note to go straight to her shower once she left here.

"You are doing really well," Zeke said.

She opened her eyes and found him staring at her. Something crossed in his eyes she couldn't put a finger on. He blinked and looked down at the water in his hands.

"Thanks. I've had a great teacher," she said. It was the truth; he had the patience of a saint. She had thought fighting with a staff would be easy, but it was anything but. She could do basic self-defense now, but there was no way she could run out into battle with the warriors. "I don't see how you all can train and wield weapons like you do. I have great respect for you and the other warriors."

Stormey knew she would never be able to do what they did. Violence wasn't something she had in her, and it took a special person to be able to inflict harm and kill another. She was glad the men and women who served Hegna and her family were so dedicated to their calling as a warrior. She'd visited their training sessions before and could barely keep up with how fast they moved.

"It is an honor to work with you, my lady," Zeke said. His gaze dropped down to her exposed neck where Hegna had drank from her. He swallowed hard a few times then turned away.

This was odd. She didn't know what was going on, but he had been acting weird the last few weeks. She checked around the room and saw it was only the two of them, the others having left.

"Is something wrong?" She wanted to clear the air between the two of them. She liked Zeke as a friend, and he was always kind to her. She watched him, sensing something was wrong. "If I've done something to—"

"You can never do anything, my lady," he interjected. He flicked his gaze to her before glancing down at his hands. "You are perfect."

Her eyes widened as he stood from where he sat. He peeked at the door where Jasper appeared. Her guard stood glaring at Zeke who faced her and held out a hand. He helped her up from the floor. She wasn't sure where this had come from.

"I can assure you that I'm not," Stormey said softly.

He offered her a strained smile, his eyes falling back to the bite mark. The bruising was slowly fading but was definitely noticeable. She had lost count of how many of the vampires around her had taken notice of it.

"I have a gift for you," he said. He jogged over to where his duffle bag lay. He came back holding a small device. It was a silver-looking cylinder that held a button on the center of it.

"What is it?" she asked. She reached out hesitantly and picked it up. It had some weight to it. It had beautiful designs on it, and as she looked closer, it had the crest of Riskel family.

"A collapsible staff." He grinned. His eyes lit up, and he motioned to the button on the cylinder. "Press that and it will go from three inches to five feet. Here, watch."

He scooped it back up from her and demonstrated. He tapped the button, and instantly, the device grew in length. Stormey's eyes widened at the weapon. She grinned and reached for it. It was certainly deceiving, and she loved it.

"This is amazing," she gushed. She twirled around with it, swinging the weapon in the air. She pressed the button again, and it withdrew to its smaller form. She looked back up at Zeke and flew across the mat to hug him.

His body stiffened slightly before relaxing, and he returned the gesture. She pulled back and took his hand. She had a feeling what was going on with him, but she didn't want to embarrass him in front of Jasper. If he even spoke of caring for her more than he should, he'd lose either his tongue or his life.

"I really appreciate this gift, Zeke. You are a true friend," she said gently.

Sadness appeared in his eyes, and it confirmed her assumption.

She stepped back and peeked at Jasper, showing off her new weapon. "Did you see that?"

"Yes, my lady." Jasper nodded.

The guard stood straighter and tossed Zeke a look, switching his attention back to her. Each warrior who guarded her were the best and each were handpicked to watch over her. The fact they were all willing to give up their lives for her sent a shudder down her spine.

"But I wouldn't be doing my job if you ever needed to use that," he said.

"You are absolutely right, Jasper." She glanced down at the weapon in her hand, enclosing her fingers around it. She peered back up at him with the grim reality of why Hegna had insisted she train and learn to protect herself. No one was invisible, and if her guards fell to the enemy, she could at least buy herself more time and have a chance of survival.

CHAPTER EIGHTEEN

Hegna swiped at the blood trailing down the side of her face. It wasn't hers but that of a lycan she had decapitated. The animal had refused to give her any information, so he'd paid for it with his life. She strode through the small makeshift camp her men had created. They had been gone for a full week, and Hegna wasn't thrilled about it. Just one week ago, she'd had her first taste of her mate's blood. The power and energy she had gained from it was unspeakable. She had never experienced anything like it.

They had returned to the castle, and she had been immediately swept away by Bijou with word that lycans were on the attack. All across the country, the lycans were creating chaos.

Just as Azura had promised.

Hegna and her men had immediately deployed.

When she should have been at her mate's side, claiming her, giving her everything she deserved, Hegna had been pulled away for battle without being able to say goodbye to Stormey. It didn't sit right with her, but she was bound by her duty to her people.

One taste of her mate, and the last part of her resistance to mating had dissolved. She ignored the fact Stormey had been brought to her because of the matching results. Yes, the test result confirmed it, but that wasn't what Hegna sought. She'd wanted to make her own decision, and being around Stormy, sensing how her body reacted to her, the taste of her and Stormey's personality, all was what had won her over.

That had been what she'd wanted.

Had she desired to wait until later in life, once the world was safe for her people? Yes. But she was quickly learning time was of the essence. Her mate was with her now, and she would reward her human for being so determined.

But now, she had these damn lycans to take care of.

They were deep in the plains of Nebraska. Lycans had gone on a rampage in the city of Grand Island. The once-thriving city was now a shell of what it had once been after the war, just like most major cities.

Their camp was located on the outskirts of the city underground. Hegna stalked along the rough terrain and headed toward the opening of their lair. Soon, the sun would rise and they would need to take cover. A few human guards who were employed by her would remain. Throughout history, they had created these caverns as a means to survive during the years. Sunlight was a threat to her kind, and they had constructed their below-ground facilities without humans being aware.

"Your Grace." A warrior bowed his head and thumped his chest with his fist. He reached down and pulled open the doorway that led to beneath the earth's surface.

"Thank you." She rested a hand on her daggers and descended the stairs. They were located in the earth's belly, safe away from the sun.

The stairs curved slightly with her arriving at the opening of a hallway. The tunnels were much larger than one would assume. The stone-and-brick walls were constructed to withstand the test of time. Small lanterns lit the way, hanging from the ceiling.

There were underground lairs constructed for vampires all across the world. It was a way they were able to function during the daylight. This particular tunnel had been built during World War II when many other tunnels were being constructed. The air was cool and the walls slightly damp. It wasn't pretty or luxurious, but it allowed vampires to survive during the day when away from home.

Hegna strolled through the complex hall, arriving at her destination. Bijou and a few warriors were gathered in a room. The men and women were the top warriors and answered directly to Bijou. Her general stood before a map posted on the wall. The room fell silent as she moved to join her.

"What do you have?" Hegna growled. Her temper was on a short fuse, and she was ready to return to Black Hollows. Since arriving in Grand Island, they had captured and eliminated lycans who had been terrorizing the inhabitants of the city.

"I think we were able to flush out the majority of the wolves," Bijou said without looking over at Hegna. She tapped on an area, the northern part of the city limits, on the map.

The tension was thick. Hegna and the warriors had been going nonstop since they'd arrived.

"The few lycans that remain, I believe they are holed up in this area. We burned down the one abandoned warehouse where they had been squatting. The human fire department finally extinguished the fire. The building is not hospitable any longer."

Hegna stared at the area and nodded. She agreed. It would seem they had another den in town. Once they took care of this threat then she could return to Black Hollow.

"Check the weather reports. I want to know if the sun will be out, and if it's not, we're going to hunt during the day. They won't expect that from us," Hegna said.

Bijou turned to one of the warriors and jerked her head. He walked over to a desk and took a seat in front of a laptop.

"It's been a while since we attacked during the

day," Bijou said. She folded her arms in front of her chest. She eyed Hegna and gave an approving nod.

The general never questioned Hegna's decisions. They had fought by each other's side for years, and besides her sisters, Hegna would have it no other way.

"We are lucky it's wintertime," Hegna said. She already knew what the warrior was going to find before he even turned back to them with the report. Hegna glanced over at him when he spun around in the chair.

"Your Grace. Today's prediction is cloudy and windy. Wind gusts are expected to come from the northwest," he stated.

Then it was final. Cloudy in the middle of winter meant they would be safe from the sun's rays today. With the lycans' current position, they wouldn't scent the vampires coming.

"Just what we need." She eyed the room. Her men would leave now if she ordered it, but that wouldn't be best. She needed them to be at the top of their game. "We will go hunting. Get a few hours of rest and blood in you."

They all thumped their chests and bowed slightly before leaving the room.

Bijou assessed Hegna.

"Are you good?" Bijou asked.

Hegna scowled at her friend. Nothing ever escaped her.

"I'm fine," Hegna grumbled. She moved over to the abandoned chair and took a seat. She rested her feet up on the table and glanced at the computer. She marveled at how they were able to gain information now from something so small and portable. Throughout her years, technology had improving quite dramatically. Her favorite part of living through time periods was the advanced weaponry that got developed.

"You're looking pale again." Bijou came over to the table and leaned back against it. Her eyes narrowed on Hegna.

Hegna rolled hers and exhaled loudly. She had been holding back the twinges of pain and focusing on their fight with the lycans. She'd fought just as hard as she always did. Her fangs had been descended for the past two days and refused to go back inside her gums.

"Why didn't you claim Stormey?" Bijou asked quietly.

"You would have wanted me to claim my mate in the midst of a feeding club? Something that is to be intimate, private, and special in front of a club full of people we don't know?" Hegna smirked. She may not have wanted a mate but she'd always figured that when she did take one, she would be traditional about it. Her claiming room in her castle had remained unused by her. She'd had employees over the years request to use it when they wanted to claim their mates.

The traditional claiming of one's mate was similar to a human wedding, only there were no witnesses. It was an intimate ritual, vows, the sharing of blood, and most ended with the two newly bonded mates consummating their union. Afterward, it was said that mates could sense each other. She'd heard rumors some could sense each other's heartbeat or emotions.

"But you drank from her. You didn't feel any urge to just continue?" Bijou asked. The look of disbelief was evident on her face.

It had been hard, but Hegna had been trying to refrain from draining Stormey dry. The taste of her mate's blood was even sweeter than the cream that flowed from her cunt.

"I was too focused on the energy and strength I felt rushing through me while the wound on my shoulder healed completely," Hegna tried to explain. What she'd experienced was hard to put to words. She had drunk from countless humans, male or female, and it was nothing like what had happened when she'd taken the first sip from Stormey.

"Well then, we must wrap up here and get you back home so you can claim your mate." Bijou smiled and tapped on Hegna's boots. She pushed off the table and strode to the door. She paused and glanced back at Hegna. "Take your own advice. Get some rest and blood. I have a feeling we will need it."

* * *

HEGNA SET the hologram device on the floor of her bunker then moved back to sit on the edge of her bed. She for once took her own advice and was able to sleep for a few hours. Her stomach even allowed her to drink a bag of blood. It was as if her body knew that the quicker she could get home, then she could get to Stormey.

Two figures filled the small area.

Her sisters.

"Where are you?" Velika asked immediately. The youngest of the three sisters never bit her tongue. She scanned the enclosed space with her hard gaze.

Hegna held back a smirk.

"Hello to you, too, sister." Hegna chuckled. She ran a hand along her face, sensing she was more tired than she thought. She wouldn't get any good rest until she returned home. The cot in the room was tiny and the mattress hard. It was nothing like the soft mattress she had back in her castle. Before her nap, she'd washed up in one of the shower rooms to erase the grime and blood from the battle. She'd donned fresh clothing and was ready to go back out in the field.

"You know Velika doesn't have a filter." Lethia laughed. Her hologram figure took a few steps around the enclosure before spinning around. "Did you take care of the problem?"

Hegna stood and folded her arms in front of her chest. She and her sisters had trained together since the moment they could wield a sword. As the heir to the throne, Hegna never thought less of her sisters. She valued their opinion and expertise. The three of them had always been stronger working together, and that would continue when she was made queen.

"To answer Velika, I'm in a bunker in Nebraska.

Lycans were on the attack here, and we came to take care of it," Hegna snarled.

When they had arrived, lycans had roamed the city, putting it on lockdown. Vampires and humans were afraid to leave their homes. As warden of this territory, it was Hegna's responsibility to keep all safe. The human police were not powerful enough to fight against the lycans. It was best for all humans to stay inside and away from the beasts. Their main intention was to capture humans and turn them.

"Do you need assistance?" Velika raised an eyebrow.

Hegna chuckled and shook her head. Her sister was bloodthirsty and wouldn't hesitate to come to fight.

"Seriously?" Hegna snorted but then became serious. "If I needed you, I would have called."

That was one thing they all had in common. They would never take on more than they could handle. One call was all it would take to bring the three sisters together. But for now, Hegna didn't need help. It was touching that her sister was prepared to drop whatever she was doing to come to be at her side.

"So why the call?" Lethia asked.

"There is something I needed to share with

you," Hegna said. She hadn't had a chance to update them on the situation in Sanlow. They needed to be brought up to speed on what had been discovered.

"What? That you've claimed your mate?" Lethia leaned back against the wall. She tossed her long blonde hair over her shoulder and wagged her eyebrows.

"What? No," Hegna growled. She didn't want to update her sisters yet on the situation between her and Stormey. If she did, they wouldn't let her get to the reason for her call.

Velika whistled. She had once shared the same views as Hegna. She hadn't wanted a mate and tried to resist her human, Quinn. But her sister eventually gave in and claimed her mate.

"I'm not sure if your will is better than mine or you're just an idiot," Velika said.

"Fuck off," Hegna snapped. She rolled her head around, feeling tension in her neck muscles. Everyone always wanted her to do things at their pace. She would determine how and when she would claim her mate. Just for once, she wished she was a normal vampire with no rules or traditions she would be forced to follow. Being a royal meant she would always be in the eye of the public.

"Nezera has been tracking lycans for me, and I will need your assistance."

The room fell quiet. The smiles disappeared from her sisters' faces as they waited for Hegna to continue.

"What's going on?" Velika asked. Her icy-blue eyes, same as all the sisters shared, narrowed on Hegna.

"There is a human town, just over the border in Canada, that has been overrun by the lycans," Hegna announced. The fact the lycans were able to attack a human town pissed her off. She may be a vampire, but she wouldn't wish a forced turning on the poor humans. They were the weaker race, and it was her job to protect all who were under her rule, be it vampire or human. She was immediately going to have new protocols put in place for other human towns. This could not continue to happen. Thankfully, they had the informant who was willing to share everything with them.

"Are there any humans left?" Lethia asked quietly. Even though her sisters were only there by way of hologram, the tension in the room thickened.

"Negative. They were all turned. At least the ones who survived the change," she replied.

Curses flew around. She had a plan to try to flush out the alpha that involved her sisters. The alpha would not be able to defeat the three of them. They were too powerful.

"There is one lycan who I am willing to give amnesty to as long as he continues to provide us with information."

"And why would you want to give one of those beasts amnesty?" Velika growled.

It was eerie how much Velika's tempter was similar to hers. Hegna shared the story of the informant and the death of his wife and child. Velika, who was mated and a mother herself, settled back and gave a nod. By the look of her facial expression, this hit home. Something like this could happen to not only her mate, but to Lethia's and Hegna's as well.

"You made a sound decision. He will be able to infiltrate places we will never be able to go."

"Lethia, do you still have those two humans in your dungeon?" Hegna asked.

Lethia's mate had been a part of the human resistance group. It was later discovered that the leaders of the group who were supposed to be helping humans escape their matches—lied. The males were actually taking the humans away and hand-delivering them to lycans. The poor humans had been turned against their will by the lycans.

"I do," Lethia confirmed. "What are you thinking?"

"We need to flush out the alpha, and I think you having those humans will help. We will go to Sanlow and use them as bait." It was time to end this between the lycans and vampires. If they had an entire town full of lycans, then that's where the alpha had to be. No one had been able to pinpoint her location. Each broadcast led to a dead end. What better way to draw her attention, then, by humans?

"I have no problem with that. It's what I had planned to do. When?" Lethia shrugged.

She was the calmest of the three of them, but it didn't make her any less deadly. She liked the finer things in life and took advantage of everything they gained as being vampires. Hegna could learn a few things from her. She had always focused on her people and trying to make the world a better place for vampires. Maybe it was time for her to indulge in life's pleasures.

Stormey came to mind.

Yes, it was time to show Stormey what it really meant to be a member of the vampire society.

"After I finish my business here, then I plan to go home for a moment. Await my call." Hegna walked over to the hologram box and ended the call. She picked it up and tossed it on the small table in the corner. She stalked out of the room, ready to hunt lycans.

CHAPTER NINETEEN

"When will I know what is going on?" Stormey laughed.

It had been over a week since Hegna had left, and she'd had no word from her. Stormey tried to keep busy around the castle to stop herself from going crazy with worry. Was she okay? Was she injured? Did she need blood? Did she think of her?

Stormey's brain raced with questions that were hard for her to turn off.

She sat impatiently while Cici worked on her makeup. She had been whisked away to her quarters where she was forced to shower and have her hair and makeup done. The black dress Cici brought her was breathtakingly gorgeous. It had a wide neckline that showcased the column of her neck and her deep cleavage. It was skintight and flared out around her ankles.

"Soon," Cici said. She narrowed her eyes on Stormey's lips as she painted ruby-red lipstick on them.

Stormey rolled her eyes and huffed. She liked surprises, but she didn't like being in the dark.

Cici stepped back from Stormey with a wide grin. "There, I'm done. "

Stormey took in her reflection in the mirror and froze. She almost didn't recognize herself. She was never one to wear makeup before due to not being able to afford it, and honestly, there was no point. She blinked and leaned forward, slightly in awe of Cici's handiwork. Her eyes were highlighted and accented by the eyeshadow, her skin appeared bronze-like, and her lips were pouty and full.

"You are amazing," Stormey murmured. She admired her hair that was in an updo style, putting her neck on display. A bit of sadness filled her when her gaze dropped down to where Hegna had drunk from her. The bruising was barely visible. She reached up and brushed the spot with her fingers unconsciously. "When will I know where we are going?"

A knock sounded at the door. Cici giggled and motioned for her to go answer it. Stormey inhaled a breath, sensing butterflies fluttering in her belly. She pushed up and stood from the chair and ambled over to the door. She smoothed a hand along her dress and glanced down at her shoes. She'd had to walk a few times around her suite to get used to the three-inch heels. She refused anything higher than that.

Stormey glanced over at Cici one last time. Her attendant was busy cleaning off the vanity where she'd prepared Stormey. Stormey laughed softly and opened the door. She froze in place.

Hegna.

Her vampire was dressed in her infamous black leather attire, only this tunic was cut low, allowing Hegna's cleavage to be visible. Her arms were bare, showcasing her defined muscles. A zipper ran down the front of the tunic that gave Stormey ideas. Her mate was dressed in soft, supple leather pants and black heeled boots.

"Hegna." Stormey flew forward into Hegna's arms. She wrapped hers around Hegna's waist and held her tight. She bit back a cry, not wanting to ruin Cici's work with her tears. She sucked air in, taking in Hegna's scent. She smelled of warm, soothing vanilla. Hegna lifted her chin and pressed her lips to Stormey's.

They may not have had their goodbye when she'd left, but Stormey welcomed their hello. Hegna's tongue pushed forward past her lips. Hegna was dominant, as always, with her kiss. Her tongued stroked Stormey's, eliciting a response from her body that only she could draw out. Stormey leaned into her, returning the kiss with the same fire and fury that came rolling off Hegna.

Hegna broke the kiss and leaned her forehead against Stormey's.

"You are safe and unharmed?" Stormey asked breathlessly. She reached up and cupped Hegna's face with her hand. She marveled that her mate was back and had apparently orchestrated something.

"I am." Hegna opened her eyes. She stepped back slightly and raked her gaze over Stormey's figure.

Stormey exhaled and smiled at the pure lust burning in Hegna's eyes. She playfully stepped farther back and swirled around so Hegna could get the full effect of the dress.

"Do you like it?" she asked. She'd lost some

weight from her workouts with Zeke, but she still had her curves. Her breasts, hips, and ass hadn't been affected from the weight loss. She'd noticed her stomach was a little flatter and her thighs were more toned.

"I do," Hegna replied. She rested a hand on Stormey's hip and backed her into the room. "I have something for you."

Stormey then saw a long rectangular box in her hand. Her heart fluttered at the sight of it. Was her vampire softening and had brought her a gift? Stormey grinned and had to keep from bouncing in place.

"Turn around, *miere*."

There was that word again.

Stormey turned around, her heart racing. Hegna slid behind her, reaching over head. Stormey gasped at the sight of a row of diamonds passing her eyes. The cool gems rested on her skin. Her hand immediately came up to feel the necklace. Hegna pressed a kiss to the nape of Stormey's neck, sending a shiver down her spine.

"Go, look at it," Hegna whispered.

Stormey didn't need to be told twice. She raced over to a mirror on her wall. Cici grinned at her as she scurried from the room. Stormey made a note to mess with her for not letting on that Hegna had returned. Cici was supposed to be loyal to her.

Stormey paused in front of her reflection. Her vision became blurry. She moved closer to it, her gaze locked on the row of diamonds. They looked flawless. A larger one was centered, resting on her chest.

"I…I don't know what to say. It's so beautiful," Stormey whispered.

Hegna came to stand behind her, wrapping her arms around her. She pulled Stormey against her. She leaned down and dropped another kiss on the side of Stormey's neck. It was near where she'd bitten Stormey.

"I've never even seen something so beautiful before."

"I have," Hegna murmured. Her eyes held Stormey's.

A wave of desire slithered through Stormey's body, ending at her center. Wetness seeped from her core. Hegna's nostrils flared as if she sensed Stormey's arousal. Stormey glanced over at the bed. Hegna's hand tightened on her.

"Hold that thought, *miere*. We have somewhere we need to be."

"Where?" Stormey spun around in Hegna's

arms. Maybe now she could find out what was going on or where they were going. It was almost ten o'clock in the evening.

"There is a dinner party being held in our honor," Hegna said.

"Wait! I have something for you." Stormey broke away from her and rushed over to the night-stand by her bed. She had almost forgotten she had purchased this gift for Hegna. She opened the door and pulled out the small velvet bag the witch had given her. She walked over to Hegna. This was the perfect time to give this to her. They were now working on their relationship, and Stormey wanted to give her the gift.

"What is this?" Hegna appeared shocked.

Stormey grew nervous. She placed the soft pouch in Hegna's palm.

"I saw this and knew I wanted to gift it to you," Stormey whispered.

She watched as Hegna opened it and reach inside. She brought out the ring and paused, studying it. Stormey's heart raced. She couldn't read Hegna's expression.

"Do you like it?"

The aquamarine stone was flawless and the same color as Hegna's eyes. Hegna slid it onto her finger, and it fit perfectly. Something flashed in her eyes that Stormy was unable to read.

"It is the most beautiful and thoughtful gift I have ever received," Hegna said.

Stormey's heart skipped a beat. Hegna tossed the empty pouch on the table nearest them before turning back to Stormey. She pressed a soft kiss to her lips again.

"Now, let's get your cloak. We wouldn't want to be late."

"MAY I TAKE YOUR CLOAK, my lady?" A woman approached Hegna and Stormey as they descended a stairwell that led underground.

After leaving the castle with their entourage of security guards, they were driven to the other side of Black Hollows. The structure that was their destination would have been easily missed had Stormey been looking for it. Once they entered the building, they immediately descended a stone spiral staircase that took them far beneath the earth's surface.

Stormey was beginning to learn vampires truly had spent a lot of time underground. How did humans not know there was an entire civilization that existed not only beside them, but also underneath them?

Her most recent lesson with Miss Lavana had centered around the underground society and structures that had been built centuries ago. She was still in awe at what she had learned and pictures she'd seen in their history books.

Stormey spun around and allowed the woman to assist her out of her cloak. Hegna handed the woman hers as well. The woman disappeared into what looked like a coat room.

"Come, *miere*." Hegna wrapped a possessive arm around Stormey's waist.

They were in an open grand foyer. It was shocking how high the ceiling was. The decor was warm with rich woods, cream-colored walls, and priceless artwork hung. A few sofas and tables were arranged around the area. Tasteful music floated through the air. Hegna led her through the space and down a short hallway.

The doors to a few rooms were open. Stormey caught sight of feedings in one to her right. The other was darkened, but the moans and sighs coming from it alluded to the acts being performed. Hegna's hand lightered on her waist. Stormey bit her lip. She once would have been shocked at what she was being exposed to, but now it was becoming second nature.

Cezar strode forward and paused in front of the double doors at the end of the hallway. Stormey grew nervous and faced Hegna once they arrived behind him. She just had to know what she was about to walk into.

"What is this?" she asked.

Hegna rested her hands on Stormey's shoulders. Her vampire relaxed slightly with a small smile gracing her lips. Stormey trusted Hegna completely. Her vampire would never place her in danger. Their guards stood around them, and Stormey could admit she had never felt safer than she did at this moment.

"If you are to be at my side as a princess and my mate," Hegna began.

Stormey's heart pounded at her chest. Hegna was actually speaking of a future with Stormey at her side. Stormey remained silent so Hegna could continue. So many thoughts were flowing through her mind that it was hard to concentrate on what Hegna was saying.

"Councilman Vilson insisted that we have a

small soirée to officially introduce you to members of the coven."

"This party is for us?"

"Really it's to welcome you, *miere*." Hegna dropped a soft kiss to her lips. "Tonight is for you to shine. Let's enjoy the festivities."

Stormey nodded. Her heart thumped away. If she didn't know any better, she would swear it was trying to drill its way out. She swallowed hard then stood to her full height. If Hegna could go off and face down lycans, then she could go in this room and face the vampires who made up their coven.

"I'm ready," Stormey announced.

Hegna turned to Cesar and nodded. He opened both doors and stepped to the side. Hegna slid her arm around Stormey's waist. They walked through the door and paused. Stormey would have never taken Hegna as person who made a dramatic entrance at a party.

Cesar strode forward before them with his head held high. He and the others were dressed in a different uniform. One that Stormey assumed was their formal dress.

Stormey leaned into Hegna while waiting for her to move. The dim room fell silent as she and Hegna became the main focus. Stormey was shocked to see a ballroom. She would have never guessed that a room this size would be underground. The ceilings had to be about ten feet tall, giving the sense they were aboveground.

"Her Royal Highness, Princes Hegna Riskel, heir to the throne, warden of middle America, and her mate, Miss Stormey Jaymes," he called out. He stepped to the side and gave a deep bow to her and Hegna.

Light classical music played again, floating through the air from the live musicians who were in one corner. The decor was dark and bold with no expense spared on it. Multiple large crystal chandeliers hung along the trayed ceiling. Tables covered in black cloths, with spectacular centerpieces, adorned the surface. A dance floor was in the center where couples moved around in a fashion of dance from the nineteenth century. Stormey recognized the dances from old movies she'd watched.

Vampires dressed in formalwear were scattered around the room. A few platforms were arranged with scantily clad human men and woman dancing as entertainment.

"This is for us?" Stormey whispered. She eyed the amount of people. "This is small?"

"Yes." Hegna snorted and gave her a squeeze.

"According to Councilman Vilson, this is small. Come, *miere*. Let's go and mingle."

Stormey smiled and walked along with Hegna. There wasn't anywhere she wouldn't follow this woman. This was to be her life. At Hegna's side, serving their people.

A tall gentleman who appeared to be around sixty approached them. "Your Grace. You have impeccable timing." He bowed to her and then leveled Stormey with his gaze. His lips curved up into a smile. "And your mate is as beautiful as I've heard."

He reached out a hand to her. She took it in a light shake. Surprisingly, his hand was cool to touch. Hegna was completely opposite, always being warm.

"Thank you." Stormey smiled. She wasn't sure who he was, but from his suit and the cape swinging behind him, she assumed he must be one of the council members.

"Councilmen Vilson. I see you have gone above and beyond yourself as usual," Hegna said. She kept her arm around Stormey's waist. She brought Stormey flush to her once he dropped Stormey's hand.

"But of course, Your Grace. It would be an

insult if I did not honor you and your mate in this fashion. We want to make sure Miss Jaymes feels welcomed." His smile revealed his fangs. He turned to Hegna. "May I escort you around?"

"I don't think that is necessary, Councilman," Hegna said. She glanced away from him, scanning the room with her sharp gaze. "My mate and I will be okay. I'm sure you have much to attend to with this size of a party."

"Ah, you are right. There is always something that will need to be addressed. Now that you are here, our live entertainment can begin."

There was a devilish glint in his eyes, and Stormy was curious on what he had planned. He gave a deep bow to the both of them and disappeared into the crowd.

"Come, *miere*. Let's continue."

They made their way around the tenure ballroom. Time flew past. Stormey lost track of how much time it took for them to mingle and speak with a lot of the vampires. She felt welcomed by all but was unsure if it was because Hegna was at her side or if they were being true with their warm greetings.

Stormey would not be able to remember everyone's name. There were too many people who wanted to meet her and have a moment of Hegna's time. Stormey watched Hegna and was in awe of what she saw. This was another part of her she was learning about. The woman was a true royal. The vampires clustered around her, vying for her attention. They were kind to Stormey, and some even asked her questions about herself, but the true star was Hegna, their future queen.

Stormey slid away from Hegna, needing a little breathing room. She stood at the bar nursing a non-alcoholic drink. She inhaled and slowly breathed out. A year ago, she was just a lowly housekeeper working in a small inn trying to make ends meet. Now fast forward, and she was the mate of a vampire princess where she had any and everything she could ever dream of.

Stormey glanced to her side and took in a female vampire standing with her back to the bar sipping on a large goblet. She looked over to Stormey as if sensing her gaze. Her lips lifted into a smile. She came over to Stormey.

"Miss Jaymes, how do you do?" she asked, her words slightly accented.

"I'm doing well. I'm sorry, you seem to know my name, but I don't know yours." Stormey returned her smile.

"My name is Monica." Her hair was dark, pulled away from her face in a loose bun with tendrils escaping. Her form-fitting red dress hugged her slim figure, and high heels shod her feet. "So you are the mate of our princess."

It wasn't a question but a statement. The narrowing of her eyes was sending an alert through Stormey. For some strange reason, she was getting a weird vibe from her. The woman's gaze swept down Stormey before returning to meet hers.

"I am." Stormey expected to be tested by some of the vampires. She wasn't going to back down and appear weak to any of them. If she were to rule beside Hegna, she needed to be just as strong as her vampire. "Are you a member of the council?"

"No, I'm an old friend of Hegna's." She sipped her blood and looked out at the dance floor.

"Oh, you mean the princess?" Stormey corrected her. Her smile slipped from her lips. She wasn't a fool. Hegna had a life before Stormey was drawn and brought to her. This must be one of her prior lovers.

"Oh, I'm sorry. Yes, the princess. I forget in public I need to be formal." Monica rolled her eyes and barked a laugh that was faker than her eyelashes.

"From this day forward, you need to remember to be formal at all times." Stormey sniffed. She took a drink from her glass before setting it down on the counter. Hegna was her vampire now, and it would be best for this woman to remember. Stormey didn't care the woman was a vampire and would be stronger than her. The training she'd received may have been for self-defense, but it would come in handy kicking some random vampire's ass.

"Why did you leave my side?" Hegna murmured, drawing Stormey back into her arms.

Stormey relaxed, her body melting back against Hegna. She hadn't heard her until she'd spoken. Her arm draped across Stormey's abdomen with her hand hovering near Stormey's center. Stormey arched her neck slightly, allowing Hegna to lean down and drop a kiss on her exposed skin. Her lips brushed the spot where she'd bitten Stormey. A shiver rushed through her.

"You appeared to be needed, and I didn't want to interrupt." Stormey's voice grew husky.

Hegna's warm breath brushed her skin as she dropped another kiss on her neck.

Stormey raised her glass to hold it up where Hegna could see it. "Plus, my throat was a little parched."

"Hmm, one of the guards could have gotten you something to drink," Hegna said. She lifted her head, her eyes taking in Monica.

Stormey felt her stiffen and pause. It was hard for her to tell if Hegna recognized the woman standing next to them.

"Is there any reason you are standing next to my mate?" Hegna asked.

Her hold on Stormey tightened. It would appear Hegna didn't remember Monica. Stormey smirked, a feeling of satisfaction racing through her. Monica's confidence faltered slightly. She recovered, a smile reappearing on her face.

"We were just making small talk." Monica shrugged. "I was just mentioning that we were old friends."

"We were never friends," Hegna snapped. Her fangs were bared, while her chest rumbled with a low growl. "I would appreciate if you didn't spread such lies."

"But, Hegna—"

"Is there a problem, Your Grace?" Kendrick, one of the royal guards, appeared. He was massive in size, standing well over six and a half feet tall. His dark hair was pulled back in a low ponytail. He glared at Monica, resting a hand on the sword that was sheathed at his waist. "You will respect your princess and call her by her official title."

"No, there is no problem, Kendrick," Hegna replied. "This woman was just leaving our presence, and she won't be speaking to my mate ever again either."

Monica stared at Hegna momentarily. She took a step back, gripping her goblet.

"Yes, I was just leaving." She spun around on her heel and disappeared into the crowd.

Kendrick turned to them and pounded on his chest. "Is there anything you need from me, Your Grace? Miss Jaymes?"

"We are fine, Kendrick. Thank you," Hegna replied. She twirled Stormey around and brought her flush against her. She pressed a soft kiss to Stormey's lips, blazing a trail along Stormey jawline and down to her neck.

"So we aren't going to talk about your little ex-girlfriend?" Stormey asked. She bit back a moan, feeling Hegna's hand slide along the curve of her bottom.

"She was never my girlfriend." Hegna lifted her head and cupped Stormey's cheeks. Her thumb lightly stroked Stormey's face. "I don't even know her name."

"Well, she certainly knew yours and even used your first name," Stormey snapped. She couldn't help but feel jealousy rear itself inside her. She reached up and ran a finger along Hegna's bottom lip. Stormey was learning more about herself, and jealousy over Hegna's old lover wasn't something she liked experiencing. Yes, she was aware Hegna had been with countless women before her, but to see one in front of her had her turning into someone she wasn't normally.

"Was my little human about to break out her claws?" Hegna smirked. She glanced over Stormey's shoulder. "Maybe I shouldn't have sent her away. I would have loved to see my mate beat the hell out of someone."

Stormey relaxed. Of course Hegna would want violence. She was a warrior princess, one of the most dangerous vampires to breathe. Stormey glanced up at her and saw honesty in her eyes. She didn't remember the woman. Hegna may be many things, but she wasn't a liar.

"You would have loved that, wouldn't you?" Stormey trailed her fingers from Hegna's lips, down her neck, and stopped at her cleavage. "Me putting what I've learned to the test."

"There is no doubt in my mind that you would

have won," Hegna breathed. Her eyes bored into Stormey. "I am drawn to you and no one else. My past is what it is. My past. You are my present and future."

A warmth spread throughout Stormey. Her vampire was giving in to what was between them. Stormey smiled and leaned in, kissing her vampire. It was that moment Stormey knew she was officially in love with Hegna Riskel.

Hegna took Stormey's hand and led her away from the bar. They maneuvered their way through the room to the dance floor. The music was slow and romantic. Hegna placed Stormey in front of her. Their bodies swayed with the rhythm of the music.

Stormey's heart rate increased. Hegna's warm body was flush against Stormey's. Her hands smoothed along Stormey's body and came up to cup her breasts. Stormey leaned back into Hegna's embrace.

Her eyes fluttered closed. She always felt safe in the circle of Hegna's arms. Her body was relaxed, but her core was slick with need. She swayed her body, brushing her ass back against Hegna. Her vampire's hands tightened on her mounds, keeping her in place. Stormey's eyes fluttered open and scanned the others around them. Her breath caught in her throat at the sight of feedings going on around her.

Bodies writhed against each other. The air grew thick with lust and the scent of copper. Vampires took what they wanted; humans basked in the pleasure of being bitten. Bare flesh greeted her as clothing disappeared from those around them.

The party had certainly taken a turn.

It would seem Councilman Vilson had brought in more humans for the vampires to feed on as entertainment.

Hegna's hand slid up to her chin and tilted her head to the side. Stormey's breaths turned into pants. Hegna's warm breath skated along her skin. Her other hand bunched up Stormey's dress, dragging it up her legs. She slipped her hand underneath it and arrived at Stormey's center. Stormey leaned completely back against Hegna, about to beg for her touch and bite.

Hegna glided her tongue along her skin, sinking her fangs deep into the side of Stormey's neck. Stormey's mouth opened, and a silent scream escaped her. Hegna's finger parted her labia and found her clit. She slid past the swollen bundle of nerves, gathering some of Stormey's wetness. She brought it back to her clit and strummed it while she drank.

Stormey's body immediately detonated. Her muscles grew taut as she rode the waves of her orgasm. Hegna's firm grip on her chin tightened. She pulled harder, drinking in Stormey's nourishing blood. Her pants grew more rapid while Hegna continued playing with her clit. She pinched it, sending Stormey into another hard orgasm.

Her body was racked with tremors. She didn't want the feeling to go away. If Hegna needed to take all that she had, she would give it to her.

No questions asked.

CHAPTER TWENTY

In the back of the vehicle, Hegna stared down at the ring on her finger. As the eldest child of the king and queen, she had been gifted many things over her lifetime from the most treasured and priceless heirlooms to the simplest of gifts from a constituent.

But none of them had ever held such an emotional attachment before.

A gift from her mate.

She stared at the flawless aquamarine jewel that sat atop the vintage ring. It was easy to see that Stormey had been attracted to it because it matched Hegna's eyes. But the emotions that had rested in Stormey's had Hegna feeling something she had never thought she would ever feel.

Love.

Did she love the human?

She had never been in love before and wasn't sure if this aching feeling in her chest was that. Hegna glanced down at Stormey who rested her head on Hegna's shoulder. Her eyes were closed, and her breathing was languid and even.

Hegna's fangs broke through her gums, wanting another taste of her mate. She made a mental note to have Stormey started on kenaf weed. She wouldn't want her to experience any side effects from her feeding from her. The power and strength she experienced from drinking from Stormey solidified that the woman was her mate.

Hegna made the decision she would claim her. She would notify Ellanora so she could prepare. The claiming of a mate for humans could be dangerous. The molecular change that happened to them which allowed their aging to slow could be harmful and painful to them. The healer needed to ensure the vampire didn't take too much blood during the claiming bite. The claiming room would need to be readied. Hegna's mind was racing with everything that would be needed to ensure this would be a special moment for her human.

The vehicle arrived at the back entrance of the castle. Hegna sat up, recognizing Bijou and a few warriors standing at the door. Hegna tensed. Something was wrong. She could feel it.

"*Miere*, wake up. We are home," she murmured.

Stormey snuggled closer to her, apparently not hearing her. A soft snore escaped her.

Hegna chuckled and gave her a light shake. "*Miere*?"

Stormey moaned, and her eyes fluttered open. She sat up, a yawn taking over her. Hegna was captivated by her beauty. She hated she had to awaken her, but it was necessary.

"We're home?" Stormey's voice was husky, and it sent a wave of desire through Hegna.

"We are." Hegna eyed Bijou who walked toward their parked vehicle.

Cezar left the driver's seat and opened her door. Hegna exited and held out a hand to Stormey whose small hand slid into hers. Stormey stepped from the car and lifted the hood of her cloak over her head. She scowled as a hard wind blew. Stormey shivered and moved close to Hegna.

"General." Hegna turned toward Bijou and

glared at her. She escorted Stormey toward the building.

"I do apologize for interrupting your private time with your mate," Bijou said.

She walked along with Hegna. From Bijou's fierce expression, Hegna's sense that something was wrong grew. They entered the building where the heat met them. Hegna entwined her fingers with Stormey's.

"What is it?" Hegna asked.

"It's the town of Sanlow. Our presence is needed immediately," Bijou announced.

A muscle in her jaw tightened. If Bijou felt they were needed there, then Hegna would not second-guess her general.

Dread filled Hegna. It was the place they had been keeping an eye on that was now a lycan town. She eyed Stormey who must have sensed this was important. Hegna grew frustrated she would have to abandon her plans for now. Duty called, and this was one of those times she wanted to ignore all of her responsibility and focus on her mate.

But she couldn't do that.

"When do we leave?"

"The helicopter is waiting for us. I've already

sent troops from here and our Minnesota and Montana outposts ahead."

Hegna cursed. This was not what she wanted to hear when arriving after a wonderful time with her intended.

"It's okay. Go," Stormey said. A small smile appeared on her lips. She leaned into Hegna and gave her hand a squeeze.

Hegna reached up and pushed back her hood so she could see her face. Her gaze dropped down to the new bruise and twin scabs from her bite.

"I'll be here when you return."

"Move your stuff to my quarters," Hegna ordered.

Stormey's eyes widened, and her smile grew. That ache in Hegna's chest intensified, and she knew this had been a right decision. No longer did she want to sleep away from her. She wanted to feel her naked curves next to her while she slept. Waking up with her mate at her side every day would be a new experience, and she yearned for it. "Alert Edward so the servants can take care of this for you."

"Okay," Stormey whispered. Her eyes were full of tears that sat on the edges of her eyelids.

Hegna cupped her cheek, hating that she had

put her through hell when all she wanted to do was be claimed by Hegna. She leaned up on her tiptoes and pressed a small kiss to Hegna's lips before stepping back. Her guard, Desmond, came to stand behind her.

"Just make sure you come back to me, princess."

"Don't worry, mate. There is nothing that will keep me from you," Hegna vowed. She turned to Desmond. "Have the healer send Stormey some kenaf weed."

Ellanora would take care that Stormey would be started on the herb and tailor the drink to her taste. It could be bitter, and the healer would ensure Stormey would be on a daily regimen.

"Yes, Your Grace." Desmond bowed his head. He spun around and tailed Stormey.

Hegna watched her until they turned the corner and disappeared from sight.

"Give me five minutes to get ready," Hegna growled.

"Of course, Your Grace." Bijou grinned, flashing her fangs.

They headed to the armory so she could outfit herself. This was a battle where she would be a victor and then return home to claim her mate. Cezar and Kendrick silently followed them. Her guards would travel with her. They may be assigned to her detail, but they were still warriors in her army and would fight by her side.

"I'm to assume that I will receive a full report once we've taken off?" Hegna asked.

They arrived at the lower level of the castle and stalked down the hall.

"Yes, Your Grace," Bijou replied.

They entered the room and were greeted by enough weapons that could outfit a small army. Hegna immediately changed her clothes and was dressed in her fighting leathers. She walked over to the wall of blades and took notice of her favorite twin daggers waiting for her on the table. She grabbed them, sliding them into their sheaths on her waist.

The room was silent as they all prepared for the impending battle.

These lycans would pay. They were making her leave her mate when all she wanted to do was claim her. Hegna would descend upon the lycan town and destroy it.

HEGNA STARED out the window of the helicopter as it descended. The dreadful sky matched her mood. Morning was upon them, but the sky was too murky to allow for sunlight. A winter storm was brewing. The angry-looking clouds were about to unleash their wrath. The helicopter landed, whipping snow around to make the visibility hard.

Hegna unbuckled her seatbelt and stood. Cezar was a step ahead of her, opening the door. The entire ride to Sanlow had been spent going over the briefing Nezera had sent them.

"Fuck, it's cold," he cursed. The big vampire drew the hood of his coat onto his head.

Hegna grimaced, the chilly wind slapping her on the face. Canada in the wintertime was much colder than Oklahoma.

Hegna was focused when she stepped out of the helicopter. It was suspected the alpha would be appearing in Sanlow. Her gaze landed on the captain standing next to a large, dark SUV. Hegna strode over to her and the armed warriors with her.

"Captain." Hegna arrived to stand in front of Nezera. The chilly, howling winds were rushing past them. The cold bit into Hegna, but she ignored it. Her fur cloak provided slight protection.

"Welcome, Your Grace." The captain was

dressed in similar fashion to ward against the weather. Even vampires could be victims of frost-bite. Her mouth was pressed into a tight line, and she motioned to the SUV. The two groups separated into the awaiting vehicles. They were on the road in minutes.

"Do you have any updates?" Hegna asked, not wasting any time. She was already being pulled away from her mate and she didn't want to be gone any longer than necessary. The roads were surprisingly clear at the moment.

"Yes, our informant has been able to collect intel that I felt was imperative. They are in talks of attacking neighboring cities and towns. They are planning to go after small towns that are vulnerable and replicate Sanlow," Nezera said. She pulled a folder from the pocket behind the passenger seat and handed it to Hegna.

She opened it and eyed the papers in front of her. She scanned them and took in the notes of the towns that were being targeted. Most were in her and Velika's territory. Her younger sister would need to be notified of this information immediately.

"Have you sent word to my sister?" Hegna asked.

"I have, Your Grace. She is sending troops to those towns as we speak," Nezera replied.

Hegna gave a slight nod, pleased with her captain's response. She handed the papers off to Bijou who was in the passenger seat.

"General, I'll leave it up to you on how to cover the areas. I don't want any weak spots," Hegna said. She trusted Bijou to take care of these issues. The last thing they needed would be to run off to protect one area while leaving another one open and vulnerable. Bijou was a master strategist and would handle the situation.

"Before I left, the informant sent in word that he heard the alpha would be arriving tonight," Nezera announced.

Hegna's hands formed into tight fists. Her fangs broke through, and she welcomed the slight pain.

"Good. We can end all of this," Hegna growled. This was the news she needed to hear and would be worth delaying the claiming of her mate. She would kill the alpha and then return to her. They would then move on with their lives.

"Did you see this note?" Bijou remarked. She turned around and pointed to the paper she was reviewing.

"What is it?" Hegna asked.

"In this report, it looks as if the information states that the alpha uses the term 'we' when speaking about the plans that were developed," she said.

"Could she have meant her and her lycans? I'm sure she has plenty of lycans backing her who are pure-born," Nezera suggested.

Hegna remained quiet, her thoughts racing. Why would the lycan say 'we?' The alpha was cocky enough to want to claim all ideas as her own. She was the ruler of their people.

"Do we know anything about the lycans working with her? We've only seen her on the broadcasts," Hegna said. Lycans moved in packs, and just like vampires, they would keep someone close to them whom they trusted. If Azura was the alpha, was there a beta? And if so, who the hell was it? "Is the informant in the barracks?"

"No, Your Grace. We didn't want to chance someone seeing him come to us. We meet him aboveground in person where the information is exchanged," Nezera shared. She glanced out the window. "We are almost there. Once we arrive, we can send a message to arrange a meeting with him."

"Yes, I want to speak with him." Hegna settled

back. The use of compulsion would be useless on a lycan. Most of them were strong enough to push back against the powers of the vampire, but none could prevent the stories that were hidden deep inside their blood. One bite, and Hegna would be able to see what he'd seen.

Then she'd be able to see if this lycan was telling the truth. She had a hard time trusting anyone and hoped that this leniency wasn't offered due to a lie. If that was the case, he would pay with his life.

"What the hell is that?" the warrior driving their vehicle muttered.

The SUV in front of them slowed to a halt. The hairs on the back of Hegna's neck rose. She pushed her cloak aside and rested a hand on the hilt of her dagger.

They were paused on a long road with rocky, snow-covered hills on either side of them. Hegna scanned the area and cursed. Her gut was screaming for them to get out and defend themselves. This time, she wouldn't have to worry about her mate in the car.

"It's a trap," Hegna growled. The moment she'd uttered the words, dark imposing figures leaped from the hills and slid down toward them. "Lycans."

Hegna pushed open the door and threw her cloak inside. She withdrew her duel swords and spun around on her heel. She scanned the area and saw her warriors were ready for battle.

"For the crown!" Hegna hollered, holding a dagger in the air.

"The crown!" her warriors cried out, racing off to meet the lycans.

She took off running toward the slope without a doubt that they would be victorious. As a welcome to Sanlow, Hegna would present the alpha with each one of her lycan warriors' heads.

CHAPTER TWENTY-ONE

A feeling of dread filled Stormey. It had been with her since the moment Hegna had left. From the information shared with her, there had been a human town that had been attacked and taken hostage. Stormey couldn't believe an entire town had been forcibly turned into lycans.

Those poor people.

Her heart went out to the families and friends of the humans who were either now lycans or had died from the change. Hegna was the defender of their territory, and they were under attack. Stormey understood being the mate of the warden would be nerve-racking. She believed and prayed to every god she could think of for Hegna to make it back to her safely.

But what did provide her comfort was sleeping in Hegna's private quarters. It was now officially theirs. The bed had felt so empty without Hegna. Stormey inhaled and drew up to her full height.

She was currently at the orphanage with Emily. They were visiting with the architect who would be in charge of renovations. She had been excited they were able to come midday to visit the orphanage for the meeting. The day was gloomy, and the sky was gray and filled with plenty of clouds.

"We will definitely need to bring in an engineer to make sure the structures in some of these rooms are sound," Zach Singleton said. He pointed to the ceiling of the room they were standing in. "We want to make sure that if we were to knock certain walls down that the floor above us doesn't collapse."

Emily and Stormey shared a look.

"Are they safe living here?" Stormey asked. What he was recommending sounded scary. There was a potential for the ceilings to fall down. Someone could get seriously injured.

"Oh, no. Everyone is fine here. I'm just saying when we start tearing down walls, we want to make sure that the structure won't be affected by removing the wall," Zach clarified. He held his clipboard to his chest.

Stormey believed him. He had been recommended by Hegna. His father and grandfather had worked on Hegna's castle with restorations over the years. If he was trusted enough to work on the royal property, then he could be trusted with the orphanage.

"That sounds good. You were worrying me for a moment." Emily chuckled.

They exited the room and strolled down the hall. Sounds of giggles echoed through the air. Stormey smiled softly to herself. She hadn't seen Maisie since they'd arrived and she was anxious to see the little tyke. There was something about that girl that just touched her heart and soul.

"Let's go over the plans I have designed. I had picked up the original blueprints to review them and the past renovations," he said. He nervously glanced over Stormey's shoulder at Desmond who was with her.

The guard had yet to say two words but had remained at Stormey's side the entire time they had toured the orphanage.

They walked into a room off the kitchen where

a table and a few chairs sat. Emily retrieved them some tea and snacks while they pored over the designs Zach offered them. Stormey grew excited looking at what was planned for the older mansion. Once they were done with it, it would truly be a home for the children until they could find families to take them in.

"What about the playground?" Stormey asked. This was an important part of the renovation they couldn't forget.

"Ah, yes. We certainly wouldn't want to miss out on something like that." Zach laughed. He pulled out another paper and rolled it out on the table before them.

Desmond suddenly spun around and held a hand to his ear. Someone must be speaking with him through his communicator. His voice was low while he walked over to the doorway.

Stormey turned back to the table, and Zach explained the children would not only get a playground but a basketball court and a pool.

"This is amazing," she gasped. She clapped, excited for the children. It was Stormey's hope that more kids would come to get off the street. They would employ more people to help Emily and her team of volunteers. Their plan would be to get all little ones off the streets and give them a safe place where they would enjoy being.

"Miss Jaymes, we need to leave," Desmond announced. His face was devoid of any emotions.

Stormey took one look at him and nodded. She offered a smile to Zach and Emily.

"I do apologize," she said. She pushed back from the table and stood. She hated she hadn't had a chance to see Maisie. "Can you tell Maisie I said hello?"

"Of course, Miss Jaymes. Thank you for coming." Emily stood from her chair.

Stormey waved her down. "I'm sure Desmond will know how to get to the front entrance." She chuckled. They would have to stop by the coat closet to grab her cloak. The temperatures outside were quite chilly. "I will give you a call later to discuss what I missed."

Stormey followed Desmond through the kitchen and to a hallway. Her smile slowly disappeared as she walked alongside her guard. He kept a hand on the hilt of his sword that was sheathed on his waist.

"Am I to assume that you will tell me what this is all about?" she asked.

"As soon as we are in the truck," he replied.

He was on high alert, and her anxiety level shot through the roof.

Stormey's heart rate quickened. Something must be wrong. She hated this feeling of unknowing. Had something happened to Hegna? Were they under attack? Question upon question kept flooding her mind. They arrived at the coat closet near the front door. Desmond assisted her with putting her cloak on. She pulled the hood over her head and followed him out the door. Their SUV was waiting for them. She shivered, a chill sliding down her spine.

Stormey settled into the backseat of the truck. Desmond shut her door and got into the passenger seat. Their driver, Henry, was a warrior she hadn't met before today. He was just as large as Desmond and had barely spoken two sentences.

"Keep your eyes sharp," Desmond said.

Stormey's widened. She gripped her hands together as worry grew. She grimaced, sensing her hands had grown damp. She wiped them on her cloak to dry them.

"Can you please tell me what is going on?" she asked, unable to wait for Desmond to decide when he was ready to tell her why they had to leave suddenly.

"Ever since the princess left, we've spread out around town and upped security. There was a lycan attack near Madam Rice's club. A few vampires were leaving, and lycans attacked," Desmond said. "And just an hour ago there was an attack a few blocks from the orphanage. We need to get you to the castle."

"Oh my," she breathed. She swallowed hard and fought to keep from fidgeting. She tried to remain calm. A future princess and ruler would not panic but keep a level head. She thought of Hegna and prayed she was safe. She wouldn't want Stormey to cower in fear. She'd want Stormey to defend herself. She'd trained for a reason, but she still hoped she wouldn't have to be tested with a real-life attack.

She took in the scenery as it flew past. Even with the cold, there were plenty of people out and about, strolling along. All appeared to be quiet and like any other day. She relaxed slightly. It was better for her guards to be cautious and get her home.

Henry slowed the vehicle to a stoplight. She stared out the window but didn't see anything outside. She inhaled, getting lost in her memory of Hegna telling her to move her items to her room. That was the best thing she'd heard. It had been what she had hoped for. She had a feeling when Hegna returned, they would complete the bond. She hadn't needed to say the words. It was evident by the look in Hegna's eyes. Stormey smiled, a warm sensation washing over her. She reached up and rested her fingers on the bite mark on her neck.

She blinked, not wanting to get too emotional. Poor Desmond and Henry probably wouldn't know what to do with a crying woman in the backseat of the truck.

The light turned green, and Henry guided the truck through the intersection. A roaring sound filled Stormey's ears. Their vehicle jerked from something slamming into them. A scream tore from her; the truck rocked onto its side and rolled. Stormey clenched her eyes shut, and her body jerked with the motion of the SUV until it went still.

She groaned and found herself hanging upside down in her seat. The seatbelt was tight across her chest. Her ears were ringing, and she couldn't hear anything else. She whimpered, not knowing what had happened. Something warm was sliding along her temple and her forehead. She closed her eyes, feeling faint. She tried to hold on. Desmond would get her—

Desmond! She hadn't heard anything from him. Was he and Henry okay?

She tried to open her mouth to speak, but no words came out. Something jerked at her, tugging on her cloak. She fell free, landing on a hard surface. Stormey fought to open her eyes, but they didn't cooperate. Her body was being dragged, and she couldn't lift a hand to protest. Instead, the darkness completely consumed her.

STORMEY EXHALED AND FROWNED. The bed was not as comfortable as she remembered. The mattress was much harder, and the scent coming from it was unfamiliar. She had been extremely comfortable the night before. Her only complaint was that Hegna had not been with her.

She paused.

When did she get home, and much less in the bed?

The last thing she remembered was riding along in the truck with Desmond and Henry after they'd left the orphanage.

Oh no.

She squeezed her eyes tight, afraid of what she

would see once she opened them. Her body shook with fear. She opened one eye, then the other. She blinked several times to try to get her vision to clear. She finally held them open and wished she had kept them closed.

Stormey was no longer in the SUV with Desmond and Henry.

She was on a cot in a room where the ceiling had exposed pipes. It was filthy and didn't seem as if anyone had cleaned in years. She turned her head and took in two men sitting in chairs watching television. These men were large and looked dangerous. Both of them had wayward hair that stood up on end everywhere.

Where were they?

The building must have been abandoned. There were plenty of buildings that were run-down in all cities across the country due to the war. She bit back a whimper, not wanting to alert them she was awake.

Stormey tugged at her hands and feet and found them bound to the bed. There would be no escaping. A door to the right opened, and a woman strode through. She held an air of power to her. Then men jumped to their feet when they saw her.

"Alpha," they said simultaneously.

Stormey swallowed hard.

Alpha.

No, it couldn't be.

The woman's gaze landed on her, and Stormey's heart all but leaped into her throat. She had seen this woman before. On television, threatening their entire world.

It was Azura Michaels.

"Well, you have awakened." Azura smirked. She walked over to Stormey with a dangerous glint in her eye. She was dressed in jeans, a white button-down shirt, and boots. Her dark hair was pulled back in a low ponytail. Her amber eyes bored into Stormey. "I was beginning to think that we'd caused real damage."

"Let me go," Stormey whispered. She tugged at her wrists, but the rope surrounding them was firmly in place. If she was here with lycans, then what had happened to Desmond and Henry? She frantically pulled at the ropes. She had to get out of here.

"Keep doing that and you'll just hurt yourself." Azura chuckled.

"Then let me go," Stormey demanded. She didn't know where this bravery had come from, but she had to find Desmond. "Where are my guards?"

"You'd better watch your tone, human," Azura snarled. She came over to the cot and reached down, gripping Stormey's chin in a tight hold.

Stormey fell still, fear taking over her. Her breaths were coming in pants.

Azura bared her large and extremely sharp fangs. "You are in no position to demand anything from me. Do you know who you are talking to?"

"A dead alpha," Stormey spat. Once Hegna knew Stormey had been taken, she wouldn't rest until Stormey was returned safely. Hegna would ensure this lycan would pay with her life.

"Brave human who is now on very borrowed time." Azura smirked again. She leaned down and reached out to touch Stormey's hair.

Stormey turned her head away, not wanting the lycan to touch her.

"Brave, but a fool," Azura said.

What did she mean Stormey was now living on borrowed time?

"You are a wanted enemy of the crown," Stormey said. Everyone knew the queen had a bounty on this lycan's head. It was shared all around on the news stations, and Stormey had even heard warriors talk about it and what they would do with the money.

"Ah, yes, the queen's bounty on my head." Azura lifted her hand with another smirk on her lips. The glint in her eyes sent a shiver down Stormey's spine. "I had heard the queen had placed a hefty sum on my head, but she will be sorely disappointed. My head likes its place on my neck and shoulders."

"Hegna will kill you," Stormey warned. There was no doubt in her mind that Hegna would deal with this lycan.

"The heir to the throne, she's no better than her father," Azura said.

Stormey's hands clenched into fists. If she were free, she would wipe that irritating smirk from the woman's face.

"You poor human. You don't even realize that the mate you are matched with is from a family of murderers."

"You lie," Stormey cried out. Hegna and her family did what they needed to for their people. She refused to believe anything Azura had to say. She would say anything to try to turn her against Hegna. For all Stormey knew, Azura wanted to change her into a lycan. Tears blurred her vision. Stormey grew angry at herself that the waterworks were about to spill. She didn't want to appear weak, she was pissed.

"And don't let me start on this matching system they came out with. It's just another way for them to snatch humans. I wish I would have come up with such a brilliant scam." Azura barked a sarcastic laugh. She bent down, her hand shifting into a massive paw.

Stormey leaned away from her. She watched Azura break through the ropes latched on to the cot to keep her in place. Both her arms and feet were free within seconds.

"The matching test works," Stormey said. She didn't know why she felt the need to argue with the lycan, but she refused to listen to her deny the authenticity of the test. She and Hegna were prime examples, as were Hegna's sisters and their mates. There was plenty of documentation that it was a valid test.

"Whatever. You're just a brainwashed human who has a kink for vampires." Azura stood back, her hand returning to human form. She narrowed her gaze on Stormey who was frozen in place, staring at the lycan.

"Excuse me?" Stormey gasped.

"I know all about you. Do you think I would go

through all of the trouble to kidnap the mate of the future queen of the vampires without checking into you? You are a human who wanted to be drafted and was lucky to be drawn to be the mate of the heir to the vampire throne," Azura sneered. She motioned to Stormey. "Get up."

"What are you going to do with me?" Stormey asked. She slowly slid her legs around and rested her feet on the floor. She didn't know how long she had been unconscious. Her muscles screamed as she slid forward to the edge of the cot. She took notice that her cloak was gone, but the same clothes she'd worn to the orphanage were still on. She eyed the two other lycans who were staring at her. Their eyes flared bright with something that she couldn't interpret. They stood as if they were dogs waiting on their master to give them an order.

Azura grunted and reached out and took Stormey by the arm. She dragged her to her feet and towed her behind her. Stormey winced from the tight hold Azura had on her.

"You, little human, will help me get the attention of the world," Azura said.

Stormey immediately didn't have a good feeling about this. Azura guided her across the room to the doorway through which she'd entered. They stepped through it and were in a small warehouse. The two men followed them without saying a word.

Stormey scanned the area and found more lycans milling around. Some of them threw glances at her but didn't say a word. It was a little daunting seeing them all gathered near. Would they want to attack her? It had fallen silent as Azura led her through them.

The room was filled with boxes, crates, and workbenches. It was divided up into different sections. There was an area with long metal tables and chairs as if used for dining, and an area with a bank of computers with a few men sitting before them. Stormey's gaze fell on the direction they were headed. There was a setup with lighting and a camera with a chair and a backdrop that looked very familiar.

Had Azura been doing her broadcast right under Hegna's nose? Was this their headquarters? Stormey had so many questions. Azura took her to a chair by the camera.

"Sit," Azura ordered. She thrust Stormey toward one of the chairs that was off camera.

Stormey leaned back in the seat as Azura bent down toward her.

"Don't even think of running. My wolves would love to get a taste of fresh meat such as yourself."

Stormey wordlessly nodded. Azura walked over to the men working on the computers and talked to them in a low tone. Stormey strained to hear what they were saying, but unfortunately, her human hearing wasn't that good.

Stormey's hands balled into tight fists. She felt all eyes on her. She may be putting on a brave front, but she wasn't stupid. Her bravery waivered slightly. She glanced down at her hands and tried to keep cool.

Hegna would come for her.

Whatever emergency that had caused her to leave, was that a sham? It had to be. Azura had stated she had organized her kidnapping. Stormey shivered, not wanting to think what the lycan alpha had planned for her. She just hoped that Hegna would be arriving soon. She had never wished violence on anyone, but she did now.

Stormey hoped Hegna came and chopped the lycan's head off.

"Where is she?" Azura asked a female who stood by her.

The woman kept her eyes down. She swallowed

hard and hesitated to answer as if afraid of what Azura would do to her. "I don't know."

Azura growled and stepped closer to her. She brandished long, sharp fangs. The woman whimpered, attempting to make herself smaller. Stormey watched, almost feeling sorry for the female.

"What do you mean you don't know where my sister is?" Azura snapped.

Her hand whipped out and took the woman by the neck. She dragged her near her, and Stormey was sure she was going to bite the woman or snap her neck.

"You go and get her on the phone for me now."

"Yes, Alpha."

The look of terror on the woman's face sent a tremor through Stormey. Azura released her. The woman stumbled back and quickly righted herself. She spun around and scrambled to get away. She ran past Stormey as if the Devil himself was behind her.

Azura turned back to the men she had been speaking with as if nothing had happened. Stormey's breaths were coming rapidly. Fear was officially gripping her.

Azura spun toward her and sniffed the air. She smirked and walked toward Stormey.

"Ah, is someone afraid?" Azura chuckled. Her golden eyes grew more menacing as she got closer to Stormey. She stopped in front of her, lifting a hand and brushing the tendrils of hair away from her face. "Having doubts that your murdering vampire will save you?"

"She will." Stormey refused to believe anything else. Her mate would come for her. She and her warriors would rain down hell on these lycans. She refused to cower away from Azura.

Something that looked like respect passed through Azura's eyes.

"Let me tell you about the royal vampire family. My people were enslaved for centuries. Serving them. Protecting them. Promises were made to my people that one day we would see our freedom. We would be treated as equals." Azura snarled. The room fell quiet with everyone listening. The woman's face darkened while she paced. "We fell for their lies, and the moment we demanded our freedom and all that was promised to us, they refused. So the uprising began, and do you know what they did?"

Stormey shook her head. She was too afraid at this point to say anything. Her heart was racing fast watching Azura pace in front of her. This was history that certainly wasn't in any of the books she'd reviewed with Miss Lavana.

"Of course you wouldn't know. They have brainwashed the entire world. But I'm going to tell you what they did. They tried to erase us from existence. They went around killing our men, women, and children." Azura yanked Stormey from her chair and pushed her toward the one in front of the cameras.

Stormey's fear had taken control of her. She barely sat in the new chair, almost falling out of it. She straightened and sat still.

"You heard me right. The king ordered the killing of young babies. My mother was lucky to survive, and you know what we are going to do for payback?"

Stormey shook her head once again. Her body was trembling uncontrollably. Her eyes went blurry from the gathering of tears. She blinked, and a warm trail of wetness ran down her face.

"We have you, the mate of the future vampire queen, and we will kill you on live television for the entire world to see."

CHAPTER TWENTY-TWO

Hegna stood and eyed the large fire that blazed before her. The flames grew, reaching for the dark sky. The past few days had been one bloody battle. She had planned for Lethia to arrive with her two human captives where they could try to lure the alpha out of hiding.

But plans had changed the moment they'd come under attack.

She was proud of her warriors. They were victorious and had driven most of the lycans back and had them running. They were now in the middle of what would have been known as downtown Sanlow. Buildings that once stood busy and full of life were hollowed shells of what they once were. Where once had stood the town's Christmas tree was a makeshift pyre, with the bodies of those lycans who'd fought for their alpha.

The scent of burning flesh filled the air. Hegna was now immune to it. Bodies of lycans needed to be burned to ensure their death. Hegna and her army had used the latest weaponry to combat the lycans, but Hegna wanted to be sure they crossed over to the afterlife. Even with the snow that covered the ground and the icy cold wind that blew, the heat from the fires provided only a slight warmth.

She bit back a growl. Azura thought she would eliminate her, but the lycan had failed. The lycan alpha was growing bolder. She knew eventually Hegna would come to this town that they'd overrun. Too bad the alpha was too cowardly to meet her on this battlefield.

Blood coated Hegna's fighting leathers. Her daggers had tasted the flesh of many lycans. She rested a hand on the hilt of one of them, circling the handle.

"There are more bodies, Your Grace." Nezera grimaced, coming to stand next to Hegna. The captain had been vital in their defeat of the lycans. Her attention to detail had been key.

Hegna would ensure the woman was rewarded. She believed in making sure her warriors were compensated for doing their jobs well.

"Burn them," Hegna replied. Their business here in Sanlow was almost complete. They had done a full sweep of the town, and there were no humans to be found. If any had survived, they must have escaped. "I want to speak with this informant of yours."

"Yes, Your Grace. We were also able to capture a lycan to be questioned, but he's not giving up any information."

"I'll get it," Hegna growled. There was no hiding from the memories that lingered in blood. She turned and followed Nezera.

They walked along the pathway that led to the main road. Her men were patrolling the area, checking it was safe for them. They didn't want to be caught off guard with another lycan attack.

"I want to make sure what happened here gets out to the masses. If Azura wants to put everything on television, then we will do the same."

“Are you sure that is wise?” Nezera asked quietly.

Hegna paused and faced her captain. It wasn’t often her officers questioned her.

Another gust of cold air blew past them. Hegna shivered slightly from it. She reached up and held on to the fur cloak that rested on her shoulders. She didn’t like being cold. The minute she got a chance, she would go and shower to wash the lycan blood off her and relax her muscles. Her stomach felt hollow. The small amounts of bagged blood she was able to consume gave her little strength.

Another reason for her to hurry home and bind herself to her mate. Stormey’s blood gave her such a thrilling rush of power.

“Do you think I am wrong?” she asked. She was reining in the rage that was burning inside her. Because of this lycan issue, she was apart from her mate. She should be at home with Stormey, sinking her fangs into her throat while offering her own blood to Stormey to bind them to each other forever.

“I’m only thinking that if we did, we could be causing a worldwide panic with the humans if they see we are warring with the lycans.” Nezera stood tall and met Hegna’s gaze head-on.

Hegna appreciated that her captain was looking at the greater picture, but there were some decisions that Hegna would be the one to gamble on.

"I appreciate your opinion, Captain, but that's just what the humans need to see. They need to understand that we are still the top of the food chain. We are in control, and there is no one who can take that from us." Hegna glanced over Nezera's shoulder at the midnight sky with the trails of smoke drifting across it. "There are going to be times we need to remind the humans of our power. If not, they may take us as weak and may try to rise above us."

It had been the same for the lycans. No matter how Azura spun it. The lycans thought they were more powerful than the vampires. Their lives had been good. Vampires had treated them well when they'd been slaves. Their alpha had convinced the masses that they were of a higher race and deserved to rule. It was the lycans who'd attacked first, starting the war. Azura had been fed lies by someone. Hegna was convinced of it.

Had the wretched animals stayed in their place, things may have turned out differently.

"Yes, Your Grace. Now I understand your point

of view." Nezera slammed her fist on her chest above her heart.

Hegna jerked her head in a nod and continued walking along with Nezera. They had requisitioned a storefront and used it as a command center in the midst of town. Her warriors were swarming the town. There was no way that a lycan could get past them. It would be a death sentence if they did.

Nezera jogged a few steps ahead of Hegna and held the door open for her. Hegna stalked inside, thankful for the warmth that greeted her. Vampires may be powerful beings, but they had to submit to the weather just as any other creature walking the earth.

At one point, this particular space had been used as a restaurant. Old tables and chairs remained strewn around. Nezera had brought in some of their communication and computers, where they would have access to outside the town. Some of her warriors were working and showed their respect to her as the passed them.

"The new prisoner is downstairs," Nezera reported. "And our informant is in the back room. Who would you like to see first?"

"The prisoner," Hegna replied automatically.

She and Nezera cut through the kitchen that

appeared as if the place was just closed for the night. It had been cleaned, and everything was still in place. The lycans must have struck during the middle of the night. Had they attacked the humans during the day or evening, this kitchen would not be this clean.

They arrived at a stairwell near the back entry where the shipping dock was located. They were greeted by a warrior standing at the bottom of the stairs. He pounded his fist on his chest when she passed. The basement was open with storage along the wall and a few refrigerators and freezers lining it. It was damp, cool, with little light. There was a lightbulb hanging from the ceiling above the prisoner.

There were five vampires standing with their guns loaded with argentite bullets pointed at a large lycan kneeling on the floor. He was in his human form. Dark hair hung in tangled strands, brushing his muscular bare shoulders. Dirty jeans covered the lower half of his body. His wrists were held together by silver handcuffs that were chained to the collar around his neck. If he were to shift, the collar would inject a lethal dose of argentite liquid directly into his bloodstream.

Hegna stopped in front of him. His amber eyes

rose and met Hegna's. He appeared familiar to her, but at the moment she couldn't place him. Hegna slid her cloak off her shoulders and handed it off to one of the warriors. She stepped closer to the prisoner, and he tilted his head back.

"Hegna Riskel," his deep voice rumbled. A smirk appeared on his lips.

"You will greet the princess with respect," the warrior directly behind the lycan snapped.

The five of them raised their weapons higher, waiting for Hegna to give the command.

"My apologies." The lycan chuckled. His smile disappeared, and his amber eyes darkened. "But she is not who I bow down to."

"Where is your alpha?" Hegna rested a hand on the hilt of her dagger. She didn't have time for games. If he wasn't going to tell her what she wanted to hear, then he would die.

"Even if I knew, I wouldn't tell you."

Hegna closed the gap between them and grabbed him by his face. Her grip was punishing as she glared into his eyes. His body vibrated from the growl echoing through his chest. He narrowed his gaze on her. She felt his fangs elongating underneath her fingertips.

"There is more than one way for me to gather

information from you," she said. Hegna's fangs pushed through her gums, descending. Blood was the key to everything. Not only was it life for her kind, but information was able to be obtained from it.

"I don't know anything. I'm just a soldier." His words were muffled due to her grip on his face. From the size of him, he was more than what he let on. Lycans who were bitten and turned didn't get to his size. They were learning that the true-born lycans were much larger. Maybe it was due to evolution or genetics or breeding.

It didn't matter.

Vampires would still prevail.

"Then you won't mind if I have a little taste." Hegna signaled to her men and stepped back.

They all came and converged on the lycan.

"I said I don't know anything!" he shouted.

He fought against them, but her men were able to bring him to his feet. His chest rose and fell rapidly. Hatred was evident in his eyes, but Hegna couldn't care less. She would take what she needed from him and be done with him. The lycan would give her all the answers.

Compulsion would not work on him. He was strong and put up a valiant fight until her men were able to pull his arms away from his body and keep them outstretched for her. She was going to have to move fast. He wasn't going to tolerate her biting him for long.

"And you call us savages," he spat.

He struggled even more, but they held him for her. One of her warriors had an arm around his head now, locking him into place.

She smirked at him. Ignoring the jab. Throwing out names wouldn't get him anywhere. She grabbed the arm nearest her and leaned her head down, sinking her fangs into his wrist. The moment his blood touched her tongue, she was hit with memories. It flashed before her eyes as if she were there with him.

The memories flew by, like flashes of light. Meetings in darkened caves. Ring fighting amongst lycans. A caravan moving along a familiar street. A truck slamming into an armored sedan. Images of Hegna standing before him with her dagger drawn. Her back while fighting another lycan. Then him grabbing her and sinking his fangs into her shoulder. Him running off at the sound of a howl. Lycans running through the woods. Standing before a woman who looked eerily similar to Azura. But it wasn't her, and this woman appeared to be in charge.

Hegna lifted her head, now recognizing him. It was the large lycan who had bitten her. She glared at him, releasing his arm. His blood slid down her chin, but she didn't wipe it away.

"Who is the woman? The one who called you lycans away that night?" she demanded. Hegna already knew. If she would have kept drinking from him, she would have probably got her answer. Too bad the memories didn't come in sound.

His lips curled up into a devious grin. He jerked forward, but her men held him back. Hegna licked her lips and reached for her dagger. Her men held his head back, brandishing his throat to her.

"I am loyal to my kind," he growled. His eyes were crazed, burning with rage as he stared at her. He continued to struggle against her warriors' hold. "You're going to have to kill me."

"Very well then." Hegna shrugged.

She swung her dagger rapidly across his neck. Blood gushed from the wound. His eyes widened as he struggled to breathe and swallow. Gurgling soon followed. Her men let him go, his body falling to the floor.

She spun on her heels and walked past Nezera. "Put a bullet in his head and burn his body."

"What other woman did you see?" Nezera asked, following behind her.

The sound of a gunshot echoed behind them. They jogged up the stairs and once again were in the kitchen.

"There was another woman in his memories that looked just like Azura," Hegna announced. She spun around and faced her captain. Hegna's mind was racing with all different possibilities. If the daughter of Ariston had survived, then that would be how Azura was related to the deceased alpha. And if her mother had Azura, then there were quite possibly other children. "It would seem as if Azura has a sister. There may be two alphas we are dealing with."

"Your Grace." Bijou stormed into the kitchen.

Hegna spun around and immediately sensed something was off.

"What is wrong, General?" Hegna reached up and wiped the drying lycan blood off her chin. She walked toward Bijou. Something passed in her friend's eyes that she didn't like.

"You need to come with me," Bijou said.

The hairs on the back of Hegna's neck stood up

on end. She glanced over at Nezera who appeared to be unaware of what Bijou was about to share with them. She followed Bijou out of the kitchen and back into the dining area. Someone had placed a television on a table. It was on, and immediately, Hegna recognized the voice of the person speaking. The warriors surrounding the television parted to allow her, Bijou, and Nezera through. Hegna stopped directly in front. She folded her arms and listened to what the alpha was rambling on about.

"I'm sure some of you are wondering what life would be like once I take over." Azura grinned. The camera zeroed in on her. The lycan alpha's hair was combed for once. Her long dark locks flowed over her shoulder. Her amber eyes were bright, and she almost looked manic as she spoke. "Just imagine life where you don't have to be afraid to go outside your home after dark. You'd be able to walk down the street without the fear of not knowing if a bloodsucker compelled you, taking your blood."

"And they would be safe from lycans?" Bijou muttered.

Hegna didn't respond. There was something about this broadcast that didn't sit right with her. She couldn't put her finger on it, but this was different than the last one.

"Are we trying to track this down?" Hegna asked.

"Our men have been on it since the moment it started a few minutes ago. Since the last one, we've been monitoring the airwaves, waiting for the moment she did another one," Bijou reported.

"Good." Hegna didn't take her eyes off the screen. She watched Azura as she continued to speak. The woman in the lycan's memory had a very close resemblance, and she was willing to bet they were not only sisters, but twins.

Fucking twin alphas.

Working together, they would be more powerful.

"Your Grace. There is an urgent phone call on hold for you." A warrior walked up to her with a phone in his hand.

Hegna held hers up. They would have to wait. She couldn't miss what this lycan was talking about.

"Wait," Hegna snapped.

"But it's Lord Apostu. He said you need to take his call now," the brave warrior said.

Hegna ignored him. Corbin could wait one more minute. She was in the middle of a war zone. Her friend didn't understand that what she was dealing with was top priority at the moment.

"King Niall," Azura called out. She grinned,

brandishing her fangs for the entire world to see. Her eyes narrowed on the camera. "You will relinquish your throne. It's time a lycan ruled. How you will give it up? Why, death, of course."

"Over my dead body," Hegna growled. This lycan was making too many threats against her father. This was going to end with that lycan's head hanging from a spike. Hegna would have one specially built just for the occasion.

"And as for the princess. Your heir," Azura continued.

Hegna growled again, moving closer to the television screen. She didn't want to miss one word that would come out of her mouth.

"Princess Hegna Riskel, the future queen of the vampires. I hear congratulations are in order."

A sudden chill slithered down Hegna's spine. She didn't like the glint in Azura's eyes. The lycan was certainly up to something, and Hegna hated it.

Corbin's voice was shouting through the phone, but she couldn't take her eyes off the screen. Azura went out of sight for a moment before pushing forward the one person Hegna would burn the entire world down for.

Her mate.

Stormey's eyes were wide with fear. She didn't look harmed, but her human was straight terrified. Azura grinned again while yanking Stormey close to her.

"It's time that we start treating the vampires the way they did my people. In two days' time, this woman, the mate of Princess Hegna Riskel, will be executed right here on national television."

The screen went blank.

Hegna's heart had leaped into her throat. The room around her was dead silent. Anger boiled inside her. Why hadn't anyone notified her that her mate had been kidnapped?

Hegna yanked the phone from the warrior and put it up to her ear. Corbin was yelling her name.

"How long has that fucking lycan had my mate?" Hegna's voice was surprisingly calm. A coolness radiated through her as she thought of all the ways she was going to kill not only Azura, but her sister as well. She was going to make them wish they had never crawled out of whatever hole they'd come from.

"It's been maybe an hour or two," Corbin gasped. Her friend sounded frantic which was not like him. He usually was cool, collected, and holding all the knowledge she would need to possess. "There was an ambush when she was leaving the orphanage. They took her then."

"I don't care what you have to do, who you have to have killed, I want to know where they are," Hegna ordered. She glanced over at Bijou who was shouting orders to prepare the helicopter. "I'm on my way."

CHAPTER TWENTY-THREE

It had been one day since Hegna had watched Azura drag her mate before a television camera. Hegna strode down the hallway toward the war planning room. Her vampires had been working ever since the broadcast had ended. Sleep had evaded Hegna. There was no way she would be able to sleep when her mate was in the hands of their enemy. She had gone to her private quarters, and the scent of her mate was everywhere.

Hegna's hands balled into tight fists. They were going to find her mate and that wretched alpha.

She would not rest until Stormey was back in her arms.

Hegna made a promise that she would end that lycan's life. The moment she'd taken Stormey, Azura had signed her death warrant.

The guards in front of the double doors took notice of her walking toward them. They rushed to open the doors for her. They bowed and thumped their chests. She nodded and continued on. The room was buzzing with vampires scurrying around trying to find some clue as to where Stormey could be.

The round table that held the electronic map of the country was in the center of the room. Rows of tables with computers lined the back wall with men and women hunched over the keyboards. Bijou and Corbin stood at the table, conversing.

"Let's review everything we know," Hegna demanded. She arrived at the table and leaned her hands on it. She tapped on the screen of the map and shifted it to their town. She marked the street where Stormey had been taken. It wasn't far from the orphanage. Stormey had fallen quickly in love with the orphanage the moment she had first stepped foot in it. Hegna wanted to give her mate whatever she wanted, and for Stormey, that was to ensure the forgotten children were taken care of.

Hegna would move the heavens and earth to ensure she got her mate back. She didn't like this feeling of helplessness. Never in all of her years had she experienced emotions like this. Stormey held more of her heart than she had known. As much as she'd tried to push the woman away, she had taken possession of it. Her mate was the calmness to her rage. The light to her darkness. Stormey was a vital part of her life, and she needed her.

Hegna never thought she would be in a place such as this. She had always figured that when she did have a mate, she would keep that person safe. She was one of the deadliest vampires in the world, and while fighting the lycans, she had failed her mate.

She vowed that when Stormey returned, she would make this up to her. She would never fail her again.

For now, she had to focus. Hegna's gaze traced the route Stormey had taken leaving the orphanage and rested her hand on the virtual representation of the building.

Stormey had gone to the orphanage to meet with the head mistress, Emily, and the architect,

Zach Singleton. Who else had known her mate was going there? The lycans apparently knew exactly where they were and had drawn them away from the orphanage.

"Who all knew my mate's whereabouts that day?" Hegna asked.

She focused on Corbin who pulled out his tablet and swiped the screen.

"Aside from the security detail, myself, the orphanage, and the architect," Corbin responded. He continued typing commands into the table before looking up at her. "I have reviewed the videos taken by the street cameras, and it didn't appear they were followed."

"At least not in a vehicle," Bijou said.

The general had returned to Black Hollow with Hegna. Nezera had assured them that she could finish up in Sanlow. They had devised a plan for the now-vacant town once their army pulled out. Bijou tapped on the screen and revealed what the cameras had captured five minutes before Stormey's vehicle had come down the street.

"For all we know, the lycans could have been in their human forms blending in with humans."

"That is true. Newly turned lycans won't stick out like sore thumbs," Corbin said.

Hegna studied the street, and it would be hard to distinguish between humans and any lycans trying to blend in with them.

"Look into the volunteers at the orphanage and the architect. I want to know everything about their financials, their loved ones, and if there has been any recent changes." Humans had a way of turning on their own kind. Some of them were honorable until they became desperate.

"Already in motion. So far, everyone is clean," Corbin announced.

Hegna gave a nod, thankful her advisor was so thorough. Corbin had many contacts with the human who would give him whatever information he desired.

Hegna folded her hands together behind her back and paced as she thought of the events that had been shared with her. The men who were with Stormey had been attacked and left for dead, but thankfully, they would make a complete recovery. Ellanora worked tirelessly to ensure those men survived.

"What caused them to leave the orphanage?" Bijou asked. She made the screen return back to the image of the orphanage.

"According to Desmond, they had received intel

that there was a lycan attack nearby, and for Stormey's safety, they felt it was necessary to leave and return her to the castle," Hegna replied automatically. She had spent some time in the infirmary with her warriors. It had been Henry's first assignment that included her mate, but Desmond, like everyone else, had a close attachment to Stormey. Desmond was already ready to dive into battle for his charge.

"Who sent the communication?" Bijou frowned.

"Not I." Corbin shook his head. "The only reason I knew they had left the orphanage early was because of Emily calling to confirm the next meeting with the architect."

The room fell silent.

Hegna wanted to throw something. Was there a traitor in her house? A red veil slid in front of her eyes. She would tear whoever it was limb from limb.

Who would have the technology to hack into their system?

"So you are telling me that someone may have infiltrated my system? How is that fucking possible?" Hegna roared.

The tension in the room thickened. Her gaze fell on the vampires sitting at the computers. Her computer specialists were top-notch. She stalked over to them and stood in front of her lead technology vampire.

June Kline was a computer hacker who had once been human. She had been one of the most infamous illegal hackers before the beginning of the war. She had been a wanted woman by countless governments until she'd died at the hands of a rogue vampire and then turned.

Hegna had hired June in the midst of the war. June had been vital in overrunning the human technology. It wasn't as advanced as vampires', but the woman could work magic.

"Explain how this could have happened?" Hegna growled.

June swallowed hard. Hegna had to give it to the woman. She met Hegna's gaze without flinching.

"I'm going to look in on it now, Your Grace. This has never happened to me before. I'm the one usually hacking, not getting hacked." June's fingers flew across the keyboard. She concentrated on the laptop screen. "Give me a few hours, and I'll have something for you."

"You have forty-five minutes," Hegna said. She glanced down at the row of computer techies, and none looked up at her. She paid them all very well to ensure they had first-class cyber security, and this happened on their watch? Someone's head would roll if they didn't figure it out.

"Yes, ma'am," June murmured.

Hegna spun on her heel and strode back to the table. Her rage was boiling inside her, and she didn't know how much longer she would be able to hold it in. She needed to kill something or someone soon.

"There is no way that they could have moved Miss Jaymes that fast. What was the time frame from when she was left until the broadcast?" Bijou asked.

"From the time Emily called to the broadcast was about three hours," Corbin answered.

Hegna fell deep in thought. Could they have still been in town during the broadcast? Hegna slid her hand along the computer screen and zoomed out to review all parts of Black Hollow. Because of the war, there were plenty of abandoned buildings in and on the outskirts of town.

"Weren't there purchases of abandoned buildings recently?" Hegna asked. She remembered hearing that someone had bought some of the buildings and there were rumors of plans of renovating and reopening. She had been impressed but hadn't looked too closely at the company who had acquired them. The world was starting to get back on its feet. The devastation from the war was great, and they were going in the right direction. "June."

Hegna spun around and eyed her hacker.

"Yes, Your Grace?" June paused what she was doing and looked up from the laptop.

"I want to know who was behind the purchases of any properties from the last five years," Hegna said.

"I'll put Peter on that task," June said.

The tall male sitting beside her gave a nod to confirm he'd heard her.

"Are you thinking that lycans bought those buildings?" Bijou murmured.

"Yes, and if they did, we know the first place to go look." Hegna stood back from the table and folded her arms in front of her. Ringing from the hologram box on the edge of the table sounded.

"It's the king," Corbin announced.

Hegna motioned for him to answer. He walked around the table and tapped on the box. Her father's and mother's images appeared in the room. Everyone knelt and bowed to the royal couple. Hegna bowed her head to her parents.

"I won't ask how you are doing, daughter," the

king's boisterous voice came across the room. His ice-blue eyes, the same as hers, watched her. His form walked over to her and came to stand in front of her.

She tilted her head back to meet his gaze.

"I can see in your eyes that you want blood," he said.

"I will do what my sister failed to do and kill the lycan," Hegna hissed.

"I received your disturbing message," he said. His infamous scowl appeared. "Are you sure there are two of them?"

She had sent word to her father immediately when she'd been in Sanlow. News that there were two alphas, twins, was not anything she wanted to hold back.

"I saw it in his blood memories," she replied. "You know as well as I do that memories do not lie."

"Well, be that as it may, it matters not that there are two of them. We will defeat them," the king snarled.

This man who stood before them was a vicious vampire who had led thousands of vampires to war. For Hegna and her sisters, he was everything. He was the one who would go to Hell and face down the Devil himself for his children and wife. The world didn't see him as they did. He was a loving father and husband who ensured his daughters were tough warriors trained from childhood to defend their people and everyone they loved.

"You have the full backing of the royal army," the queen said. She came to stand by her husband.

"Thank you, Mother." Hegna was thankful for her parents and appreciated them, but at the moment, she could handle getting her mate back. She had been through many tests in her life. She considered them all trials to prepare her for the day she would be queen.

This was going to be no different. She would succeed and get her mate back.

"I am going to do my own broadcast," the king announced.

Hegna arched an eyebrow at him. He had refused to do one before, not wanting to stoop to Azura's level.

Her father had always been larger than life. He was a force to be reckoned with. When he spoke, everyone listened. The human government was terrified of him, which they should be. They hadn't believed that Niall had armies and millions of vampires under his rule. According to the human leaders, vampires didn't exist.

Her father and the six other kings had taken the world by storm.

Hegna had a feeling they were going to do the same against the lycans.

"We will do it together, *miere*," the queen murmured. She rested a hand on her husband's arm. She had stood by her husband's side since the moment they'd been mated.

Hegna felt a tug on her heart. She wanted what her parents had. To be able to spend an eternity with the one person who completed her.

It had taken her too long to understand that. She promised that she would do all she could to make up for it when she got Stormey back.

If one hair was harmed on Stormey's head, Hegna would lose it.

No doubt about it.

She would kill anyone who dared to harm her mate.

"Like I would have it any other way," Niall said. He covered his wife's hand with his. Something passed between the two of them. He turned back to Hegna, his eyes hardening. "We will get on national television. Azura wants to play games. She wants to make threats against me. The lycan better damn well be able to back up those threats. She's a pup compared to me. I've fought larger and older lycans and won. I will squash her and her twin like the vermin they are."

Hegna's heart raced at the thought of fighting alongside her father. Niall Riskel was a legend in the vampire world, and he was well respected as a warrior and as a king.

"Don't lose your focus, daughter," the queen said.

Hegna turned to her mother, surprised. "I am focused," she bit out around her fangs. It had been extremely difficult to walk around their private area, scent her mate, but not have her to hold. Hegna wanted Stormey in her arms again. She wanted to be able to nuzzle her neck with her face and breathe her in. Her voluptuous body belonged pressed against Hegna's muscular frame. "So fucking focused that I have imagined all of the ways I will kill Azura."

A glint appeared in her eyes that alluded to the queen's own bloodthirsty need for vengeance. The same lycan had threatened her mate and would not go unpunished.

"There will be time for bloodshed, daughter. I

promise you this. The lycans will pay for everything. Spreading lies, attacking our towns, threatening your king and taking your mate." The queen held her head high, a devious grin appearing on her lips. She was just as dangerous as her husband. The lycans didn't know how truly fucked they were. They wanted the attention of the royal family on them.

They had it.

Her sisters were a phone call away. Their armies were ready to go at a moment's notice.

Her mother was right. No matter how much she wanted to go out and kill every single lycan who crossed her path, it would not do her any good. They were loyal to their alpha—alphas—and would not roll over and give away their position.

"If you need us, don't hesitate to call for backup," her father growled. He glared at Hegna.

She was known to be a hothead and had been told she was just like her father. She bit her lip, denying she would need them.

"Yes, Father."

Her father stared at her for another moment before he motioned for the call to end. The room appeared to breathe once the royal couple's hologram images were no longer present. Hegna glanced over at Bijou who gave her a comforting nod.

"Your Grace!" June rose from her laptop. The hacker stood, determination lining her face. She held papers. "We have what you asked for."

"What do you have?" Hegna strode over to her. She was immediately hit with the slight scent of fear coming from some of the techies. She eyed them but dismissed their fear. If they gave her what she wanted, then there was no need to be afraid of her. This was a critical time, and there was no room for mistakes.

"First, I found traces of the hacker who got into our system. I assure you that we will seal it and this will never happen again." June lifted her chin and met Hegna's hard gaze. She handed the papers over to Hegna. "Second, I found the recent purchase agreements of two warehouses and I was able to trace them back to multiple dummy corporations. But lucky enough, our team is the best, and we were able to zip through all of the red tape. The owner of the properties listed on those papers is Rayna Vaughn."

"Who?" Hegna asked.

"Rayna Vaughn is the sister to Azura Michaels."

Hegna flipped through the papers and took notice that Rayna Vaughn owned three large buildings in Black Hollow and countless within her territory alone.

"Good job," Hegna said. She looked up at June who appeared relieved. "Take care of the break in our system."

"Yes, Your Grace," all of the techies echoed.

Hegna moved back to Bijou and Corbin and tossed the papers on the table. She leaned down, gripping the edge of it tight.

"How bad is it?" Corbin asked. He picked up the papers and eyed them. A whistle slipped from his lips before he passed them to Bijou.

The general glanced down at the papers. "Your Grace. The warriors are ready. We can separate and coordinate this within twenty minutes."

"Good." Hegna stood to her full height. She trusted her second-in-command would do as she promised. The men and women who served her were highly trained and would not rest until they had accomplished the mission. "We have less than twenty-four hours to find my mate. I will not accept failure in this."

CHAPTER TWENTY-FOUR

Stormey closed her eyes and leaned back against the wall. After her debut on national television, she'd been dragged away and thrown into a little room. It wasn't the one that she'd woken up in, but it at least allowed her to be alone. There was a small cot that was harder than the cement floor. A hole in the floor in the corner was her toilet. She grimaced thinking of the scent that rose from it.

She had lost track of time and didn't know how long she had been in there. Someone had brought her a tray of food. It was bland chicken, rice, and a cup of water. She wasn't sure when the next meal would come so she'd forced herself to eat it. She had to keep up her strength for when Hegna rescued her.

And she would come for her.

That was what kept Stormey going. She knew Hegna would not rest until she had brought her home.

Stormey tried to not think that Azura's plan was to execute her on television. This was not how she'd imagined her death. Stormey saw herself growing old, with several generations of family members surrounding her. She and Hegna would pass through time together.

Dying at the hands of a lycan was never a consideration.

A shiver rippled through her at the thought. She wondered how Azura planned to do it. Would she shoot her? Stab her? Slit her throat? Poison her? These dark thoughts kept filling her mind, and she had a hard time pushing them away.

The one thing that scared her the most was, would there be pain?

She bit back a cry and opened her eyes. She stared around her prison and wished there was a window. Her sense of time was thrown off. She had no way of knowing if it was day or night or even how much time she had left.

"She's going to come save me," Stormey whispered. She inhaled deeply and forced all of the negative thoughts back. She had to be strong. She *was* strong. She exhaled, and her heart rate slowly declined. "My mate is going to kill that lycan and take me home."

The door handle jiggled, and she practically jumped from her spot on the floor. Her heart slammed against her chest. Was this it?

The door opened, and a man with disheveled blond hair, large amber eyes, a muscular physique, wearing only jeans that rode low on his waist, and boots, entered. He carried a tray that signaled it was time for her to eat. He set the tray down in the middle of the room a few feet from her.

"Eat," his deep voice cut through the air.

He turned his back on her and walked out of the room, slamming the door. The lock engaged, and then there was silence outside the door. Her stomach chose that moment to make itself known. She hadn't realized how hungry she was.

Stormey crawled to the tray and dragged it over to her. She returned to her seat and eyed the food. She bit her lip and wondered if she was to die by poison, had they already started? Was this food tainted?

"Stop it," she groaned. She closed her eyes and tried to draw in strength. She eyed the food again and sighed. She had to eat it. No matter that it looked like. There was a bowl of what appeared to be oatmeal, two cold pieces of toast, and water. Her captors weren't kind enough to give her anything to try to doctor the food.

She lifted the spoon and brought it up to her lips. There was slight steam to it.

"At least it's warm," she murmured. She grimaced at the first taste. It was oatmeal and was downright horrible. How did one mess up oatmeal? She grabbed the cup and took a sip of her water. "Eat. You'll need your strength."

Stormey continued eating until it was all gone. She held back a belch, hit by a wave of nausea. She pushed the tray away and stood. She would hate to vomit on herself or where she sat.

She focused on her breathing and walked around in her small room. Her thoughts turned to Hegna. Had she'd seen the broadcast? It was obvious Azura was taunting Hegna. She wanted the princess to come after her. But why the games? Why not just demand a fight and the best woman wins—and lives?

Stormey continued to pace her tiny prison until she grew tired. She went over to her cot and got on it, scooting back until she was in the corner. She leaned her head against the wall to wait.

"Hegna is coming," she chanted softly to herself. Her eyes drifted shut. She tensed and opened them, but again felt them close. "Just a short nap."

Her eyes fluttered closed, and she fell asleep. She didn't know how long she was asleep, but the sound of someone unlocking her door awakened her. Stormey sat straight up, fear clutching her. She blinked a few times, trying to clear the blurriness from her vision. The door opened, and Azura herself stalked inside.

The alpha had her hair tied up into bun on top of her head. Her amber eyes glowed bright as she stared at Stormey.

"Let's go," Azura growled.

"Where are you taking me?" Stormey whimpered. The strength and bravery faded away fast.

Azura moved over to the cot and snatched Stormey by her arm. The woman's strength almost had her ripping Stormey's shoulder out of the socket. Stormey winced and followed behind Azura.

She tripped over her feet before righting herself. "You're hurting me."

"Quit your whining," Azura snapped.

She dragged Stormy down a hall. Her grip tightened even more, bringing tears to Stormey's eyes. They arrived at the end of the hall and took a left. Sounds of growls and shouts filled the air.

"You humans are only good for one thing for the vampires. But you steadily bow down to them as if they are gods."

"And lycans would be better? You'd force us to become one of you—"

"You'd gain power." Azura spun around suddenly.

Stormey crashed into her. Azura's eyes were crazed, narrowing on Stormy. Her lips arched up into a sadistic grin.

"The vampires don't share their gifts with the world. They just take what they want from humans until there is nothing left. Literally draining the life from you."

"You don't know what you are talking about," Stormey whispered.

Azura had no idea. Vampires and their mates

were happy. They felt the bond and honored that they were meant to be together. Hegna and her family were building bridges with the human government. They just needed more time for them to fully trust vampires.

“They don’t go running around changing humans because not all the humans would survive.”

“Same for lycans, but we are still willing to give our power to you puny humans. Imagine a world where everyone was strong, powerful, and lived long lives. You wouldn’t have to hide from the sun. The world I want to create would be heaven.”

“You’re crazy.” The words escaped Stormey’s lips before she’d even thought about it. But she wasn’t going to take it back. It was the truth.

The woman standing before her was downright loco. Azura threw her head back and barked a harsh laugh that sent chills down Stormey’s spine.

“I don’t know what I’m talking about?” Azura gripped Stormey’s chin and forced her head both ways.

A growl escaped the alpha as she leaned in and sniffed Stormey’s neck. She lifted her head, and Stormey hated the smirk on her lips.

“The princess who is supposed to be your mate

has fed from you but hasn't claimed you. Why is that?"

"That's none of your business." Stormey refused to explain her relationship with Hegna. No matter what the alpha thought, she was wrong on all counts.

Azura took her by the arm and dragged her behind her again. The sounds of growls and shouting grew louder. They bypassed an open door where a crowd of lycans gathered. She shivered, thankful they weren't going in there. From what she'd heard, lycans must have been in there fighting for sport with onlookers.

Stormey lost track of where they were going. They burst through a set of double doors, and she froze in place. They were in the same warehouse as yesterday, only things were different. An area was set up as a studio, with bright lights aimed at the white backdrop. They had altered the studio from before, and what she saw had the fear in her skyrocketing. There was a mat on the floor, and next to it was a small table. A sword sat on it, and immediately, Stormey's fight or flight instinct kicked in.

Azura truly planned to kill her on national television.

"No!" Stormey screamed. She struggled and fought Azura's hold.

The alpha laughed, wrapping an arm around Stormey's waist. She lifted her as if she weighed nothing.

"Let me go!" Stormey continued to kick and scream.

Azura carried her over to the mat. The other men and women in the room didn't even try to help her.

They wouldn't.

They were lycans and loyal to their alpha.

Tears flowed down Stormey's cheeks. Azura dropped her on the mat. Stormey scrambled to move, but the alpha's foot planted in the middle of Stormey's back, holding her in place.

"Give me something to restrain her," Azura growled.

Someone knelt next to Stormey and yanked her arms behind her. She cried out from the burst of pain that rippled through her shoulders. Her hands were forced together, and rope was tied around her wrist extremely tight.

Stormey let go and allowed the sobs to take over her. There was no way she could fight these lycans. She thought of all the things in life she wanted to accomplish. It wasn't fair that her life would be shortened due to someone's hatred. She'd had goals. Complete the bond with her mate. Motherhood. Fighting for the orphans and taking on the government to lower adoption fees. Helping bridge the gap between human and vampire relations. Have a long, fulfilling life with her mate.

Was that too much to ask?

Azura grabbed her by her arms and hauled her up into a kneeling position.

"Someone bring a towel and wipe her face," Azura shouted.

Stormey didn't care what she looked like. If her death was to be on television for the world to see, then she wanted them to truly see how this was affecting her. How this was torture and cruel.

"We want our star to look her best."

A woman arrived in front of Stormey and wiped her face. She was gentle while she cleaned off Stormey's skin, but it didn't matter to Stormey. She inhaled shakily and wanted to think of all the people who'd brought joy to her life. She didn't want her last thoughts to be of anything else. She thought of Maisie and her smile. Stormey had connected with the little girl. Maisie was full of life and happiness, even though she had been dealt a shitty hand. Stormey wanted to keep seeing her smile, but now—

Happy thoughts only, Stormey Jaymes.

Then Hegna's image came to mind.

They had made such progress in recent weeks. Even though she'd had a short time with her mate, Stormey would cherish it. Hegna had finally come to the reality that they belonged together and that fate had designed them for one another. An ache settled in Stormey's chest. She would have loved to complete their bond and go through life as Hegna's partner and mate.

"We're ready, Alpha," a deep voice said. A large man stood behind the camera. His hand adjusted the lens.

Stormey blinked and looked around. She had been so lost in her thoughts that she hadn't realized so many people had been working around her. Cameras were now focused on her. The lights were brighter. A small crowd stood watching. Azura stood at her side with an evil gleam in her eyes.

Stormey's heart raced again.

This would be it.

"Good. I want this on every outlet across the world," the alpha snapped.

Stormey jumped at the force of Azura's words.

The alpha stood tall, making her demands known. "I want patrols upped while we are doing this broadcast. Once we are done here, be prepared to break this building down. We will be moving to join my sister."

Azura spoke as if she wasn't about to take a life. She acted as if this was just a daily task for her, not something horrific. The alpha already had plans for once she left this building.

"Let's begin," Azura announced.

Stormey's vision blurred as fresh tears accumulated. They spilled out and ran down her face. She held her head up and refused to cower. If this was how her life ended, so be it. A red light slowly blinked on the camera. Stormey tried to focus on that.

"Good day, world. It is I, Azura Matthews," the alpha proclaimed.

There was an uplift to her words. She actually sounded excited for this. How could someone be so cruel as to want to kill an innocent woman? Stormey had done nothing but fall in love with her vampire.

Stormey felt it in her soul.

She was in love with Hegna Riskel.

She just wished she could tell Hegna to her face,

be held by her, kissed by her. She now regretted that she hadn't told Hegna. She'd die, and her mate would never know how she truly felt about her. Sadness filled Stormey. She swallowed hard and continued focusing on the red light, blocking out Azura's crazed rambling.

"There will be a new world where lycans rule. You've cowered to the vampires because you were weak. Well, me and my lycans are far from weak. We are powerful and will decimate the vampire rule. Join us, and I promise you there will be glory," Azura spat.

Stormey was sure humans were afraid, nervous, and feeling threatened. She knew her people. Some would run and hide, trying to avoid the clash between lycans and vampires, while there were some who still had fire in them. They would fight this. At least vampires didn't try to control every waking movement of the humans.

If Stormey had to choose between the two, she'd pick vampires every single time.

Humans wouldn't survive another war, and their leaders would more than likely bend to the will of whoever the victor was. Azura's crazed plan was to change as many humans to lycans as possible.

And she didn't care who died in the changing

process.

Stormey cried out from Azura latching on to her hair. The lycan laughed, entwining her fingers into Stormey's thick strands.

"Today will be the first of many televised executions. My ancestors were the victims of public executions. Killed like animals in front of crowds. The vampire king didn't want to allow the lycan alpha to rise to power and guide his people to a better life. Instead, he killed my grandfather, his wife, and sons." Azura tugged Stormey's head back and forced her to look straight ahead. "Tell the world your name, human."

Stormey swallowed hard and pushed her shoulders back. She straightened up and blew out a deep breath.

"My name is Stormey Jaymes, mate to the heir of the vampire throne, Princess Hegna Riskel, and warden—"

"I didn't ask for all of that, bitch," Azura growled. She yanked on Stormey's hair again.

Tears fell from Stormey's eyes from the sharp pain that exploded on her scalp. She blinked, trying to clear her vision. The warmth of tears slid down her cheeks. She tightened her jaw and dug down deep, finding strength she didn't think she had in her. With millions of people watching, she refused to cower.

And if Maisie happened to see this—

She prayed Emily would keep the little ones from watching something so horrific.

"As you can see, I have the mate to the king's daughter," Azura said.

The male behind the camera lifted his head, a puzzled expression on his shocked face. He turned back to look at the other guy who was sitting behind a computer.

Azura took notice, too. "What is going on?"

"Somehow our signal is blocked. The vampire king is now on television," the man behind the computer said.

"What?" Azura roared. "Get it back. Knock him off the air. Now!"

"I'm trying, Alpha."

"Try faster, or I will personally gut you," Azura threatened.

What color the man had vanished. He bent down and focused on the computer screen. Tension grew higher as they waited. Azura paced in front of Stormey before she froze and tilted her head to the side. Everyone else must have picked up on whatever caught her ear.

The wall behind the lycans across from Stormey exploded. Stormey fell back on her bottom due to the force of the explosion. Her ears rang, muffling the sounds of shouting and fighting. Stormey shook her head and tried to focus on what she was seeing before her. The men and women who had been in the audience had shifted and raced toward the wall.

Azura barked orders as more lycans rushed into the warehouse from the back. An alarm sounded through the building. Azura spun around, her glare landing on Stormey. She stalked toward her and yanked her to her feet.

"This changes nothing," Azura snapped.

Her amber eyes were practically glowering at Stormey. Her fangs were out, and slight hair was sprouting along her arms. The woman was close to shifting, and Stormey didn't want to be anywhere near her when she did.

"Vampires think they will stop me, but they are sorely mistaken."

Hope leaped into Stormey's chest. Was that Hegna? Had she found her? Stormey struggled against Azura's hold.

"Stop fighting, you dumb bitch." Azura tightened her grip on Stormey's arm and brought her in front of her.

She backed away as her lycans raced forward, engaging in the fight. She brought her free hand up and wrapped it around Stormey's neck. The sensation of sharp claws at her throat had Stormey pausing. It wouldn't take much for Azura to slice her arteries.

Azura bent down, her lips resting near Stormey's ear. "Look who it is."

Stormey's lip trembled while her heart raced. She caught sight of a familiar dark-haired vampire warrior taking down lycans with her twin daggers. Her movements were swift yet graceful. She swung her arms, sending the lycans' heads tumbling on the floor. She spun around, her gaze landing on Stormey.

She felt the connection to her vampire immediately.

Hegna had come for her.

"Azura!" Hegna shouted.

She stalked toward them with an expression so dark, Stormey was concerned about her vampire's mental state. Splatters of blood covered Hegna's face. She ignored it and advanced toward them.

"That's far enough, vampire," Azura warned.

Stormey whimpered from the piercing pain that appeared on one side of her throat. Something thick slowly trailed down the side of her neck.

"Withdraw your warriors."

"No," Hegna said.

"Then your mate will die right here," Azura threatened.

The lycan kept her other arm wrapped around Stormey's waist, holding her against her. Stormey held on to Hegna's gaze. She trusted that her vampire would rescue her and take her home.

"This building is surrounded by more vampires than lycans, Azura," Hegna said.

"Is that supposed to frighten me?" Azura threw back her head and laughed. Her hand dug into Stormey's side.

Stormey winced, feeling another set of claws on her stomach.

"You aren't in a position to threaten me. Let me and my wolves go, and I'll let your mate live."

"Not going to happen." Hegna shook her head and dropped down in a fighting stance. She was downright vicious with her request. Her fangs were on full display, and her laser focus was on Azura. "Let my mate go and come fight me like a woman."

"I don't think so," Azura snarled.

Her body jerked with force, her grasp loosening

around Stormey. It jerked again, the distinct sound of gunfire coming from behind her. Stormey tried to break out of her hold, but the lycan held on to her and brought her back to her.

Stormey screamed; pain lanced her belly and her neck. Azura's claws dug into her flesh, and agony like nothing she'd ever experienced surged through her. Her cry filled the air as her body grew weak. Azura flung her to the side. Her body flew through the air, landing hard on the floor. She rolled onto her side, cradling her stomach with one hand while her other one covered her neck.

She pulled her palm away from her stomach and lifted it. Blood covered her hand completely.

This was not good.

Weakness crept into her. Her vision blurred, but she tried to hold on. She twisted her head to the side and saw her mate engaged in a fight to the death with the lycan. Azura must have shifted fully into her beast form.

Stormey didn't want to distract her mate. She felt herself fading.

"I love you, princess," Stormey whispered. With all of the commotion, she doubted that Hegna had heard her, but she still needed to verbalize the words. At least the universe would have heard her.

She rested back on the floor, her gaze on the ceiling. A chill overtook her, and darkness clouded her vision. Wetness covered her skin and soaked her clothes. A peaceful feeling overcame her.

She closed her eyes momentarily; a bright, blinding light appeared suddenly. She blinked several times, her eyes needing to adjust. She turned her head and paused. A Black couple stood in the light. The woman appeared similar to Stormey while the man was handsome and tall.

Her parents.

Without even being told who they were, she just knew.

She smiled and tried to reach for them. She focused on their warm smiles and stood. She didn't feel pain anymore. Nothing but love filled her.

She took a step toward them but sensed she was leaving something behind that was important. Stormey glanced over her shoulder and was met with white clouds and a bright-blue sky. It was a beautiful sight to behold. She stood still and took it all in. She looked back at the couple who waved to her. Their welcoming smiles and open arms drew her to them.

They were still a distance away, but she would go to them.

CHAPTER TWENTY-FIVE

Hegna roared, sending her twin daggers directly into Azura's neck. The larger animal had been slowed down by the argentite bullets, but she had put up one hell of a fight. Hegna stared into Azura's eyes as the light began to fade.

"Know that you die at the hands of a vampire, lycan," Hegna growled. She gave a yell and pulled them out. Blood sprayed everywhere, but Hegna would not be satisfied until Azura's head rolled. She spun around with a hard force and sent the alpha's head flying through the air.

"Your Grace," Bijou's voice rang out.

The urgency had Hegna's head whipping around. She had never heard this tone in Bijou's voice before. She turned and found Bijou kneeling beside Stormey's eerily still body. Hegna sheathed her weapons and rushed to her mate's side.

She fell to her knees near Stormey, in shock. Stormey's injury was far worse than she'd thought. Her mate's blood was pooling on the floor underneath her. It was so much blood that Hegna feared Stormy was already gone.

"We need a healer," Hegna hollered. She reached out and swept a hand along her mate's cool face. Stormey's chest was rising and falling dangerously slowly. She tried to listen for her heart rate, but each beat was too far away from the next one. Her mate was dying before her.

Hegna's heart raced as fear crept inside her. She couldn't lose her mate. Not when she hadn't claimed her yet. Hegna bit back the rage and anger that exploded inside at herself. How had she not protected her mate again? She had been so focused on Azura that she hadn't realized the lycan had fatally wounded her mate.

She leaned forward and took in the wound on Stormey's neck. It was angry-looking with blood seeping from it. She moved down to Stormey's stomach where her shirt was drenched in blood. She lifted the material and bit back a curse at the sight of Stormey's belly. Azura's claws had mangled her flesh.

If she could kill Azura again, she would.

"She's not going to make it. She's lost too much blood," Bijou said quietly. Her friend rested a hand on Hegna's shoulder. Bijou's eyes were full of sorrow. They had lost plenty of warriors on the battlefield, but this was different. Stormey was an innocent. Even Bijou had connected with her mate. "Unless you try to turn her."

"She may not make it then," Hegna murmured. Panic swirled around inside her. Hegna never lost her cool, but seeing her mate standing on death's door had her close. She lifted her wrist and bit into her flesh. She held it over Stormey's stomach and allowed her blood to flow into the wound. She hoped her enzymes would staunch the flow of blood.

What Bijou had said was correct. The only way she could potentially save her mate would be to attempt to turn her. It had been a long while since she had done it. Her sister, Lethia, had turned her guard, Lane, saving his life. He had been on the brink of death when her sister had given him the choice.

Death or eternal life.

But Stormey was not conscious to be able to make the final decision. Hegna, as her mate, would have to make it. If she didn't attempt to turn her, then she'd lose her. If she did risk turning her and she didn't accept the change, then at least Hegna had tried her best.

She moved her hand and allowed her blood to flow onto Stormey's neck wound.

"I'm here, Your Grace." Aries, their combat healer, arrived at her side. The pale-skinned vampire had traveled along with Hegna for many battles over the years. She had trained under Ellanora and the king's personal healer. She sat next to Hegna, setting her bag down beside Stormey's head.

Hegna removed her hand and licked the holes on her wrist to seal them shut.

Aries began her assessment of Stormey. She paused once she got a good look at Stormey's abdomen. "Oh, no."

Aries immediately set to work going through her bag. She pulled out gauzes, soaking them with a fluid from a dark glass bottle. She pressed the bandages to Stormey's neck and motioned to Bijou to hold them in place. The general didn't hesitate. She, too, looked as helpless as Hegna felt.

"Do you think you can save her?" Hegna asked. Her voice was low, and even she heard the tremor on her words. She reached out and took Stormey's cool hand in hers. She needed to feel her mate, only Stormey was always warm to touch.

Hegna and her warriors had searched long and hard for the location of Azura's hideout. The lycan had grown bold and was still in Black Hollows. Hegna bit back a growl at the balls the lycan had. Azura was taunting her with her mate right under her nose. June was able to pinpoint a high amount of electricity being utilized in a building that was supposed to be abandoned in town. While Bijou had dispatched warriors to other known properties owned by Rayna, Hegna had felt it in her gut that she needed to look into this particular building. She'd always relied on her instincts during battle, and they never let her down.

Her father's tech vampires were even able to find the signal Azura's lycans were using and knock it out, replacing her broadcast with his. The king would assure the humans and vampires that he was still in charge and that they would take care of this new threat. Knowing her father, his message was probably filled with his own threats. None of the human government officials were bold enough to try to cross him.

"I can make her comfortable," Aries answered softly. Her hand rested on Stormey's stomach, pressing a bandage to the wound.

Hegna squeezed Stormey's hand at her honesty.

"She's lost so much blood and she's human. Their bodies are much more delicate than ours. We have the ability to regenerate, but she does not."

Hegna's mind was made up.

She was going to save her mate by turning her. It was the only way, but if she passed on to the afterlife, then Hegna—

She shook that thought from her mind.

No. Her mate was strong and would survive. Stormey hadn't survived a hard, human life to not be able to accept the change.

"I'm going to change her," Hegna announced. She stared at Stormey's still face and felt more confident. Yes, her mate would survive this. "Can we get her stable enough to get back to the castle? I don't want to do it here."

Hegna glanced around at the filthy warehouse the lycans had been utilizing. This was no place for her mate to transition. When she woke up, Hegna wanted her to be in the comforts of home.

Their home.

Then she would claim her mate.

"We'd have to move quickly," Aries replied. She reached into her bag and brought out an ampule and syringe. She drew up a medication and injected it into Stormey's arm.

Hegna trusted the healer to do as she'd promised.

"This medication will keep her heart beating. We need to move now."

Hegna leaned over Stormey, resting her lips near her ear.

"Hold on, mate. Stay with me. I need you."

"ARE YOU REAL?" Stormey whispered. She stood before the handsome couple in awe. She had dreamed of one day seeing her parents. As a child she had imagined that she had been removed from her parents and they would come swooping in and take her home where they could live happily ever after.

But that day never came.

She had been so young and moved around to so many foster homes and orphanages, records had been misplaced. She didn't even know their names, but she knew without a doubt this was them in front of her.

"Oh, baby girl. We are real," her mother said.

Her smile was familiar. Stormy remembered her tilted grin and warm eyes. Her father wiped the tears spilling down his cheeks.

"You are as beautiful as your mother." His voice grew gruff as he stared at her.

She took him in, recognizing some of her own features in him.

"You were so young when I left. Look at you, all grown up."

"Come here," her mother urged.

Stormey didn't hesitate and rushed into their open arms. Tears flowed down her cheeks. She wrapped an arm around each of them as tight as she could. What she wouldn't have given to be able to speak with them, hear their voices, and feel them in her arms while growing up. Now she finally had them.

"I've missed you so much." Stormey's voice was strained.

Her mother pulled away first, cupping

Stormey's cheeks. She brushed Stormey's hair away from her face while her gaze raked over Stormey as if she were memorizing her features.

"We've watched you grow up into a beautiful woman. There's not a day that doesn't go by that we don't peek in on you. We are so proud of you," her mother said. Her eyes suddenly took on a sad glint. She glanced over at her husband and sighed.

"You've faced such adversary in your life head-on. I can't wait to see what you do with the rest of your life." Her father pressed a kiss to her forehead. His smile wavered slightly.

Stormey sensed something was wrong. She paused and stared at both of them.

"There is something you aren't telling me." Dread filled her.

They were keeping a secret from her, and she wasn't sure if she would like it or not. Their nervous smiles and shared looks left her worried. She glanced behind them into the white light and felt the desire to go walk into it. Her curiosity was getting the best of her. What would she see if she entered it?

"Stormey, baby. Look at me." Her mother's soft voice gained her attention. She took Stormey's hands in hers and squeezed them tight. "It's not your time."

"What?" Stormey was confused. What was she talking about? She was here in this beautiful area where the energy drew her to it. She sensed peace, calmness, and love coming from the light. That was where she wanted to go. "But I'm here now."

"You are too early, baby girl." Her father's deep voice washed over her. He rested a hand on her shoulder and released a sigh. "As much as we would love to keep you here with us, we can't. You are needed back there."

"Where? I don't know what you are talking about. Don't I belong here with you?" she asked, confused. Why would they say such a thing? They had been apart for so long. Her neck itched slightly. She reached up and rubbed at it, trying to soothe the skin. Her hand moved to her stomach where the same sensation appeared. She used her nails to relieve the irritation that grew more intense before dissipating.

"One day it will be time for you to come here, but today is not the day," her father said. He cupped her cheeks and stared into her eyes. "Stormey, know that we have and will always love you. We will be here when you return."

"But, Dad—"

"Go to her." His thumb stroked her skin softly.

She leaned into his touch, the tears that were pushed back flooding her eyes. Her vision blurred as she gazed up at her father. She had the faint memory of riding on his strong shoulders while he jogged around their yard. Her giggles echoed in her ears. She closed her eyes and allowed the tears to run down her face.

"To whom?" she whispered. The itching of her neck and stomach returned. The skin grew warm to touch. She gasped, running her nails along her flesh. She stepped back away from her parents, wanting to memorize their faces. She'd never had any pictures of them. Did she truly have to go? Why wouldn't they want her to stay with them? They had so much time they needed to make up, and she didn't want to lose them again.

"Go to your mate. She's waiting for you," her mother said.

Stormey's gaze flicked between them. Confusion rattled her. She scratched at the annoying irritations. What was wrong her? She glanced down at her stomach and didn't see anything but the white gown she was dressed in. Had she been wearing a white dress all day?

Matter of fact, where had she come from before she'd found her parents?

"My mate?" Stormy frowned. An image of a beautiful, pale-faced brunette with a fierce scowl appeared. Stormey's hand paused on her neck as memories flooded her mind.

Hold on, mate. Stay with me. I need you.

The woman's voice appeared close to her ear as if she were standing beside her. Stormey recognized her voice. The pleading had Stormey's heart pounding. She took another step back, torn. She glanced behind her, and suddenly the urge to go in that direction filled her.

Her parents were right.

It wasn't her time.

She glanced at her parents again. Her father wrapped an arm around her mother's shoulder. Tears streamed down their faces, but their smiles remained. She vowed to always remember what they looked like.

"Go, my dear. Hegna is waiting for you," her mother said.

Her father nodded in agreement.

"I love you," Stormey whispered. She didn't know when she would see them again, but she had to let them know that she had always loved them.

She had always wondered if her parents would be proud of her, and now, she knew. She looked around again at their surroundings.

"We love you more than you could ever know," her mother responded. She leaned into her husband, and they waved at her. "We will see you again."

Stormey lifted her hand to return the wave. An unseen force pulled her backwards, away from them. Her parents grew smaller as more distance was put between them. Wind whipped around her, and streams of light flowed. She rested her hand in front of her eyes, trying to block out the brightness.

A silent scream flew from her lips, and she was yanked even faster. Her body coasted along the winds until she fell, landing on something soft. She lay still for a moment, shocked. She was afraid to open her eyes.

Then suddenly, pain ripped through her.

Stormey writhed around, every inch of her body heating to an almost burning temperature. She couldn't escape the pain. Her gums appeared to swell and ache; something pierced them. She threw back her head and screamed, unable to take any more.

CHAPTER TWENTY-SIX

Hegna sat on the edge of the bed watching over her mate. It had been almost a week since she had brought her home. It had been touch and go with Stormey, but her mate had survived.

Just as Hegna knew she would.

Now they needed for her to awaken from her slumber.

"She will need to feed immediately when she awakens," Ellanora announced. The healer had been at Stormey's side constantly since they'd arrived home.

"She can feed from me," Hegna murmured.

Stormey looked angelic lying in their bed. Her hands were folded on top of the blanket that covered her body. Her hair was plaited into two braids to keep it neat while her body healed. The traumatic and almost fatal wounds had healed perfectly, and there was a faint mark where each one was.

Her mate had been on the brink of death.

Now, she would continue to live by Hegna's side forever. Hegna only wished her mate wouldn't regret being changed. She would spend the rest of her days as a vampire.

"We may need more blood than what you have, Your Grace." Ellanora's voice held a slight hint of amusement. She came to stand next to Hegna and rested a hand on her shoulder. "Newly turned vampires have ravenous appetites. We will keep some on standby."

Hegna nodded. For all she cared, Stormey could drain her dry. It would be due punishment for failing to keep her safe.

"No live donors," Hegna said.

"Of course not. That would be for a later lesson, not when she first awakens," Ellanora said. She squeezed Hegna's shoulder before releasing her.

"Will it be you who would be helping her with the transition—"

Hegna turned and faced Ellanora. Her cold expression must have been the answer Ellanora was looking for. The healer backed away and bowed her head.

There would be no other vampire to teach her mate how to be one of them. Stormey was her responsibility, and she would see to it that her mate would have a smooth transition from human to vampire.

"I will be claiming my mate the moment she awakens," Hegna announced. She turned back to Stormey and moved closer to her on the bed. She reached up and brushed her finger along the softness of her mate's cheek.

"Yes, Your Grace. Please let me know if you need anything."

"We shall be fine. I will be able to handle my mate," Hegna said. Her gaze landed on the box resting on the nightstand. They would no longer need the traditional knife that would have been used during the claiming ceremony. Her mate was now vampire and would have her own fangs to bite Hegna.

A shiver rippled through Hegna at the thought

of feeling Stormey bite her. A jolt of desire shot straight to her core.

Slight movement of Stormey's fingers captured Hegna's attention.

"You may leave us," Hegna ordered. Was her mate about to awaken? If so, she only wanted the two of them in the room. There was no telling how Stormey would react when she woke up. The newly turned vampires all reacted to their new lives differently. Some angry, some violent, while others were afraid or in denial. Hegna didn't know what to expect from Stormey.

"Yes, Your Grace." The healer padded away from Hegna.

It wasn't until Hegna heard the suite door open and close that she leaned forward.

Hegna watched Stormey's fingers move. The rate of Stormey's breathing increased, as did the pulse at the base of her neck. She was coming around.

"Wake up, *miere*," Hegna whispered. She needed to see her eyes open. Would they remain her beautiful brown or would they now be like Hegna's, vampire blue?

She continued to watch her. Stormey's plump lips were pushed out slightly from the recently developed fangs. Hegna ached to see them, watch them sink into her flesh. Her arousal grew with every thought of her newly turned mate.

"Stormey, come to me, *miere*. Your mate needs you." Hegna slid closer to Stormey. After she had awakened this evening from a power nap, she'd showered, slid her robe on, and returned to her mate's side. She hadn't wanted to be away from Stormey any longer than necessary. Hegna had rarely left Stormey's side. Ellanora had forced her to drink prepackaged blood so that she could keep up her strength. For some reason, her body was accepting it as if it understood she would be unable to feed from her at this time.

Bijou and Corbin had been in charge while she'd attended Stormey. The entire territory knew of the attack on their princess's mate. Gifts and flowers had arrived daily, the cards wishing Stormey well. Hegna was unsure of how she had become so popular amongst their constituents, but word must have gotten around about her kindness and love of all. Hegna was proud of her and couldn't wait to see her ruling over humans and vampires.

Stormey's lips parted, revealing the tips of her pearly-white fangs.

"That's right, *miere*. Follow my voice," Hegna

urged. She ran a finger down Stormey's cheek. The muscle underneath her finger twitched.

Yes, her mate was slowing awakening.

Hegna removed her finger and rested her hand on the blanket. She would join her underneath it until she was fully conscious. They would then have a long conversation about what had happened that would include an apology from her. Hegna would never stop apologizing to her. She had been a horrible partner and would repay Stormey until she took her last breath.

A brown hand shot out and gripped Hegna's wrist with a strength that had never been there before. Hegna's gaze flicked to Stormey's face and found her new icy-blue eyes locked on her.

A growl rumbled from Stormey's chest. Her lips curled up, revealing her fangs.

Hegna had never seen anyone more beautiful.

"*Miere*," Hegna said softly. She slowly stood from the bed with her wrist still held in Stormey's grasp. Hegna's gums stretched from her fangs, breaching through them. Her heart rate spiked with the sight of her mate.

Stormey pushed up into a sitting position on the bed.

"Welcome back."

Stormey's growl grew louder. She yanked on Hegna's arm, sending her flying onto the bed with Stormey's body landing on top of her. Fear was far from Hegna's mind. Instead, her core clenched, dripping with her arousal. Stormey's new powers were attractive, and Hegna was getting a kick out of this aggression.

Stormey's hands rested on both of Hegna's wrists, pinning them to the mattress. Her thin gown that covered her body did little to hide it from Hegna. Stormey's big brown areolas were visible through the material. Her soft, thick thighs rested on each side of Hegna.

Hegna's robe slipped open in the tussle. Stormey's gaze roamed Hegna's face, drifting down to her exposed breasts. The cool air kissed Hegna's pebbled nipples.

"What's happened to me?" Stormey rasped.

She blinked, and confusion filled her eyes. The grip on Hegna's wrists lightened. Hegna could have escaped her hold at any time. Even a newly turned vampire wasn't as strong as a pure-born royal. Hegna didn't feel threatened by her.

Hegna broke her hold and pushed up into a sitting position. Stormey remained on her lap, her legs sliding forward where her core rested on

Hegna's stomach. Hegna slid a hand along Stormey's ample bottom to hold her flush to her. Stormey's arms came to rest on Hegna's shoulders.

She reached up with her free hand and trailed a finger along Stormey's lip. Gazing into her eyes, she saw her mate. Not the newly turned vampire, but her beautiful, thoughtful mate.

"I failed you," Hegna admitted softly. It pained her that Stormey had almost died because of her negligence.

"How?" Stormey whispered.

Her eyes widened, and her hand flew to her mouth. She prodded her mouth, feeling her new fangs. She jerked her finger back, having pricked the tip of it. A small bubble of blood formed on it. Hegna's vision locked in on it. She reached up and took Stormey's hand in hers and brought the finger to her lips. Hegna licked the small drop of blood, a groan escaping from her.

The taste of her blood remained just as sweet as it always had been. Hegna's core clenched with need. She desired her, but now they had a lot to discuss. Sex would come later, after they'd spoken about the past events.

"How do I have fangs?" she asked.

The sight of her sharp little teeth mesmerized

Hegna. She had to fight to concentrate. Unable to resist, she brought Stormey's head down to hers. She covered Stormey's lips with hers. It had been entirely too long since she'd kissed her. Their mouths fused, their tongues dueling together. Hegna slowly brought hers back and traced Stormey's fangs with it.

"Azura almost killed you." Hegna tore her mouth from Stormey's. She reached up and cupped Stormey's face. "I did not protect you like I should have."

"It wasn't your fault," Stormey replied. She closed her eyes momentarily before they reopened. "I'm having a hard time remembering everything, but I distinctly remember you arriving to save me."

"You were mortally injured. You were going to die," Hegna growled.

It should have never come down to her having to choose to let her mate die, or risk turning her. She tightened her hands on Stormey's face then released it. Her hand skated down to the neck of Stormey's gown. The offending material had to go. She gripped the thin fabric and ripped it off her, leaving Stormey naked.

Stormey hissed, brandishing her fangs. Hegna loved how fierce she was now. She was going to love training her and teaching her about her newly gained strength. She looked forward to educating Stormey on how to be a vampire.

"And how does that lead to me having these?" Stormey's hands pushed the robe off Hegna's shoulders. Her icy-blue eyes darkened with lust.

Hegna could read her and saw the need for blood and sex. Hegna was ready to teach her all that she needed to know about becoming a vampire.

"You were dying, and I couldn't lose you," Hegna admitted. She took notice that her mate's gaze was now locked in on her neck. Hegna's pulse rate rose in anticipating teaching her mate to drink from her. "I was selfish and needed you, so I took a risk."

Hegna reached up and tilted Stormey's chin up so she could look her in the eyes. She just hoped Stormey wouldn't hate what she had become.

"You needed me?" Stormey whispered.

"Yes. In order to keep you with me, I turned you."

The silence was broken by Stormey's sexy little growl. Her new nature was overtaking her. The need to feed was going to consume her until her body was satisfied. Hegna turned her head and offered her neck to Stormey. She wasn't worried about her hurting her.

"Bite me, *miere*," Hegna said.

Stormey's tense body trembled. She needed to take her first drink to cure the edge. If she didn't, Stormey would hurt someone, and she would never be able to live with herself if she caused someone pain.

"Hegna," Stormey's voice shook with fear and doubt.

"Do it, *miere*. You won't hurt me. You need to consume blood before the thirst gets out of control," Hegna said. She kept her voice as calm as she could. She, herself, trembled on the inside. She wanted Stormey to pierce her neck with her fangs. She wanted to feel the pull of her mate drinking from her. She was so aroused, wetness coated her thighs.

Stormey leaned in, resting her nose at Hegna's throat. It took all of Hegna's restraint to not reach for her. She gripped the blankets in a tight fist. Stormey needed to do this.

"What is that smell?" Stormey inhaled sharply.

Hegna groaned at the sensation of her mate's tongue sliding along her skin. The scaling of her fangs almost had Hegna becoming undone.

"It's sweet with a slight musk."

"You are using your new sense of smell, *miere*," Hegna replied. Her eyes fluttered closed as Stormey continued to tease her with her tongue and fangs. "It is my wetness that you smell. My cunt is slick and ready for you, *miere*."

"Is this what happens to you when I'm aroused? You smell it?" Stormey lifted her head and looked Hegna in the eye.

Hegna gave a slight nod. Stormey smiled softly, revealing her fangs. It then faded as she studied Hegna.

"Did you claim me? Is that part of the turning?"

"No, *miere*. It is separate. I needed to make sure you survived the change. When I claim you, I wanted you to be awake."

"Can we do it now?"

Hegna's heart stuttered. She, who had failed her mate, didn't think she'd want to do it right away. Hegna wanted to repay her for everything she had done to her.

But here was Stormey, wanting her first taste of blood to be even more special by including it as part of their claiming.

"Are you sure, *miere*? Once we seal the bond, it is

forever," Hegna said.

"I've been in love with you forever. I think from the first time I got to see you fighting in person," Stormey whispered.

Hegna's breath caught in her throat.

Stormey's cool hands rested on her face. "I don't care if I'm human or vampire. I just want to be with you, and forever would never be long enough."

Hegna stared at Stormey. She didn't deserve the love of this woman, but she would always cherish her and everything she stood for. Without a doubt, she was in love with Stormey. She didn't need fate to tell her that without Stormey, her life would be over. There would be no purpose to breathe or exist.

Stormey was her entire world.

"I love you, too, *miere*," Hegna whispered. She reached up and covered Stormey's hand with hers.

Stormey's eyes filled with tears.

Without thinking, the words to the bonding vow flowed from Hegna's lips. "Fate has willed the two of us together."

Funny how she hadn't believed fate deserved to carve out her future, but now she was recognizing it in her vow to Stormey.

Hegna nicked her wrist with her own fangs; it bled. She spread some of the blood on Stormey's forehead, marking her. Stormey's body grew still, her eyes locked on Hegna. Fat tears streamed down Stormey's face. She blinked them back, a small smile ghosting her lips.

"We thank the fates for the bond that has formed between us." Hegna paused, swallowing the lump that had grown in her throat. Her stubbornness had almost cost her this woman. She made herself a promise that she would always listen to fate from this day forward. Maybe fate did know what she was doing. "We shall forever be joined together."

She painted Stormey's lips with more of her blood. Her mate's tongue snuck out and tasted it. Her icy-blue eyes widened, the first taste fueling her thirst.

"Through our bond, you shall live throughout time standing by my side," Hegna rasped. She brushed Stormey's bare chest with her wrist, coating her in the blood.

Stormey's chest rose and fell swiftly. Her hands were balled into fists. It was evident her mate was fighting the thirst so they could seal their bond. Hegna was so proud of her. Controlling one's thirst after the change was very uncommon. She was just as strong as Hegna knew she would be.

Hegna tilted Stormey's head back, exposing the smooth column of her neck.

"I vow to protect you. To honor you," Hegna continued. She ran her tongue along Stormey's skin. The taste of her woman comforted her. It had been touch and go, and she'd almost had this ripped from her.

"I vow to protect you and honor you, as well," Stormey murmured. She closed the tiny gap between them.

Her hot core burned against Hegna's stomach. The scent of her arousal flooded Hegna's senses.

"I vow to please you."

"I vow to please you," Stormey moaned. Her hands came to rest on Hegna's shoulders. She rocked her pelvis against Hegna. "Please. Do it. Claim me."

Hegna couldn't resist any longer. She sank her fangs deep into her mate's flesh. Stormey's gasp sent a bolt of desire to Hegna's core. She drank in her mate's sweet blood. Stormey groaned, holding Hegna to her while she drank from her. Pure strength and energy filled Hegna. She could leave their room and go fight a thousand lycans and she would defeat them.

She lifted her head and licked the wound, taking another taste. Her mate's blood was so delicious, but she had to stop. Stormey leaned in and covered Hegna's mouth with hers. The kiss was hard and feral. Hegna gathered Stormey close, holding on to her ample ass. She squeezed it, loving how it overflowed her palms.

She tilted her head, deepening the kiss. Stormey thrust her hips forward in a rocking motion that drove Hegna crazy. Her slickness was coating Hegna's stomach.

It was now her mate's turn to feed, and it would complete their bond.

Hegna pulled back slightly, breaking the kiss.

"Come, mate. Take your first drink from me," Hegna urged.

Stormey's hand turned Hegna's face away. She leaned in confidently and trailed her tongue along the side of Hegna's neck. Stormey didn't hesitate, sinking her fangs into Hegna's skin. She drank almost immediately. The sensation had Hegna teetering on the edge of her climax. She gripped Stormey to her and rolled them until Stormey was on her back. Stormey's grip on Hegna's neck didn't lessen. She continued to drink while Hegna positioned them where their two slick cunts pressed together. Hegna groaned and rocked her hips, sliding her clit against Stormey's.

Hegna shuddered from the hard pull. She didn't care how much of her blood Stormey took.

She was in heaven.

Stormey's hand settled on her ass while she thrust her pelvis toward Hegna's. Their moans and gasps filled the air. Their movements became frantic as they took pleasure from each other.

Stormey released Hegna's neck with a cry. Hegna swooped down and covered her mouth with hers. They continued to writhe against each other. Their cunts slid effortlessly from the slickness that coated them. Their two nubs danced together, creating a delicious feeling that was coursing through Hegna's body. She forced Stormey's head to the side and sank her fangs into the other side of her neck.

Stormey's body shuddered, and a scream escaped her. Hegna was right behind her. She released Stormey's neck and roared. Their hips slowed to gentle arches and rubs. Hegna's clit was sensitive, but the feeling of Stormey's brushing hers was so good, she didn't want to stop.

"We're mated," Stormey whispered in awe.

Hegna moved to lay on her side, bringing Stormey into her embrace.

"We are." Hegna lifted her arm and offered her mate her wrist. "Come, *miere*. You are a newly turned vampire. You need to drink."

Stormey's eyed her wrist for a moment, bringing it to her lips. She opened her mouth wide and bit down. Hegna moaned, her head falling back on the pillows underneath them. Stormey suckled from her for a few minutes then released her. She licked Hegna's wrist. Hegna smiled. Her mate was a fast learner.

"To celebrate our mating, we'll just feed and fuck?" Stormey's lips tilted up in a devilish grin. She moved to straddle Hegna but almost flew off the bed.

Hegna caught her leg before she went crashing to the floor. Her laughter filled the air as she hung upside down.

"Is that so bad, that you'd risk breaking your neck?" Hegna chuckled, dragging her mate back onto the bed. She helped Stormey get into the position she had attempted. "Someone is going to have to learn that they are no longer human. We are going to have to teach you how to move as a vampire."

"Oh my," Stormey breathed. Her smile was wide, revealing her sexy fangs. "So you have to watch how you walk? You don't just walk?"

"I don't know how to answer that because I was born a vampire. But the quick movements you used to do will be made extremely fast due to your new vampiric speed." She rested her hands on Stormey's waist. She was already losing her train of thought with Stormey's beautiful brown breasts sitting in front of her face. "Now I'm going to answer your question with a question. Is fucking and feeding not how you would want to celebrate our mating?"

Stormey's eyes darkened and narrowed on Hegna. She leaned in and softly pressed a kiss to Hegna's lips. She slid down Hegna's body, leaving a trail of kisses along the way. Once she reached Hegna's center, she pushed Hegna's thighs far apart. She eyed Hegna's cunt and licked her lips.

"The scent of your pussy is driving me crazy." Stormey slid her tongue through Hegna's slick slit. She closed her eyes and repeated the motion.

Hegna watched her mate through hooded eyes.

"Well, if this is the way of vampires, then I'm all in."

CHAPTER TWENTY-SEVEN

Stormey strolled through the party feeling many sets of eyes on her. Tonight was the celebration of her mating to the future queen of vampires. Their coven had gone all out, sparing no expenses to celebrate their union.

It had been about six weeks since her change. She felt she had acclimated to her new life well. She was struggling with the fact that she would no longer be able to eat food. Hegna explained to her that her stomach wouldn't be able to digest or process it. Blood would be her primary source of nourishment.

She was sad about this, but lately was finding that she wasn't even craving it as she'd once thought she would. It didn't keep her from the kitchen and cooking. Hegna hadn't allowed her around humans without guards to ensure the new thirst wouldn't overtake her. She'd agreed because she would never be able to live with herself if she had attacked Val, or a kitchen attendant, or any of the human employees.

So far, so good. Hegna ensured she had plenty of blood to keep her thirst at bay. Many had thought that she would change after becoming a vampire. Some of the humans were nervous to be around her but soon saw she was still the same person, only now she had fangs and was sensitive to sunlight.

Stormey didn't harbor any ill will toward Hegna for making a delicate decision. It now explained where she had been when she had seen her parents. She'd been in limbo and literally standing outside Heaven's door. It comforted her to know that her parents were together in Heaven.

One day, they would be reunited. Stormey believed that, but it would be a really long time before that day would come.

Stormey paused near the bar and took in the

hundreds of people filling their ballroom. Everyone was dressed in their finest clothing, enjoying the party. Music floated through the air, bringing a smile to her face. The decor theme was based on their house colors of purple and gold. The ballroom was turned into that of a dark fairy tale.

She felt as if she were living in one. She had captured her princess and was going to live happily ever after in their castle. Stormey was still in awe of everything she had gained. She would never take it for granted.

Her new family accepted her with open arms. She had become fast friends with Quinn and Alima, the mates to Hegna's sisters. They spoke via hologram at least four to five times a week. They decided to work together on bridging human and vampire relationships. They were also bringing much attention to the way of life for the less fortunate humans. It was time the vampires became more involved in the human politics and government.

The human leaders did not care what happened to people. They were greedy and only out for themselves. Since the three princesses were mated to humans, they were stepping up to the responsibility.

The king and queen had agreed after speaking with her, Quinn, and Alima.

"Your Grace. You look beautiful tonight," a familiar voice said.

She turned to see the person standing next to her and smiled. She had to agree with the newcomer. She felt downright sexy in her dress. Hegna had impeccable taste and had it made for her. It was a deep-plum dress that hugged her curves. It was an off-the-shoulder design with a slit that came practically up to her navel. It didn't allow for any panties or even a thong. It was amazing she was able to find body tape to hold the front in place to not expose her pussy for the world to see.

"Why, thank you, Corbin. You look dashing yourself." She smiled and turned to him. "Now if you are here with me, where is that mate of mine?"

Corbin lifted the bronze goblet in his hand and took a sip. With her newly enhanced senses, she scented the blood in his cup. She'd had to learn a lot over the past few weeks. From controlling her thirst, her movements, and speed to her strength. Her workouts with Zeke were much different. She got a kick out of being able to toss a grown man across a room.

"Oh, she's around. The last time I saw her, she was speaking with Lord Vilson." Corbin smirked.

"And you know she's not supposed to be doing any business tonight and you're here to tell on her." Stormey arched an eyebrow at her mate's personal advisor. She now understood why Hegna kept Corbin close to her. He was loyal to his princess, and in doing so, he was loyal to Stormey. He agreed Hegna worked too much and needed to enjoy her life. One thing he'd said to her not long after her change had stuck with her.

Why be immortal if you aren't going to enjoy the pleasures in life?

"I wouldn't want my friend to be in the…what do humans say? Be in the doghouse?"

Stormey barked a laugh at his attempt at an innocent look. She had learned a lot about the vampire, and this man before her was anything but innocent.

"Point me in the direction of your princess, and I will take care of her," she said. Her gums burned. A signal she had learned meant that her fangs wanted to descend. She hadn't quite mastered how to control them yet. They broke free and slid down into place. She playfully flashed her fangs at him. "I know what will distract her away from business."

He tilted his head toward a small crowd near the far corner away from the orchestra.

"Thank you, Corbin. You are so good to my mate. I appreciate it." She reached over and squeezed his arm.

A shirtless man, with a toned body dressed only in dark linen pants, approached them. She didn't remember the waitstaff not wearing shirts. As the night grew later, the human donors would start appearing. The night was young, but it would seem one of the males wanted to claim Corbin early.

"I'm glad someone knows it." He tossed her a wink, turning his attention to the male sidling up to him.

Stormey shook her head and made her way to her mate. She had promised to not discuss business. She didn't want to have lycans being deliberated about at their mating celebration. She shivered thinking of the animals that had almost taken her life.

Azura Michaels' death had been talked about all over the newsfeed. Her vicious vampire mate had ensured the lycan's dead body had been publicly displayed on national television. She had planned to kill Stormey before the world, and

Hegna had ensured her death was proved in the same fashion.

The human Stormey would have been appalled at the thought of showcasing a headless body lying next to its head to be barbaric and cruel. The vampire Stormey didn't think it was good enough.

So Hegna had Azura's body burned.

On national television.

Since the killing of Azura, lycans had retreated in hiding. No one had heard word from Azura's twin sister. Hegna and her sisters were preparing their armies for retaliation. But for now, all had gone quiet. There weren't any recent reports of lycan attacks since they went into hiding. It was only a matter of time before Rayna acted. Until then, the royal army would be waiting.

"We are going to install cameras on every street corner and increase security. I want humans and vampires to feel safe. It was because of the few cameras we already had that we were able to pinpoint my mate's abduction," Hegna said.

There was a small crowd of men and women around her mate. They were all hanging on to every word the princess said.

"Going into the future, we will do all that we can to protect our humans and lower-class vampires. My mate has opened my eyes to the importance of living in harmony with the humans."

"But they are our food." An older-looking vampire bristled.

"Ah, Lord Hampton. The humans are only your food if they allow it." Stormey arrived at her mate's side.

Hegna turned to her with a guilty expression. She brought Stormey flush to her side and snaked an arm around her waist. Stormey faced the wealthy vampire lord and arched an eyebrow at him.

"Your Grace," murmurs went around as they all bowed their heads to her.

Stormey held back a grin, still getting used to the notion that she was royalty now.

"Better living environments, secured employment with decent wages, and healthcare would enhance their lives. By doing that, you'd have not only an increase of donors at the blood bank but healthier ones. Our economy can and will thrive once humans are able to better themselves, open businesses, be creative, and prosper as they once did. All of this will be possible with the help of vampires." Stormey met the stares of her audience. She tilted her head to the side and leveled Lord

Hampton with her gaze. "Don't you agree, Lord Hampton?"

"Um, well, yes, since you put it that way." Lord Hampton swallowed hard. He pulled a handkerchief from his jacket and wiped his brow.

"Then I'm sure I can expect a sizable donation for the medical clinic we are going to be opening. I'll make sure to have someone contact your office." Stormey leaned into her mate and glanced up into her eyes. She could admit she had grown bold since becoming a vampire. Hegna loved her spunk and her sassiness, and that was all that mattered.

"Yes, Your Grace," Lord Hampton muttered. His angry footsteps sounded as he stomped away.

"You all won't mind if I take Her Royal Highness away from you, would you?" Stormey innocently glanced over her shoulder at the remaining members.

Lord Vilson bowed to her as well as the others before they walked away.

"How much trouble am I in?" Hegna grimaced. Her hands skated along Stormey's torso with one resting on her hip while the other landed on her bottom.

Hegna was in her formal leathers that were different from her fighting ones. Stormey had wanted her to wear something fancy such as her gown, but Hegna was not having it. She insisted on her formal uniform that had their family emblem on it. She met Stormey halfway and had her hair styled in a braidless manner that left her hair flowing along her shoulders and back.

"I'll have to decide. Why don't you escort me to the dance floor?" Stormey asked. She pressed a soft kiss to Hegna's lips.

Her vampire's nostrils flared out, her eyes filling with desire.

"Of course, *miere*. Anything you want." Hegna dropped another kiss on her lips, taking her hand and leading her out to the dance floor.

The sea of dancers parted to allow them to walk to the center. Stormey eyed her mate, and a rush of desire filled her. She was one lucky woman.

Hegna swung her around, bringing her into the circle of her embrace. Stormey tilted her head back to meet the gaze of her love. Hegna's icy-blue eyes warmed as they met hers.

"New medical center?" Hegna asked.

"Yeah, I made that up right then and there. I guess I need to put that on my list of things for me and the girls to work on." Stormey giggled. She pressed closer to her mate, loving the feeling of her vampire against her. Hegna always would have her back. If this was something she wanted, then Hegna would move mountains to ensure she got it.

"I love when you get all fired up about what you believe in," Hegna said. She twirled Stormey around.

Applause came from their audience. Stormey smiled at their spectators, not realizing the dancers had given them the floor. She inhaled softly, detecting a hint of her mate's desire.

"I can scent how much you love it." Stormey smiled. She embraced her new life as a vampire. She could have cried, thrown tantrums, or fallen into deep depression, but that wasn't her. She was always a fighter. If fate determined that she become a vampire, then so be it.

A single bell sounded, ringing through the air. Stormey frowned, unsure of what it meant. She glanced around, and no one appeared bothered by it. The dancers now joined them on the floor, crowding around them. She pressed closer to Hegna and dropped a kiss on her chin.

"I do love you," she whispered softly.

The lights lowered even more around them, but it didn't bother Stormey. She was now able to see in the dark. It was one perk that she loved. Even in the low light, she watched Hegna's pupils constrict.

"And I love you, too, *miere*," Hegna murmured. She cupped Stormey's cheek and held her in place as she covered her mouth with hers.

Stormey's lips parted, welcoming Hegna's tongue. Stormey had never felt so loved and cherished. This was now her reality and her life. Hegna ensured that she honored all of her vows she'd made to Stormey.

Hegna broke their kiss and spun Stormey around. Her arms came around Stormey and held her back against her chest. They continued to sway with the rhythm of the music. Stormey rested her head back, tilting her head to the side.

"What was that bell for?" Stormey asked.

Hegna's lips danced along her neck, leaving a trail of kisses on her skin.

"The human entertainment," Hegna replied.

Her fangs slid over Stormey's neck, eliciting a moan from Stormey. Her eyes fluttered closed as she rested back against Hegna. She basked in the feeling of her mate's arms around her. Hegna's hand slid down her stomach and was dangerously low where Stormey's slit began.

"You know how much vampires love feeding,

miere. I ensured our coven had plenty of entertainment and food."

Stormey smirked. She was sure she knew what type of entertainment her mate was providing for their coven's entertainment. That male who had approached Corbin had definitely not been a part of the waitstaff. She wouldn't have put it past Corbin to get first look at the entertainers or donors and had picked who he wanted. Corbin certainly took advantage of being the personal advisor to the princess, and he deserved it.

"I'm sure you did, and that's why our coven loves you," Stormey murmured.

Hegna nipped at her ear, her warm breath sending a shiver down Stormey's spine.

"I care not that they love me," Hegna said. "The only person I need to love me is you."

Stormey gasped, feeling Hegna's hand part her dress open. Stormey had suspected that Hegna had this dress made for a reason, and now it was confirmed. Hegna's talented fingers parted her labia and dipped into her wet heat. Stormey's pussy was primed and drenched.

Hegna drew some of her slickness up to her clit and stroked Stormey's protruding bud.

"Hegna," Stormey moaned. Her head fell back to rest on Hegna's shoulder.

Her mate took advantage of the move and sank her fangs into Stormey's neck. Her hips undulated toward her hand in the rhythm Hegna set. Her eyes flew open, and she took notice of vampires openly feeding from their mates or human donors.

Her eyes fluttered closed once again. Her focus was now on the woman drinking from her and pleasuring her. Stormey had the woman of her dreams and a life she could have only imagined. She couldn't ask for anything more.

EPILOGUE

Hegna strolled behind Stormey as she walked through the orphanage. She'd ordered her men to stay outside guarding the building while she and her mate were inside. Hegna didn't need help guarding her own mate. The kids always seemed to get a kick out of having vampire guards roaming around the grounds.

The first phase of the renovations had begun. Stormey and Emily were excited with their talk. Hegna had given Stormey full rein to do whatever she and Emily felt was necessary for the children and everyone who lived there. The construction workers were currently rebuilding one of the other wings and, once complete, everyone would move to that one so they may start on the other half of the house. It would be completed in a few stages.

They arrived at a staircase, and Stormey was lost in her conversation with Emily. The two women ascended the stairs. Hegna felt a presence behind her in the hallway. She turned and found Maisie standing there watching her.

"Hello, Maisie." Hegna smiled at the child.

"Hi, princess." Maisie skipped toward her and stopped next to her. She glanced up the stairs at Stormey and Emily who were paused at the top.

"Will my princess be okay?" Maisie asked, worry taking over her features. The smile she had disappeared from her lips.

Hegna didn't like the look of worry on the child's face. Children her age should be out playing and enjoying life.

"Of course. Why do you ask?" Hegna knelt before the little girl so they could be eye to eye.

"We had heard that the princess was now a vampire," Maisie whispered. She turned her wide eyes to Hegna. "But she doesn't act different."

"Would that bother you? That she is a vampire now?" Hegna asked softly.

Maisie shook her head without hesitation.

Relief filled Hegna. It would have pained her mate to think that Maisie thought differently of her. "Good. A very nasty woman hurt Stormey really bad. Turning her into a vampire was the only way to save her life."

Maisie's eyes grew round. Her audible swallow was the only sound that came from her at first. "Did you turn her?" she asked.

"I did." Hegna nodded cautiously. "Had I not, she wouldn't be here with us today."

"It's a good thing you did." Maisie glanced down at her hands and bit her lip.

Hegna could tell something else was on her mind.

"Some of the big kids said that she wouldn't want to hang with us anymore now that she was a vampire."

"I'm sure those big kids were being asses," Hegna said, then instantly regretted her choice in words.

Maisie grinned at her slip-up. Hegna may not be a mother or around children often, but she was sure her mate nor Emily wouldn't appreciate her cussing in front of them.

"You said a bad word." Maisie giggled. "Miss

Emily said that bad words are not allowed. She washed out Julian's mouth with soap for saying one."

"Rightfully so. Children shouldn't say such words." Hegna grinned.

Maisie glanced back up the stairs at Stormey. The girl was taken by her mate. Stormey talked non-stop about the little girl as well.

"But you do know the princess cares very much for the orphanage, everyone in it, and even you."

Maisie turned to her and sighed. The girl suddenly appeared much older than her age.

"I wish the princess was my mommy." Her voice was small, and her shoulders slumped.

The sight of the child tugged at Hegna's heartstrings. She rubbed Maisie's shoulder, taking her hand in hers.

"What if I can make that happen?" Hegna whispered.

Maisie's eyes lit up immediately. Hegna held up a finger to her lips. Her mate had been so busy the last few weeks that she'd barely rested.

But there was one thing Hegna knew her mate wanted in life.

A child.

They'd spent plenty of time learning about each

other's pasts and what they wanted in the future. One of Stormey's goals in life was to become a mother. Through all of the time that Stormey had spent at the orphanage, Maisie and Stormey had formed a bond. One that only a mother and daughter could share.

This was something that had been on Hegna's mind for a while. She had wanted children, but she'd been busy protecting and fighting for her people. Now that she had a mate, it was time for her to think of the next generation. Her mate would make a wonderful mother, and this was something Hegna could give her.

She had spoken with Emily a week ago, and the adoption was already completed. It paid to be wealthy and the future queen of vampires. The human government had rushed everything though in record time.

Stormey had already begun tackling the adoption processes for all children across the country. It helped that Hegna was her mate and she had the backing of the royal family. Human government officials didn't want to come under the radar of Hegna, her sisters, or the king and queen.

Hegna was just waiting for the perfect time to share the news.

Maisie was now a Riskel.

A princess.

"Come, Maisie." Hegna held out her hand.

Maisie slipped her smaller one in hers and allowed her to lead her up the staircase. Hegna's heart swelled with the thought that this girl was now her daughter. She had wanted to do something special, and now was the time. When they left the orphanage today, Maisie would be going home with them.

Emily's gaze landed on Hegna and Maisie as they reached the final step.

"I see you found company." Stormey spun around and smiled.

Maisie released Hegna's hand and raced over to her. Stormey bent down and hugged the girl.

"Where have you been all day?" Stormey asked.

"Around." Maisie shrugged. She glanced over at Hegna before standing to her full height. "Princess, can I ask you a question?"

"Of course you may." Stormey bent down to Maisie's level. She brushed off a piece of lint from Maisie's shirt. "What is it, my dear?"

"Can we go to the kitchen and get ice cream?" Maisie asked.

They all laughed at her question.

"We will have to see if there is some ice cream here." Stormey grinned. She leaned over and pressed a kiss to Maisie's cheek. She stood back up and motioned to Emily. "I'm sure Miss Emily will know for certain."

"I believe we have some in the deep freezer." Emily laughed. She glanced at Hegna and gave her a nod. She was ready to share the secret as well as Hegna was.

"That won't be necessary," Hegna said.

All eyes turned to her. Stormey frowned at Hegna.

"Why not?" Stormey asked. She took Maisie's hand in hers and pulled the girl close. "I'm sure a bite or two of ice cream won't hurt me."

"That's not what I'm talking about." She held back a grin at the frustrated look that appeared on her mate's face. She walked over to stand before Stormey and Maisie. "I heard the chef at our castle has ten different kinds of homemade ice cream stored in the freezers."

"Really?" Maisie shouted. She bounced around in place, excitement lining her face.

"What are you talking about, Hegna?" Stormey asked softly. She probably hadn't realized that she nervously tugged at her bottom lip with her fang. It was a cute move she had come to do. "You want to take Maisie to the castle to visit?"

Hegna reached out and cupped Stormey's cheek and shook her head.

"No, *miere*. I mean for us to take Maisie home with us because she's ours."

Stormey's eyes filled with tears. She glanced down at Maisie whose mouth dropped open.

"For real? I get to go home with you?" Maisie's voice ended on a screech. She turned to Emily, tears falling down her cheeks. "I'm adopted?"

Stormey had yet to take her eyes off Hegna. She stepped closer, a hiccup escaping her.

"She's ours? You—we—adopted her? How?" Stormey's tears streamed down her face.

Hegna gathered Stormey to her, pressing a kiss on the top of her head.

"Yes, *miere*. Maisie is our daughter. She is coming home with us. Today," Hegna announced. She turned and opened her other arm for the little tyke.

Maisie flew to her, joining their hug.

"I love you so much." Stormey lifted her head, a wide grin on her lips. She bent down and picked up Maisie. She nuzzled her neck and pressed kisses on her cheeks. "You hear that. You are coming home with us."

"Does that mean I'm a princess now, too?" Maisie asked.

Hegna returned her smile and gave a nod. Since the adoption had been completed, her father would officially announce Maisie to the world. The Riskel family was growing. They now had two members of the next generation. It mattered not that Maisie was not hers biologically. Legally, she was now a Riskel and would be awarded everything a biological child would.

"That you are, little one," Hegna replied.

"I have to go pack and tell everyone that I'm a princess now!" Maisie scrambled down from Stormey's arms. She raced over to the stairs and paused, spinning back to them. "You're not going to leave me, are you?"

"Never," Stormey replied. She leaned into Hegna, wrapping her arms around her waist.

Maisie sped down the stairs. Stormey faced Hegna and arched her eyebrows.

"You and I are going to have to talk about some decisions you make without me."

"Was this a bad decision?" Hegna asked.

"Of course not. It's just that I have so much to

prepare for Maisie at the castle. We need to pick out a room, go shopping for her—"

"It will be fine, *miere*. She has us now, and that's all that really matters."

"She certainly is lucky to have you two as parents," Emily said. "Stormey, I think we are done for now. We can continue later. I'm sure you have much to do."

"Thanks for your assistance, Emily." Hegna offered her hand to her.

The woman came over and pulled Hegna into a hug.

"This is worth a hug, princess." Emily stepped back with a laugh. "I'll speak with you later, Stormey."

She waved then walked over to the stairs. When she was halfway down, Stormey turned back to Hegna. She reached out and tugged her mate to her. Hegna wrapped her arms around Stormey and never wanted to let go.

"When we arrive home, everyone is going to be waiting for your orders, princess," Hegna said. "Whatever we need for our daughter will be provided."

"We are what Maisie needs." Stormey's eyes

misted over again. She sniffed and smiled through her tears.

Hegna vowed to continue to do what she must to keep her mate smiling at all times.

"You are all I need."

"And you are everything I need."

FROM THE AUTHOR

Dear Reader,

Thank you for reading Royal Bite. I am blown away by the love this series has received. I can't say thank you enough. It warms my heart that so many people love the Riskel sisters and their mates.

Because of the love The Immortal Reign series has gotten, I will be giving this series a few more books. It had been my intention to only write three stories, but I feel my readers deserve more from this world.

If you love my sapphic paranormal reads, make sure you sign up for my newsletter. I'm revamping it (no pun intended, lol). Click HERE to join my newsletter.

Again, thanks so much for the love and support!

Happy reading,

Ariel Marie

P.S. Don't forget to leave a review of this book on the platform you purchased it. All reviews matter! That's how I know if you want me to keep this series going!

Hot for Her Bear

THE MONTANA GRIZZLIES 1

She was warned to leave the grumpy bear alone, but she couldn't help herself. Her curiosity was piqued. She wanted to see the bear roar!

Saffron Dakota knew she shouldn't have specific thoughts about her best friend's older sister. It was forbidden, but it didn't keep her from smiling at her.

Or making sure she was dressed up nice when around her.

Or randomly showing up to her cabin in the woods.

All of this, hoping the beautiful grizzly would show her just a wee bit of interest. Her friend would be pissed if she knew Saffron was crazy over her sister.

Dasha Prime couldn't believe the strong reaction her bear had to Saffron. After all of these years, it was clear what her bear was trying to tell her. It was something she had thought all along, but now her bear was roaring loud and clear.

Saffron was her mate, and Dasha would defend her woman against anyone who had a problem with it.

If you love steamy, wlw paranormal romance with a grumpy bear shifter and her sassy human mate, then you will enjoy Hot For Her Bear. This story was intended for mature readers only.

Hot For Her Bear releases on February 14, 2023. For more information, visit www.thearielmarie.com .

Claimed by the Orc Queen

WARRIORS OF ASTOVAR 1

Orcs were supposed to be mythical creatures. How can one stand in front of her claiming to be her mate?

Unexplained occurrences have been occurring on Earth. Everything was being blamed on global warming. Tornados and hurricanes wrecking cities in the off-season, dangerous electrical thunderstorms are documented around the globe, and now portals to another realm are opening.

Cherish Little woke up in a forest and didn't know how she got there. The last thing she remembered was jogging in her neighborhood, darkening skies, and a violent gust of wind.

Somehow she was transported to another realm where massive, green, muscle-bound warriors with thick tusks protruding from their mouths captured her.

Orcs.

These brutal, vicious monsters didn't know what to do with her, so they took her to their queen. Ghorza, the slayer, was an intimidating and powerful orc determined to claim Cherish.

The fierce queen who led armies, seized lands, and tormented her enemies, had a soft spot for Cherish.

The queen vehemently proclaims she would never let her go. She swore to always please her, provide for her and protect her. As much as Cherish wants to return to her world, her heart and body long to stay. She found herself falling for Ghorza, her green protector.

A human in their realm was uncommon and drawing unwanted attention. Ghorza was willing to meet any challenger to remind all of her name and keep Cherish by her side.

Claimed by the Orc Queen is a sapphic orc fantasy romance with a fierce, possessive orc who falls for her beautiful, stubborn human mate. If you love wlw fantasy romance with plenty of heat, then you will love the first book in the Warriors of Astovar series.

This book is for mature readers only.

Claimed by the Orc Queen releases on May 2, 2023. For more information, visit www.thearielmarie.com .

The Nightstar Shifters

A FF WOLF SHIFTER ROMANCE SERIES

No wolf can resist the call to mate.

Strong female wolves are in search of their mate. The desire is strong for these women who long to find the one person meant for them.

They are fierce and determined, putting their trust in fate.

If you love lesbian wolf shifter romance filled with action and adventure, then you will love the Nightstar Shifters series.

Start the series today!

ABOUT THE AUTHOR

Ariel Marie is an author who loves the paranormal, action and hot steamy romance. She combines all three in each and every one of her stories. For as long as she can remember, she has loved vampires, shifters and every creature you can think of. This even rolls over into her favorite movies. She loves a good action packed thriller! Throw a touch of the supernatural world in it and she's hooked!

For more information:

www.thearielmarie.com

ALSO BY ARIEL MARIE

The Immortal Reign series

Deadly Kiss

Iced Heart

Royal Bite

Wicked Allure (TBD)

The Nightstar Shifters

Sailing With Her Wolf

Protecting Her Wolf

Sealed With A Bite

Hers to Claim

Wanted by the Wolf

Taming Her Mate

Warriors of Astovar

Claimed by the Orc Queen (TBD)

Blackclaw Alphas (Reverse Harem Series)

Fate of Four

Bearing Her Fate (TBD)

The Midnight Coven Brand

Forever Desired

Wicked Shadows

Paranormal Erotic Box Sets

Vampire Destiny (An Erotic Vampire Box Set)

Moon Valley Shifters Box Set (F/F Shifters)

The Dragon Curse Series (Ménage MFF Erotic Series)

The Dark Shadows Series

Princess

Toma

Phaelyn

Teague

Adrian

Nicu

Stand Alone Books

Dani's Return

A Faery's Kiss

Tiger Haven

Searching For His Mate

A Tiger's Gift

Stone Heart (The Gargoyle Protectors)

Saving Penny

A Beary Christmas

Howl for Me

Birthright

Return to Darkness

Red and the Alpha

Printed in Great Britain
by Amazon